"Johnson uses the background of conflict and culture clash to tell an unusual love story."
                    —*The Chattanooga Times* on *The Island Snatchers*

"Recommended."
                    —*Library Journal* on *The Island Snatchers*

"Historical romance at its best, with characters that breathe [and] a plot that makes sense. Not a scene rang false."
                    —*The Honolulu Advertiser* on *The Island Snatchers*

"[An] explosive, fast-paced thriller."
                    —*Romantic Times* on *Lifesaver*

By Janice Kay Johnson
from Tom Doherty Associates

The Island Snatchers
Winter of the Raven

WINTER
of the RAVEN

Janice Kay Johnson

TOR®

A TOM DOHERTY ASSOCIATES BOOK
NEW YORK

This is a work of fiction. All the characters and events portrayed in this book are either products of the author's imagination or are used fictitiously.

WINTER OF THE RAVEN

A Tor Book
Published by Tom Doherty Associates, LLC
175 Fifth Avenue
New York, NY 10010

www.tor.com

Tor® is a registered trademark of Tom Doherty Associates, LLC.

ISBN: 0-812-52435-7

First edition: August 1995
First mass market edition: September 2000

Printed in the United States of America

0 9 8 7 6 5 4 3 2 1

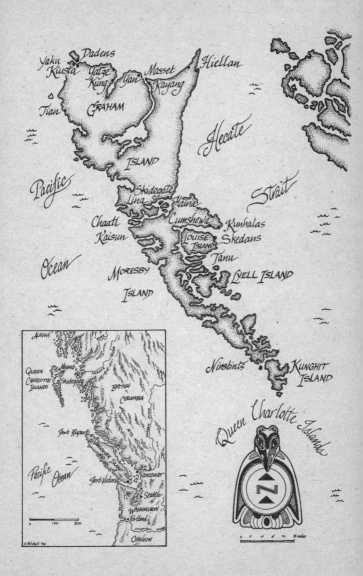

Yaku
Kiusta
Dadens
Yatze
Kung
Yan
Masset
Kayang
Hiellan
Tian
GRAHAM
ISLAND
Skidegate
Lina
Haina
Cumshewa
Kunhalas
Skedans
Chaatl
Kaisun
Louise
Island
Tanu
Ninstints
MORESBY
ISLAND
LYELL ISLAND
KUNGHIT
ISLAND

Pacific
Ocean
Hecate
Strait

Queen Charlotte Islands

ALASKA
Queen
Charlotte
Islands
Masset
Skidegate
BRITISH
COLUMBIA
Fort Rupert
VANCOUVER ISLAND
Pacific
Ocean
Fort Victoria
Vancouver
Seattle
WASHINGTON
Portland
COLUMBIA RIVER
OREGON

0   100   200

e. Mitchell '66

0 5 10 15 20 25 miles

Prologue

The signs promised well for tomorrow. Fine-Weather-Woman blew gently, and the long, narrow clouds agreed with her. Though the water of the Skit-ei-get inlet rolled, the surface was as shiny as the small mirror Gao's mother had owned.

Gao worked behind a cedar-bark screen at the end of the village, so that the people would not see the house pole he was carving before it was raised. It lay faceup on cedar braces, staring at the sky. He had one helper only: his sister's son, who was young but revered Master Carpenter and wanted to do as his uncle did. Yesterday they had smoothed the carvings with stone and polished them with the rough skin of Dogfish. Today they painted, using black for eyes and eyebrows, and red for the tongues and nostrils of the crest figures and Watchmen at the top.

Tomorrow the pole would be raised, the first in too many years. Perhaps the last, too. Not many chiefs owned enough to potlatch anymore. This feast and the giving away of goods would not be like some Gao remembered from when he was a child, or had been told about by his parents. Coppers would not be broken or thrown into the sea; blankets to be given away would not be piled so high in the house that the roof boards had to be taken off to allow room.

But Gao thought it would be a good ceremony still. The feasting—he smiled at the thought. At this season, when ice first lay in thin sheets between the canoes, there would be fresh crab apples and cranberries, and other berries preserved in cakes. There would be potatoes and salmon and other fish. All could be dipped in great bowls of oolachen grease, more than a man could eat. Yes, tomorrow would be good, a time to remember.

But first, the pole must be finished. Gao did not want to disgrace the chief who had asked for the house to be built and the pole to be carved. He did not want to disgrace himself.

He ran his hand over the smooth wood and watched critically as the boy, his nephew, carefully painted the eyes of Dogfish. Above were the three Watchmen, to call warning of visitors who would approach the beach. Frog was there, to keep the pole from falling down, and Eagle and Killer Whale, to represent the chief's lineage. Gao had seen carvings on house poles that winked with their eyes, so skillfully were they rendered. His own carving—he stood back and appraised his work—his own did not wink, he thought, but was not totally without worth. He had not his uncle's skill; his uncle had died of the smallpox before Gao had learned enough, just as his uncle was not the master his grandfather had been.

There were so few carvers left. The boy might be the only one when Gao was gone. But even the boy might not be left. If he listened too long to the missionaries, he might tear down poles rather than raise them. He might catch the smallpox himself or die from some other pestilence that came from the white people's towns. He might have the skill, but not be asked to display it. So many now were without ears; they listened only to the white people and not to their own people.

But just for today they had warded off what might come. They did not yet have to say, "Here it comes to a stop," as they might when a story ended. This latest missionary, Richardson, did not have the power that the other one had possessed. His preaching was not so much about the great Chief of the Heavens as it was about what kind of church building they should have, and whether they should potlatch. How could they show the respect their families had earned if not by giving away great possessions? Richardson asked for gifts instead of giving them. That was not the way of a chief. Yes, this white man could be fought, Gao thought, if quietly.

"Enough," Gao said, and the boy started. "We are finished. Let us find the ropes and be sure they are ready." The boy nodded and Gao smiled. "Your painting is good. The day will come when I will be worthless next to you."

Now the boy smiled, and Gao was glad he had spoken. "I'm hungry," he went on. "Shall we see what we can find to eat? Perhaps my sister will give us a taste of what she prepares for tomorrow."

"Yes!" the boy agreed, a child again and no longer serious. They walked around the screen and along the gravel beach. The day was warm after the chill of night. Mostly naked children played everywhere, chased by dogs. The smell of cook fires hung in the air, and women bustled by with baskets laden with roots and berries. Gao and the boy circled canoes pulled almost to the houses that sat just above the high-water mark. All faced the inlet; who would want to look toward the ghosts that inhabited the inland?

The paint had faded from the elaborately carved poles that still stood, and from the cedar boards fronting the houses. All were gray, like the bones in a chief's burial. As Gao's bones would be someday, and the boy's after his. Perhaps he and the boy would come back in another generation, but maybe there would not be one. How could he come back if no baby was born to give him a shell?

Gao made himself quit thinking such dark thoughts. This

was a joyful time, a time for feasting and celebration, for dances and women's songs. The people who had gone south had returned, as had those who worked in canneries for the summer. Winter was the time for stories and dances. The white men's ships would no longer arrive during this time, and the people would draw into themselves until spring. Each winter there were fewer of them, though the people had once been as many as salmon eggs. Skit-ei-get seemed alive only because its empty houses had been filled by those who had left other towns to the dead.

And so Gao listened to the boy's chatter, and while his sister slapped at their hands with mock ferocity, pretended to steal a berry cake from a cedar box she had set out for tomorrow. They ate as they looked at the newly built house, its pungent wood red like blood against the gray of the village, and at the hole dug in front for the pole they had finished today. He explained to the boy how the pole would be raised with long ropes and how the beat of drums and songs would mark the moment. Describing something the child had never seen and Gao himself not so many times, he felt like an old man. But he had lived for only twenty-three summers and was not even married! Yet how could he help but feel old, a line between past and future?

Hearing the hoarse call of a raven, he turned to see the bird sitting on the highest beam of the new house. Huge and black, it might have had the dignity of an eagle but for the ruffled feathers around the neck that made it easy to see The Trickster. The bird cocked its head and looked at Gao with a beady dark eye. Did he laugh? Gao wondered with sudden bitterness, to see all that he had given the people slowly taken away? Did he admire the greed of white men, greater even than his own?

Or was he jealous? Did he play tricks on the white men? If so, Gao would not want to be Richardson. That man was so greedy, it was a wonder his hands had not shriveled to black claws like Raven's.

Gao stood there in the midst of the village, no longer hearing the laughter, the scrape of a steel adze against wood,

For Mom, with love and thanks for being my best friend.
This book, like all the others, would never have been written
without your encouragement, suggestions, and support.

the crackle of cook fires, and the hum of voices. He watched as Raven spread his great black wings and flapped his way aloft. And he wondered: had The Trickster not liked Hewitt, either?

Chapter One

With long, impatient strides, Luke Brennan crossed the hard-packed street to the wooden boardwalk. He ignored the fine mist that dampened his dark hair and the clatter of horses' hooves as a heavily loaded wagon passed just behind him. Frustration burned in his throat like rotgut whiskey, without the salvaging kick.

He was awaited on the covered sidewalk by a russet-haired man who leaned comfortably against a post, a cigar clamped between his teeth. Dr. Alistair Meade and Luke Brennan were old friends, though until this past week, they had not met in four years.

When Alistair saw Luke's face, his expression changed and he slowly removed the cigar from his mouth.

"Something wrong?"

Luke grimly extracted the crumpled telegram from his coat pocket and handed it to Alistair, who read it in silence.

"This is a setback," he said at last, handing the telegram back to Luke, who pocketed it again.

"Setback? You're a master of understatement, Alistair."

Scowling, Luke turned his back on a gaggle of young ladies who paused to admire the display of fine dress goods in the window of Victoria House, the large department store in front of which he had arranged to meet Alistair. His interest in completing the purchase of supplies for the coming expedition had abruptly vanished.

He hunched broad shoulders and stared unseeing at the busy street, which the drizzle had turned into a gray watercolor. He had spent the entire last year planning this expedition for the museum, coaxing money from benefactors, scheming to acquire the services of the finest photographer he could lure away from the government surveys. The fog-shrouded, mysterious Queen Charlotte Islands off the coast of British Columbia were his destination, his object to collect what remained of the material culture of the vanishing Haida Indians. But the photographs were to have been the coupe de grâce, the centerpiece of the museum exhibit. In shades of light on paper, they were to have immortalized the Haidas, providing a link between a dying people and the remnants of their culture that would lie lifelessly in the museum's glass cases. Now, with time running out, the photographer had failed to arrive in Victoria, his apologetic telegram serving as an inadequate substitute.

"Damn Thompson," Luke said bitterly.

"The man could hardly help becoming ill."

Luke ignored the doctor's annoyingly rational observation. "What the hell am I going to do, Alistair?"

His portly friend smoothed cinnamon side-whiskers and looked thoughtful. "There are several studios here in Victoria," he suggested. "Perhaps you could persuade a local photographer . . ."

"Working in the field is different. Even the equipment is not the same." Luke grimaced. "Let's forget the damned shopping. I can do it tomorrow."

Hired hacks waited in a sodden line along Government Street, but by unspoken agreement, the two men passed them. The walk to Alistair's comfortable Gothic-style house on Fort Street was not far.

The friendship between Luke and Dr. Alistair Meade had been one of shared interests, conducted primarily by correspondence. They had met on a South American expedition for which Alistair had served as doctor while indulging his own interest in plant collecting. This past spring, when Luke had first written of his intention to stop over in Victoria, Alistair had promptly sent a letter by return post volunteering his home. Since Luke's arrival, the portly doctor had conducted him about the fledgling city with every appearance of pleasure. A sense of vicarious adventure, Luke had thought. Since his marriage, Alistair had become more settled.

Others were on foot, too, despite the damp day, which made conversation difficult. Women with baskets over their arms and skirts that swept over the muddy sidewalk chattered as they went into shops; Chinese laborers passed like silent, self-contained shadows. A well-dressed businessman with a fat gold watch chain draped over his paunch stared down the Chinamen, who bowed obsequiously and stepped out of his way. Luke made a point of jostling the complacent fool when he reached him.

They had proceeded in silence for nearly a block before, sounding oddly diffident, Alistair said, "I know of an amateur photographer who might consider going with you. Although," he cleared his throat, displaying a hint of unease, "it would be somewhat out of the ordinary."

"What does that mean?"

Alistair didn't look at Luke. Instead, he gave every appearance of being fascinated by the sight of a muddy brougham that had stopped down the street to discharge a stout gentleman who handed down an equally stout lady wearing a walking suit of bilious green. "Actually," Alistair ventured, "this particular photographer is a woman."

"A woman?" Luke stopped dead on the wooden walk to stare incredulously at his old friend. "Are you insane?"

Alistair blinked, as though in surprise. "I don't believe so. I'll admit that photography is an unusual hobby for a young woman, but Miss Hewitt has earned an enviable reputation. Besides which . . . ah, you recognize her name."

Luke snorted and turned to glare after a passing wagon that had splattered the two men with mud. "The Reverend Hewitt's daughter, I presume. I recall her father mentioning her photographic interests."

"Indeed." Alistair spoke more quickly as they made way for a group of miners, then resumed walking. His rising enthusiasm was apparent in his voice. "Luke, she's an unusual young woman. We became acquainted when I wrote her father about collecting some plant specimens for me. There are many that exist only in the Queen Charlotte Islands, you know. Miss Hewitt was kind enough to oblige, and delivered them to me herself on a visit to Victoria. Since then, we have become friends of a sort." His tone again became persuasive. "She speaks the language, doubtless even has friends among the Haida. She could save you from hiring a translator as well as take photographs. Perhaps even help you acquire some unusual pieces not commonly shown. She could be a godsend."

Luke's laugh was harsh. "I gather she isn't married? Have you a chaperone in mind as well? Good God, Alistair."

"The trip is important to you." Heedless of the cold drizzle, Alistair stopped this time in mid-street, his gaze holding Luke's. "You knew the risk in going so late. If you don't catch the steamship in two days' time, you'll have lost your opportunity for this winter. And in another year . . ." He shrugged.

That was the trouble with old friends. Luke growled the rest of the sentence. "More fine objects will be irretrievably gone."

Damn Thompson, Luke thought again. He would have to go without the photographer. Detailed notes on the words of songs and ceremonials ought to be sufficient. . . .

"There's more," Alistair said bluntly. "I hear that Durham is in town. I assume that he plans to go north. If so, he'll be on the same steamship."

It was the worst possible news. James Durham was determined to make the Field Museum's Northwest Coast collection equal to any. Luke despised Durham's methods, and as the rival museum's curator, the man had become Luke's nemesis. To think that Durham might beat him to the Queen Charlotte Islands, claiming the finest objects the Haida were willing to sell! It was insupportable.

The rattle and clatter of an approaching carriage spurred the two men to resume their walk, though they had now left the covered sidewalk behind. Victoria was growing in peculiar fits and starts, with the result that handsome masonry buildings stood cheek by jowl with ramshackle wooden structures, while sheep or pigs might still wander down Government Street. The Christ Church Cathedral rose out of a field, and the roads were abysmal. Ridiculous, considering the pretensions of the city's finest citizens, who, with their mansions and tennis parties and regattas, aped English nobility.

Alistair interrupted his brooding. "A call on Miss Hewitt wouldn't take you long."

Luke's blue eyes narrowed. "You're very persistent," he observed. "I can't help wondering why."

"Her work is superb," Alistair said simply. "She's single-minded in the pursuit of her craft."

Luke grunted. It was ludicrous to suppose that some young lady who dabbled in photography, however successfully, could take the place of George Thompson, whose images of the southwest were nationally admired.

But Alistair said with sudden passion, "Good God above, Luke, surely you aren't so conventional as to refuse to consider her only because she's a woman? That would be ironic in view of the fact that Mary accompanied you everywhere."

Muscles tightened in Luke's jaw, though his tone was carefully unemotional. "Mary would still be alive if I hadn't dragged her to the Yucatan. Disregarding the fragility of the female sex is not a mistake I care to make twice."

"It was an accident!"

The cold rain that dripped down his neck suited Luke's

mood. "An accident that would not have happened had she been home in Boston where she belonged."

"Nonetheless, the two cases are not comparable. Mary was gently reared, not accustomed to a primitive lifestyle. Miss Hewitt, to the contrary, followed her father where his missionary work took him. Why, she lived among the Haida for over four years!"

Luke accepted the ache that came with any reminder of his young wife, gone for nearly the same four years now. Their marriage had been too brief, but he had not forgotten her, or his own culpability. He could scarcely believe that Alistair, long a friend, could shrug the past aside so easily. Luke spoke coldly. "Nonetheless, I was responsible for Mary's death. I will not be responsible for your Miss Hewitt's."

Turning in at the picket gate of his handsomely decorated clapboard house, Alistair raised his brows. "So you plan to throw your expedition over?"

"What I plan is to hire an Indian guide who can translate for me. I will simply do without the photographs."

"Which were to be the heart of your display, what separated it from those of rival museums."

The two men paused on the porch to shake off the rain and knock the mud from their boots. Luke said impatiently, "The life figures I plan will be effective enough."

Alistair opened the front door. Glancing back, he said, "And how will you have authentic figures sculpted without photographs to work from?"

"I'll take ample notes." Seeing that his friend was about to speak, Luke shook his head. "No, Alistair, no more. You can't persuade me. Aside from my deeper qualms, it simply wouldn't work. I intend to travel around the islands, even to the seldom-visited west coast. The only transport will be Indian canoe. To be of any use, a photographer must be able to accompany me. If I were going only to Masset, where Miss Hewitt might stay with the Hudson Bay Company factor, or to Skidegate, where her father's home was . . . But as things stand, the practical difficulties in taking a woman would deter me in any case."

"Perhaps there is something in what you say," Alistair conceded grudgingly as he led the way into the gaslit parlor, where a low fire still burned on the grate. "She's an unusual woman, however. I hope you'll agree to at least call on her. You knew her father, after all. Extending your sympathies on her loss would be only courteous."

"The man hated me and all of my kind! I can't imagine that my sympathy would be welcome."

"Ah, but has it occurred to you that she might have some photographs of the Haida in her files? Perhaps you could persuade her to part with some of them."

Luke's automatic stubbornness was checked by a glimmer of hope. Even a few photographs of everyday activities would achieve his purpose in part. He said thoughtfully, "I don't suppose that she was allowed to attend any of the ceremonials. The Reverend disapproved heartily of shamans and the old ways. His entire goal in life was to obliterate the Indians' culture. He would scarcely have permitted his daughter to photograph such pagan ceremonies."

"Permitted?" The word appeared to amuse Alistair. "Miss Hewitt strikes me as a determined young woman. I doubt she would have heeded such a ban."

Luke accepted the glass of deep red port wine proffered by the doctor. "You make me grateful that I'm not seriously considering taking her. A headstrong young woman sounds like a highly unpleasant travelling companion."

"I intended a compliment. I think you'd find her a kindred spirit, if you would only give her a chance."

There was steel in Luke's voice. "You're asking for the impossible, Alistair. I'm prepared to risk myself for the cause of ethnology. But not a young lady."

"You will call on her?"

Luke threw up a hand in mock defense. "Very well! You've worn me down. If nothing else, I look forward to finding out how she gained such a fervent advocate. Is Miss Hewitt a stunning beauty? Tell me, what does your esteemed wife think of her?"

Alistair settled into an armchair beside the fire with an air of satisfaction. "A beauty? To the contrary, I'm afraid. Her face is too strong, and there is something in her eyes . . . a sort of distance, perhaps even an indifference. Well, it may be only the photographer in her, always observing. As far as Caroline goes, oddly enough, I believe she admires Miss Hewitt. She has no reason to feel jealousy, if that's what you're implying. No, no, I prefer to hold the reins in my household. For a man willing to run in tandem, however—"

"With a homely, headstrong spinster? Thank you, but no."

"I wouldn't describe her as homely," Alistair countered. "Not pretty, but intelligent, alive, certain of herself. Not qualities that appeal to every man, but you . . ."

Luke flung himself into a matching armchair, stretching out long legs to the fire. His wet boots began to gently steam. With raised brows, he studied the good doctor. "Trying to marry me off?"

Alistair only smiled. "Wait until you see her photographs, my friend. Marriage might be a small price to pay for such talent."

Luke became very still. "No, Alistair. The price would be entirely too high. Trust me. I've paid it."

There's a gentleman here to see you, Katherine. A Mister Brennan. He is apparently staying with Doctor Meade. He claims to have known your father."

Katherine Hewitt glanced up at her aunt, a handsome woman with dark hair only faintly streaked with silver, coiled atop a proud head. The cool disapproval in her crisp voice piqued Kate's interest.

Not that it took very much to do so. Kate was desperate for diversion. During the past year and a half since her father's death, she had sometimes thought she would go mad confined to the circumscribed life of a well-to-do young lady, with no other goal in life but to capture a husband, the last thing Kate wanted. That life, this house, had become a prison that had defied her every effort to escape it.

Now, with relief from the proffered crumbs, she set aside her despised needlework and rose, shaking out her skirts.

"I don't believe I know a Mister Brennan," she murmured thoughtfully. "Unless—"

"Unless?" Mrs. Fitzgerald interrupted sharply.

"Father wrote about a museum collector," Kate said. "A Mister Lucas Brennan. Perhaps he has heard about Father's collection."

"You mean those heathen objects? I'll never understand how a man who disapproved of the Indians' savage practices could admire such crude work."

Kate stepped ahead of her aunt into the hall. "But then, you and Father had very little in common, didn't you?"

Mrs. Fitzgerald's voice became tinged with ice. "Naturally I respected the work he did. But dragging a child along was unpardonable. Worse yet was keeping you with him even after you had grown into a young lady. Why, you should be married, with your own household by now. But he was too selfishly concerned with his own comfort!"

The subject was an old one, the refrain well worn. Kate contented herself with saying, "If he had been selfishly concerned with his own comfort, he would scarcely have been a missionary among savages, Aunt Grace."

Before her aunt could do more than give a disdainful sniff, Kate opened the door to the parlor and swept in. Her caller had his back to the door, although he could hardly have failed to hear her entrance. A tall, broad-shouldered man in a dark suit, he stood in front of a marble-topped table on which were displayed a number of Kate's more conventional photographs. It was the one concession her aunt made to Kate's unusual vocation.

When the man at last did turn to face her, in his unsettlingly blue eyes there was a look of startled respect that Kate had come to recognize. Clearly, he had known about her hobby; equally clearly, he had not expected her standards to be high.

It was not his expression that shook Kate; rather, it was the man himself. She could see why her aunt had disapproved of him, though the disturbing quality was difficult to define. His black-serge suit was perfectly correct, the crisp white collar a foil for his darkly tanned countenance. So what about him so unsettled her? Perhaps it was the directness of his blue gaze, suggesting that there was something untamed about this man. She tried to tell herself that it was only his bronzed skin that gave such an impression, coupled with a small scar on his chin and hair that was just a little long, brushing his collar.

The frisson of awareness she felt disconcerted Kate. She could only hope that her aunt, standing silently at her elbow, had not observed her reaction. It was absurd in any case. Kate had no illusions about her own appearance; men's gazes passed over her without pause. Nor did her lack of feminine graces cause her more than an occasional pang. As surely as iron bars, beauty would have trapped her.

She would not know the smell of the wind and its speed as it skimmed the waves, the primitive beat of Haida drums, and the flickering shadows of dancers on the firelit walls of the longhouse. She would have learned to manage servants rather than to swim; she would now be ruled by a complacent man and the demands of children as well as by those of society. No! She would not long for something she did not possess and did not want. She would not allow herself to wish that this stranger's eyes held more than respect.

Her back very straight, Kate inclined her head. "Mister Brennan," she said. "How do you do?"

Frown lines showed between his dark brows. She had the sense that he was disconcerted, that she was not what he had anticipated. Why he should have held any expectations about her, she couldn't imagine. When he spoke, Kate was not surprised that he didn't bother with the usual courtesies. "These photographs are very good," he said brusquely. "Yours, I take it?"

"Yes, they are. Have we met, Mister Brennan?"

Those curiously penetrating blue eyes had not once left

her face, not even to acknowledge her aunt. "No, we haven't. I did know your father, however. I was sorry to hear of his death."

"Murder."

The single word, calmly spoken, did not elicit the usual reaction. He only nodded in turn. "Yes, so Alistair said. I gather the authorities haven't arrested the culprit."

"What authorities?" she asked with a hint of bitterness, before her aunt bustled forward, her tone and glance repressive.

"Please, Mister Brennan, let's have a seat. How is it that you were acquainted with my brother-in-law?"

He glanced about and chose a gold sofa abundantly draped with satin fringe. Seated upon it, he looked singularly out of place. "I'm a museum curator, Mrs. Fitzgerald. Miss Hewitt's father was kind enough to put me up last summer. We had a number of quite interesting discussions." He hesitated. "I'm afraid he didn't agree with my purpose, nor I with his."

Since Kate was well aware that Aunt Grace had despised her brother-in-law but could hardly say so, following up this remark would have taken the older woman into dangerous territory. Instead, she asked with rigid courtesy, "Can we offer you tea, Mister Brennan?"

Kate doubted that he had come for the purpose of sipping tea with two females, but he said only, "Thank you."

Her aunt said stiffly, "If you'll excuse me for a moment, then."

Kate was relieved at Aunt Grace's departure. She was beginning to feel a good deal of curiosity about Mr. Lucas Brennan. His expression of sympathy had struck her as too perfunctory to be the sole purpose of his visit. She would have been certain that this visitor had designs on her father's collection but for one thing: How could he have known of it? Her father rarely showed it, and he was particularly unlikely to have done so to a museum curator. He considered the entire breed to be scoundrels.

She was quite certain that she had not mentioned the collection to Dr. Meade. Had the doctor called here more often, she might have succumbed to the temptation to show the collection to him—as she had shown him her photographs before her father's death—but to her regret, they most often met in company in other people's homes. And no wonder! Society little condoned a friendship between a married man and a young lady.

She tried to recall what she knew about Mr. Brennan. Nearly a year and a half ago, she had been on her annual visit to Victoria when her father had been murdered. Only a few days before his death, he had written her a letter that was to be their last communication.

"This latest visitor is unswerving in his determination," the Reverend Hewitt had written, "although at least he does not rob graves. It may be my presence rather than respect for the dead that deters him, however." Her father had almost sounded as though he had enjoyed their arguments, perhaps because Mr. Brennan was both well educated and passionate in his convictions.

Now she clasped her hands in her lap and studied him curiously. "I'm familiar with my father's opinions, Mister Brennan. In what way did you disagree with his purpose?"

He spoke quickly, almost impatiently, making no effort to soften his opinion. "Unlike the missionaries, I don't automatically assume our culture to be superior to all others. Only different. In the process of converting the Indians to our way of life, we are shaming them and annihilating their history. What smallpox has not accomplished, missionaries such as your father have. Soon there will be nothing of their culture left."

"A process that men such as you are hastening," she pointed out tartly.

He paid her the compliment of not appearing surprised that she should have given the matter any thought. "Perhaps," he conceded. "But it is a process that will take place with or without us. Our intent is to salvage, not to destroy. At least in museum displays, some small part of the material culture of North American Indians will be available to future ethnologists. We will have a window to the past that would be gone altogether were it not for our efforts."

Kate was unwillingly impressed, as much by the intensity of his belief as by the actual words, just as her father had been. "Tell me, Mister Brennan," she said with a calm she did not feel, "why do you think my father disapproved of your work?"

He didn't hesitate. "Your father denounced and belittled the traditional ways of the Haida Indian. The pieces that I sought to collect symbolized the beliefs he would have his converts forget."

Would that her father's convictions had been so simple! Perhaps then he would not have been murdered. Or at the very least, she might have known what to do with his legacy, and with her own life.

Kate came to a sudden decision, although there was no time for her to examine her motives. "I should like to show you something," she said, abruptly standing. "If you would humor me."

His eyes narrowed, but he rose as well, seeming to sense the challenge she had silently offered. "Certainly," he said, his tone scrupulously polite.

In the wide hall, they met her aunt, carrying a tray that bore a steaming porcelain teapot and a plate of scones.

She looked startled and, Kate thought, relieved. "Are you leaving already, Mister Brennan?"

Kate interceded. "Mister Brennan expressed an interest in seeing my darkroom. If you'll excuse us for just a few minutes?"

A frown marred her aunt's ordinarily smooth brow. "Perhaps I should come with you . . . ."

"Aunt, you know how the odors overpower you. Aren't we to go out tonight? I'd hate to be responsible for giving you a headache."

Mrs. Fitzgerald's gaze was unexpectedly shrewd, but after a moment, she inclined her head. "I'll just pour the tea, then. Don't keep Mister Brennan out in the cold for long, Katherine."

As Kate led the way toward the back of the house, she was uneasily conscious of her silent follower. He had a way of moving that reminded her more of the Indians than of the usually heavy tread of the civilized white man. With a prickle at the back of her neck, she could feel his gaze resting on her. The blue taffeta of her skirts rustled with each step, and she held her slender shoulders very straight, her head high.

For once, she was grateful for her modish appearance, though it could not gild the plain oak beneath. Still, she knew the bustle that belled her skirts made her waist appear tiny, the striped overskirt and high-buttoned collar were crisp, and the chignon gave an illusion of elegance to her mass of curly dark hair. In the young lady he met today, he would not see the girl who had dressed and behaved as best suited her fancy in another world, a far more primitive one. She had no doubt of the contempt with which he would regard that girl; all men were the same, even her own father. He had given Kate her freedom only because he *was* selfish, and knew that bowing to society's dictates would have meant the loss of her companionship. And perhaps also because he had seen her talent as God-given, a gift more important than her femininity.

Cloaks hung on hooks beside the back door, but Kate ignored them. The sky was gray and heavy, the air damp-smelling, but for the moment, the incessant autumn rain held back. A narrow brick path led across the sweep of lawn, past the waterlogged tennis court to the former gardener's cottage, tucked in a back corner. She had been grudgingly permitted to convert it into a refuge, which on some days was all that saved her sanity.

But when she opened the front door and stepped inside, she made no move toward the second door, behind which lay her darkroom. Instead, she stood silently, allowing the man who had entered behind her to take in the shelves of objects, the masks that hung on the white plaster walls, the decorated baskets and bent-cedar boxes that cluttered the floor. Amongst them she had displayed her photographs of the Haida. She heard his sharp intake of breath as he turned slowly to view the contents of the small room, many of them grotesque, all of them a poignant reminder of that other world, of a nearly vanished way of life.

His voice was rough, as though to disguise his emotions. "Your father's. And the photographs are your own."

"Yes." Not looking at him, she stepped toward the wall of masks, some of them with huge, carved beaks, others astonishingly human appearing. She let her finger trace the painted cheek of a transformation mask. Hanging there on the wall, it seemed dead to her, the paint fading, the spirit and the hunger for understanding that had brought it to mysterious life lacking. The masks, the room, all that surrounded her brought an ache to her chest for which she was very nearly grateful. It countered in a small way the emptiness of her present life.

She only regretted that all of her father's collection wasn't here. The Reverend Hewitt's successor had shipped the bulk of it to her, but her letters of inquiry about the missing portion had thus far not been answered.

She didn't protest when Luke Brennan stepped forward to touch a wooden bowl carved into the shape of a frog, to shake a shaman's rattle, to caress the texture of a very old, painted hat. Goat's-horn spoons, the ceremonial ax that white men had with repugnance labeled "a slave killer," fishing hooks, a heavy hammer representing a thunderbird—none escaped his touch or gaze. He muttered to himself as he examined the pieces and the photographs that accompanied them. In his face she saw the exhilaration of a man presented with his heart's desire. Kate was startled into wondering whether he had ever looked at a woman that way, and what it would feel like to be that woman.

He tried to hide it, but his eyes glittered covetously. She had to admire his straightforwardness, however. "Will you sell this collection to me?"

"No." Her tone was flat. "This is all that I still possess of my father. I showed it to you so that you might understand him. You are quite right that he sought to convert the Haida, but he had respect for what they had been. He was a realistic man, Mister Brennan. He recognized that the tide of the white man's progress would destroy the Indians were they not helped to adapt. Nonetheless, he wanted them to value their artistic heritage and the land to which they had a right. He had only contempt for those such as you, who take advantage of the Indians, even steal from them. It was your methods he despised, Mister Brennan, not your goal."

"Adapt?" He uttered an incredulous laugh. "Is that what you call it? I have long read about the magnificent chants used by the Haida to greet honored visitors. When my steamship tied up at Skidegate last year, *we* were greeted by the dismal strains of Protestant hymns played badly on brass horns, with your father conducting. Adaptation? Cultural robbery is closer to the mark."

Flushing, she said, "I did not agree with everything my father did. But he at least was not content only to destroy. He sought to replace what was lost. That is surely more than you are doing, Mister Brennan. You have such noble aims— that of salvaging the Haida culture for future ethnologists." Kate mocked his own words, then continued bitterly: "But what about the Haida *people?* What do they have left when you take away their ceremonial dishes and masks, the memorial poles that celebrate their ancestors? Do they care that those rest in glass cases in Boston? They know only that when the next winter comes, they must do the dance without a mask, or not do it at all. They know that somehow they are supposed to remember great warriors when they see painted crosses in a white man's cemetery."

She was not surprised when he did not back down. "What is it you would have me do?" he asked. "Leave the memorial poles to rot? The dishes and masks to be bought by unscrupulous collectors who don't care what part they played in a dance or what food was eaten from them? Or perhaps I ask the wrong question." His tone became silky. "What would *you* do, Miss Hewitt?"

He seemed very large in the small room, his personality a force that crackled in the air like a summer storm. Kate held her head proudly high and did not flinch from his provocation or allow her gaze to shy from his intense blue eyes. "I would leave them alone," she said in a voice that shook only slightly. "Let them find their own way into a new world."

He was silent for a moment, then lifted his hands and let them fall in a strangely helpless gesture. His expression was compassionate, his voice gentler. "It's too late for that," he said. "Prostitution and smallpox are killing the Haida. There will be none left to find their own way if they are not helped."

"And who is to help them?" she asked on a rush of anger. How dare he? "My father is dead. Murdered. His successor cares only about extracting enough money to build a grander church. The Hudson Bay Company cares only about profits. And I . . ." She turned away, angered to feel tears burning in her eyes. "I am forever exiled, because I am a woman. I envy you, Mister Brennan—you are free to follow your own convictions."

"And you are not? What is stopping you, Miss Hewitt? You are a fine photographer. Can you not support yourself with portraiture?"

She gave a choked laugh and turned back to face him. A part of her was shocked that she had so bared herself before this man. Another part of her felt reckless. What did it matter? He was a stranger; she would probably never see him again. Why not, just this once, insist on the truth?

"Surely you don't think any self-respecting man would bring his business to a woman? For me, it is a barely acceptable hobby. I am fortunate that my aunt has been so tolerant." She did not tell him that in her desperation, she had even considered marrying a missionary who worked with the Tsimshian, only a day's sail from the Queen Charlotte Islands. Until, that is, she had discovered that he regarded her photography as a "masculine" hobby that had no place in a wife's duties.

Frowning again, Luke Brennan was silent. Indeed, what was there for him to say? She had only stated reality. Because she was a woman, she could do nothing to help herself, far less the people her father had sought to guide. She could not even avenge his murder.

"You've seen what I wanted to show you," she said, conscious suddenly of their aloneness. "We had best go back to the house now. My aunt will be anxious."

On the way to the door, she had to pass him. When his hand shot out to stop her, Kate's heart gave an uncomfortable lurch.

"Wait," he said in an odd voice. "Tell me something, Miss Hewitt. Would you return to the Queen Charlotte Islands, given a chance? Would you risk your reputation, even your life, to go back one more time?"

Kate stood very still in his grasp, staring at the door in front of her. She was suddenly light-headed with hope.

"I would risk anything," she replied.

"Very well." His face expressionless, Lucas Brennan released her. "Then I have a proposition for you, Miss Hewitt. I seem to have lost the photographer who was to have accompanied my forthcoming expedition. For what I assure you is a generous remuneration, would you consider taking his place? Despite my infamous purpose?"

On a great rush of relief, Kate closed her eyes. Against the darkness of her eyelids, she had a vision. She saw a rocky inlet lined with silent totem poles and empty longhouses, while above, the towering cedar forest rose deep green into the mist that shrouded the heights. She heard the waves singing against the shore and the voice of Raven speaking to her, though she could not seem to understand him.

Nor did it matter. This man, this stranger, was giving her a chance to do what she must. Kate opened her eyes and smiled at him.

"Thank you, Mister Brennan. I would be delighted to join your expedition."

Chapter Two

I f you go, this is no longer your home." Aunt Grace's voice
was as unbending as her spine. Forbiddingly framed in the
doorway, she had not stepped over the threshold of Kate's
bedroom, as though doing so would be an admission of
weakness.

The ultimatum was not a surprise to Kate, though it hurt.
She stood beside the bed in the gracefully feminine room
that had always seemed a rebuke to her. Declining the help
of her maid, she had begun to lay out the most appropriate
costumes for the journey. An elderly, battered steamer trunk
sat open to receive them. With less than twenty-four hours
to pack, Kate was filling the trunk with more haste than care.
Now she faced her aunt, but made no effort to close the distance between them.

"I hope you will change your mind, Aunt," she said quietly. "I'll be amply chaperoned on the steamship, and I
expect to find Annie at Metlakatla. I'm sure she'll be willing
to accompany me. You know she'll guard me with her life."

"That does not make her respectable. She is an Indian,

with no idea of civilized behavior. Another instance of your father's heedlessness."

Anger and nausea mixed in Kate's throat. She would not allow Annie, kind and plump and with a sense of dignity as strong as Aunt Grace's, to be scorned. Nor did Kate wish to part with her only family so harshly. "You've been good to me, Aunt," she tried again. "Perhaps you are right that Father should not have kept me with him. But he did, and it changed me. I feel . . . stifled here. I need something more, something . . ."

It was useless. She could see that on her aunt's face. "If you care at all for me," Aunt Grace said coldly, "you will write a polite letter to Mister Brennan declining his offer. You will not disgrace your uncle or your cousin or me by accompanying an unmarried 'gentleman' "—her tone implied that he was no such thing—"beyond the reach of civilization. Even your father would not have permitted this."

"Aunt Grace, Father was *murdered*. Haven't you the least interest in who did it? Can't you understand that I must know?"

Alarm subtly changed the uncompromising lines of her aunt's face. "You cannot intend—"

"I want to know where his body was found." Kate's hands curled into fists. "I want to see his grave. How can I say good-bye . . ." Her voice broke, but she caught herself. "I must know."

"Kate, this is foolishness! Asking questions is . . ."

"Unladylike? Do you think it will reflect badly on you?" Scornful, Kate turned away to fold one of the split skirts she had sewed for herself long ago as a compromise between function and appearance.

"Dangerous." The word was both unexpected and melodramatic. Surprised, Kate looked back at her aunt, to find her face as grim as her voice. "This is life and death," her aunt said. "Not a parlor game."

"I didn't know you realized that," Kate said softly.

Aunt Grace still stood in the doorway, the long, white fingers that twined before her the only sign of perturbation. Her answer was indirect. "I could hardly be expected to mourn him," she said with disdain. "He treated my sister shamefully."

The marriage of Kate's parents had certainly been an unusual one. At nearly thirty years of age, her father had become ordained in Birmingham, England, and been sent by the Missionary Society to western Canada. Forced to wait out the winter in Victoria, he had met and married seventeen-year-old Amy Stapleton, Aunt Grace's younger sister. Pretty and sweet, accustomed to being cosseted, Amy had admired the minister's dedication, thrilled to the fire of his passion for Christ as well as for her. Why she had not foreseen what this meant for their future, Kate had never understood.

The outcome of this mismatched marriage was inevitable, if unorthodox. Newly wedded, Amy Hewitt had accompanied her husband to Bella Bella, far up the British Columbia coast. The living was primitive, smallpox rampant. The Indians, whom she had romantically imagined evangelizing, proved to be smelly, drunken, and hostile. Amy had not learned courage or determination; instead, she had clung hysterically to her husband. The Reverend Hewitt's love turned to pity and impatience, and the next spring when Amy became pregnant, he had taken her to Victoria to stay with her parents. She never traveled north again.

Now Kate let the skirt drop back to the bed. "What about Mother, Aunt Grace?" she challenged. "You often speak of a woman's duty to her husband. What about her? Didn't she owe my father a duty?"

"A husband has an equal obligation to provide and care for his family. Expecting a delicate young woman to set up housekeeping amidst squalor and with savages as her only near neighbors was scarcely reasonable."

"She knew his calling when she married him."

"He could have done God's work here in Victoria just as well."

As a child, Kate had often thought the same. She had

watched her mother dwindle into a helpless, weeping creature who at last accepted her lingering death from consumption gratefully. Surely, being the husband his wife needed would have been God's work, too. But Kate had come to believe that her father had failed his wife not by his absence, but by allowing her to stay behind. Why had he not insisted that she *live?*

Sometimes Kate wondered if man and woman had a duty to each other at all. Had God indeed set it into stone that woman shall live thus and man so? If her parents had been happy in their unconventional marriage, Kate knew that she would not be speaking now about duty. She did not care for something so passionless, something required and not given freely. She had watched her aunt and uncle with their obligatory inquiries after comfort, the dry touch of lips to cheek. Duty, it seemed to her, was a refuge for those who lacked love.

"Perhaps Mother was frail because everyone allowed her to be so," Kate said, knowing that the assessment was harsh, but determined to say it, if only once.

"She tried . . ." Was there some lack of conviction in Aunt Grace's voice?

Kate's eyes met her aunt's gray ones. "Did she?"

"Your father left her without a purpose. She had nothing."

"She had me." Kate shocked even herself. It was the child in her who had spoken, the child who had hopelessly wept into her pillow because she had known that her mother did not love her enough for life to be worth living. "Now I need a purpose," she said. "Can't you understand that, Aunt?"

For the first time, she saw past the older woman's stern mask to the puzzlement beneath. "If you are so determined to live amongst heathens, why did you not marry that young missionary?"

"Because the work would not have been mine." Once again she had shocked her aunt, she saw. Well, perhaps speaking the truth was like a sickness in the bloodstream, spreading and gaining strength until it was impossible to resist. And why should she try to? It *was* the truth she spoke.

"He didn't want a partner. He wanted a woman's body, a housekeeper, a mother for his children. He didn't want *me*."

She had almost done it. She was frightened to think of how close she had come. To her shame, Kate had encouraged him, not because she loved him, but because he could give her some of what she sought. He had been appointed to assist Mr. William Duncan at the Metlakatla Mission, not so very far from the Queen Charlottes. He might well be sent on missionary work to the Haida, for Mr. Duncan did not care for assistants. He had a habit of fobbing them off elsewhere.

The life would be familiar, Kate had told herself; she would have escaped *this* life. She would be closer to her father's murderer.

The missionary was not a handsome man; had he been, he would have courted a more admired young lady. Still, she didn't find him physically repugnant. She wasn't attracted to him, either, but then, she didn't expect to be. The truth was, Kate thought little of him one way or the other. He was merely a means to an end.

Until, that is, the day she had shown him some of her photographs. He gave a cursory glance through them, then cleared his throat. "I'm surprised that your father encouraged you in such an unusual . . . pursuit." She heard clearly the unspoken implication: He would not criticize her father, but he thought him misguided. "We will soon have you too busy for such things," he murmured confidently.

He was standing very close to her, and his eyes, a rather pale blue, focused on her mouth. He leaned toward her, his tongue moistening his lips. Kate discovered quite abruptly that he was repugnant to her after all. And what had looked like escape, she saw suddenly as another trap. An eternal one. *'Til death do us part*, she had thought, shuddering. To bring her father's murderer to justice, she was prepared to sacrifice a great deal, but not her entire life. Not her soul.

Her aunt's sniff recalled her to the present. "Ridiculous," she snapped. "The only proper work for a woman is her husband. Love is hardly required. I had no idea you held such romantic notions."

"I've seen Alice sighing over her books of poetry." Kate was on safe ground here; her cousin at seventeen was excessively romantic.

"Alice can afford to demand romance," Aunt Grace said acerbically. Her face then softened and she stepped into the room, the crisp taffeta of her skirt sweeping over the floral carpet. "It hardly seems fair to you, I know, but there is no use our pretending. Alice is both pretty and charming. She is also an heiress. Nonetheless, the men who protest their love to her will do so as cold-bloodly as your young missionary chose you. She is perhaps too young to realize that. You, Katherine, are not."

"I didn't ask for love," Kate said. "Only respect."

"That's why you are accompanying this American? Because you fancy he will offer you respect?"

"Because I will be able to respect myself," Kate said. "I'm the only one who cares that somebody murdered Father. He did his best for me. I must do my best for him."

Her aunt inclined her head. "Then so be it. You must understand, Katherine, that you cannot expect to defy your uncle and me on such a grave matter and receive our blessings. We've done our best to treat you as a daughter. We would not permit Alice to do something that is both scandalous and dangerous. We cannot permit you to, either."

Kate's lips felt stiff. "I do understand, Aunt."

"Very well." Aunt Grace turned to sweep out. On the threshold, she paused. "Be careful, Katherine. Very, very careful."

Kate departed her aunt and uncle's house without a backward glance, down the allée of rhododendrons that flanked the drive. She did not let herself think about the fact that she would never see the great blossoms bloom again. Her uncle had permitted her the use of the family's coachman and the carriage, which was fully loaded with her trunks. Perhaps Uncle had been anxious to speed her on her way, Kate thought ironically.

She scarcely knew what she felt. She was exhilarated, frightened, determined. She had schemed and prayed for this moment, but not foreseen the cost. Mr. Brennan planned the expedition to last for four or five months, depending on when steamship service resumed in the spring. That seemed in the distant future now, but Kate knew better. When her current employment was over, what would she do?

He had indeed offered her generous pay for her services, enough to attempt setting up business as a photographer. But not here in Victoria, where her doing so would be an embarrassment to the Fitzgeralds. By their lights, they had been kind to her. The Reverend Hewitt had left his daughter nothing. What little the Missionary Society paid him, he had used on medicine and books for his parishioners. After his death, Kate's aunt and uncle had clothed and fed and housed their niece. They *had* treated her like a daughter: a pampered and protected young lady. Something she was not.

She had felt especially sad saying good-bye to Alice. Despite being greatly admired and flattered, Alice had remained sweet and rather naive. She was easily led, which worried Kate. This morning Kate had hugged her and felt Alice's slender arms cling tight.

"I wish you weren't going," Alice said tearfully.

"I shall miss you," Kate admitted. "Perhaps you'll be married by the time I see you again."

Alice gave a watery chuckle. "Heavens, no! I don't want a winter wedding! When I marry, it will be in the garden, with roses in bloom and the sun shining."

"And have you chosen the groom?" Kate asked with some amusement. Alice seemed quite certain that no rain would dare fall on *her* wedding day.

Her young cousin crinkled her nose. "No, how can I? Mister Scott is so dashing, but sometimes brusque. Mister Grubb writes splendid poetry, but I cannot become Amy Grubb! And Mister Collins—" here she hesitated, looking troubled "—he claims to admire me excessively, but then he pats me on the hand as though I were a child and refuses to worry me with business, though I know he and Father have dealings. I would like a man to *talk* to me! Do you know what I mean, Kate?"

"Indeed I do!" Kate could not resist hugging Alice again. Her cousin had more sense than she had realized. "You are absolutely right! Promise me you won't marry a man who will not at least confide in you his worries."

"I promise," Alice said solemnly. "And you must do the same, Kate."

She had felt ridiculous, but promised anyway. Men were generally willing to talk to her, she thought now. What they did not do was listen. Women, after all, were not expected to hold opinions.

Though it was early morning, the waterfront already bustled with activity. Despite new competition, Victoria remained the principal port north of San Francisco. Sailing vessels and steamships were lined up in the inner harbor to load and unload, while a frigate of Her Majesty's Navy stood offshore. The week's rain had turned Wharf Street to mud, so that drivers cracked their whips to persuade weary horses to haul loads through the slippery muck. The carriage rumbled past the new Custom House with its mansard roof and lurched and slid to a stop beside a warehouse. Beyond it stretched an L-shaped wharf, with the white-painted steamer alongside. Smoke already curled from its stacks, rising to meet the overcast sky.

Kate was grateful to see Luke Brennan waiting for her amidst the chaos at dockside, his friend Dr. Meade with him. She was disconcerted by the pleasure she felt at the sight of Mr. Brennan, though perhaps relief was a better word. Throwing away all security to accept his casual offer had begun to seem like madness. What if he had regretted it and sent a note around to her that she hadn't received? What if her impressions of him had been false and he was not to be trusted? What if . . .

Kate pulled herself up short. At least he was here, reassuringly solid and clearly impatient for her arrival.

He had abandoned any pretensions to fashion, she saw, wearing a shapeless brown frock coat and a felt hat pushed to the back of his head. Dr. Meade was considerably nattier, with a checkered suit and a silver-headed cane.

The coachman came around to open the door for her, and Kate carefully gathered her heavy skirts before she stepped down to the wooden boardwalk. The salty air assailed her nostrils, and a brisk breeze tugged tendrils of her hair loose.

"Good morning, Mister Brennan, Doctor Meade."

"You are prompt, at least," Luke said in what he very likely imagined to be an affable tone. His approval appeared to dissipate, however, as he looked her over with something less than approbation. "I trust you brought more practical garments."

Kate was rather fond of her traveling dress. Although it required a corset and bustle beneath, the wine-colored wool was warm and easily cleaned. She would not have chosen it to ride in an Indian canoe. Their passage, however, had been booked on the steamship *Skeena,* named for the river and owned by the mercantile company in which her uncle was a partner. The new stern-wheeler's dining saloon and state-rooms were admired for their elegance. Kate could scarcely dine with the captain in a man's jodhpurs.

Nettled, she responded sharply, "Would you care to inspect my trunks?"

"I'm depending on your good sense."

"How nice to hear that," she retorted, then turned to his companion. "Doctor Meade, it's kind of you to see us off."

The plump doctor bowed over her hand. "I'm suffering the pangs of envy, Miss Hewitt. I begin to wish I were accompanying you."

"You would miss the comforts of home," Luke contributed.

Alistair smiled. "I trust you'll ignore Luke's manners. He's been a bear for the last twenty-four hours. He seems to be quite certain something else will go wrong before your expedition sets out."

Luke growled a response under his breath.

"Did you expect the *Skeena* to run ashore?" Kate asked him sweetly.

His face had a distinctly sardonic cast. "I expected your uncle to offer a meeting at dawn with pistols."

"The fault is being laid entirely at my door, Mister Brennan," Kate said. "You've been absolved of all responsibility."

"Actually, I expected you not to show up," he admitted. "Your uncle is the one who should be shot for agreeing to such insanity."

Kate glared at him. "Fortunately, my uncle's agreement was not required."

"What did you do?" he asked. "Sneak out?"

"Why did you invite me if you feel this way?"

"Lord knows," he muttered. "I frequently regret my impulses." He turned his head, and his dark brows drew together. "What the devil . . ."

Kate glanced over her shoulder. "Those are my trunks. Surely you were aware that photographic supplies are bulky."

"Do you still use the wet-plate method?" Dr. Meade asked hastily, with a sidelong glance at his friend.

"No, but I thought it wise to bring my developing solutions, since we will be there for several months. That way, I can be certain of the quality of the photographs. Though I could store the dry plates, I should hate to find out next spring that the chemicals had failed for some reason. And, of course, I needed to bring an ample supply of plates."

Luke cleared his throat. "I apologize. Most women seem unable to travel without every gewgaw they own. For a moment, I imagined—"

"You forget that I know the Queen Charlotte Islands intimately," Kate said, her tone cool. "I don't need to be told that fashionable clothes would be out of place there. And you may rest assured that I don't intend to travel with all these trunks. Most of them can stay in Skidegate or Masset, wherever you intend to set up base."

Kate was aware of another carriage that had pulled up

behind her uncle's but amidst the stir of loading, she paid little attention. Passengers were parting from friends and family, stores were being loaded, and puffs of steam could be
heard popping from the ship's escapement valve. The seeming chaos was familiar, and Kate felt rising excitement.

"I believe we'll settle at Skidegate between excursions,"
Luke said. He waved to a deckhand, who summoned
another to carry the first of Kate's boxes aboard.

Skidegate! She was beginning to think God had chosen to
take a hand in her plans, so perfectly had every obstacle
been removed from her way. To hide her exultation, she
turned to the crewman. "This one to my cabin," she said,
indicating the familiar, battered steamer trunk that had made
this journey so many times, and the young man nodded.
"The contents of these others are quite breakable. You will
use care?"

"Of course, Ma'am."

Kate knew better than to believe him, but she had packed
the photographic plates in swathes of cotton batting. Fortunately, she had already possessed a fair supply of plates, and
a hurried trip to the store where she purchased supplies had
produced ample. Her previous success in transporting the
delicate apparatus allowed her to watch with only slight
anxiety as her baggage was hauled aboard by crewmen,
where it would no doubt ride in steerage. She only hoped all
could be found when they reached Metlakatla.

"Skidegate is centrally located," Luke continued. "We'll
visit Masset, of course, although the village has been
stripped of anything worth collecting."

"Certainly the more portable objects," Kate agreed. "The
steamer lets in so often there, and at Skidegate. Tell me, had
you contemplated trying to take one of the smaller poles?"
But she saw that he was no longer attending to her. He had
stiffened and was looking over her shoulder, his blue eyes
narrowed so that she could no longer read his expression.

"Hell," he muttered just before she heard footsteps
approaching behind her.

Kate's heart took an unpleasant leap, and she turned slowly. Had her uncle decided to prevent her going after all?

But it was a stranger who stopped just before their group. Urbanely dressed in a bowler hat and pale gray cutaway frock coat, he was a handsome man of perhaps thirty-five with a close-cropped dark beard and luxuriant mustache.

"Luke," he said warmly. "How do you do? I'd heard you were in town."

"Durham." Luke accepted the proffered hand without enthusiasm, his dislike all too obvious. "I expected you."

"Splendid. We must have a brandy together. I hear that you went to Polynesia last spring. I hope your expedition was successful. I should like to hear about it." The new-comer's velvet-brown eyes moved to Kate's face, and the finely shaped mouth beneath the mustache lifted at the corners. "Might I be introduced to the lady?"

A malicious note crept into Luke's voice. "You're not already acquainted? Very well. Miss Hewitt, may I make you known to James Durham? I believe your father and he had a small . . . skirmish."

A muscle in Mr. Durham's cheek twitched, but he smiled ruefully. "A misunderstanding, I would call it. You must be the Reverend Hewitt's daughter. He spoke of your photographic skills."

Kate was surprised; her father had mentioned Mr. Durham in that last letter, but with none of the indulgence he apparently felt for Luke. Also a museum curator, James Durham had apparently tried to abscond with the skeletal and ceremonial contents of a memorial pole. The dead chief's relatives were irate. The Reverend Hewitt announced his intention to kick Mr. Durham by the seat of his pants onto the first steamer that called. Kate wondered if her father had indeed done so. Or had his violent end come first?

She meant to say something trivial and conventional, saving the serious for another moment, but she surprised herself. "Were you there when my father died?" she asked.

A less close observer would have failed to see that betraying muscle jerk again. "I had departed a day or two before," he said. "A brutal business. Please accept my regrets."

"Thank you," she murmured, aware of Luke's gaze on her face. He was frowning again, she saw, although this time, he looked more thoughtful than annoyed.

"I think we'd better board," Luke said. "We'll no doubt see you there, Durham."

Nodding, the other man expressed his delight that Miss Hewitt was to be on the voyage, then made his way toward the ship.

Luke frowned after him for a moment before he seemed to recollect himself. "Miss Hewitt, you have everything? Alistair, my thanks for your hospitality."

Kate said her own good-byes to Alistair Meade, conscious that he was her last tie to the familiar and secure. He had nearly been her salvation this last year, the only person she knew in Victoria who approved of her photography.

Kate had forgotten James Durham by the time she thanked the coachman, tipped him, and collected her umbrella and large, brocaded carpetbag from the carriage. Luke took the bag from her. A moment later, she stepped up the gangplank, taking care not to catch the narrow heels of her buttoned boots.

The deck shifted subtly under her feet with the motion of the tide, and her spirits instantly rose. Freedom! The steam engines puffed, the brisk sea breeze tossed the flags strung from the pilothouse and wrapped her skirts about her ankles. She longed for the gangplank to be lifted, the lines to be cast off.

"Would you like to go inside?" Luke asked once they had made their way to the second deck, but she gave him a distracted smile.

"Thank you, but no. I enjoy departures."

"Very well." He deposited her bag on the deck, and she leaned her umbrella on it, then took hold of the railing. Luke remained beside her, his hands shoved into his coat pockets. Kate gazed at the city sprawling in every direction, stolid and overpoweringly respectable. Would Victoria look the same to her when she saw it again, she wondered, or would she have irreparably changed? She felt a sadness that surprised her, and which she was grateful to abandon when at last there was a stir below as the plank was pulled aboard, the lines gathered.

"All clear, sir!"

The gong sounded, the engines sighed, and the paddle wheel thundered. The deck shuddered underfoot. With a shrill scream of the whistle, the steamer edged away from the dock. Turning her head astern, Kate could see misty, gray-green water foaming against the wharf pilings. A seagull answered the scream and banked above them, riding a wind current. Kate realized that she was smiling idiotically.

She was wrenched from her silent contentment by a startled exclamation. "Katie, is that you?"

She turned. A burly, bearded man in heavy boots and rough clothes dropped a duffel bag and strode toward her. Only from long acquaintance could she tell he was smiling. His voice boomed above the steady slap of the wheel. "By God, of all people! It's Katie Rose! Coming to throw in your fortune with me?"

She laughed and allowed herself to be engulfed in an embrace. "Sims! Oh, I'm so glad to see you!"

Huge hands held her at arm's length for an inspection. "You've changed! But it never takes you more than a few days to let down the braids and be back in boy clothes." His glance became more comprehensive. "Though I'm not so sure they'll fit you now. By God . . . !" He stopped, then said awkwardly, "I should have written, but I'm not much of a hand . . ."

Kate had almost forgotten Luke's presence. His gaze was very cool. "A friend?"

"What?" Kate blinked. "Oh, yes." She raised her voice so that the rumble of the paddle did not drown it out. "Mister Lucas Brennan, this is . . . why, I believe I don't know your first name!" Amazing. She had been friends with the big man since her first winter at Skidegate, when she was fourteen, lonely, and scared. The miners had dubbed her Katie Rose because Sims had declared that she reminded him of a wild rose: skinny, prickly, and on rare occasions, pretty. Kate had not known whether to be flattered or insulted. She still didn't. No one else had ever called her pretty.

The miners had otherwise ignored the fact that she was a girl; probably not hard to do, she thought, since she had been shaped like a board. They had not moderated their language at all, but at least that language was English, if somewhat crude. She had chipped at rocks with them, helped lay explosives, cooked up a meal. Her father had not approved, but he was too busy to keep track of her whereabouts.

"Sims'll do. Hardly remember anything else myself." The two men eyed each other with all the enthusiasm of tomcats being introduced. Through Luke was dwarfed by Sim's mountainous size, somehow his presence still dominated. "And who are you?" Sims rumbled.

Kate intervened. "Mister Brennan has kindly hired me to take photographs for his museum. And Sims—" she smiled at one of her few true friends "—Sims is a miner. He is determined to discover gold on the Queen Charlottes."

"I've found some investors who have me looking for copper, too." He grinned, apparently losing interest in Luke, who stayed beside Kate, his expression imperturbable. Kate could not tell whether he disapproved of her rough-hewn friend or not. "So you're on your way home?" Sims asked.

"Yes, indeed. Though it's no longer home," she said sadly.

He gave a gusty sigh. "You know, the Reverend and I . . ." Uncharacteristically, he hesitated.

"Detested each other?" Kate suggested. She wished it had not been so.

Sims clapped her vigorously on the shoulder. "Maybe so, but I almost miss the stiff-rumped . . ." He harrumphed. "That is, the Reverend. At least he kept life interesting. Richardson lets us alone, all right; too busy squeezing the natives. Church your father built ain't good enough, not for him. Wants stained-glass windows, by God." He shook his head. "Gives the Indians communion. Even I know that'd make the Reverend roll over in his grave."

"Richardson?" Luke inquired.

"He was my father's assistant," Kate said absently. "The Missionary Society asked him to stay on. Though I don't believe he is ordained yet." She turned back to Sims. "How very strange. I thought that Mister Richardson entered into my father's feelings on communion. How can he reasonably forbid alcohol and then give it to them himself in church? And Father thought even the bread . . ." When she hesitated, Luke finished her thought.

"Smacked of cannibalism?" He gave a hearty laugh. "I've never heard of any other Christians incited by their Sunday Mass to rend flesh with their teeth."

"The Haida have a history of such conduct," Kate said stiffly.

"Surely the Cannibal Dance is symbolic." Luke appeared to be enjoying the discussion. "I've seen no convincing evidence that they ever actually ate human flesh. In any case, the dance seems to have originated with the Kwakiutl."

"Far as I can tell," Sims added, "Richardson hasn't explained what the bread and wine are supposed to be, anyway. Thinks they won't understand, I suppose. All that happens is, they try to sneak back a couple of times for the wine. No wonder, after he's done preaching fire and brimstone. Gets 'em all excited."

"Oh, dear." It was probably not her business, but Kate was dismayed at the loss of so much her father had believed in. Surely, giving wine to the Indians was not a good idea. She would make a point of attending a service to see for herself. Perhaps she could influence Mr. Richardson.

"Where are you located?" she asked Sims.

"Kaisun. We're finding flakes, there's a seam of quartz. I swore I'd find gold, and by God, I will."

"Are you employing Haida men?"

"Can't afford to employ anybody, except for transportation. How do you plan to cross over?"

Luke spoke up. "By canoe, if need be. I'm hoping that

we'll be fortunate enough to come upon the steamer from the Oil Works, or meet the *Otter* making one last call before winter."

"Sunk, you know."

"The *Otter*?" Kate said, astonished. "No. I hadn't heard. Are they attempting to raise her?"

Sims didn't know, and like them, he was hoping for a chance encounter to save him from the necessity of crossing Hecate Strait in a canoe. Reassured that he would see Kate at dinner, he swung his duffel bag to his shoulder and disappeared below decks.

Kate sighed. The wind was sharpening as they passed the natural arms of the harbor and she was beginning to feel chilled despite her woolen gown. She shouldn't have packed her coat in the trunk. Gusts of sea wind whipped her curls across her face. The fir-shrouded Gulf Islands looked forbidding today, their gray rocks sloping into the choppy, iron-gray water.

She had already seen several Indian canoes effortlessly cutting the waves, though none so fine as the Haida war canoes. Those had always seemed to her to have wings, so swiftly did they fly. Up to seventy-five feet long, they could carry as many as forty people with two tons of baggage. Should Luke be forced to hire a canoe, however, it would be one considerably smaller than that.

Kate didn't look forward to that stage of the journey. Much of the way would be out of sight of land, and the currents in Hecate Strait were treacherous. Storms rose unpredictably; one could set out on water as smooth as glass, then, within hours, be in the midst of nature's violent rage. Kate disliked feeling frail.

As though to underscore her changed mood, a harsh call made her turn her head in time to see a black sweep of wings as a raven passed like a dark shadow over the ship and headed toward the rocky point. The Haida would have seen an omen in its appearance—whether good or bad, she did not know. Perhaps she did not want to know.

"I believe I'll go in now," she said, resolutely turning from the railing. "There's no need for you to accompany me."

Luke picked up her bag. "I'll see you to your stateroom."

They passed through the Grand Saloon, opulently decorated in gilt and red plush, with gaslit chandeliers hanging above clusters of curved rococo sofas, many of them already occupied. Laughter drifted from the Gentlemen's Saloon, where Kate had no doubt that a card party had begun.

Luke followed silently as she climbed the wide staircase to the gallery above, where the Ladies' Cabins were located. It occurred to Kate suddenly that she had not thought to ask Sims about her father's death. He must know where the body had been found. There would have been talk; he might have heard what the Indians thought. She wondered how Sims had felt about her father's death. Had he disliked him enough to be glad? The idea was disturbing, for it led to a corollary: Could Sims have hated the Reverend Hewitt enough to murder him?

She wanted to reject the notion out of hand. Not Sims. Surely not! The two men had clashed, it was true, and the Reverend Hewitt *had* incited the Indians against the miners. He had felt that they had an historic right to their lands, that the minerals beneath them belonged to the Indians. He did not like the miners' use of whiskey, nor their attempts to trade it for Indian women.

But even drunk, Sims had always been kind to her. And what did he have to gain by killing her father? More comfortable relations with the Indians? Not worth murder, surely. But then, what was? she wondered bleakly. Her father had been a man of dogmatic opinions firmly voiced; those who had not loved him had hated him. But murder?

And yet, somebody had killed him. What she was determined to find out was why. When she knew that, surely she would have found the murderer.

Chapter Three

The five-day voyage up the northwest coast gave Luke ample opportunity to rue his folly. He'd felt sorry for Miss Hewitt; she had made him freshly conscious of the injustice done women by the rarely questioned roles allotted the sexes. But he didn't run a charitable institution and should not have jeopardized this expedition by burdening himself with a young, unmarried woman.

That first night, he lay sleepless in his cabin, the brass bed vibrating with the motion of the ship. He was disturbed to find his thoughts taken up by Miss Hewitt, rather than by the adventures ahead. His feelings toward her were too complex for comfort, defying analysis.

He admired her boldness; he was dismayed by the same quality. Several times that day, he had caught himself reacting to her with physical admiration, seeing the narrowness of her waist, the mist-gray color of her eyes, the full curve of her mouth; at other moments, he could not help thinking her mannish. There was nothing *soft* about her. She did not pretend to be anything but capable and made no attempt to disguise her long, thoughtful gazes with maidenly shyness. She was too tall, too thin. Like a bundle of springs, her mass of wiry hair crackled with energy, and her hands, stained with chemicals, were long-fingered and strong.

She was nothing like Mary, who had been utterly feminine, and yet she made him think about his wife. Since Mary was the only other woman with whom he had ever traveled, perhaps he should have foreseen such a consequence. He had not, however, and the awakening of memories was unwelcome. Luke scowled into the darkness. Despite her remarkable photographs, he should not have brought Miss Hewitt.

Mary had been equally talented at a different art. The museum was nearly empty the day he had come upon her sitting on a bench amongst the wood-and-glass cases, gazing with complete composure at a fierce Aztec god carved in stone. The contrast between the two figures had been striking. Even at first sight, she had seemed to him gentle, her soft ringlets of strawberry-blond hair brushing a round cheek, her mouth like a child's, freckles disarmingly scattered across creamy skin. In her concentration, she did not hear his approach, so he had been able to look over her shoulder at her sketchbook. The Aztec god no longer sat stoically beside a mahogany case, the light cast by tall windows too harsh and gray, his sneer a trick of the stone-cutter's art. On her pad, he lurked behind a tangle of vines that sought to devour an ancient civilization, yet did not quite succeed. With subtle shades of her pencil, the young woman had made him mysterious, evil. The light in her drawing was filtered by the jungle thickness, and she had somehow managed to suggest the lushness and the decay of vegetation. Through her imagination and skill, she brought the stone god to life. He had appeared just so when Luke had first brushed aside the vines and seen him.

Luke fell in love with the young woman, and he had not even looked into her eyes.

He had been madly, gloriously, happy during their brief marriage. Only after her death did he suffer from the realiza-

tion that he had used her. He had wanted a partner, an expedition artist, a cook. He had wanted an intrepid lady explorer
who could wield a shovel as well as her sketching pencil and
watercolors, who could entertain to his advantage in Boston
and yet glory in the adventure of primitive living. Mary had
tried. Only in retrospect did he remember how often she had
flinched, how pinched her face had become in the firelight
when the jungle darkness closed about them and the sounds
began—the screams and rustles, the soft pad of footsteps,
the snarl of a predator.

He had thought her gallant. Perhaps she had been more so
than he had known, because in dying, Mary had shown the
fear she had never expressed in life. He could close his eyes
and see the moment of her death.

He felt again the humid heat, the sweat that soaked his
shirt and blurred his vision. With a machete, he chopped at
the vegetation that smothered the stone steps—huge slabs
smooth and closely fitted—as the temple rose precipitously
toward the gods. His arm ached, but exultation had him in its
fierce grip. A city lost in the jungle! What might he find?

The native guides waited at the foot of the pyramid. They
had been willing to come this far, but no farther. Mary
climbed behind him, a wide-brimmed hat set jauntily on her
head and a parasol shading her delicate complexion. He
heard her small gasp and turned. In this waking nightmare, it
all happened so slowly, as though the humid air had thick-
ened to water. From several steps above, he saw a shiver of
movement at her feet, slim and black and lethal. An adder,
disguised by the twisting vines, awakened perhaps by
Luke's passing. Mary wore high, sturdy boots. If she had
stood very still, the snake might have slithered away. Even
had she forged clumsily on, the bite would probably not
have penetrated the heavy leather. She did neither. Terrified,
she stepped back.

He could still see her face. His heart raced as he lunged
for her. There had never been any hope. He had felt so
damnably slow, but she had been falling even as he turned,
clutching the parasol as though it could save her. She

screamed, and then her scream was cut off when her body thudded against one of the narrow, steep stone steps, then another and another.

Luke had descended at foolhardy speed. Perhaps he had trampled the adder. He didn't know. He knew only that he was too late. At the bottom, Mary lay in a twisted heap, the crumpled parasol beneath her. Her neck was broken, and those wide green eyes stared into eternity. Her fear had killed her.

Luke kicked the bedcovers off. He was breathing in great gasps and sweating, though the cabin was not unduly warm. His own bellow echoed still in his ears.

"Mary! *Mary!*"

Damnation. He had not remembered so vividly in a long while. He had wished never to do so again.

His anguish had been dulled by time, though not his repentance. Mary should not have climbed that temple. She should not have been in the jungle at all. If he hadn't expected her to be a woman at night and a man by day, she would not be dead. She would be awaiting him now in Boston, filling her days with sketching and housewifely arts.

He dragged in another breath and moved restlessly. The jungle canopy formed again before his eyes, gaudy and smothering, the ancient temple, the *whack, whack* of his machete. He looked back and she was behind him, though *she* was no longer Mary, but Katherine Hewitt. What he had thought to be a vine writhed at her feet, subtle and deadly. She gasped. . . .

His body jerked in an involuntary spasm and he clenched his teeth. Mary had stepped backward to her death. Would Miss Hewitt have done the same?

All hope of sleep lost now, he thought back to the day, trying rationally to assess the stuff of which Miss Hewitt was made. He had discovered quickly that she had a wide and interesting acquaintance. Her father's collection had made him reassess the Reverend Hewitt's character. Otherwise, he might have been even more surprised at the motley collection of people she apparently considered friends.

She had given every appearance of brooding as they mounted the stairs from the *Skeena*'s Grand Saloon. Just as they reached the top, he had felt compelled to make some conventional, meaningless comment. He saw, however, that he had lost her attention, if he had ever possessed it. An altercation was taking place ahead in the corridor.

Miss Hewitt's stride lengthened and she called sharply, "Suzette, is that you?"

"Kate!" The young Indian woman tried to pull free of her captor, but failed to break the uniformed steward's grip. The small, plump woman was dressed in European clothes; she might have been pretty were it not for the scars of smallpox on her round face.

"Is something wrong?" Miss Hewitt asked straightly.

The steward, red-faced and bullish, was foolish enough not to see that he was outmatched. "This . . . person does not belong up here, Ma'am. If you'll excuse me . . ." He bodily turned the Indian woman toward the stairs.

Miss Hewitt's umbrella smacked down on his hand, which jerked open. A passing couple stared, but she ignored them and her voice remained pleasant. "Suzette?"

"I pay fare. He . . ." The young woman visibly groped for words. "He tells I not. I have paper. See?"

Miss Hewitt scanned it. "Why, this is outrageous! She's been grossly overcharged! I shall certainly discuss this with the captain!"

"I don't know anything about that," the steward said sullenly. "I just know she don't belong here. Shouldn't let 'em on the boat at all."

Luke was not surprised by the attitude, however ugly he thought it. The Indian camps around Victoria were scenes of terrible squalor, with disease, violence, and prostitution rampant. Encountering these pathetic examples of the Indian populace inclined many otherwise well-meant people to bigotry. It was easier to blame the victims than to accept responsibility for the effect of the white man's vices. Profiting from the Indians' ignorance, however, was not the work of a well-meaning individual. Luke was entirely in sympathy with Miss Hewitt's indignation, and was prepared to lend his support should it be necessary. Thus far, she did not appear to require any assistance.

"You have not assigned Miss Edwards a cabin." Miss Hewitt's icy stare would have quelled a more intelligent man. "She will share with me. I shall expect her baggage to be delivered to our cabin. She will be politely treated at all times, and the monies due her will be refunded. Is that clear?"

The young woman's black eyes darted from one speaker to another, though she probably understood the emotion more than she did the words. The burly, uniformed man flushed a deeper red and took an impetuous step forward, his hands curling into fists, his belligerent gaze turning to Luke. Luke set down the carpetbag. He had no doubt of who would be the victor of this skirmish, but thought he ought to be prepared for a deepening of the hostilities.

The steward growled, "I don't know who she thinks she is."

Kate did not acknowledge his attempt to transfer responsibility to a man, nor did she flinch. Perhaps she would not have flinched from the snake, either. "I am Katherine Hewitt," she said coolly. "It might be of interest to you that my uncle is a majority stockholder in the company that owns this ship."

"I have orders—"

"I'm sure you do. They have just been changed." She took Suzette's arm and swept past him, drawing the Indian woman with her.

The steward had little option but to retreat in disorder. Luke admired her tactics, not to mention the set of her long, slender back. No wonder her father had kept her with him! She must have been a formidable addition to his missionary arsenal.

Feeling somewhat extraneous, Luke delivered Miss Hewitt's bag to her stateroom, which was furnished with surprising elegance. A plush red carpet covered the floor, and handsomely framed pictures hung above the brass bedstead. The cabins here even had commodes with running-water jets. He and Miss Hewitt were fortunate to be able to travel in such comfort, though the museum trustees would not like the cost.

When he attempted to make a hasty escape, Miss Hewitt said, "Please, call me Kate. It's absurd for us to work together and remain formal."

"Very well," he agreed. "Kate."

Luke saw nothing of the ladies before dinnertime. The steamer docked at Nanaimo to take on coal, then proceeded up the Inland Passage without any further stops that day. Most of the passengers were bound for Wrangell or Sitka, in Alaska, so the *Skeena* would not anchor at every trading post along the way, as the Hudson Bay Company's *Otter* usually had. The scenery was magnificent, though painted today in shades of gray. The inland sea was a maze of islands and gorges, from which mountains rose sharply to peaks capped by early snow. The land was cloaked in the forbidding dark green of fir and cedar, and the water was uncannily smooth, without the deep swells of the open ocean.

Although feeling cowardly for it, Luke spent the day avoiding Kate by lurking in the Gentlemen's Saloon, with its spare furnishings and brass spittoons. He felt uncomfortable in her company, did not know what to say to her. He would somehow have to learn to pretend she was a man and deal with her accordingly. He tried to convince himself that he was obsessed with her only because he lacked occupation; in the field, she would become merely an adjunct, translating and photographing scenes of more compelling interest than the presence of any woman.

Even his masculine refuge failed him when he was forced to go into hiding in his cabin by Durham, who looked determined to corner him. What did the man imagine they had to say to each other? Were they supposed to enjoy a professional exchange of ideas on how to extract a native's last possessions with the smallest recompense? Durham was utterly without conscience, but he was also the agent of a respectable museum. Luke had thus far reluctantly avoided the scandal that would result in their circle were he as rude to the man as he would like to be. Still, Durham was surely aware of his distaste.

Luke did change before dinner and escort Kate and her companion to the dining room. Suzette, it developed, was a Haida woman who had married a Kwakiutl chief, and thus was traveling only as far as Fort Rupert, on the north end of Vancouver Island. Her European dress indicated her conversion to Christianity; her English, however, was very limited, though Luke was able to communicate with her to some extent in Chinook, the local traders' jargon that he had made it his business to learn on his last visit to the Northwest.

Their small party was unavoidably joined by both Sims and Durham. Luke gritted his teeth and strove to be polite. He had to admit that Durham unblinkingly accepted the addition at their table of an Indian woman who spoke only broken English. The bastard probably imagined he could charm her into coercing her husband to sell some family heirloom, Luke thought dourly.

The tablecloth was crisp white linen, the dishes china, and the goblets crystal. The service was impeccable, and the waiter brought a number of courses: baked chicken and salmon, creamed onions and a bean salad, followed by a very fine apple shortcake.

Suzette ate timidly, with frequent glances at Kate for direction. Sims, who had clearly not bathed in some time, ate with gusto, calling frequently in a loud voice for more wine. Other diners cast disdainful looks at their motley assemblage. Luke doubted that there was a person beyond their table who had ever actually dined in the same room as an Indian. They would have been astonished to know that his discomfort came not from Suzette Edwards or Sims, but from Durham, eminently civilized and utterly despicable.

From the first sip of wine, Durham went on the attack. "I hear you're contemplating a Northwest Indian display separate from the rest of the museum." He quirked an amused brow. "But perhaps my source was misinformed."

There had been a trend in museums toward displaying objects by type, no matter what part of the world they had come from, with the result that spears from Kenya lay in cases with Eskimo harpoons, baskets from the Australian aborigines beside those from the American Southwest. Luke thought the principle absurd.

However, he answered with an attempt at civility. "You heard correctly. The artifacts can be understood only within the context of the people who made them. We must understand the people to understand the objects we collect."

"Surely ethnology is the study of *all* peoples! The evolutionary sequence—"

—was in the minds of fools like Durham.

"Balderdash." Luke abruptly lost patience and set down his fork. "Let's take a rattle as an example. We're agreed that all rattles are constructed to make noise. But think of the intended usage. Some tribes make rattles merely for the children's pleasure, others to play a role in a religious event. Placing the two side by side assumes that they vary only in decoration, where in fact, they represent quite different aspects of very individual cultures."

Durham's eyes narrowed and he leaned forward. "I think it obvious that inventions of both customs and things spring from prior inventions. There is a pattern that is lost if you separate like objects in your display. It is the similarities that are of interest, not the differences."

Kate had abandoned eating as she listened, her fine gray eyes gazing from one man to the other. Oblivious to the conversation, Sims refilled his wineglass and tucked his napkin into his shirt collar to make a bib. Crumbs already dribbled down it. Suzette had apparently had enough to eat, for she sat quietly with her hands folded in her lap, her dark eyes following the speakers despite the language barrier.

Luke snorted. "You've determined the pattern before you collect the objects, far less study them. You merely set them in their predetermined places, no matter whether they fit, like an infant who doesn't care that one puzzle piece is round and another square."

This outrageous insult earned him a supercilious smile from Durham. "I fear it's you who are the infant who doesn't even attempt to discover the true shape."

Before a growl could erupt from Luke's throat, Kate said with amusement, "I believe the analogy is apt. The two of you do seem very like two infants—well, perhaps toddlers—arguing over a toy."

Durham turned a smile of infuriating charm on her. "Have we bored you? I must apologize. It was hardly a discussion appropriate for ladies."

A crackle of ice chilled the atmosphere, but Kate's voice remained gentle. "I'm afraid *ladies* are all too accustomed to infantile discussions. This one was very interesting, however. I must say that I'm inclined to agree with Luke. I think that the coastal Indians have a very long history. I doubt that their course of cultural development is at all comparable with that of early European man's, for example. The environments are so different. Living is quite easy here, you know. If white men had not appeared, I wonder whether the Indians would have changed. They seem to have had a very satisfactory culture. The land wasn't overpopulated and food was ample. Their dances are marvelous, their artistic efforts magnificent, if somewhat frightening. Unless the climate changed or something drastic befell them, would they have continued to 'evolve'? And if evolution comes about because of changing conditions, can you truly compare the stages of people faced with vastly different circumstances?"

"I congratulate you on your perception," Luke said triumphantly. "Would you care to answer the lady, Durham?"

Durham's smile was thin. "That was a very thoughtful exposition, Miss Hewitt. But I wonder, have you ever seen the artifacts of any other native civilization?"

"I'm afraid not," Kate said with no evidence of apology. "Which part of my thesis do you think that would disprove?"

"I merely think you would find that the similarities are quite striking," Durham said. He smiled again at her, the expression in his brown eyes warm, even caressing. Luke was irritated at the familiarity.

"Are they?" Her answering smile was bland. "Tell me, Mister Durham, did you have much success in collecting from the Haida on your trip last year?"

Luke studied her face closely. Her eyes were wide, no more than inquiring. He was coming to know her well enough to doubt that her interest was as innocent as it appeared. But where did she intend to direct the conversation?

"I was there for only a few days," Durham said. "Not long enough to travel about." His tone became rueful. "I'm afraid I was forced to depart somewhat sooner than I'd planned. In any case, I hadn't realized that so many Indians would be away working at the canneries in the summer. I had enough success to pique my interest, but not enough to satisfy me. Thus my return. Why do you ask, Miss Hewitt?"

"Oh," she said vaguely, "I had wondered whether my father assisted you. He could be . . . somewhat unpredictable."

"I fear I found him so," Durham agreed. "He incited feelings against me among the Indians. That made my work difficult."

"But you did stay with him?"

For the first time, Durham had the sense to look wary. "I did."

"Father wrote me—" Kate said. With a fingertip, she traced the gold rim of her plate. "—perhaps a day or two before he died."

The silence was absolute. With narrowed eyes, Luke noted the reaction to her announcement. Sims' head came up sharply, as though he were an animal scenting danger. For the first time, Luke was struck by how difficult the man was to read; with shaggy hair, a full beard, and bushy brows, much of his face was hidden. He stared at Kate with muddy brown eyes, and Luke felt a prickle of unease.

More experienced than the miner at dissembling, Durham took a slow sip of wine, but his tension was visible in the fingers that tightened on the delicate stem of the glass and in his elaborately casual mien. With enviable control, he did no more than smile wryly. "The closest to friendship your father and I came was in agreeing to disagree. I'm sure he had nothing good to say about me."

"Nothing so very bad, either," Kate said unrevealingly, and turned the subject.

Luke no longer listened. Though still observing the other two men, he could not help but wonder what the Reverend Hewitt had said about *him*. Luke had rather enjoyed arguing with the man. He'd had a practical bent unusual for his kind, and at least some empathy for the natives, even believing that they had partial claim to the land that had once been inarguably theirs. Perhaps inspired by Mr. Duncan at Metlakatla, Kate's father had been putting in motion several schemes to gain financial independence for the Haida. He had talked of buying a steamer so that the Indians were not forced to sell their furs to the Hudson Bay Company for a pittance. He had not liked the Skidegate Oil Works, which had borrowed the Indians' method of extracting oil from the dogfish to profit the white men, who were able to ship and market the valuable oil. The Reverend Hewitt had contemplated going into competition with the Oil Works, which had not made him popular in that quarter.

It was from Alistair Meade that Luke had heard of Durham's conflict with Mr. Hewitt. Luke could not imagine that the two men had cared for each other even before the contretemps. As he had read Alistair's letter, which told of the Reverend's death as well as of Durham's visit, Luke had even briefly speculated. . . . But no. The idea seemed as ridiculous now as it had then. Durham might have faced embarrassment had he been caught a second time in raiding a burial, but that was nothing compared to the disaster had he been arrested for murder. Scoundrel that he was, Durham was too self-serving to do something as foolish as committing a murder, even in a hot-blooded moment. No, there must be some other explanation.

If *he* had speculated as much, however, it was safe to assume that Kate, too, had imagined a similar scenario. Had she been deliberately fishing for an odd reaction, imagining that Durham might betray himself? And if so, had she noticed the way Sims still stared at her?

But Luke would have liked even more to know whether Kate had cast her lines in the water on impulse—or whether this was the reason she had accepted his offer. Did she travel to the Queen Charlottes not for adventure or feminine equality or concern for the Haida, but because she sought her father's murderer?

The *Skeena*'s whistle, somewhat muffled, jerked Luke back to the present. He lay in bed, the tattered remnants of his earlier waking nightmare still fluttering dismally about him. Punching his pillow, he sought a more comfortable position, all the while trying to dismiss the evening from his thoughts. Recollecting the last few hours had been no more than a diversion, to keep his mind from memories older than those of today. Mary . . . But the anguish had faded, and he could not deceive himself.

No, Mary's ghost was not responsible for robbing him of sleep. That blame could be laid with Miss Katherine Hewitt, who no doubt reposed peacefully in her own stateroom. Luke groaned. *He* was responsible for her presence. Had he loosed a vengeful Amazon who intended to exact satisfaction for her father's murder?

His eyes closed and he felt Kate again, climbing the pyramid behind him. He heard her small gasp, swung around and . . . nothing. He could not see the outcome.

Damnation. Luke flung himself out of bed, then groped for his pocket watch on the bedside table. He felt as though he had lain here for an eternity, and it had been less than two hours. A brandy would help him sleep, help him to forget the thud of Mary's body striking the ancient stone steps, the gasp that was no longer Mary's . . . and the Pandora's box that Kate had so foolishly opened, which might contain a murderer.

* * *

Fort Rupert came and went, their brief stop there achieving little of moment but the departure of Suzette Edwards and the opportunity for Kate to embarrass herself.

The passengers had been given several hours in which to stroll past the fort and its surrounding stockade—vertical logs driven into the ground—toward the Indian village clustered beyond the Fort's walls. Constructed of huge cedar planks, the Kwakiutl houses were impressive, their fronts vividly painted. Canoes were drawn up along the curve of the gravel beach. At the sound of the steamer's arrival, natives had gathered to squat beside blankets laid out and laden with merchandise. Silver bracelets hammered from dollar and half-dollar coins were eagerly presented, along with toy canoes, baskets, and crudely carved goat's-horn spoons.

"Twenty-five cents," called an old woman, her face webbed with wrinkles. She was wrapped in a dirty, coarse blanket for which Kate knew quite well the Hudson Bay Company had charged fifty marten furs. So unfair. If only her father had had time, some improvement might have been wrought at least for the Haida . . . But the regret was an old one.

"Twenty-five cents! Beautiful, see?"

Luke ignored the cheap items manufactured for the tourist trade. His longing gaze was directed at the village. "If only we had more time," he muttered. "Perhaps Miss Edwards—"

"Her husband has been a Christian for a number of years," Kate said, holding her skirts in one hand as she picked her way along the rough path. "I doubt that he has any objects of interest left."

"We have an adequate collection from the Kwakiutl. Though I would have liked some fishing hooks, even a pole . . ."

"I know of an interesting one," Kate said, then immediately regretted her impulse.

"Yes?" His vivid blue eyes took in her blush. "Nothing suitable to display in the museum, I take it?"

"I'm afraid not," she said in an absurdly constrained voice. "I don't know why I—"

"Can you direct me?"

She refused to allow herself a maidenly escape, and hoped he hadn't noticed her brief hesitation.

"Certainly." Kate led the way between cedar longhouses to one that had stood concealed from their view.

Her hope that the pole might have disappeared since she had last seen it was soon extinguished. Luke silently regarded the house support, which represented a man who stood with legs slightly apart, his erect sexual organ in his hands. Though Luke's arms were crossed, his stance somewhat echoed that of the carved man. Kate indulged in some highly improper speculation. Was that what he would look like at such a moment? Had the pole been carved in scale? Its appendage seemed rather large. . . .

At that precise moment, Luke turned to look at her. A fiery blush spread across her face. Dear Lord, could he read her thoughts?

His eyes narrowed, but not before she had seen a flicker of something quite unnerving in them. "Interesting indeed," he conceded. His voice sounded rough, and he cleared his throat. "Do you know of other similar . . ." He hesitated.

Kate tried to make herself aware of the world beyond them. The day was bright and breezy. The hum of voices came from just on the other side of the longhouses. A mongrel lay idly scratching fleas in a mud hole near the entrance to the house. A young woman shuffled past, carrying a laden basket, and gazed curiously at them. There was nothing unusual about the scene. She had seen the pole before. Ridiculous to feel so self-conscious, so tinglingly aware of that crude carving and of Luke's tall, muscular body.

"Indecent pieces, do you mean?" Her voice was too high, a soprano that wanted to crack. "I saw a potlatch dish once. It was a man lying on his back, knees drawn up. His stomach formed the dish. I believe his . . . his organ was meant to be a handle."

"Haida?"

"No, traded from the Kwakiutl, as I recall."

"I wonder, is it intended to be humorous?" Luke clasped his hands behind his back and returned to his contemplation of the house pole. "If we had more time—"

"Ah. There you are." Durham succeeded in startling Kate, who had not heard his arrival. In contrast to Luke, he was finely turned out in well-tailored tweed; with an ivory-handled walking stick in hand, he looked rather like a Scottish lord wandering the moors. Kate tried to imagine him unclothed, too, and utterly failed. Strange. He was far more handsome than Luke, but less . . . less *masculine*.

"What are you—" he began before his gaze followed Luke's. "Ah," he said again. For a moment, there was a profound silence before he seemed to recollect himself. "Surely this is no sight for Miss Hewitt! I'm astonished that you permitted—"

A wave of annoyance made Kate feel more like herself. "Do you imagine I have no idea of the male anatomy? I'm afraid I lost such prudishness while living amongst the Indians. They don't regard modesty as such a virtue."

"Still . . ." Frowning severely, he turned to Luke. "I wonder that you should bring her—"

"She brought me." A sudden, infectious grin slashed across Luke's face, softening its hard lines. "You're accusing the wrong party."

Kate could not recall seeing him smile before. At the sight, her throat seemed to close. "Perhaps we should start back."

"That's why I came looking for you," Durham said. "We're being summoned. A pity, though." He and Luke turned as one for a last, regretful glance. "With more time, we could arrange for its purchase."

"And then split the spoils?" Luke's devastating, rather wicked grin flashed again. "But who would get which half?"

In a rare moment of accord, the two men laughed. Kate tried to turn her involuntary giggle into a cough.

Later, remembering the incident, she felt again that odd tingling. Such self-awareness had increased her sense of awkwardness with her employer. For the moment, they could avoid each other—in fact, she would have sworn he *was* avoiding her—but the fact remained that eventually they would have to work together. Closely.

Well, she could understand his motivation. But Sims, too, appeared to be avoiding her. Had he guessed that she wanted to ask him questions? But why wouldn't he want to answer them?

Kate saw him slip out of the Gentlemen's Saloon just as she descended the stairs from her cabin. The wind snatched at her hair and skirts when she followed him outside, but the sharp, salty breath she drew in was refreshing. Though it was only late afternoon, dusk had begun to cast deep, purple shadows that made the steep shoreline indistinct. Gold and peach glowed to the west, from whence, according to Haida stories, Raven had come. There was an immense stillness about the scene, defied only by the beat of the stern wheel and the laughter and voices coming from behind the ship's lighted windows. Kate felt very small as she looked out at the swells of sea that glowed as though lit from within until they faded into the shadows of the coming night.

At the sound of the door opening, Sims had turned to face her. Now he stood with his back to the rail, seemingly resigned, though as always with him, it was difficult to be sure of what he thought.

"I should like a minute of your time," Kate said. "We've had no chance to talk alone. I have questions. . . ."

"Your father," he said gruffly.

Her breath came out on a long, shaken sigh. "Yes. I hoped you could tell me about his death. The authorities seemed to know very little and to care less."

He shrugged. "Probably think an Indian did it. Hell, the government's probably afraid to do anything to stir up the Haida."

"I suppose so," she said. "What do *you* think?"

"I don't know," he said. "Did they tell you about it?"

"Only that—" she bit her lip "—that he had been bludgeoned from behind. Judge Begbie didn't seem to know where his body was found."

"Kiusta."

Sims said it without any particular inflection, though the news was startling. The abandoned village of Kiusta was around on the northeast end of Graham Island, far from Skidegate. Even had the Reverend Hewitt gone to Masset, what reason could he have had to continue in the opposite direction from home, toward the unpopulated, wild western coast? And *how* had he made his way?

"He went missing, though nobody was worried, I guess. Thought he'd been called to Tanu or Cumshewa. Some Indians from Masset were stormbound at Kiusta, found him between a couple of houses, facedown. No canoe, no sign of how he got there. Recognized him by his clothes. His body had started to—" He stopped abruptly.

Kate's stomach lurched. She preferred not to think about the state of her father's body. She hadn't enough faith in the hereafter to bulwark her from the hideous reality of his death. "But *why?*" she cried, unsure of whether she asked Sims or a mightier power.

"Why did somebody do him in?"

"Why was he there?"

"If you knew that, you'd probably know who killed him."

She swallowed painfully. "And the Indians?"

"Aren't talking. I think they know something."

"But what?" Kate whispered.

"That's the question." Sims' face was shadowed as the sunset faded behind him, and his voice was peculiarly flat. "I don't know if asking it is such a good idea."

A cold finger seemed to touch the back of Kate's neck as she stared at him. Had he just issued a warning—or a threat?

She was suddenly chilled, aware of the darkness overtaking them. The water's surface was smooth and black now, a length of satin that rippled at the *Skeena*'s passing. The color of mourning, Kate thought. Would a small splash even be noted?

No! She was being ridiculous once again. Sims meant her to be cautious, that was all. Aunt Grace had said the same.

"No doubt you're right," she agreed, almost evenly. "Now, shall we go in to dinner?"

"Why not?"

Odd, she thought, accepting his arm. His voice had lightened, as though he were pleased with himself. Why? Because he had scared her?

But that was only the smallest of the questions he had given her to ponder. As she accompanied him into the safety and sanity of the lighted saloon, she was silently demanding answers.

What had led her father to Kiusta? *Who* had led him there? And why, *why* had he had to die?

Chapter Four

Metlakatla had grown with such astonishing speed that Kate was invariably surprised each time she visited. In just seventeen years, an entirely new town had been built upon the site of an abandoned Tsimshian Indian village by the missionary, Mr. Duncan, and his few Christian followers who had chosen to flee the numerous evils and temptations of Fort Simpson. The first years had been difficult, but now Metlakatla appeared both prosperous and well-inhabited. Rows of absolutely tidy houses, each surrounded by a picket fence, fronted a wide, bare street leading toward Mission Point, where stood the enormous church. Kate understood that it was capable of holding twelve hundred worshipers: the entire population of Metlakatla, and visitors as well.

It was midafternoon when the *Skeena* blasted her whistle and dropped anchor offshore of the missionary village. Kate stood at the rail, drinking in the familiar sights. The water had a cold blue sheen, snow dusted the mountaintops, and yet grass was still green and the sun was warm on her face. The "in-between month," the Haida called this time; past "ice month," but not yet to the month when "bears dig roots to prepare for hibernation."

The whistle brought Indians pouring from the village, all of them garbed in European clothing. Amongst the distant figures, Kate recognized Mr. Duncan, his hair whiter than she remembered. She saw him gesture vigorously to prompt the launching of several canoes to meet the steamship.

When the first canoe eased against the creaking side of the *Skeena* amidst shouts of greeting, Mr. Durham bowed to Kate. "Ladies first."

"Waiting to see if she'll get dunked before you chance it?" Luke inquired.

Kate said hastily, "Thank you, Mister Durham. I'm quite certain, gentlemen, that we're in no danger of being dunked." However, she couldn't help but watch with a degree of anxiety as her trunks, which had been brought up from steerage, were shifted to the first canoe.

Beside her at the rail, Luke raised a brow. "Your confidence does nothing to bolster my own."

"I've had boxes dropped overboard before," Kate admitted. "Clothing can be dried out, but I don't believe a camera would care for a saltwater bath."

"So far, so good," Luke said a few minutes later when all had been safely transferred. Ready hands pushed the first canoe off and a second took its place. Luke lowered himself agilely into the swaying craft and held out his arms. "Miss Hewitt?"

Kate hiked up her skirts and allowed him to grasp her around the waist as she made an awkward descent down the short ladder. She was uncomfortably aware of the warmth of his hands and his nearness before he released her. If only women, too, could wear trousers, so that they were not so at the mercy of men! Why hadn't she thought to change to a split skirt?

Wet paddles lifted, shedding droplets that glittered in the sunlight before the paddles slid into the water, propelling the canoe swiftly toward the shore. Nearly there, the Indians

turned the craft about so that the crest of a wave carried it
stern-first onto the gravel beach.

Luke jumped out to help drag it above the watermark.
"Do they ever beach a canoe bow-first?"

"Only in an emergency," Kate said, rising and shaking
out her skirts. "They prefer to take the extra time now, so
that they can launch quickly if need be. Their warring days
aren't so far past, you know."

Without waiting for Luke, Kate stepped over the high
gunwale and went forward immediately to meet Mr. Duncan, who was well up the beach but hurrying toward her. In
contrast to the village, he had changed little. A missionary
here among the Tsimshian Indians for nearly twenty-five
years now, he was a short, stocky man with a broad face
framed by a close-trimmed white beard. Bright blue eyes
glittered with energy and intensity. One either liked and
admired him, Kate reflected, or detested him. No one, having met him, would make the mistake of taking him lightly.
He and her father had been much the same in that respect, as
well as in their opinions about the Indians and the Missionary Society.

"Miss Hewitt!" He clasped her hand in both of his. "I had
not expected to see you! Unless perhaps you've changed
your mind about my young assistant? He could not have
chosen better. A good Christian woman like you would set
such an example for the young women in my charge."

"Why, thank you," Kate said, smiling. "But I'm merely
passing through. Mister Brennan—" she glanced over her
shoulder to find that Luke strode even now across the grav-
eled beach toward them "—has hired me to take photographs of the Haida for his museum. I'm hoping to find
Annie here, and passage for the three of us across the strait."

Mr. Duncan's white brows rose, though he contented
himself with, "Ah. Yes, Annie is here, and will be delighted
to see you. We can talk more at dinner. I trust that you and
Mister Brennan will dine with me?"

"With pleasure," Kate assured him.

She winced at the sight of her steamer trunks being tossed ashore, where they crunched and tipped on the sloping beach. With rumbled comments that Kate couldn't quite make out—perhaps mercifully so—Luke reversed direction to chastise the Indians unloading. A large duffel bag over his shoulder, Sims was climbing out of the third canoe to beach, followed by Durham, who stayed to supervise the unloading of his own trunks.

"You didn't mention your fellow travelers," Mr. Duncan said quizzically.

Interpreting the scowl Luke cast toward the other curator, Kate sighed. "Mister Sims and Mister Durham are not with our party. Though I suspect they will somehow end up being so."

It was immediately obvious that Sims had found an old friend among the Indians gathered on the beach. Mr. Duncan's work had been done among the Tsimshian Indians, but a few Haida had been gathered into the missionary fold as well. Sims swung his duffel bag over his shoulder, but stopped beside Luke and repeated his offer to share the cost of hiring a canoe. "These men say they may know of someone willing to take us. I'll let you know. You'll do the same?"

"Certainly," Luke agreed. "You have somewhere to stay?"

"Yes, but I'd rather be on my way as soon as possible."

He departed in company with two Indians, making a wide berth around Mr. Duncan. The missionary liked miners no better than Kate's father had, and for the same reasons.

Luke came to Kate's side. She had scarcely introduced him and mentioned their plans when Mr. Durham insinuated himself into the group. "How do you do?" he said, holding out a hand. His countenance was guileless, his tone amiable. "I'm James Durham, with the Field Museum. I've long looked forward to seeing Metlakatla. I was sorry indeed not to have an opportunity to stop here last year when I was on the coast. Dare I hope you have time to show us around?"

Clasping Durham's hand, Mr. Duncan declared, "I enjoy

nothing more than showing off our accomplishments here. I hope in turn that you will join me for dinner. And you, too, of course, Mister Brennan."

"Thank you," Luke said. "I was hoping to have the chance to ask whether you know of any interesting relics for sale. Perhaps you have recent converts . . ."

Durham's gaze sharpened until the missionary shook his head. "We're visited often by steamships. The Indians know only too well the value of the possessions they are casting off. I think you would be wise to wait until you reach the islands."

They proceeded up the street, having left their baggage to the mercy of several Indians who were stacking it in a small cabin. Luke took Kate's arm to slow her so that they lagged behind the missionary, whose attention had been seized by Durham. Nattily attired in tweed, the museum man was punctuating his points with expressive waves of his ivory-handled walking stick. He appeared to be commenting at flattering length on the energy and industry of Metlakatla, discernible at first sight to anyone with eyes. Kate began to understand why Luke disliked him so.

"This place looks alarmingly like a prison yard," Luke murmured. "Do they even sweep the dirt?"

Kate couldn't help but agree with his assessment. "It is rather . . . stark, isn't it?"

The houses were all two-storied, of uniform dimensions. Each had a small flower garden in the front; bushes, a young fruit tree, and a vegetable patch in the back. The houses were laid out as exactly as squares in a quilt, without the attraction of varied fabric. More were under construction.

"What if someone wanted to add a wing to his house?" Luke asked. "Or put a memorial pole up in front?"

"I believe the residents here at Metlakatla are the genuinely faithful," Kate said. "I doubt if they would think to defy Mister Duncan."

"I understand he is magistrate, too."

"There are those who believe he has too much power," Kate admitted. "I take it you're among them?"

"I would not care to live under his thumb." Luke sounded thoughtful. "On the other hand, I see much to admire in the man. He has certainly given his life to these people."

Ahead, the object of their conversation stopped to wait for them. "Mister Brennan, would you care to have a look about, too? Miss Hewitt, you might like to see the changes we've made."

"Yes, of course," she agreed. "The town has grown so. And I understand you are considering a salmon cannery?"

"Indeed. And see the gaslights. Why, this street is as fine as any in Victoria!" Standing at regular intervals along the street, the standards had already caught her eye. "The first night they were lit," Duncan said almost gaily, "the men were so proud, they insisted on a parade!"

Kate was not alone in noticing the ironic juxtaposition of two constables who passed just then, truncheons in hand. They wore military uniforms, with high hats that strapped beneath the chin.

"*Clah-how-ya,*" one said, nodding civilly.

"*Clah-how-ya,*" Luke responded. The greeting was in Chinook, and Kate wondered how well Luke had learned it during his last visit. Quite well, she would guess, given that trading had been his entire purpose.

"How do you choose the constables?" Luke asked once they were out of earshot.

"Of course they must be men I consider trustworthy," the missionary said. "Beyond that, they are almost all individuals with high status among their people. Chiefs are the hardest to convert, you know; they are reluctant to lose the power and wealth they hold. The office of constable, which is greatly respected here, is one way to recompense them."

"And of course the Indians are inclined to accept their authority already," Durham said admiringly. "I assume the idea has worked as well as one would expect?"

"I have been criticized by those who don't understand how important lineage and status are to these people, but I consider the experiment a success."

The tour progressed, encompassing the blacksmith shop,

the trading post, and the looms on which young Tsimshian women were weaving rough blankets.

"And of course," Mr. Duncan continued, "the lumber for all of our building comes from our own sawmill. I have plans for us to begin manufacturing bricks as well."

"Do you hope to employ all of the residents locally?" Luke asked.

"The more economically independent we can be, the more successful becomes spiritual conversion. I consider my greatest enemy to be other white men, not the Indians' own traditional ways. Those who must travel to Victoria to earn a living fall easily into sin. They sell their women, drink themselves into a stupor . . ." He shook his head. "Even here, we have constant trouble with traders willing to exchange liquor for furs." His sonorous voice deepened. "Temptation is too great at this stage. The Indians are like children, in need of guidance and protection."

Her father had felt the same. Kate had often wondered— and still did—whether white men would have behaved with any more maturity, thrown into a new world with all that was familiar wrenched from them.

She was not surprised when Luke spoke up. "Surely there is a danger in treating grown men and women like children. People usually give us what we expect."

Kate thought instantly of her mother. Would the young Amy Hewitt have matured into a capable woman had those around her assumed she was one?

Mr. Duncan treated the minor outbreak of doubt with condescension. "You don't know the natives as I do. You said you are to winter on the Queen Charlottes? Perhaps by spring, your outlook will have moderated."

"Perhaps," Luke conceded. Kate hoped that Mr. Duncan couldn't read Luke's expression as she could.

The centerpiece of the tour, the church was an impressive achievement, if appearing peculiarly out of place against the untamed backdrop of dark evergreens, with rocky beach and cold blue water at its feet. Its architecture hinted at the Gothic windows and flying buttresses of a European cathedral, though it remained quite plain. Narrow windows were topped by fanlights, and delicate scrollwork edged the dormers. Within was a great high-ceilinged space filled with hard wooden pews. Kate was reminded more of a barn than of the elaborate church her aunt and uncle attended in Victoria. The only decoration here consisted of banners across the front, behind the pulpit, which proclaimed: "Thou shalt call His name. He shall save His people from their sins."

"If only we could be here on Sunday!" Durham exclaimed. "I should very much like to hear you preach."

"You would be welcome to stay, of course," Mr. Duncan said, appearing gratified, "though unfortunately, I can't recommend it. A party of Haida plan to leave in the morning for Masset, and I believe they could be persuaded to take you with them. I know of no other opportunity to cross to the islands soon."

"We would prefer not to delay," Luke said. "If you could direct me to the leader of this party . . ."

"I will send word for him to call at my house after dinner." The missionary's tone was repressive. If Luke had wanted to find a way to his good graces, an echo of Durham's regret at not hearing Mr. Duncan preach would have been politic. Kate suspected that Luke Brennan was seldom politic. Fortunately, for the sake of Kate's father, Mr. Duncan would be sure to do all he could to advance their expedition.

Her certainty proved true. The small party turned to retrace their steps to the Mission House, where Kate was to share a room with one of the young Indian women Mr. Duncan boarded. He felt that his personal protection was required to keep the older girls virtuous, but the fact that he was not married made his living situation scandalous and weakened his support among the churchgoers of Victoria. Though the Reverend Hewitt had believed Mr. Duncan's motives to be innocent, still he had not hesitated to make a moral judgment. The presence of the young women boarders in Mr. Duncan's own home had been a deeply divisive issue between the two men, who otherwise shared so many goals.

Kate and the others were nearly to the plain frame house, no grander than any other at Metlakatla, when Kate saw a small, stout figure ahead entering through the front gate. Her steps quickened until she was running. "Annie!" she called, and her old friend turned. They tumbled into each other's arms.

The first five minutes were filled with tears and hugs and incoherent cries. The men tactfully left the two women alone in the front parlor. But when Kate broached the subject of Annie resuming her duties as chaperone, the Indian woman shook her head, and Kate's heart sank.

Annie was the possessor of an expressive face and a volatile personality. Enveloped in petticoats beneath a dark, long-sleeved, high-necked dress, her plump form appeared nearly as wide as she was tall. Now her face fell. "I thought you wouldn't need me anymore, so this summer I married again. And already I am pregnant."

"Oh, dear. Of course you can't come." Kate bit her lip, aware that she hadn't hidden her chagrin. No, worse yet, her panic! What would she do? But she mustn't make poor Annie feel guilty; if her friend's new marriage was happy, Kate knew it was the best thing for her. "I'm glad for you," she said simply.

Annie was searching her face. "I should come. You are like a daughter to me."

"Oh, Annie." Kate felt fresh tears flow. "I've missed you so. I feel as if I'm going home, but without you, and Father . . ."

Annie gathered her into a voluminous embrace. Fiercely, she said again, "I will have Mister Duncan talk to George. You should come first. This one—" she shrugged "—he is not born yet."

Kate collected herself and stepped back, swiping at her damp cheeks. "I'll manage just fine, Annie. You mustn't worry. Besides," she added firmly, "remember how you get seasick."

Funny that she hadn't thought of that until now. It was an irony that Annie was prone to seasickness, considering how dependent her people were on the sea, and how they excelled at canoe-building. Annie had most often stayed behind at Skidegate when Kate made her trips back and forth to Victoria.

The Reverend Hewitt would wait until a steamship stopped that had among its passengers an apparently respectable white woman, and entrust to her care his daughter. Aunt Grace had been incensed at his carelessness with Kate's welfare; appearances were only skin deep, she had pointed out with a sniff.

Kate was fifteen the year she had discovered that her aunt was right. Her temporary guardian on the six-day voyage was a handsome woman of middle age and comfortable manners. Seeking her, Kate had knocked on her cabin door and opened it without waiting for an answer. The apparently respectable woman was not alone, nor were she or her guest clothed. The scene within was still imprinted in Kate's memory as surely as any photograph she had ever taken. The picture was not a pretty one, but it was highly educational. Later, Kate had agreed with her aunt that appearances could be deceiving, without admitting that they *had* been deceiving on that particular voyage.

The question now was what she should tell Luke. What if he refused to take her unchaperoned? She was so close to Skidegate and the task she must accomplish! What was it Luke had said? *Would you risk your reputation, even your life, to go back one more time?* She had answered that she would risk anything. It was too late now to develop qualms, or to permit him to do so.

Annie had been watching her with shrewd eyes. "You trust this man?" she asked. "This Luke? Enough to go alone with him?"

Kate did not allow herself to hesitate. "Yes," she said. More slowly she repeated, "Yes. Of course I do."

The party of ten Haida, which included two women, had stopped over on their way home from Victoria. Though they were from Masset, they proved willing to detour via Skidegate—for a fee. A substantial fee. Through Kate as a mouthpiece, Luke attempted to bargain, but without success.

"For each of you, twenty dollars." The Haida leader was a man named Gats, who told Kate that he was one of Those-Born-at-House-Point. She did not know the northern Haida, but recognized the family name. "We have been away from home all summer. To go so far out of our way now . . ." He gestured, palms up.

"He has us over a barrel," Luke grumbled in English, "and he knows it. Perhaps your friend Sims could do better."

Gats waited with an air of complete relaxation. Behind him, others loaded the two seagoing canoes. The men were dressed in a peculiar assemblage of European and native clothing. Some looked conventional enough in trousers and coats. One of the men wore a conical spruce-root hat and around his shoulders, a Chilkat blanket. Kate did not like to think where Gats had acquired the uniform of an officer in Her Majesty's Royal Navy. It would have lent him more dignity had he not added a blanket wrapped around his waist. The two women had scarves over their heads and huddled inside blankets.

Unfortunately, Sims did not know these men and proved to have no influence whatsoever with them. He and Luke reluctantly handed over the price in gold coins.

Kate's trunks and boxes were being loaded into the larger of the two canoes when Durham strolled down to the beach. "I see you struck a deal with these fellows, too."

"You're going with us." Luke appeared resigned to the inevitable. He couldn't really have hoped to escape his rival; Duncan's well-meant intervention ensured that their group stayed together.

"I saw no alternative to their price," Durham said, "outrageous as it is."

"What'd they soak you for?" Sims asked.

"I beat them down to twenty-two dollars. We could take a comfortable steamship to Wrangell and back for less than that!"

Luke's gaze met Sims'. There was a moment of silent communication. Then Luke said in a far more pleasant tone than usual, "Many a New York businessman would have driven a harder bargain. When there's no competition for a service . . ." He shrugged.

Durham's nostrils flared. "Did you take a close look at these canoes? There's half a dozen cracks in each!"

Kate thought the two vessels looked sturdy enough for the journey. The Haida made canoes superior to any of the other northwest tribes. Because they most often crossed stretches of open sea, theirs tended to be the largest, with a high prow meant to withstand deep swells. These were typical: one perhaps thirty-five feet long, the other forty, each with flaring sides and a painted prow that rose well above Kate's head. The gunwales were crowned by long planks designed to prevent high waves from breaking over the sides. Each canoe was carved from a single cedar log, hollowed out by an adze and then filled with hot stones that softened the wood until it could be bent to the desired shape. Simple thwarts formed the cross-hatching inside that served as seats, too.

It was true that the painted designs of Eagle and Killer Whale had faded and that obvious cracks had been repaired with cedar withes and then coated with spruce or fir gum. Such repairs, she knew, were amazingly strong, adding years to the life of a canoe.

"They've come all the way from Victoria," Luke said. "They surely wouldn't set out if they didn't think it was safe. And I for one would choose these over the rest of the canoes here."

Kate wholeheartedly agreed. Most of the others drawn up on the beach were designed for coastal travel; smaller, they lacked the high prow and the capacity to have a mast lashed into place to take advantage of a favorable wind.

It would clearly be midday before they embarked. The Indians had to finish loading the bent-cedar boxes of oolachen grease, for which they had traded. Along with trunks and crates brought by Kate, Luke, and Durham, the cedar boxes were being carefully distributed over the length and width of the canoes.

Luke turned to Kate. "Does Annie have a trunk?"

The moment of truth had come. Kate stiffened her spine and said, "Annie won't be coming with us."

It was as she had feared. His voice rose. *"What?"*

"She's with child," Kate continued. "She can hardly travel with us in her condition."

His eyes narrowed. "And you just discovered this?"

Foolishly, she hesitated.

He snapped, "So you intend to cast off all the strictures governing a young woman's behavior? I should have known better than to—"

"Hire me?" she interrupted without compunction, "*You* are the one who asked whether I was willing to risk my reputation! Are you suffering from second thoughts?"

"It is *your* reputation that concerns me," he said stiffly.

He had taken it better than she expected. Chin high, she said, "Then allow me to worry about it!"

Kate retreated to the Mission House, where, with only small regret, she packed away her bustle and wool traveling dress. Several years ago, she had designed and sewed for herself a more practical gown with a split skirt. She had since duplicated it several times. Even the color was utilitarian: the serviceable blue seldom showed stains.

The only mirror in her room was small. However she twisted her neck, she couldn't see below the stiff, high collar. Perhaps that was just as well. She knew the gown to be unbecoming, which had never mattered before.

Now it seemed to. Had Alice's innocent vanity been contagious? she wondered in dismay. Of the European men here, Mister Duncan had seen her looking worse and she didn't even like Mr. Durham, or care what he thought of her appearance.

However, Kate had never been given to self-deceit. She knew perfectly well that she *did* care what Luke thought of her. But he had given no sign of admiring her as a woman anyway, so she might as well resign herself to gratefully accepting crumbs. He would approve of this dress. Besides, a day and a half spent bailing seawater from a canoe was unlikely to have a felicitous effect on whatever she wore.

Predictably, Luke spared her no more than a glance when she reappeared on the beach. "No, no!" he roared. "Put that box in *this* canoe!"

"Does it matter?" Kate inquired, stopping at his side.

"If we survive the journey, I want all our possessions with us. What if we become separated from the other canoe? I don't trust that scoundrel Durham. And should he go down in a squall, I don't want to be forced to repine because he took my razor with him."

"Surely that box contains a good deal more than a razor."

Luke turned his head and for the first time in some days, really looked at her. The intelligence in his eyes was frank and unpatronizing. "I thought I might host a potlatch or two of my own. I can hardly do so without something to give away. What do you think? Will it work?"

"Work? Of course it will." She turned her head as though to watch the increasingly tumultuous proceedings. Several boys were helping load the canoes, though they seemed to be getting in the way more often than not. The dogs that slunk hopefully behind them didn't improve matters.

She didn't know whether to be impressed or dismayed by Luke's scheme. How perfectly designed it was to win him a cordial reception from the Haida, who demonstrated their status by giving away possessions. Even her father had not understood how central the peculiar institution of the "potlatch" was to the Indians. He had felt that it was no more than an excuse for chiefs to ruthlessly tax their subjects. He had been determined to convince his converts that each man should work for his own benefit, and for that of his wife and children, not for the greater glory of some chief whose claim on his minions was at best hazy. The Reverend Hewitt had considered the destruction of property to be criminally wasteful, while the giving of great wealth to a hated rival was foolish.

When Kate had argued that breaking coppers and throwing them into the sea was far better than warring, her father had said impatiently, "Deciding which is the greater of two evils serves little purpose. It is absurd for a man to let his wife and children go hungry because he has given everything he owns to a chief, to be distributed to total strangers!"

On the face of it, he was right. And yet, surely pride counted for something. The Haida would have no pride if they were thought to be so poor they couldn't afford to potlatch. Was a potlatch given on the occasion of a daughter's marriage any more wasteful, really, than the extravagant weddings and receptions given by wealthy Victorians? If her father had attempted to make a distinction between *kinds* of potlatches—between those that celebrated marriages or births, that paid back kin who had helped build a new house, that erected a pole in memory of a respected man, and those that served only to humiliate a rival—she thought he might have gotten farther. As it was, he had made very little headway in his battle against the potlatch.

And now Luke intended to use the Haida's own institution to establish his reputation amongst them. The scheme was ingenious—and underhanded, she thought.

He was watching her, his eyes clear and so blue that she almost felt the need to shield her own from the brilliance. "You expected me to fail," he said, sounding thoughtful. "Or at least hoped I would."

"No," Kate said. "Yes."

"Which is it?"

"I hope that you and others like you will not succeed entirely. If you do, what will be left?"

"There may be nothing anyway."

She nodded toward the canoes. "They are not all dead yet. You sound as though you hope they soon will be, so you can claim credit for having the foresight to 'salvage' the bones before the meat has been picked clean."

"I knew you didn't approve of me," he said. "I was not aware that you despised me."

Kate struggled for an answer, aware that she had sounded disagreeable, even quarrelsome, when in fact, her feelings were far more mixed than that. "Perhaps," she said, "it's only that I don't want to admit that the end you envision is inevitable."

His brows drew together. "Just when I've decided that you're as unreasonably emotional as any other woman, you confound me."

There he went again, annoying her at the same time he sparked a ridiculous little glow of pride. "I take it you don't like being confounded."

Luke gave her a peculiarly searching look. "Then you take it wrong."

They were interrupted by an eruption from Sims, who strode up. "Blast it, I don't want to travel with that idiot! He'll hurt somebody with that stick."

Luke's good humor was restored. "I seem to recall that the top screws off to reveal a sword."

A rumble rose in Sims' chest. Kate shot Luke a stern look as she patted Sims on the arm. "He's baiting you. For heavens' sake, what possible harm can the man do? He's more likely to whack himself in the head." She lowered her voice. "They detest each other, you know. I'm grateful that they'll be separated."

His beard twitched, and she thought that Sims might be smiling. "I'm going to be sorry you talked me into this."

"Talked you into what?" she asked innocently.

"Putting up with that tomfool." He grunted. "Looks as though we're wanted."

Indeed, the chaos seemed to have sorted itself into order of a kind. The boys had retreated, the dogs were barking, and the pile of boxes on the beach awaiting disposal had vanished.

Annie, who had come down to see her off, hugged Kate as though she expected some monster of the deep to swallow her. With only a little trepidation, Kate joined the Haida women aboard. The younger of the two shyly gave her a smile, which she returned. And then, with a scrape of cedar on gravel and the shouted *"hu-u-u-u-i!"* of the men shoving her free, the canoe drove into the first wave. Kate clutched the cedar crossbar beneath her and lifted her head to catch the rush of salt air.

She was on her way home.

Chapter Five

With the open sea ahead, they stopped just before nightfall at one of the small, outermost islands. Canvas sails were transformed into crude tents, wood gathered for fires, and as the tide withdrew, the two Haida women took digging sticks and collected clams, which they then steamed in an iron kettle above the fire. One of the men clambered onto the rocks and had the good fortune to shoot a fur seal. The roasted meat was surprisingly palatable.

"By Jove," Durham said, "this isn't bad. I had seal the last time I was here and could hardly stomach it."

"Probably an ordinary hair seal, whose meat is rather oily," Kate said.

Her own appetite was excellent, and she was almost grateful that Annie wasn't along. This first leg of the voyage had been accomplished with no more motion than a child might feel on a rocking horse, but it would have been enough to make her ill. How she would have dreaded tomorrow!

Kate herself was conscious of some apprehension; she had only once crossed the strait in a canoe, and they had been blessed that time with serene weather. At this season, the chances of a rough crossing were vastly increased.

Shortly thereafter, she retired for the night. She and the other two women slept on mats in one of the tents.

She was roused in the darkness by Luke. "Up and at 'em!" he called cheerfully. Kate groaned and tried to bury herself beneath the furs. His infuriating voice pursued her. "The Indians mean to make an early start. If you want any coffee or breakfast, you'd better leap."

Groggily, Kate forced her eyes open. The two Haida women were gone; probably they had been responsible for building the fire. Kate managed to wriggle into her clothes beneath the seal robe, motivated not by modesty, but by the cold; this late in the fall, frost lay on the ground in the morning.

Mr. Duncan had sent them on their way with provisions for the journey, so they were able to share biscuits, cheese, and jam with the Haida.

Pale light streaked the horizon as they packed for the next stage of the journey. "Why do we leave so early?" Kate asked Gats.

"The wind is good. We can use the sails. But there are clouds there," he pointed south, "that will bring a storm. We must hurry."

Kate looked for Luke, to find him stalking the Haida man who wore the handsome spruce-root hat. She arrived at Luke's side in time to hear him say, *"Nika makook . . . ?"* He muttered under his breath, then in English asked, "What the devil is 'hat' in Chinook?"

"I don't speak it very well," she said. "In Haida, hat is *ta'tsung*."

Understanding, the Indian shook his head. *"Wake."* He spoiled his curt refusal by adding hopefully, *"Konsick mika hoey-hoey?* What will you give me for it?"

Luke countered by asking what he wanted for the hat; the Indian suggested that perhaps later they could gamble for it.

Kate tugged at Luke's sleeve. "Gats fears a change of weather. Can't you discuss this at Skidegate?"

"Will there be time?"

"You'll see other hats," she pointed out.

"This one has a particularly fine design," Luke said obstinately.

The Indian's head swiveled back and forth. Kate wondered how much English he understood.

"I recognize the style. It was painted by Mister Edenshaw," she said. "He lives at Masset and, I understand, accepts commissions."

"Ah." Luke turned back to the man. *"Tu-mallow?"* he suggested. "Tomorrow?"

The man was agreeable, and the others were ready to embark. The surf was low this morning, allowing an easy launch, thank the Lord. Kate had seen canoes even as large as this one break apart in heavy surf.

The Indians wasted no time in raising sails, made of cotton sheeting to take advantage of the stiff, following wind. The effect was odd, quite different from a masted schooner. It was rather like a gray shorebird that had been floating quietly and now spread its wings, dazzlingly white. The wind caught the sails, sending the long canoes skimming over the water. They were fortunate indeed in its direction; since the canoes lacked keel or rudder, they could not quarter or sail into the wind. Should it shift, they must revert to paddling.

Kate turned her head to watch the land recede faster than seemed possible. A dark bulk to the east, the mountain range was backlit by purple. Spruce and cedar cloaked the small islands, whose rocky shores dropped precipitously into the water. Seagulls sat on isolated rocks; a dark shape swooped and snatched a fish from the sea. Kate made out the snowy head that marked the bald eagle.

To the west lay open water. The sky was dark still, but the purple dawn behind them was reflected in the deep swells of the strait. Even with favorable winds, the voyage would take six or eight hours. She would not care to arrive after nightfall. If they wandered too far to the north, the treacherous shoals of Rose Spit would tear the canoes asunder. Even worse was the secret fear Kate harbored, that they might miss the islands altogether.

A last, rocky isle rose ahead of them. From a distance, it seemed to undulate, its very surface shivering like a great beast rippling its skin.

Seated near Kate was the oldest man in the party. Lines carved into his forehead and beside his eyes and mouth lent him at least the appearance of wisdom. Seeing Kate's fascinated stare, he smiled. *"Teipon."*

"Sea lions," Kate repeated for Luke's benefit. "I've never seen so many at once." Or heard so many. The deep-throated roar might have come from some supernatural being as it rose to suck the canoes beneath the sea.

Their route took them quite close to the rock and its denizens, whose fat, dark bodies glistened as their heads swiveled to watch the canoes' approach. The bulls crowned the highest point. Enormous and powerful, they looked to be the kings they fancied themselves.

The other canoe was just ahead, nearly abreast of the rock, when Luke swore. Kate turned her head. "What?" And then she, too, saw what had alarmed him. Durham had risen to his feet and was leveling a rifle at the rock. One of the Indians lunged at him and knocked the barrel up, but too late. Kate heard the one sharp crack, even amongst the roar of the sea lions. Crimson splashed one of the bulls and it lurched in a death spasm.

More frightening yet was the chaos that followed. The entire rock looked like a moving mass as the panicky herd bellowed and struggled to reach the water. Ungainly on land, the sea lions hit the water with huge splashes, until the sea was alive with the beasts. They circled the canoes, rising from the water so close that Kate could have touched them. The canoe shuddered as the great bodies bumped it.

The Haida had reacted while she was still stupefied. Amidst cries of alarm and the snap of orders, they grabbed paddles and used them to fend the creatures off. Luke found a pole and followed suit. With the other two women,

Kate could only cling to the thwarts and watch the drama in horror.

Miraculously, the wind seemed to freshen, and the sails made a popping sound as they filled. The rock was left well astern, though for some distance, the more aggressive sea lions chased the canoes. At last even they fell back, and the Indians lifted the paddles from the water.

In the momentary silence, no one spoke. Then, quietly, the old man said, *"Up willa wahl wa-ka-koad."*

Kate automatically translated: "That is the way fools act."

The others nodded. He added, "I have known when a wounded *teipon* has wrenched a canoe apart with its teeth and caused the loss of all on board. We are lucky."

"Damn fool," Luke muttered.

Gats, who was the steersman, turned. He nodded at Luke and said to Kate, "Does his friend ever think before he acts?"

"Mister Durham is no friend of Mister Brennan's," she said firmly. "It is only chance that we both sought passage at the same time."

"Ah." To the others, he said, "They should throw him out and let him swim to the islands."

The Indians laughed. Sotto voce, Kate translated for Luke. He smiled grimly. "Perhaps he could use his umbrella for a canoe and his stick as a paddle."

Kate translated, to the merriment of all. She sensed a relaxation toward her and Luke, as though the two of them had passed a test. She was grateful they were not in the same canoe with Durham. Relations there would not be friendly.

Hour passed into hour. The wind increased until the masts groaned and the ocean was covered with foam-crested waves. Kate became a trifle queasy as gray-green swells rose above the canoe. On Gats' instructions, the passengers huddled on the goods in the hull, where they couldn't be thrown out at a fickle toss of the waves.

They lost sight of the other canoe, though it might have

been no more than yards from them. The Indians discussed whether to bring down the sails, but the wind still held firmly behind them. The discussion became academic when one of the sails suddenly tore, its sturdy fabric rent to ribbons that twisted and writhed in the wind.

"Take down the other," Gats called. His order was followed, the masts unlashed. The Indians unshipped the paddles and fought to turn the craft into the waves. As the sea became rougher, waves broke above them, drenching the canoe.

"We must bail," one of the Haida women said. She scrambled to the stern, where she found buckets carried for this very task. Already they sat in several inches of seawater; as each wave broke, the level rose.

Both Luke and Kate accepted a bucket. If the previous hours had seemed to run into each other, now time blurred. Walls of water rose around them; the canoe bucked and groaned. If the craft should split under the strain, they had no hope of survival. Kate did not even let herself worry at the possibility. She quit thinking, simply scooping and emptying the bucket over the side. It began to seem hopeless as the water was replaced by the next wave. She was drenched and bitterly cold; all of them were. Her arms and shoulders first ached, then screamed for relief, but she could not stop. They would quickly be swamped if they ceased to bail.

She was dimly conscious of Luke beside her, moving twice as fast as she could; she began to feel as though death had found her but was held off by the rhythm she would not interrupt.

At some point, the Indians began to sing, a powerful chant punctuated by the sound of paddles striking the gunwale.

"Ocean Spirit, calm the waves for me. Get close to me, my Power. My heart is tired. Make the sea very calm for me, *ye ho ye ho'lo!*"

Despite—or perhaps because of—her upbringing, Kate did not often pray, but now she did. Her prayer was very nearly wordless, but heartfelt. She thought wildly that she had claimed to be prepared to risk her life to go home once more, but she had not really understood what that meant. She might easily have had Annie's safety on her conscience as well! Had she been driven not by a need for justice, but by a selfish longing to return to an easier time in her life?

In their exhaustion, no one noticed the gradual change in wind and sea, the diminution of the waves as they lost their crests of foam and instead became long, slow swells. Kate bent to fill her bucket and found too little water. Her weary brain did not respond to what her eyes saw; it told her to bail though there was no longer a need. At last her head fell and she slumped into a heap in the bottom of the canoe. An arm came around her and she leaned against Luke, whose expression was as tired and incomprehending as hers.

And then Gats shouted, *"Tl-ga!"*

Land. Could it be? Kate lifted her head, rose to her knees. The canoe rode high on the next swell, and she saw it, too. Across the horizon stretched the mountains of Graham and Moresby Islands, blue-gray and solid. Home.

Excited voices broke out. Kate hugged the Haida woman who sat nearest her, and then Luke. "We made it!" he shouted jubilantly, lifting her until she dangled from his hands. "By God, we did it!"

"So we did," Kate agreed, laughing. "Now will you put me down?"

"I suppose so." He complied, still smiling at her. "I should hate to tip us both out, so that we had to swim for it."

Kate glanced down at herself. "We look as if we've already been for a swim." She was unlikely to have anything dry to change into; her trunks were not waterproof. In sudden horror, she turned to scramble astern. "My camera! My plates! Dear heavens, they must be soaked!"

Luke's hand caught her arm. "They were packed carefully, neither on the bottom nor on the top. Gats understood that they must be kept dry."

She sagged. "I would give anything for a hot bath."

"Unlikely to be forthcoming, I assume."

"Well, not for a while. We still have some way to go, you know."

But Luke was not attending. "I wonder where the others are," he said, scanning the horizon that rose and fell with each sea swell.

Although he had not intended it as a reproach, Kate immediately felt selfish that she had not thought of the other canoe. The Indians looked understandably anxious. After some discussion, they decided that they had veered too far south. Perhaps the others had maintained a more accurate course.

By an hour later, the land ahead was coalescing into a familiar coastline of inlets and small, rocky islands crowned by a few spruce or cedar. They still had not spotted the other canoe and could only hope it had arrived ahead of them.

At length, they rounded the long, low northeast point of Moresby Island, which protected the Skidegate Inlet. Kate was grateful for what was left of the fading light and the long, quiet swells of the strait, because Spit Point, or Kil'kun, as the Haida called it, could be nearly as treacherous as Rose Point to the north, with its vicious crosscurrents.

She saw the poles before the canoe was properly in sight of the long, curving beach. A forest of them rose along the shore, their grayness in sharp contrast to the forested slope behind. Many were elaborately carved, while others were simpler but topped with the stylistic figure of some supernatural being.

The visitors had been spotted; by the time they passed the two islands in front of Skidegate, dogs had begun to bark and a small crowd was gathered on the beach. Kate's heart swelled with something close to pain, and she had to blink away tears. It was ridiculous to be so glad that nothing had changed: the plank houses and their frontal poles, the high-prowed canoes drawn up on the beach, smoke curling from the smoke holes, gray mist shrouding the point beyond the village. Children scampering behind the dogs, the mingled odors of sea and cooking.

Of course she would not know these children. The girls she had played with when she first came here had long since had children of their own. After their puberty seclusion and a potlatch celebrating their new womanhood, Haida girls were ready for marriage. Her friends had teased her because her menstruation had not started until she was sixteen. They claimed that one family had given the potlatch for a daughter whose menstruation never started, and everyone pretended that it had; perhaps Kate's father should do the same, they laughed. Kate had pretended not to mind, but at fourteen and fifteen, she had minded very much. Still as skinny as a pole, still Katie Rose, she had felt left behind.

What an odd thing to remember. Heaven knew, she hadn't envied them! She had known perfectly well that she wasn't ready for marriage and motherhood. Especially when the marriage was arranged without consulting the girl, as was often the case.

At one end of the curved beach stood the Mission House and the modest church, each painted white, as was the house of Mr. Sterling and Mr. MacGregor, who had established the Oil Works. The building where they processed the fish into oil stood on pilings, so that at high tide, it was possible to bring boats right up to the door.

Amidst shouts of greeting, the canoe was turned around and driven by one last forceful stroke of the paddles stern-first onto the beach. For an instant, Kate closed her eyes. She gave a silent prayer of thanksgiving. Until this second, her homecoming had not seemed entirely real. But here she was, with one more long, dark winter to comfort her in the years of exile to come.

Luke's pleasure in the arrival was somewhat dimmed by two distractions: his concern for the other travelers, including the scoundrel Durham, and his awareness of Miss Hewitt's emotions. Thus he found that instead of studying the village, wondering which pole might be available for purchase, anticipating the ceremonies he might be allowed to witness, he was scanning the beach for a canoe that was not there, and watching Kate.

He saw the moment when she blinked back tears, the

delight when she recognized old friends . . . one in particular.

"Gao!" She lifted wet skirts and hurried on unsteady legs to greet the young man who came forward. Stocky, he possessed dark skin, broad cheekbones, and unfriendly eyes. Though tattooing was seldom done anymore, Gao's shirt, open at the neck, revealed the blue outlines of Sea Wolf. This was a young man who had not given up the old ways.

Kate spoke an incomprehensible line that was answered in kind. The man nodded at Luke and clearly asked a question. Kate said, "Mister Brennan *hinu il keyang*." She rattled on, gesturing toward Luke as she did so.

Luke lifted his brows.

"He wants to know who you are," Kate explained. "I told him you are a scholar."

The man coolly looked Luke over, then said something to Kate, who translated: "He asks if you will buy things. I said yes."

The news was not well-received. Gao gave a grunt of disapproval and turned so that his back was to Luke as he spoke again to Kate.

Frowning, Luke watched the byplay. His thoughts were interrupted by a boy, perhaps ten years of age, who spoke in Chinook. "You buy? My aunt has things to sell. See? There."

His aunt—though she was not necessarily such in the way white people calculated familial relationships—was hurriedly laying out baskets and silver bracelets on a mat. She had been caught by surprise without the warning whistle of a steamship to give her time to prepare her wares.

Her graying hair was drawn back untidily, her dark face wrinkled. As with all the Haida, her eyes had a nearly Oriental cast, while her face was deformed by the carved-bone lip plug: the labret. Like tattoos, the labret had become a little used form of ornamentation. A young girl no longer automatically had her lip cut so as to install the plug. Only the older women, such as the boy's aunt, still wore the disfiguring, if sometimes quite handsome, ornament.

The woman's merchandise was unlikely to be anything

that would interest him, but Luke allowed himself to be drawn over to look. After all, he had to start somewhere, and she was as likely a candidate as any to spread the word about what he sought.

"Clah-how-ya," he greeted her politely.

"Mesika nanitsh," she said, indicating her goods with a sweeping gesture. *"Mesika nanitsh kloshe iktah. Nika mamook opekwan pee klik-wallie. Klaske elip kloshe."*

It would have been difficult not to understand her even if Luke had forgotten the simple trade jargon. "You look," she had said. "You see fine goods. I make the baskets and bracelets. They best."

Perhaps they were, but the objects had been manufactured specifically for the tourist trade. They were not necessarily the same as the baskets she might make for use in her own house, or as the bracelets she and her daughters would wear.

Luke assured her that her goods were indeed fine. But he would like to buy ordinary things, everyday things. *"Kahkwa mamook tipshin pe muckamuck ooskan.* Like a sewing needle or a food bowl."

"Mamook tipshin?" she repeated incredulously.

"Nika . . ." He hesitated, frustrated by the limitations of Chinook, which included only about three hundred words. How could he possibly describe the purpose of a museum? He looked around for Miss Hewitt—no, for Kate. He really must get used to the implied intimacy of using her first name.

She had been talking with two blanket-clothed women, but seeing his silent plea, she excused herself and came to his side. "Gwa'g!anat," she said respectfully, and he guessed that to be the woman's name. They talked briefly before Kate asked in surprise, "You want to buy her sewing needle?"

"I want to buy everyday things," he said. "So that people who come to the museum can see how the Haida truly live. How beautiful are their dishes and clothes and fishing equipment."

Kate translated what he had said and the reply. "You wish to see these things?"

"Yes, I wish to see them," Luke confirmed.

"I will talk to others," the old woman said. "We might have some things we could get rid of."

Luke bowed. "I would be very grateful."

He glanced at Kate, to see that he had lost her attention. Sounding relieved, she said, "Here comes Mister Richardson. I was beginning to fear that he was away."

Luke went with her to meet the young missionary. He felt some curiosity, since Richardson had been absent during Luke's brief stop-over here last year.

"Miss Hewitt!" the missionary called while still a distance away.

"It *is* you. I thought my eyes were deceiving me!"

Richardson's appearance was a disappointment. Luke had expected to see a zealot. It was difficult to picture this slight figure quivering with the passion of the Lord, or to imagine the pleasant, light voice booming out threats of Hell Everlasting. Why, Richardson was no taller than Miss Hewitt, with light, wispy hair that had already begun to recede, leaving a high forehead that lent him the look of a scholar. Only his sideburns, carefully tended, hinted at worldly vanity.

Closer up, it was possible to see more strength in the man's face, perhaps even intelligence, a quality Luke did not necessarily ascribe to missionaries. His hands were large and capable-appearing, almost out of proportion to his body. His brown eyes were so warm when he clasped Miss Hewitt's hands in his that Luke wondered if Richardson held her in more regard than she knew.

"I had no idea that you intended a visit!" he exclaimed. "Did you write and the letter was lost? Not that you aren't welcome, of course! This will always be your home as far as I'm concerned. But surely you were safe in the care of your aunt and uncle. Or are we behind on the news up here? Is all well at home?"

"Yes, they're fine, and vastly disapproving of my decision to come." She disengaged her hands so gently that she did not seem to be rejecting him. "Let me introduce Mister Brennan. Mister Lucas Brennan. Unless you've met before?" Assured that they had not, she described Luke's expedition and her own role. "So of course I have all my photographic equipment, and must find a space I can use as a darkroom. Is there an uninhabited house sturdy enough to serve?"

Even as she spoke, disapproval clouded the missionary's face. "You came alone with Mister Brennan? And you wonder at your aunt and uncle's disapproval?"

Her tone became cool. "I'll engage a woman here to serve as my chaperone, just as Annie always did. Nonetheless, I do understand my aunt and uncle's feelings. But I must find a way to support myself in the future, and Mister Brennan offered a splendid chance that I would have been foolish to turn down. Besides which . . ." Uncharacteristically, she hesitated. "I hope to learn more about my father's death. The authorities are so uninterested, I didn't even know where his body was found until by chance I met Mister Sims on the *Skeena.*"

Richardson did not have the face of a poker player. A stubborn desire to argue with Miss Hewitt's plans for the future was followed by alarm.

"Surely you don't hope to unmask the perpetrator! Even an attempt to do so could be dangerous!"

Kate's chin jutted in a manner that was nearly masculine. "My quest may be impossible, but I must make an attempt. I hope you can understand that."

Unwisely, the missionary said, "If you were a man, I might understand, though I still think the attempt is futile. But for a young lady to go around asking impertinent questions that might easily be resented, even by those who aren't guilty of murder . . ." Words seemed to fail him.

They did not, of course, fail Miss Hewitt. "The questions might well be less resented simply because it is a woman who asks them. In any case, I must do it. I owe my father that much."

Both appeared to have forgotten that Luke was an audience. He wondered if Miss Hewitt would have spoken so plainly had she remembered. She had certainly not warned *him* of her intentions. Perhaps she assumed that now she was here, he could not send her back. Unfortunately, she was right.

His sympathies ought wholly to be with Richardson. Yet Luke was surprised to realize that his feelings were mixed. A girl loves her father no less than a son does, so why was a determination to achieve justice—or vengeance—a masculine preserve? Even he had always believed it to be. Why else had he thought her squared jaw made her appear masculine? Because delicate young ladies were not supposed to feel the determination Miss Hewitt had been expressing?

He discovered that he had missed several interchanges between the missionary and Miss Hewitt. It would appear that Richardson was routed, at least temporarily. They were discussing the missing canoe and its passengers.

"I fear it is getting too dark to search for them," Richardson said. "Certainly, if they have not appeared by morning, we can send out a party in hopes of aiding them."

Miss Hewitt had to be content with that. "Perhaps we should be getting settled as well. You didn't say whether there is an uninhabited house that might be suitable as a base for us."

"We can find something for a darkroom, but you . . . and Mister Brennan, of course, must be my guests. If you wouldn't be too cramped sharing with a woman from the village, Mister Brennan could have the extra room."

He had earned a smile. "If you truly don't mind our unannounced arrival—"

"You must know how delighted I am to see you!" Richardson said fervently. Miss Hewitt looked startled, and his expression changed to one that reminded Luke of a basset hound. Perhaps the ability to assume a suitably mournful countenance at will was a requirement for becoming a minister. "I meant every word that I wrote you. I'm sorry I couldn't come to you personally. To hear of your father's death from strangers . . ."

Instead of receiving comfort, Miss Hewitt was required to give it. "Your letter was very kind," she said gently. "You did all you could."

"The Reverend Hewitt's death is an irreparable loss." If anything, Richardson appeared more mournful. "I feel ill-equipped to take his place. No, I shouldn't even use those words! I can't pretend to take his place, only to continue his work to the best of my ability. I often feel his presence, and his approval, or so I believe. I couldn't bear to allow the field he labored in for so long to lie fallow."

Luke was hungry, wet, and cold. Miss Hewitt looked as bedraggled as he felt. She had begun the day with her dark curls severely tamed in a bun; wet ringlets were now plastered to her neck and forehead. Her dress was soaked and clung to her breasts and thighs in a way that would embarrass her should she notice. Water no doubt squished in her boots as it did in his own. Altogether, he wished the missionary would save the breast-beating for another time, so that they could proceed to dry clothes at least, if not to a meal.

· The pat Miss Hewitt gave to Richardson's arm appeared perfunctory, her smile wan. Her words, however, made Luke forget his physical condition. "I know Father sometimes had doubts about you, but I feel sure you would have overcome them."

"Doubts?" Richardson said sharply.

"Surely he expressed them to you," she said as though in surprise. "He wrote me." Her brow crinkled. "Why, I believe it was the last letter I received from him. How sad, that he should have died while unsure of your calling. I often hope that he can look down on us now. Perhaps he knows that his original faith in you was justified."

Stiffly, the young missionary said, "I was not aware that he suffered doubts about me. I can't imagine why he should have. Did he say?"

"I must consult the letter again. I had nearly forgotten his comments until now."

"You do have it with you?"

Luke decided the time had come for intercession. "Surely

you can discuss this another time? Miss Hewitt must be wretchedly cold and weary. We had a difficult crossing. There were moments when I think we all despaired of a safe arrival."

Richardson blinked, took another look at both, and said, "My delight at seeing you must have blinded me! I sincerely hope that a hot bath will reduce the chances of your having taken a severe chill. Let us proceed to the house immediately!" He turned to the nearest Indian and snapped out what must have been orders, because the bustle of activity changed focus. However, Miss Hewitt's old friend Gao did not join in. He stood to one side, watching with a brooding expression Luke could not like.

Despite Miss Hewitt's attempt to tug away, Luke held a firm grip on her arm. "Lead on," he said, and the missionary had no choice but to go ahead.

Luke lowered his voice. "What the hell were you thinking of? You are playing dangerous games!"

"Which is my privilege," she said waspishly.

"If you are knocked in the head or drowned, I will not have photographs for my display."

"I'm glad to know that my death would at least cause you a moment's regret!"

"It would cause far more than that. I would feel responsible."

"Responsible!" She stopped on the path that led up from the beach. "Because I'm a woman, I suppose, and therefore incapable of answering for my own behavior?"

"Because you are my employee," he said impatiently. "Because you would not be here if it weren't for me. Your gender has nothing to do with it."

"Well, that's a change, at least," she said ungraciously.

He waited. Finally, she sighed. "Truly I don't intend to do anything too foolhardy. I have every intention of fulfilling my obligation to you."

"If someone doesn't murder you first."

"I'll find no answers if I don't raise possibilities."

"Miss Hewitt!" Richardson turned to find that they had

fallen behind. He frowned at Luke. "Let's not delay. We must think of Miss Hewitt's health!"

"By all means," Luke agreed. He had said all he intended to. He had known even before he opened his mouth that she would reject his advice. He could only hope that she wasn't needling the wrong man—or perhaps, from her point of view, the *right* man.

Given that she had spread her attentions indiscriminately, he was hoping for too much. He had not forgotten the wariness on Sims' face when she hinted at the content of that letter. And then there was Gao's dark, unreadable stare. What had she said to him?

Damnation! He should never even have considered bringing a woman. Why had he listened to Alistair?

Of course, there was a certain irony in the fact that it was not her womanly qualities that made him regret bringing her . . . although he felt sure it would come to that as well. He would not have minded seeing her when she emerged from the hot bath, her skin flushed becomingly.

"Bloody hell," he muttered, and followed.

Chapter Six

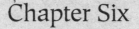

So, the missionary's daughter had come back.

Gao stayed on the beach until the sky closed and he could no longer see anything. There was a moon tonight, but it hid behind dark, scudding clouds. It would be hard for the other canoe to find its way now. Gao did not want his own people to die, but he would not mind if the two *yetz haada,* the white men, never came to Skit-ei-get. Especially the one who had shown such disrespect. The dead might not know the man had stolen from them, but the living did. He had even taken the bones of Gao's mother's father. The grandfather had been reborn in Gao's younger brother, but the bones were still his. No, the thief should not have tried to come back. Perhaps the One-in-the-Sea had been angry and had let the waves swallow the canoe.

It was the *yetz haada* who had not been swallowed who were the most worrisome. Gao had thought of the woman as a friend, though she was really his sister's friend. He had called her Katie. And now she was back with a man who wanted to take and take and take. She was to use her box with windows to write the images of Haida on paper, so that *yetz haada* very far away could see how the Indians lived.

Gao was not interested in how *they* lived. Why should they care about the Haida? He wondered sometimes what really happened to all the things that were taken away. Did a chief somewhere throw them into the sea to impress other chiefs? If it were so, Gao would not mind seeing a potlatch so grand. There would never again be one like that here. People were too poor now. They were poor because of the *yetz haada* and the pestilence they had brought. And because of men like this Luke, who wanted to take more away, paying gold or blankets in place of masks and dishes that could belong only to one family.

But what could he, Gao, do? Sometimes he was angry enough to want to kill them all, but he knew that would be futile. Even a supernatural being could not hold back a tidal wave alone. He had hoped that when the first missionary was found dead, things would change, that people would hear the chiefs and shamans again. But still they talked about the Great Chief of the Heavens and were ashamed of the dances that belonged to them by right. Gao felt sometimes like a pebble being worn to nothing by the sea.

He turned at last and went to the house of his mother's brother, where he lived. Gao was not a nobleman who sat at the rear of the house, but neither did he sit at the front, with commoners. His parents had potlatched for him two times and had been saving things with which to do it again, but the pestilence had found them first. His sister had had only one potlatch, but she had been lucky. The son of a noble had wanted her, and his family had thought she was worthy. Now she was a chief-woman, and her first son carved with Gao. Two other children had died; one drowned, and the other's thread of life was not strong enough. That one had lived for only two days. Now his sister was pregnant again, and taking care to do everything right, but Gao knew she was worried. She had hoped to have ten children, and here she had been married for ten years and had only one!

Gao ate with those he was close to, sharing dog salmon,

fresh-caught, potatoes cooked on the coals, and tart crab apples dipped in grease. At this season, it was hard to find a place to sleep; there were so many boxes stacked everywhere, all of them filled with dried seaweed and fish and berries so there would be plenty to eat when everything was scarce. He spread a mat apart from the others, but sleeping was not easy. There were always noises: the grunts and whispers of two who lay together; a baby crying; the muffled snore of his uncle, who liked to drink *hoochino,* bought from the white traders. Sometimes it was more tobacco water than whiskey, but his uncle traded for it anyway. He didn't show respect for himself in doing that, Gao thought, but Gao was not one to say so.

Tonight it was more than the sounds that kept Gao awake. He thought about the white man and the missionary's daughter. He wondered why she had come back. She seemed so glad to be here. He remembered her telling his sister that she didn't like Victoria. Maybe she still didn't. But Gao wished she had found another way to return. Because she knew so many people and because she could talk Haida, she would help the man from the museum find things he would never be shown otherwise. She had been a friend, but that was not the way a friend acted. He must be careful around her, Gao decided.

In the morning, he was heavy-eyed, as if he had not slept at all, though he had. His uncle's wife had found chitons and cooked them in the fire. He ate those, along with dried wild rhubarb with grease. Then he went out the door to the beach. Thus he was the first one to see the canoe. The sea was calm this morning, and the canoe had just passed Balance Rock. Gao knew who the craft was carrying. Part of him was glad to see it, and he raised a shout to let others know it was safe. But another part of him was sorry. He didn't care about the miner . . . but the one who took things without asking, Gao had hoped he had drowned. So now there would be two greedy *yetz haada* here, which meant that people would get good prices for the things they sold. They would be happy, but Gao was not. High prices meant that more objects would be sold, because people would offer things they would otherwise have kept.

Gao would have to talk against the *yetz haada*. He would have to think of what else he could do to stop them from buying so much. Maybe it was good that the missionary's daughter thought of him as a friend. Maybe she would tell him things that he could use to stir people up against the two men.

The canoe was almost to the beach. Dogs were barking now, and a crowd had gathered. Gao had eyes only for the white man who sat in the middle and looked as though he thought he were a chief and everybody within sight a common surface bird. It would have been better if he had drowned. But it would be interesting to see who he was friends with and who sold him things. Gao had wondered last year, when the missionary died, whether this man might have had something to do with it. They had quarreled, and Hewitt had died so soon after. Would the man quarrel with Richardson, too? Or was Richardson so eager to see people quit using their old things that he would help this one buy?

Gao thought again that he was a pebble being worn smooth. But he was not worn completely smooth yet; he still had jagged edges that would hurt a white man whose skin was soft. He was glad of that. The winter was long, and something might still happen to these *yetz haada* who thought they could trick people into selling everything.

Kate had not expected to feel like a guest. This was *home*. The bedroom was her own; the feather bed knew the contours of her body. She awakened to pale sunlight streaming in the small, four-paned window, illuminating the wall papered with roses she had chosen herself. She was alone; the woman Mr. Richardson had found to lend Kate countenance must already have dressed and gone back to her own family.

Kate turned her head to survey the room, glorying in its familiarity. The bedroom at her aunt and uncle's house had been hers alone, too, and yet for months after her father's death, she had imagined every morning that she would open her eyes to this room instead. Each morning, the shock had been fresh, even cruel. *This* was home.

And yet . . . Already she saw changes. Several dark rectangles on one bare wall had once been covered by her own photographs. The one of her father was in her trunk now. Her lens had caught him unaware, in a pensive moment. He was holding a shaman's rattle carved in the design of a killer whale. He had known she was planning to photograph him, but she had fussed under the black cloth for so long that he had dismissed her from his mind. The result was a far truer representation of the man she remembered than were the stiffer portraits she had also taken.

Her own looks had come from him, not from her mother's family. The Reverend Hewitt had been a tall, angular man with a long, gaunt face. He kept his curly dark hair cropped short, but wore a thick mustache that he liked to finger as he thought. There had been gray in his hair and beard the last few years, more all the time, which she had thought secretly dismayed him. Perhaps vanity was unavoidable, no matter how noble one's intentions. After all, what culture did not bend great resources to ornamentation?

Her gaze moved on. The wardrobe was still there, and beside the bed, the marble-topped stand with pitcher and bowl, but the flowered Turkey carpet she had chosen was gone, as was the quilt her mother had tediously stitched by hand. Of course Kate had packed away the quilt herself, so why had she expected it to be here? Because nothing was supposed to change? Had she thought time would stand still, waiting for her return?

Refusing to brood, she slipped out of bed and into her alternate dress, this one in serviceable brown. Surely she could have achieved the same purpose with a pretty muslin, she thought, wrinkling her nose at the crumpled skirt. She brushed her hair and and bundled it efficiently into a braid that she pinned up, all without benefit of a mirror.

She could hear Emmet Richardson and Luke engaging in

a spirited debate in the kitchen, but she paused in the front room, glancing around. The house was really quite small. Her father had been uninterested in his living quarters, and what few luxuries he had allowed were for Kate's benefit, not his. She had clung to some hope that she would find the missing portion of his collection still here, that Mr. Richardson would have a good reason for having kept it and ignoring her letters. But this room was just like the bedchamber, bare of all but necessities: four chairs, a bookshelf, and two small tables. Against one wall were piled the Hudson Bay Company blankets used as currency all up and down the northwest coast, often given to the missionary in place of coins. Of course her father's collection might be in storage—but where? And why?

The kitchen seemed austere as well, though pans hung on the stone chimney, and enameled-metal dishes filled the few shelves. It was the feminine touch that was missing, she supposed: the sampler Alice had embroidered as a Christmas gift, which had always served to reproach Kate for her inadequacy at that obligatory skill, needlework; the handsome lace tablecloth from Aunt Grace; the rag rugs that added color to the raw wood floor. Although Mr. Richardson was at least fastidious, so that all was clean, he seemed somehow to have stripped the house of character. No, that wasn't fair; all he had done was to ship her own possessions to her and not bothered to replace them.

"Good morning," she said.

Both men glanced at her with a similar expression of surprise. They had apparently been deeply engrossed in their conversation.

Mr. Richardson rose to his feet with a smile that seemed forced. "I trust you are recovered from yesterday's travails? You did rest well?"

"Yes indeed, thank you." She hesitated. "Is there any word on the other canoe?"

Richardson looked grave. "I'm afraid not." He moved toward the stove.

"No, let me wait on myself," Kate said, and fended off his

protests. "I assure you I'm not so frail that a little seawater causes any damage."

Luke looked impatient with the civilities. "Perhaps Miss Hewitt has an opinion she might care to add to our discussion."

"She must be aware of what poor groping souls these Indians are," Richardson said vehemently. "Don't mistake me, I would be pleased to see you buy every object of idolatry they own, thus freeing them from ties with their past. But I fear you will reawaken heathenish ways if you encourage them to recall dances and songs and stories full of superstition. Have you heard their creation tales? They make little sense, and I can't see what they would add to your museum display."

"Everything," Luke answered, apparently less interested in Kate's opinion than he had pretended to be. "In many cases, the stories are necessary in order to identify the creatures represented by the carvings."

After searching the tins, Kate made herself a cup of tea. As it steeped, she watched the two men, passionately involved in their argument.

Condescension crept into the missionary's voice. "I cannot believe your museum-goers care. Do they even read your signs, or do they merely scan the exhibits with idle curiosity?"

Luke bridled. Stiffly, he said, "I believe you underestimate the interests and capabilities of the general populace. I often hear quite intelligent questions even from schoolboys. But I must confess that museum displays are only a part of my purpose. This is a dying culture, and what we do not salvage now will be gone forever! I collect for the future, so that the human past may be studied."

"And to what purpose?" Richardson snapped. "Do you consider the Haida to be noble savages? How can people with no concept of God be noble in any way? Their salvation does not lie in collecting remnants of their ignorant, idolatrous past, but in encouraging them to cast off that past, so that the value of such barbaric possessions may be put to better use!" His tone became pious. " 'He that believeth shall be saved; he that believeth not is condemned already.' "

Real anger glinted in Luke's eyes. He shoved his chair back and stood, grasping it as though to restrain himself. "God is so merciful that he condemns those who have never been told of the Gospel? Or is it men like you who condemn them?"

Richardson rose, too. The air fairly crackled with tension as the two men glowered at each other. "I have dedicated my life to the salvation of these people. And you dare to question *my* motives or conduct?"

Kate supposed that the time had come for intervention. Such seemed often to be the case around Luke. Did he get along with anyone?

"Gentlemen," she said primly, "surely you're carrying an intellectual difference to rather personal lengths. Mister Richardson, I cannot believe that reciting the words to a song will have any profound effect on the spiritual well-being of your converts. Quite to the contrary, they may be comforted by the notion that their traditions will be preserved, thereby relieving them of guilt at abandoning the old ways."

There was a moment of silence. Richardson was the first to regain control of himself, which did not surprise Kate. "I trust you're right, and I must apologize for the heat of our discussion. It was inappropriate for the time and place."

The grim line of Luke's mouth relaxed into something approaching amusement, which Kate guessed was at her expense. "Do you not believe that women and heated emotions go together?"

Richardson's nostrils flared, and Kate said hurriedly, "I quite agree that conversation over the breakfast table ought to be tranquil."

"Coward," Luke murmured.

She shot him a look. "Tell me, Mister Brennan, what are your plans for today? Do you wish me to translate?"

He was easily distracted. "I was about to begin tromping

back and forth in front of your bedroom door in hopes I'd wake you. Richardson has dissuaded me thus far. I hope you don't care for large breakfasts?"

He looked so eager, like a child awaiting a treat, that she couldn't be annoyed. "No, though I might have some bread and jam . . ." She smiled at the missionary. "I brought you several jars of preserves. I must unpack them later today."

"Bless you!" he declared. "I confess that I loathe the diet forced upon me here. I have never cared to eat anything that swims in the sea, but I have little choice. Well, we all make sacrifices in the Lord's work, and I suppose this is one of mine."

"Have you anyone to bake bread or biscuits for you? And surely potatoes are an adequate staple?"

"Yes, I have a young woman who helps out, but her cooking is abominable. Of course she's had no experience with yeast, and nothing ever seems to rise." He shuddered. "She insists on putting out a bowl of grease with every meal, as though I would touch it."

"Have you tried it?" Luke asked in interest. "I found it surprisingly agreeable. The concept is surely no more repulsive than the lard we use in nearly every dish."

"I can't abide the smell of fish." He looked as though even the thought was nauseating.

"Then I'll rescue the preserves immediately," Kate said. "It won't take me a minute." As she left the kitchen, she tried to remember if she had known how thoroughly Mr. Richardson disliked nearly every aspect of life here among the Haida. And yet he spoke as though he were committed to the work—so committed, in fact, that he could not see even the least part of the Haida culture as possessing any worth.

Was Richardson's dislike of the daily life the only thing that had concerned her father? Perhaps the Reverend Hewitt had feared that his assistant's zeal would not stand up to the daily routine. After all, the work so often seemed hopeless; for every stride forward, there were two back. An unusually large congregation in church on a Sunday would be followed by two weeks of drunken revels when a potlatch was given. Her father had often said that one must have nearly limitless hope and determination to overcome the constant disappointments, large and small. Mr. Richardson had been passionate in his argument with Luke, but he clearly felt very isolated, and she could see within him no sense of joy in his calling. Yet if Sims were right, Richardson was collecting contributions toward the building of a grander church. Surely that argued his determination to stay here.

When she returned to the kitchen, Luke was still at the table and Richardson was at the back door speaking to someone, although she couldn't see who. The conversation was brief; he turned almost immediately and latched the door.

"The other canoe has arrived! Everyone aboard is wet and weary, but safe. They apparently found themselves too far north, but were able to go ashore at the mouth of the Tl'ell River, setting out again at first light."

Sims was safe! Kate had not realized how she was grieving until this moment. "Thank heavens!" she exclaimed.

"I suppose even I must admit to some relief," Luke said dourly.

Richardson's mouth tightened, but he said only, "If you'll excuse me, I had best go see that Mister Durham has accommodations."

Luke sat up, the chair clattering. "Gad! I won't be expected to bunk with him, will I?"

Kate suppressed a smile, but she hoped that Mr. Richardson, who had indeed departed, had been out of earshot. "A fate worse than death?"

Ignoring her levity, he shoved the chair back. "Well? Are you going to eat or not?"

She took the less than subtle hint and sliced herself a piece of bread, slathering it with plum preserves. It was true that she wasn't very interested in food first thing in the morning, even when the morning was as far advanced as this one was. However, she refused to let herself be bullied; she must begin as she meant to go on. So she ignored his looming presence and finished her tea and bread quickly, but without gobbling.

Only then did she express her willingness to accompany Luke on his first foray.

The trail went just above the beach, where coarse grass grew thick on the sandy soil. Skidegate was a large village, with thirty or more houses stretched out in a single, uneven line for perhaps half a mile along the curve of sandy beach. Most of the houses had grayed with age; the smooth, vertical planks contrasted handsomely with the large beams and round corner posts. Many of the poles showed at least the remnants of paint. A few of the structures bore signs of European contact: small windows set into the otherwise blank walls, iron tools, occasional representations of white people on poles.

The trail passed in front of the houses, winding about a variety of obstacles: poles, logs washed in by storms, canoes, and racks for drying fish. Women were already about, expertly filleting fresh-caught halibut, calling for children, throwing wash water out the doors. Clothes had been hung from beams or laid on the grass to dry. A pair of trousers dangled incongruously from Raven's beak, which protruded several feet from a pole.

Kate thought the village must resemble an ancient European town, where streets were narrow and unplanned, hemmed in by buildings that had settled with age. The cobblestone streets there would not be so different from the sand and gravel underfoot here; children would play beside ditches in which wash water was discarded, with laundry flapping overhead. Life would go on in cramped quarters much as it did here, all the disputes and pettiness exaggerated by wagging tongues, all the joys and successes eagerly shared . . . and the kinships never forgotten.

Ahead, she could see the other canoe from Masset, drawn up beside the one in which they had arrived. Both were empty; apparently the missionary had not been informed of its safe arrival until well after the fact. Frowning, Mr. Richardson was turning back already, and would be upon them shortly.

Kate had yesterday noted the new house, perhaps halfway

along the beach, fronted by an equally new and quite hand-some pole, topped by the Three Watchmen. Now Luke made an interested noise and detoured so that he could study it. Kate was aware of Mr. Richardson's passing, apparently unconscious of their presence.

Luke wore boots laced over trousers, and a dark, shape-less frock coat. He must have shaved at least, but his hair was rumpled as though he had not combed it, or had merely shoved his fingers through it. Strangely, his rough attire and lack of interest in his appearance enhanced his manliness rather than lessened it. One was more conscious of his vigor, of his broad shoulders, his easy grace. In profile, his face was strong, even forbidding, leavened only by his obvious intelligence.

Kate turned a little away, disconcerted by the pleasure she felt in observing him unseen. To distract herself, she said, "You haven't said what your principal object is. Are you looking for certain kinds of relics? Do you have limitations on size, for instance?"

He swung to face her, lifting one booted foot to plant it on the silvered trunk of a log. She felt his gaze on her for a long moment before he spoke. "We should have talked more on the *Skeena*," he said abruptly. "I regret that I didn't have you begin teaching me the language. My only excuse for the lapse is that it took me some time to adjust to the idea of working with a woman." He held up a hand when she opened her mouth to speak. "I'm not accustomed to working with anyone at all, and even you must admit that the rela-tionship we propose having is an unusual one."

"Yes," she said in a low voice. "I, too, feel some awk-wardness."

She was grateful when he said merely, "Today I'm most interested in looking around, meeting people, letting it be known what I seek to purchase."

"And what is that?"

"Everything!" His voice quickened with enthusiasm. "With the one exception being objects made for the tourist trade. Things of especial antiquity are perhaps my first choice, but even newly manufactured items, if authentic, might serve my purposes. As I said yesterday, I want items of everyday usage—fishhooks and lines, arrows, sewing needles, children's toys, a cradle, cooking vessels. I hope that I can collect ceremonial objects, complete with the stories they are intended to illustrate. Although transportation might be a problem, I intend to buy at least one pole, and perhaps a large canoe."

She was staggered by his ambition. "You realize how reluctant people are to sell such things as poles."

His eyes were shrewd. "Christian converts may well have ceased to value displays of lineage."

She looked away, across the inlet toward Maude Island. "You may be fortunate enough to find a pole unclaimed by anyone. So many families have vanished altogether."

"I would prefer to buy one," he said quietly. "That way, I can know the stories associated with it, and not feel as though I'm robbing the dead."

Kate could not help the sarcasm that crept into her voice. "Which, of course, you would never do."

"It must be done sometimes," he said, his own tone harsher. "You know how I feel; even cataloging and studying the objects I buy must be secondary to the collecting itself. Those who come after us can work out the problems if they have the data, but that they cannot provide, because it will no longer exist. Sometimes I must do things I find personally repugnant to ensure that a historical record is left."

She would not argue the point again. He might even be right. In any case, she had accepted the job and should not continually carp.

"How do you intend to get a canoe to the east coast?" she asked. Surely he did not intend for them to travel back to Victoria in it!

He was already turning away, his attention drawn by the wealth of ethnological material around him. The people were merely incidental, she thought. "Hire some Indians to deliver it to Victoria," he said absently. "From there, it will depend on the size. Although I would regret the necessity, it might have to be sawed in half to fit on two rail cars. The same, of course, for a pole. One of the shorter examples might be preferable." His gaze, however, was currently traveling covetously up a rather tall pole, crowned by the ringed property hat shared by the Three Watchmen, a frequent presence on house poles. On this particular one, Raven's beak protruded by five feet or more.

"On your previous visit, did you see the corner posts representing Judge Pemberton and Mister Smith?" she asked.

His attention and interest, wherever given, had an intensity that still disconcerted Kate. He would be a difficult man to deceive. "No," he said. "Are they represented? True to life?"

"I don't know either man," Kate said, "but I understand the likenesses to be accurate." She led the way, smiling and exchanging polite greetings with those they passed.

"*Kasino dung edung aiata?* How are you today? Yes, I've come from Victoria." The women were all friendly, even those whom Kate did not know. The men were more reserved. Two stood to one side as she and Luke passed, their faces utterly blank. They nodded in return to the greeting, but Kate was uneasily conscious of being watched until a high-prowed war canoe blocked them from sight.

Kate stopped at last before the two figures, carved to ridicule the judge and town clerk who had been instrumental in imprisoning the chief of this house some years before. Both were mustachioed, dressed in European clothing and hats, the carving distinctly different in style from any other example of Haida art Kate had seen.

"Interesting," Luke said, sounding pleased. "Not suitable for the museum, of course, but the skill here ought to refute any critics who deride the work of native carvers as crude and grotesque."

"Grotesque only when seen out of context in a museum!" Kate exclaimed. "But the poles seem natural here, in a way nothing we build ever will be."

"A champion." His eyes were warm, though his tone mocked her. "Did your father feel the same?"

"What do you think?"

"I think he was torn. Part of him admired the grandeur. Part of him wanted to tame it. He had in common with many of his kind a belief that only civilization is safe."

He was making her remember the whole man, not just the father she had loved. No, she couldn't blame her reawakened memories on Luke alone; it was this place—which her father had loved fiercely, yet worked to transform—that made her see him more clearly.

Unwillingly, she said, "He worried about the potential turbulence of native peoples if they were not contained by moral restraints. He was not alone, you know. People in Victoria are terrified of the Indians camped outside the city."

"But not so terrified that the men do not seek out prostitutes there," Luke said bluntly.

How could she deny it? She had sometimes looked at her uncle and wondered, when there was so obviously little but duty in his marriage. Had he sought feminine companionship or passion elsewhere? Might he have made furtive trips to the Indian camps, or had his wealth bought something more permanent?

"Perhaps we are all hypocrites," she said.

He looked at her, frowning, but did not make any of the expected replies. In particular, he did not deny that he was any such thing. She instantly speculated that perhaps he, too, had sought out women in the camps, or paid for the company of women when he was on such an expedition as this. Would he do so despite her presence this time? They could not constantly be together. The thought was disturbing in a way she didn't care to analyze, so she took the coward's way out.

"Shall we make some calls?" She pretended to feel a need to step carefully, lifting her skirts, until they were back on the trail. "I doubt that you'll find much until we leave Skidegate, but one never knows."

"There must occasionally be new Christian converts. Although it's hard to picture Richardson persuading anyone to change his most fundamental beliefs. Well, we shall see. I assume we have the privilege of hearing him this Sunday?"

"Yes," Kate said, her tone as troubled as her thoughts. "Yes, I look forward to that."

"Well? Lead on."

She gave her head a little shake. "Yes, of course."

They began their visits at Grizzly Bear House, a handsome and typical structure that served as home to several families. The gable end faced the inlet, with open beams supporting the roof. Its walls were made of planks that were three or four inches thick and perhaps ten inches wide, all fitted closely together. A large house pole, called a *kexen,* stood at the center; a plain *xet,* or mortuary pole, with the carved figure of a bear on top, was in front. One did not enter this house through a hole in the house pole; rather, on one side there was an ordinary door.

Before they knocked and entered, Kate asked, "Have you ever seen a pole raised? Were you aware that most poles are hollowed out to make them easier to set in place?"

"Which would make transporting one easier for me as well," Luke said thoughtfully, "but I suppose leaves them more vulnerable to rot and cracking."

"Yes, see the crack already in this one."

"Do they make any attempt to repair them?" Luke asked.

"I've never seen them do so," Kate said. "It's always puzzled me, because they certainly have the capability. Remember the cracks in the canoe, which were skillfully fixed. I have never understood why they don't do the same with the poles."

Luke grunted, his attention all for the *kexen* and the four corner posts, decorated with Watchmen. "I'd rather find one in better condition. If only I could control the temperature and humidity in the museum! Wood dries out so easily."

"Nothing dries out here," Kate said. "It rains incessantly. Enjoy today's sunshine. You may not see it again until spring."

Inside, the light was so dim that they were forced to wait for their eyes to adjust before they could announce themselves. The principal, and inadequate, source of light was a large opening in the roof; this opening also served as a smoke hole. It had a covering that could be adjusted, depending on the direction of the wind or rain. Three small windows along one wall allowed pale, golden rectangles of sunlight to lie on the plank floor.

The interior of the house was larger than appeared from the exterior. Grizzly Bear House was perhaps forty feet long, but inside, it had been excavated so that several levels, each wide enough to function as separate rooms, stepped down to the cook fire in the center. At a busier season, the house would have been nearly deserted by this time of day, but now several men were seated on a chief's bench at the back, gambling sticks laid out before them, while women worked around the fire. Children peeked giggling from behind bentwood boxes.

Seized by memories, Kate was just looking around when a woman wearing a severe dark gown bustled forward. In contrast to her dress, she wore a lip labret and a multitude of silver bracelets on each wrist. "Ah, Katie!" She spoke in Haida, not yet acknowledging Luke's presence. "I heard you had returned. You honor us with a visit. You are well?"

"Martha!" Kate felt a sudden sting of tears. This woman had been kind to her, even mothered her in a modest way. Martha Frederick—Gaudgas then, before her baptism— hadn't been able to understand how a girl could live with only her father and no female relatives at hand. "Yes, I'm well. And you? And how is your family?"

"Sarah died last year. It was not a sickness we knew. The shaman saw a spear in her but could not pull it out. She left a baby whom her sister cares for."

The grief was sharp and unexpected. Kate remembered Sarah as beautiful, her face dark and strong. They had been friends, the two girls, although the one left childhood early on, becoming a wife and then a mother. She had moved so gracefully, had worked so hard, and had never complained. Perhaps her illness was one that could have been treated by a doctor, or even by Kate's father. Kate didn't know whether Mr. Richardson had any medical knowledge.

"I'm very sorry," Kate said simply. "I didn't know."

"And your father, he is now with the Great Chief of the Heavens."

"Yes, but he should not have had to go before he was ready," Kate said. She tried, and failed, to smile. "It is good to see you, Martha."

Luke had been waiting patiently all the while, though the language had excluded him. Now Martha nodded at him. "This man, he is your husband?"

"No, I work for him." This time, the smile came more easily. "You must think I'm crazy, refusing to marry."

Martha took Kate's hand in a firm grip. "Not crazy, no. You didn't have a mother to raise you right."

Kate looked down at their joined hands. Her own looked so pale, even delicate, compared to the Haida woman's work-roughened hands. There was such warmth, such strength, in Martha's clasp that Kate felt a familiar moment of pain that she had not had a mother who could hold her so.

Surprising herself, she leaned forward and kissed Martha's dark cheek. "But I was lucky enough to have you," she said softly.

Martha's brown eyes held a wealth of pain. "I lost two daughters last year. But one has come back."

"Only for a little while," Kate said. "I cannot stay with Father gone."

"You must find a husband. Perhaps this one . . ." Martha nodded again at Luke, her eyes mischievous.

Blushing, Kate was grateful that Luke hadn't understood. "Martha, this is Luke Brennan. He works for a museum and is here to buy things." In English, she introduced the Haida woman, who insisted they must have something to eat.

They followed her down the ladders to the level of the fire, where they drank Haida tea made from the spring leaves of a plant that was a member of the heather family. It was dark and strong, the way the Indians liked it, and had probably been boiling for several days. Martha served them steamed fern roots she had recently gathered, which, once cooked, were sweet, along with the ubiquitous oolachen grease to dip them in. Luke ate his with apparent enjoyment, to Kate's relief. Martha would have been insulted had her cooking not pleased him.

Samuel Frederick, Martha's husband and the house-chief, left the group of gamblers to join them and listened, too, as Kate explained what Luke wanted. "I hope you will tell others," she concluded.

The chief, an unusually tall man with the strong features and dark skin his daughter had inherited, said, "We will do that. I have nothing I wish to sell. Even if we no longer do the dances, I cannot sell the masks and rattles that are in my care, to be passed to my sister's children."

Kate didn't doubt that he spoke the truth. Whatever household possessions that Samuel had ever owned were long gone. The chief's dress was European; even the dishes the food had been served on were white men's. Believing that the Haida were doomed if they followed the old ways, Tahow-hegelths had turned his back on them, accepting a new name and new ways with his baptism. He had been scorned by some, but was brave enough to know that someone must lead. He had been the Reverend Hewitt's first convert.

When Kate translated, Luke inclined his head. "His sister's children will be grateful. Ask him if he knows of ceremonial items that belonged to families who no longer worry about such responsibilities, or who are all gone."

Samuel's impassive expression did not change. "I know of none. I will ask others."

"Give him my great thanks," Luke said. "Tell him I hope to learn the words of stories and songs, too, because they are as important and valuable as objects that can be held in the hands."

Samuel looked at Luke for a long moment, his face still unrevealing. "It might be that there are stories we could tell," he conceded at last. "I will think about which ones."

"He is generous to give such time to me," Luke said. "Tell him I am grateful."

After lengthy civilities, they were able to depart, wending their way up the ladders past piled cedar boxes filled with food and clothing. In just the last few years, the families had added many furnishings obtained from the white people: bureaus for clothing, tables and chairs. These pieces looked odd in this great house, constructed on massive proportions, and yet they were undeniably practical.

That first visit was a pattern followed by the three others that time allowed. Their Haida hosts all professed to be pleased to see Kate again. They listened courteously as she explained what Luke sought, then denied that they had any-. thing they were willing to sell. Kate knew perfectly well that later some of them would "remember" something they no longer wanted that might interest the *yetz haada*. The price suggested would be outrageous, but out of generosity, they might be willing to accept less. Kate supposed the conversation would be similar to those taking place in any market-place where prices were flexible.

Each visit was painful for her in a greater or lesser degree. People she'd known had died, or were much changed. One friend had gone to Victoria this year and not come back; another's husband had sold the house to a different family and they had gone to live in Masset with her parents. Once-prominent families had lost status; huge houses were half empty. Nearly all wore European clothing now. The white man's ways were triumphing. That would have made her father happy, Kate thought, but she could not rejoice.

At the last house, the chief said, "Another white man was here, too. He also wanted to buy."

When Kate translated, Luke scowled. "Tell him that the other white man is from a different museum. Remind him that your father caught Durham stealing from mortuary poles last year."

Kate obliged. The chief smiled, so faintly that she might easily have missed it. "We remember. He may pay high prices, but most people won't have anything to sell to him."

"Good," Luke said. He was especially generous in his gratitude to this chief.

When they emerged from the hole in the *kexen,* Luke muttered, "So he's out prowling around already."

He sounded as though he were describing distasteful behavior. In all fairness, Kate felt obliged to point out, "So are you."

"At least I'm honest in my dealings."

"Then you don't need to worry," Kate said. "Word will get around."

He wasn't so easily pacified. "I wish I knew how much money he has to spend. All those Chicago millionaires are anxious to make their city the cultural equal of Boston and New York. Unfortunately, our trustees and friends are more complacent; they don't see the need to continue adding to our collections."

"You're afraid that Mister Durham can afford to buy things you can't?"

"If I must, I'll exceed my budget," Luke said strongly. "I won't let Durham steal away fine artifacts. Once I can show what I've been able to buy, explain the urgency, I'm sure I can raise more money."

Kate hid a smile. "It's lucky most housewives don't have that attitude."

"It's hardly the same thing!" Luke said, sounding huffy. "A woman buying cuts of meat isn't comparable to the curator of a museum who is saving a magnificent relic for the future!"

Kate made her tone innocent. "Surely a budget is a budget."

She had at least distracted him. He lectured her all the way back to the Mission House. Having heard most of it at least once, Kate let her thoughts wander.

A young Indian woman was at work in the kitchen. A kettle of stew bubbled over the fire. Kate's offer to bake biscuits was gratefully accepted.

She had to wash up first, however, so she went to her room. Surprised to see the door a few inches ajar, she pushed it open.

Her temporary chaperone wasn't there, but someone else

had been. Her steamer trunk was tipped over and its contents strewn across the bare floor. Lids had been pried off the other crates and trunks; at least one box of photographic plates had been opened, so that all were spoiled by the light. One plate lay in shards on the floor, as though smashed there in anger. Handfuls of cotton batting had fallen like snow about the room.

Kate hugged herself, feeling chilled. Her possessions had been ransacked. But why? What had the searcher hoped to find?

Chapter Seven

"It is intolerable!" Richardson paced the front room, his agitation very real. "That someone should have dared to enter my house and rummage through the possessions of a guest here!"

"The idea is certainly disturbing," Kate agreed, "but fortunately I brought nothing worth stealing, so no permanent harm has been done."

Durham, who was bunking with Mr. Sterling of the Oil Works, had accompanied Mr. Richardson back to the Mission House, while Sims was conspicuously absent. The missionary would not want to appear to condone the presence of the miners here in the Queen Charlottes, even by so small a courtesy as an invitation to dinner to one of them.

Now Durham asked, "Have you checked your own room?"

"Yes, first thing." Almost too hastily, Richardson added, "Of course, my own possessions are modest, but I hold in trust the funds to erect a more substantial church."

"So they searched only Miss Hewitt's room." It was Luke

who asked the question that had been uppermost in Kate's mind. "What could they have hoped to find?"

Now Mr. Durham said, "Surely the usual. Anyone could assume that a young lady would travel with jewelry, money . . ." He shrugged. "To the Indians, any frippery might seem worth taking a small risk for."

"More than a small risk!" Richardson snapped. "I must begin inquiries. Someone might have seen who entered the house."

Kate had already queried the girl in the kitchen. She had seen no one but Mr. Richardson himself, had heard nothing. But she had not had reason to go into the bedrooms, so the search might easily have been made earlier. Luke and Kate had been gone all afternoon, as had Kate's temporary chaperone, and Richardson admitted to having been in and out. The opportunity had certainly been there.

Kate did not have high hopes for the missionary's inquiries. Someone could too easily have entered by the back door unobserved. Without thinking, she asked, "Has Mister Sims left for Kaisun yet?"

"He is a likely possibility," Richardson said. "I'll have questions for him if he's still to be found!"

"I saw him less than an hour ago," Durham said.

"He admits to being short of funds," Luke commented.

Kate shook her head. "I've known Sims too long. I don't believe he would steal from me."

"You mean you would prefer to believe that he wouldn't." The missionary surprised her with his perception. "I have no such faith in him."

Kate wanted to argue, but didn't. The murder of her father had eroded her ability to have faith in anyone. She had never been convinced that the murderer was an Indian, as the authorities believed. She was even less convinced now that she knew where his body had been found. Surely if an Indian had been the culprit, the murder would have happened in a moment of fury, quickly regretted.

But Kiusta! Why would her father have gone there? The trip would have taken several days. The town had been deserted for some years now, except for an occasional fishing party. Even then, if a missionary had been wanted, the Reverend Collison of Masset would have been called, as he was so much closer.

Most mysterious was the fact that her father had not expressed an intention to journey there. He had simply disappeared. He must have been lured to his death, which implied cold-blooded planning. It was not impossible that the man who had done the planning and committed the deed was one of the three currently expressing indignation at the rifling of her possessions.

She did not suspect Luke; her father had written of his departure on a steamer. He might conceivably have returned, but that was unlikely. Durham claimed to have left before her father's death, too, but she had only his word for it. When she had a chance to talk to people on her own, she had every intention of asking more about Durham's visit.

It was difficult to seriously suspect Mr. Richardson, either. What did he have to gain? If he had not liked his subordinate position here, he could have gone elsewhere; missions had been opened at only a few locations, and many villages, even whole tribes, were still without. There would have been no difficulty had he wanted to strike out on his own. Too, he had supposedly been away when the Reverend Hewitt was killed. She would have to think of a tactful way of asking where he had been. Because the fact remained that though she could not understand the motive, her father *had* been murdered.

She was brought back to the present discussion when Mr. Richardson spoke to her. "Can you think of anything else the thief might have sought? Have you begun your inquiries into your father's death? An injudicious hint suggesting that you had in your possession evidence leading to the guilty party could well explain this incident."

Luke had been mainly silent. He sat in one of the room's four chairs, his legs crossed and his pose relaxed. He had been watching the others, his expression enigmatic. Now he said, as though idly, "Like a letter, perhaps?"

Richardson's face flushed. "What are you implying, sir?"

Luke raised his brows. "Implying? I'm merely pointing out that Miss Hewitt's correspondence with her father might be of interest to the murderer . . . assuming that the culprit had a rational motive at all, one that might be discovered by probing."

"Well." A muscle in Richardson's cheek twitched. "I suppose that's so."

Managing to appear languid, Durham sat across from Luke. "You did mention a letter to me, Miss Hewitt. Do I gather that I'm not alone?"

It was Kate's turn to flush. She was very conscious of Luke's sardonic gaze. "I might have mentioned it to others. It was surely natural, considering my bereavement, to want to talk about my father with those who knew him."

She did not look at Luke, but was well aware that his expression had not changed. He knew perfectly well why she had interjected mention of the letter into several conversations.

"Yes, of course," the missionary said, sounding perfunctory. "But did you have a missive from your father with you? Have you checked to see whether it is still in your possession?"

"I didn't bring any correspondence," Kate said with almost perfect composure. "I must not dwell on the past. My memories of my father are enough."

Had Luke snorted? If so, he covered the sound by scraping the chair on the bare floor as he stood. "May I suggest that you get on with your inquiries, Richardson? Sitting here wringing our hands is fruitless. Miss Hewitt, did I hear you say something about biscuits?"

"Miss Hewitt must be overcome with shock," the missionary protested. "Perhaps she should lie down."

"Nonsense. It's much better to stay occupied." Despite her brisk tone, Kate hesitated. "Mister Richardson, I wonder if I might have a private word with you."

He looked surprised. "Certainly. In the kitchen, perhaps?"

There they found the young Haida woman gone; the stew still simmered over the fire, and a fresh-baked pie sat on a shelf.

Standing, Kate grasped the back of a chair and met the missionary's gaze. "Did you receive the letters I've written you this past year?"

"Letters?" He frowned. "No. Quite honestly, I wondered at not receiving word from you. I feared that your aunt and uncle weren't willing to keep you, that you had been forced to leave Victoria. Is something wrong? Did you require my assistance? I hope you know that it is yours."

"Thank you," she said, moved despite herself by his ready answer. "I wrote in thanks for your prompt shipment to me of Father's things. And also—" there was no way to say it that did not sound bald. "—also because some of his collection was missing. A substantial portion."

"Missing?" If his shock was not genuine, he was a fine actor. "I was not aware . . . I'm certain I packed everything that was here. Could some have been misplaced in shipping?"

"I did ask," Kate said, "but the captain of the *Grappler* insisted that everything he received from you had been delivered to me. He had an itemized list, and it's true that every box on that list was delivered. Unfortunately, it was some time before I unpacked it all and discovered how much was missing."

"I swear to you—"

"I'm not accusing you," she said quickly. "I hoped only that you would have some idea of what might have happened to the rest. Was the house empty for some time after Father's death?"

His high brow furrowed as he thought. "Yes, certainly after his disappearance. I was away, and several days passed before an alarm was raised. Everyone assumed that he was on legitimate business. If there was any good fortune involved in the affair, it was that his body was found so soon. Months might have passed."

"Yes." Kate bit her lip. "I know you have considered every possibility, just as I have. But you were here to ask questions, I wasn't."

"You wonder how he got to Kiusta." Again he had surprised her with his perception. "That was the first question I asked, but no answers were forthcoming. I think the Indians know something, but they aren't talking."

"I can't believe they would shield his murderer. Father was loved!" Kate looked down at her hands and saw that her knuckles were white. Deliberately, she loosened her grip.

"Not by all." Richardson's gaze was compassionate, the hand he laid over hers gentle. "He had enemies, all those who had lost power because of him. There could well be a chief who resented having lost his prerogatives, a shaman who is now treated with more disdain than awe, who thought that the mission would close if your father was gone. Or who hated him enough to kill him whatever the future might bring."

"But if it were the former, you too might be in danger."

"That has occurred to me," he said ruefully. "I will not run away, but I do take some care. I would not accept on trust a summons to some remote place."

"We may never know," Kate said in dismay, for the first time facing the fact squarely. She had always believed that should she return, she would find the murderer, exact justice. Yet here she was, only now seeing clearly the obstacles that faced her. She had naively assumed that the Skidegate Haida would talk to her, but she was no longer sure. Gao had not welcomed her; he had been angry that she helped such a one as Luke. And others today had looked at her with eyes that showed nothing of their feelings; many had not smiled to see the Reverend Hewitt's daughter home again.

Her belief that the killer was not an Indian had buoyed her, convinced her that she and the Haida were allies, if not comrades. But in only a few words, Mr. Richardson had frayed her certainty. She couldn't deny that there were those with cause to hate her father. She remembered vividly an occasion when he had humiliated one old *ska-ga,* as the Haida called their shamans.

Kate had been newly come to Skidegate then, not yet speaking the language. Her fourteen-year-old self had been frightened of everything: the dark forest behind the village, with moss that covered the ground and wrapped the trunks of giant spruce and cedar, muffling sound, deadening footsteps; the people, dark and strange to her; the hideous creatures incised on the poles; the knowledge that dead bodies rested in cavities atop the *xet.*

That evening she had cowered in her bedroom, frightened because she was alone in the house. When her father returned to gather his supplies, she had crept into the parlor.

He looked up, his expression remote. "I must go. There's an ill child receiving no care because a so-called medicine man claims he can suck the child's soul into a tube and trap it there, saving him thus. It might be dangerous. The child's father is allowing me to try the white man's medicine, but the threat was thinly disguised: This is my chance either to prove myself or fail in his people's eyes. You're safe here, but don't come after me. The atmosphere is dangerous, the house crowded with half the people of the village, who were enjoying the show the medicine man put on. Unless I dance and sing, they're bound to be disappointed."

"Don't go," she had whispered. "Please! Don't leave me alone!"

Even then, she had been ashamed of her selfishness, yet she had not learned bravery. Who had there been to learn it from? Her mother, who was too frightened to live? Her father, a stranger until his wife's death had forced custody of his young daughter upon him?.

He had looked at her with something near disgust in his eyes before his long, bony face softened. "You don't understand—how can you? Your mother never sympathized with my purpose, my commitment. For humanitarian reasons alone, I cannot let that child suffer and die when I have the skill to save him. But this is also the opportunity I have been waiting for. My main opponents among the Haida are the medicine men. If I can discredit them, I will be listened to and at last have a chance to talk of our dear Lord. I must grasp the opportunity, Kate, even if it does endanger both of us."

She had bitten her trembling lip. "Please . . . may I come, too?"

He first refused, then succumbed to her begging. Why she had wanted to go, Kate still didn't know. Perhaps her fear of remaining alone and ignorant of her father's success or failure had been greater than her timidity. Or perhaps even then her unladylike curiosity had won out. She hadn't yet been inside one of those forbidding, gaudily decorated houses. At night she sometimes heard music, if the wild chanting and sound of drums could be called that. Her father said the Indians were dancing, and his censorious tone had made her wonder what was so very wrong with their dances.

Kate had been here long enough to recognize the terrors that her mother had described, but also long enough to accept the presence of those terrors and begin to wonder, if timidly, whether they were so very great after all. Just that day, she had sat on the back step, facing the somber forest, which the Haida believed to be the home of ghosts and which her mother had found so oppressive. At first, the silence was absolute and she sat rigid, waiting.

Slowly she saw things she had never noticed before: the way a shaft of sunlight backlit a soft wisp of moss that hung from a branch; a tiny, delicate candelabra of pink flowers; a fungus that seemed to have sprouted wings traced by a network of fine lines. And there *were* sounds after all, for one who really listened. Water running, a rustling that presaged the nervous dart of a deer mouse, a *rat-tat-tatting* that she finally tracked to a woodpecker with a bright red slash on his black-and-white head.

There was life there under those enormous trees, and Kate

felt comforted. She might not be so afraid to take a step into the forest; why, she might even explore, just a little!

Perhaps it was that comfort, that first tentative unfurling of curiosity and courage, that made her decide to see inside one of those forbidding houses, to *know* what her father did tonight that was so dangerous.

Or perhaps not. Perhaps, after all, it was cowardice, a greater fear of being alone than a fear of the dark, tattooed savages.

In any case, she had gone. Her father held his satchel in one hand, her hand in his other, as they made their way through the darkness. From some distance, she could tell which house they were going to; the fire inside it leaped so high that sparks came from the smoke hole, along with the sounds of chanting and keening that made the hair on the back of her neck prickle.

She felt the momentary hesitation in her father's stride even before her eyes made out the three men who blocked the path just before the house. The moon was high, and firelight spilled out, making them dark silhouettes. They wore skirts with fringe that rattled like a wolf's teeth clicking, and blankets with figures woven on them. Their faces were shadowed—no, she saw suddenly, with terror, that two wore masks, one with its mouth twisted up and the other with a great curved beak like an eagle's. But it was the man in the middle at whom her father was looking, the one who wore a headdress adorned with a carved raven that bent its head over his face.

But for the brief pause, her father advanced steadily, drawing her with him. The three men fell back, separating just before the doorway. The one in the middle she saw best, and could still see with nightmarish clarity: hair tangled and twisted to below his waist, a matted beard, and deep-set eyes so malevolent she had gasped. Just as her father swept her past him, the medicine man had lifted his hand and she had seen the fingernails like claws.

He laughed and said something guttural in that alien language, but her father did not answer. She whispered, "What did he say?"

Her father's voice was tight. "He is certain that I will fail."

She had not then understood why the *ska-ga* hated her father with such passion. She had not understood that her father threatened all that the *ska-ga* believed in, all that they were. She had not understood that her father would sweep back the cloak of mystery, showing their masks and rattles to be mere carved wood, their visions fantasies; that he would tear their power from them as if he had shorn their heads of the hair that gave them strength. She had not felt pity, only terror.

Her father had to duck to enter the low door beside the *kexen*. Kate's small store of courage was already long gone; when she saw the crowd inside, she wished with all her being that she had stayed behind. Her father had not exaggerated when he said that half the village was here. Men, women, and children were packed within like fish in a barrel, tiers of them. When she stole a terrified peek upward, she saw faces peering down through the smoke hole, too. She clung to her father's coat as he pushed through the crowd. It was hard to breathe; the odor of too many near-naked, sweating bodies mixed with those of rancid grease and smoke.

The child lay near the fire, his mother hovering over him. Sweat poured from his drawn face and too-thin chest. His eyes were closed, and he breathed in rapid, shallow gasps.

The Reverend Hewitt barely glanced at the boy. He strode up to a man who lounged in relative comfort on a painted bench that faced the front of the house. In Haida, he said something peremptory, loud enough so that he was widely heard. A murmur of disapproval rippled through the crowd, but her father ignored it. He waited, standing with great dignity and authority, his demeanor so assured that he might have been in a church in Victoria.

The chief slowly stood. Kate gaped at the blue tattoos that covered his torso and upper arms. His eyes left her father only once, to look at his ill son. The mother, kneeling beside the boy, did not say a word, but her pleading eyes spoke for her.

The chief nodded once, abruptly. He bellowed what was clearly an order and swept his left hand in a half circle.

For a moment, nothing happened; the two men waited. Then the crowd stirred and began to filter out. Beyond the circle of firelight, darkness closed behind the people. Within minutes, most had gone.

Speaking to the mother, her father swept the boy up in his arms and started up the steps to the next level, and the next. He stopped beside the doorway, where cool air alleviated the fetid, overheated atmosphere. The mother and a girl about Kate's age hurriedly spread out mats and a blanket, so that her father could lay the boy down. Men brought torches and held them steady to allow the missionary to begin his examination.

It was easy to see the problem: Pus oozed from a wound on the boy's leg. His entire limb was swollen to twice its normal size, and red lines streaked out from the wound. Kate knelt beside the girl, close enough that she could feel the heat emanating from the feverish boy. Her father's deft fingers felt the glands in the child's neck, gently touched the burning forehead. He discussed something with the mother, then took his case and went with her back down the steep steps to the fire pit. Kate guessed that he was going to sterilize his instruments in boiling water; he had talked to her of his work, the secular as well as the spiritual.

"I would wish I could concentrate on the last," he had said, shaking his head, "but their physical needs are too urgent. If all die, who will be left to hear the Gospel?"

Kate waited beside the girl, whom she guessed to be the sister of the patient, and whose gaze stayed fixed on the boy's face. Kate glanced down at the girl's hands, which were knotted into fists. On impulse, she reached out and gently covered one fist with her own hand. The girl jerked, and her dark eyes lit on Kate's face with the grace and wariness of a small bird. Kate smiled tremulously and said, though she knew she would not be understood, "I'm sorry. I hope my father can make your brother well again." She hesitated. "My name is Kate." She pointed at herself and said again, carefully, "Kate."

The dark eyes were still wary, but the girl repeated awkwardly, "Kate." After a long moment, she pointed at her own chest and said, "Oahla."

"Oahla."

Then her father returned and the drama unfolded. He lanced the wound, and without flinching, drained the stinking pus, from which Kate recoiled. He mixed up a poultice and applied it under a pad of cotton. With the mother's help, he lifted the semiconscious boy and persuaded him, choking, to swallow a concoction that included an antipyretic agent, designed to lower the fever.

There was nothing to do but wait then. Eventually, Kate became drowsy and her father took her home, promising to return. He tucked her in bed, his hands nearly as tender as they had been when working on the Indian boy. She was almost asleep when he said softly, "Now you understand."

She awakened in the morning to find the house empty, but only an hour later, he returned. He laughed at the sight of her and lifted her to twirl her around the kitchen in a triumphal dance.

"We've won!" he declared. "The boy will recover and Ta-how-hegelths declares that he has lost all faith in the medicine men! He wants to learn our way, he says. On Sunday, he will arrange a gathering so that all can hear me preach. At last!"

"Will the medicine men listen, too?" Kate asked when he set her down and she regained her breath.

Her father's countenance had become somber. "No," he said. "I have made an enemy there, perhaps many enemies. But gain cannot be made without risk."

She had sat in this church so many times, often the only white person amongst the worshipers. Then it had been her father, tall and bony and intense, who paced before the congregation, who raised his voice in praise or condemnation. Now Kate felt disoriented, as she often did these days, to see Richardson in her father's place.

The young missionary grasped the pulpit in both hands and leaned forward. "I repeat, you must not lounge in sinful indolence, nor degrade yourselves by vice, nor offend the laws by crime! You who come into this holy church are welcome—welcome to habits of industry and thrift, to duties of religion and piety, to obligations of law and order!"

Of course every word must be repeated in Haida. In the interlude, Kate's mind drifted.

Although she was not deeply moved by Mr. Richardson's preaching, she was reassured. While he attempted to command the attention of every man and woman in the small church, he did not speak with the wild fervor Sims had led her to expect. There was nothing here of the fire and brimstone she had feared. No, this sermon was tame, even dull. Had Sims been mistaken, repeating fallacious rumor?

Surreptitiously, she glanced around. She knew all but a few of the Indians who made up the bulk of the congregation; they were her father's faithful, unchanging in their attendance but for the months when they were away working in the canneries. Although all who had come home for the winter were undoubtedly here, the building was no more than three-quarters full. Kate wondered at Mr. Richardson's determination to build a larger, grander church.

Beside her, Luke shifted, and she stole a sidelong glance at him. He had slumped a little lower on the hard bench and was gazing at his booted feet. Despite the attempt he had made at Sunday best, his dark frock coat was rumpled and his boots scuffed. He looked supremely bored.

On her other side was Durham. He sat with a straight back, his legs crossed, the linen collar of his shirt so crisp that he must have had it ironed. His boots gleamed, and the tails of his long, checkered coat were flipped out so that he didn't sit on them. His attention was seemingly fixed on the missionary. Assuming he was absorbed in the sermon, she was startled to hear a tiny snap and see him slip his watch back in his pocket.

The small movement hinted at boredom, but it made Kate think of her father rather than of Mr. Durham. The only symbol of personal wealth that he had possessed was his pocket watch, worn on a gold chain. She could close her eyes and still see it, the initials "E. H." ornately scrolled on the cover. The watch had belonged to his father—Edward Hewitt—before him. It bore a patina of age, and the elegant swirls were worn by the fingers that had pulled it from the pocket, flicked it open, closed tightly around it in moments of stress. Henry Hewitt had always worn the watch, but it had not been found with his body, nor had it been shipped to her with his effects. It had apparently been irresistible to someone. The murderer? The Indians who had found his body? Unless he had lost it, but she did not believe that.

Something made Kate turn her head in time to meet Sims' gaze. He leaned against the rough plank wall to one side, as though seating himself among the congregation would have been a commitment too large for the occasion. She was surprised to see the bearded miner at all. Why hadn't he departed for Kaisun? What held him here? She knew that Richardson had cornered him the very evening after the search of her possessions. Surely he had understood the purpose of Mr. Richardson's pointed questions. She would have expected pride alone to keep him away! He had seldom attended her father's services. It was odd, too, that he had continued to avoid her, though he lingered in Skidegate.

Well, she mustn't think the world revolved around her. Perhaps Sims had a lady friend here. With Kaisun deserted, the miners must miss female companionship. As though in a logical extension, Kate wondered whether Sims had to pay for it. Though she still felt his gaze on her, she turned her eyes to the front for fear of revealing some small part of her thoughts. Why on earth was she suddenly so curious about male-female relations? Why did the thought of buying and selling such intimacies repulse her so? It wasn't as though the knowledge that such things were common was new to her.

She forced herself to attend to what Richardson was saying. "But of the children take special care," he declared. "Heaven has entrusted them to you for a special purpose." He paused dramatically, cast his stern gaze over the congregation. "Parents must educate their children, not depend upon the tribe or the more distant family members to do it; most of all, the education comes from the mother rather than the father.

"How important, then, that the mothers be right-minded; that our young women, of whom our mothers come, be brought up with a high sense of personal character, be taught to prefer virtue to gold, and death itself to a violated chastity."

He seemed now to be looking at Kate, to be speaking to her. Her spine stiffened in affront. Was he questioning *her* virtue? But his gaze and the lecture swept on before she could be sure that he had intended to censure her in particular.

"The women make the men; therefore the women should be greater than the men, in order that they be the mothers of great men. But this requires the transforming grace of God, requires that our mothers be women of strong faith and fervent daily prayers, requires that they live at the foot of the Cross."

Kate's mind began to wander again. How uncomfortable the corset and bustle were! After only a few days without, donning the trappings of a lady again was difficult ... although she didn't mind appearing to greater advantage in her rose-colored gown severely tailored from lightweight wool serge. The wrinkles had shaken out well, so that she was nearly as handsomely attired as Mr. Durham.

She looked well enough that Mr. Richardson had kissed her hand and Mr. Durham had offered extravagant compliments that almost sounded sincere. Luke, on the other hand, had looked startled and not altogether pleased at her transformation. He preferred her dowdy, she thought; then he was not reminded of his foolishness in hiring a woman. Did he try to pretend that she was a man? Or did he simply prefer that her femininity remain less intrusive?

Either way, it mattered little. She had noticed signs of restlessness in Luke; they would not remain in Skidegate long. If she intended to ask questions concerning her father, she should be about it. Time was running out.

Somehow, the missionary had progressed to exhorting the congregation to work, work, work! "Gain money by diligent labor. Shun no work that will bring you an honest penny. 'Tis honorable to labor with our own hands. God works, and shall man be greater than God? Only fools think labor dishonorable. Wise men feel themselves honored in following the example of God.

"But when you get the pennies, save them. Then you will soon have dollars. The dollars will enable you to buy comfortable homes for yourselves and your children, to build a church more fitting for the worship of God, whose works adorn and bless both Heaven and earth."

Mr. Richardson had begun to pace, his voice to deepen. His eyes were fierce, his hair damp with sweat. He was revealing power Kate had not suspected he possessed. The topic was an odd one to elicit it.

"Work for money; work every day, work diligently, and follow His example. Ever since the first stone in the foundations of the universe were laid by God's own hand till now, He has been working, and will continue working through endless ages. Follow His glorious example. Work, work, work, for an honest penny; but when you get it, spend it wisely, for your family and most of all, for God."

He stopped behind the pulpit, grasped it again as he moved his eyes from one to the next member of his congregation. Not even a small child stirred when he concluded, "For whatever God accepts and pronounces good, *must be good*: good in itself; good in its effects, always good; good for man, because ordained of God!"

Nobody left. The collection plate made its way down the

rows to the steady clink of coins. The offering would join the blankets already heaped in back, which Mr. Richardson would ultimately sell. Kate was dismayed to see how much was being given. Could the Indians afford it, making as little as they did from selling furs and working at the canneries? Was having a church the equal of that at Metlakatla so important to their pride?

Silently, the Indians lined up to receive the sacrament. Christ's body and blood; bread and wine. How many times had Kate's father ranted against the evil of whiskey and rum? Could not Mr. Richardson see the hypocrisy of giving alcohol with his own hands in the Lord's own house?

"The blood of Christ shed for you. The body of Christ broken for you."

She must speak to him, for her father's sake. She had avoided it thus far, determined to see for herself whether Sims' tales were true—and also, she must in all honesty admit, because she had not wanted to antagonize Mr. Richardson. Their comfort depended on good relations with him.

She did not take communion herself; her feelings were in too great turmoil. Instead, she rose and accepted Luke's arm. When he raised a brow and nodded toward the altar, she shook her head. They squeezed through the crowd, in which she recognized and greeted many friends. Martha and Samuel Frederick were there, with a young man Kate recognized as a slave—perhaps now a former slave, since he was here. If so, Richardson had done some good, at least.

She was almost ashamed of the thought, but realized that her feelings toward him were oddly soured by his emphasis on working for the purpose of collecting wealth. Was it chance that had determined the topic of today's sermon, or did he care more for the trappings of civilization than he did for the Indians' spiritual welfare?

Kate looked around outside for Sims. She spotted him leaning against a porch railing, poking a brown plug into his mouth. His jaws worked rhythmically. He saw her coming and did not attempt to evade her, though the delight he had evinced at the sight of her on the *Skeena* was nowhere in evidence.

"Good day," she said. "I was surprised to see you this morning."

His big shoulders moved. "Curiosity. I'm hoping to talk to someone before I leave for Kaisun. Have to fill my time somehow."

"Indeed." Now what? She wondered. Repeat Mr. Richardson's questions? Ask whether Sims knew anything about her father's pocket watch? The missing portion of his collection?

"Wanted to say good-bye to you anyway," Sims said gruffly. "Don't know what your plans are, whether I'll see you again."

Kate softened immediately. Sims wouldn't steal from her, any more than he would kill "the Reverend," as he had always called her father. Antagonism and violence did not necessarily go together, thank the Lord.

"We plan to circle the islands," Luke said, startling her. She had not realized he had followed her. "As soon as we can hire guides and a canoe, we'll take a short trip up the inlet first. I hear the scenery is spectacular and that several villages are deserted but have poles in reasonable condition."

"Circle the islands?" Sims was frowning. "In the winter? Do you know how foul the weather is? Never stops raining, and the seas are mighty strong. Especially on the west coast, you're asking for trouble."

"Trouble?"

"Storms," Sims said succinctly.

Kate wondered if that was what he truly meant. "I'm not unfamiliar with the winter months," she reminded him. "We'll proceed cautiously. Perhaps we can visit you at Kaisun in the early spring."

He gazed broodingly at her, that same dark frown carved in his rough-hewn face. "Be careful," he said, surprising her again. "Don't forget what happened to the Reverend."

"I'm unlikely to forget," Kate said wryly.

Sims growled, "Wouldn't want anything to happen to you."

"Thank you." She smiled tremulously. "Oh, Sims, it's good to see you again."

He frowned so fiercely, she thought he must be as moved as she was. Her suspicion proved founded when he swept her into a bear hug. "Katie Rose," he said roughly, "the Reverend'd roll over in his grave to see you, but he'd be proud, too."

"Would he?" She blinked away the moisture in her eyes when the huge man set her back on her feet. "Perhaps this is the year you'll find that gold seam."

"Why not?" Sims spat a brown stream at the ground, clapped Luke on the back, and strode away.

Under Luke's shrewd gaze, Kate tried not to betray her feelings. "Do you need me this afternoon?" she asked.

"No. I've been invited to gamble. Doesn't look like their game takes any particular skill, so I thought I'd give it a try. I might win something worthwhile. Goodwill, if nothing else."

She ought to disapprove of gaming on Sunday, but in fact, she was relieved. This would give her a chance to speak to Mr. Richardson . . . and to begin her inquiries among the Haida she knew best.

"Then I wish you luck," she said.

Luke's vivid blue eyes saw her too clearly. He lifted the brim of his shapeless felt hat and nodded. "I think you need it more than I do." He cleared his throat. "You might mention that we need to hire guides." Obviously, he knew her intentions and was making no attempt to dissuade her.

She was more fortunate than she deserved. It seemed more than ever as though God Himself was lending a hand to her cause. The thought brought with it a flush of shame for her wandering attention during the service. She must not let Sundays pass unheeded on the journey. Surely the magnificent coast of these islands on the edge of the western world, so little touched by the hand of man, was as much

God's abode as was the church. He would hear her wherever she was, if she called. She must believe that, and persevere.

As Kate watched Luke walk away, she wondered if luck was what she needed. Or was it something far grimmer? For the first time since she had come here, she heard the hoarse call of a raven; she turned to see a dark sweep of wings cast a momentary shadow over the ground at her feet. He was The Trickster, this raven, more often cruel than deliberately kind. Yet if one believed the Haida, he had given to people most of the blessings that made their lives possible: the sun, the moon, even the Haida Gwai, the islands themselves. Would he give her success in her hunt, if only for the pleasure of seeing her prey falter?

Chapter Eight

Luke had watched the game played before, so he was not at a total loss. Sharp eyes seemed to be the principal requirement, along with a certain amount of nerve. Not so very different from poker. He was not a gambler himself; life held too many possibilities to waste it sitting around a table in a smoky room watching for the turn of a card.

Or a stick. Along with six or eight Haida men, Luke pulled a chair up to the chief's bench by the fire pit in one of the large houses. Each of the men had his own bundle of gambling sticks, which he carried in a bag. The sticks were four or five inches long and perhaps a quarter of an inch thick, rounded, and beautifully polished. Each had some designating mark upon it, with the exception that in each bundle, one stick, called the *djil,* was entirely plain.

To play, the sticks were divided into two piles, each wrapped in cedar bark. One man would put the two bundles under a fine cloth and pass them rapidly from hand to hand before laying them out. His opponent must then indicate which of the parcels held the *djil*.

Luke watched several rounds before he was invited to play. He was interested to see that much of the drama and skill of the game had nothing to do with the actual winning or losing. After the opponent chose the bundle he thought held the *djil,* the dealer opened the bark wrapping and with a flourish, tossed the sticks one at a time out on the bench until the *djil* appeared. Then the watchers all murmured or released long breaths of satisfaction.

His host was a man named Nengkwigetklals, which Kate had translated as "They Gave Ten Potlatches for Him." He was obviously house-chief, and perhaps more than that; he seemed to be held in great respect, but with the language block, Luke was unable to ascertain whether he was a lineage chief, or even town-chief.

He was *not* a Christian, though like most of the Skidegate Haida, he wore European clothing, in his case, a Navy uniform with a double row of shiny gold buttons. He was darker-skinned than average, stocky, and broad of face. A scar on one cheek lent him a sinister aspect, though he seemed friendly enough. Luke had been surprised by the invitation, since he had not formerly met Nengkwigetklals. Perhaps the chief had things to sell, or was merely curious. Luke assumed that he would find out soon enough. He only hoped that Durham hadn't gotten to the man first. Damn it, he didn't like wondering where that scoundrel was at any given moment, what choice objects he'd found to buy.

The others playing tonight were strangers to Luke as well, save for one: Gao. Gao had nodded when Luke was introduced, his eyes dark and cool. He had come with another young man, Kun taos, who seemed to look to him for guidance. They sat a little apart, holding back, though presumably they were among friends.

The game had thus far been quiet. Now Nengkwigetklals sat back and smiled at Luke, revealing teeth riddled by rot. *"Mesika mamook itlokum?"* he asked in Chinook. "You want to play?"

Luke smiled. "Yes," he agreed. "I would like to play."

"What do you have to gamble?" the chief asked.

Hoping to avoid the struggle to answer with his limited vocabulary, Luke looked around. "Do any of you speak English?"

"I speak English." The words were heavily accented and came slowly, but they were clear. The speaker was Gao.

Luke raised an eyebrow, but otherwise kept his surprise to himself. Had Gao been hiding his ability to speak the white man's language? Did Kate know? Why had Gao admitted to his knowledge now?

"Will you tell the chief that what I have to gamble are trifles only, worthless." Luke held out his hands in a gesture of emptiness. "I have come from far away and could bring little."

"I will tell him." Gao switched to Haida and spoke briefly. The obligatory deprecation of the worth of anything Luke possessed was met with polite inclinations of the head. Yes, they understood. Of course. What they had to gamble was of little value also.

"I have mirrors and beads for their wives and daughters. Some knives." From his pocket, Luke withdrew a pocket knife, opened it and passed it around. Kun taos flicked the razor-sharp steel blade with his thumb. He held up his hand so all could see the beads of blood it had drawn so easily. Luke continued blandly, "I know you have knives that are sharper. But perhaps you would find these useful, if only for your children, who might otherwise cut themselves as they learn to slice fish."

Gao passed this on without expression or comment. Luke found him hard to read, wondered at his relationship with the others here.

Nengkwigetklals said, "I hear that you want to buy things. Do you see anything here that pleases you?" He swept his hand in a gesture that took in all that surrounded them.

Luke waited for the translation, then made a small bow. "I see much that pleases me. How can I not, when the chief owns such a fine house and so many beautiful things?"

Nengkwigetklals leaned forward. "I have a woman slave. She could come to you tonight. Would you wager ten knives for her?"

Gao's voice had become even flatter, more expressionless. He did not approve of the wager, Luke thought; he did not like it when a chief sold even a slave woman to a white man.

"I'm sure your slave is very beautiful," Luke said, "but I have a woman. She frightens even me when she is angry. If I should win this bet, her temper might bring lightning and thunder."

There was laughter from all but Gao. A flicker of emotion showed in the young Haida man's eyes, but he said nothing, though he must assume what Luke had implied: that Kate was his woman.

Luke continued, "I would rather gamble for something else, something that I might put in the museum to show my people how skilled your artists are." He glanced around, as though casually. "That dish you serve grease in. It is a pretty little thing. Will you wager it against ten knives?"

The dish was carved from wood; it depicted a whale's head on one end, an eagle's on the other, with an incised side that served as both wing and fin. It was an exceptionally graceful piece.

Nengkwigetklals affected a look of surprise. "You want the dish? Very well. I stake it against ten knives."

Luke agreed. The chief displayed the *djil,* then wrapped the two bundles. Beneath the cloth, he tossed the bundles from hand to hand. Luke watched intently, as did the audience. He debated whether he would be wise to win this round. Scarcely a breath was taken as the chief tossed the cloth aside, then moved the two bundles around on the bench. At last he said, "Choose."

Luke hesitated, though he was fairly certain he had tracked the correct bundle. "That one," he said, pointing at the other.

Nengkwigetklals smiled. The bundles were unwrapped, the sticks thrown out one at a time. There was no *djil* in the first bundle; it was in the other.

Luke shook his head. "You were too quick for me."

"Again?" Ten more knives for the bowl?"

"Again," Luke agreed.

The elaborate ritual was performed once more. This time, Nengkwigetklals' hands moved with such speed that Luke wondered if he had been set up, an easy mark. He leaned forward and concentrated. It was in the right hand, left, right; this time, the bundles were not exchanged, though the chief made it appear they had been. Left, right, left. Now the cloth was removed, the two bark bundles shifted around on the bench with bewildering speed.

The chief's smile was complacent. "Choose," he said.

Luke held the chief's gaze with his own. "That one," he said, touching one without even looking at it.

The smile faded; all watched tensely as the bundles were opened. The sticks made tiny clicks as they landed and rolled. The tenth stick was the *djil*, the pale color of honey.

Luke sat back in his chair. "I was fortunate."

The chief spoke, Gao repeated, "Do you want to play again?"

"I would like to," Luke said, "if the chief does not find me too unworthy an opponent."

Something had changed in the way Gao looked at him. His expression was suddenly thoughtful, even wary. Had he guessed that Luke had deliberately lost the first round?

An hour later, Luke was thirty knives and ten mirrors poorer, but he had acquired several nice pieces. They could have been bought outright at a cheaper price, but that way, he would not have also acquired the respect and amiable relationship he presently enjoyed.

The whiskey Nengkwigetklals had produced was foul stuff; Luke suspected that tobacco juice was responsible for the color, not fine whiskey. He drank moderately, thankful to see that he was not the only one who did so, though the chief consumed an astonishing quantity. Gao alone did not drink at all. Luke didn't understand what he said when he turned down the first drink, but it produced a laugh, and no attempt was made to persuade him further.

The sky Luke could see through the smoke hole had deepened to purple by the time Nengkwigetklals got down to business. The gambling sticks had been put away while they ate dog salmon dipped in grease, followed by blueberries whipped with grease into a sweet froth that resembled ice cream.

Through Gao, the chief asked, "What things do you wish to buy?"

Luke repeated his usual list: everyday utensils, ceremonial objects, a fine war canoe, a pole.

"There is an *xet* that I own at Haina," Nengkwigetklals said thoughtfully. "It belonged to my mother's sister's family, but they are all gone. What would you pay for such a pole?"

"A dollar for each foot. I will also pay workers to take it down and bring it to the shore."

The stocky man shook his head as though in disbelief. "My mother's sister's husband had such a potlatch when that pole was raised, it is still talked of. He broke into pieces the copper named 'All Other Coppers are Ashamed to Look at it' and gave them out. And the blankets! They filled the house to the roof, so that there was no room for people! It was to remember his uncle, who was a chief in Haina. One dollar a foot is not enough for such a pole."

"That is true," Luke conceded. "But it is all I can pay. Perhaps I should find a pole that was not raised to remember such a great man."

Nengkwigetklals was too wise a bargainer to show his alarm at the potential loss of a deal. He said only, "The pole is no good to me over there. I never go to Haina. But it is worth more. I will find somebody to take you to see it, if you want to go."

"I would like that very much," Luke said courteously. "I also seek a canoe and guides, who would take Miss Hewitt and me through the inlet to Chaatl."

The chief promised to let others know. Feeling that he had accomplished all he could here, Luke thanked Nengkwigetklals for his generous hospitality and the opportunity to try such a game of skill. They agreed to exchange winnings on the morrow, and Luke found his way out of the great house into the darkness.

He stretched and drew in a breath of damp, salty air to clear his lungs of smoke. The night was misty and exceptionally dark; he could just make out the shapes of several canoes drawn up in front of the house. He supposed he ought to find out what trouble Kate had gotten into today. He only hoped it wasn't fatal.

When a voice spoke his name from behind him, Luke started.

"Damn it." He rubbed the vertebrae in his neck that had cracked when he jerked around. "Oh, Gao. What can I do for you?"

The young man's face was indistinct. "I know Kate. I will be your guide."

At the risk of offending him, Luke chose to be blunt. "Why do you want to work for me? You don't approve of my buying things, do you?"

"No." As always, the tone was flat, inexpressive. "But I am saving to potlatch for my father, who is dead. I would carve a pole, if I can pay others to raise it. There was not a job for me at the cannery this year."

"And you need to earn some money." Luke supposed it didn't matter why Gao wanted the job anyway, as long as he didn't intend to slit their throats the minute they were out of sight of the village. Considering his friendship with Kate, that was presumably unlikely. "Do you know someone else who would like to work for me, too? And do you have a canoe?"

"Yes, I have a canoe. Kun taos—" he nodded toward the oval door into the house "—he has taken people around before."

"Very well," Luke agreed. "Let me talk to Miss Hewitt—to Kate—about when to depart. Is three days from now too soon?"

"No," Gao said. "I can go any time."

"Good. Come by the Mission House tomorrow so that we can discuss provisions."

Gao agreed, and they parted company.

Well, that was one problem solved, Luke thought as he made his way along the well-worn path above the beach. He would have preferred to hire someone else, damn near anyone else. But there had been no easy way to reject Gao's offer, and Luke's reasons for wanting to were vague and unsubstantiated in any case. Gao seemed competent enough, and he spoke English. He had been civil today, and there had been no sign of the unfriendliness that had been Luke's first impression of the man. What did it matter if he disapproved of Luke's intentions? He and Miss Hewitt could frown together all they liked . . . as long as they didn't get in the way of valuable purchases.

The talk with Mr. Richardson did not go well. Kate had begun tentatively.

"I was surprised to see you giving the Indians communion. You know Father's reservations about it."

They were walking the short distance back to the Mission House. Mr. Richardson offered a solicitous hand to help her over a rough stretch of ground. "Indeed I do, though this is one subject we always disagreed upon. I believe your father didn't give the Haida adequate credit. That may well be natural, given the primitive civilization he found here when he arrived. But much of the tribe is Christian now. The Cannibal Dance is as repugnant to them as it is to you or me."

Kate seriously doubted the truth of that, unless the winter ceremonies had changed greatly in a very short time. She had once seen the "ceremony," if it could be so called, in which a lone dancer, garbed only in a loincloth, his face covered by a hideous mask, ran through the village in an apparent frenzy. He had at last seized a dog and torn it to pieces. Even the memory sickened her. Rationally, she could convince herself that the act was no worse than butchering an animal for its meat, but emotionally, she failed to find any solace. She never knew who the dancer was, and she didn't want to know.

Shutting out the recollection, she persevered. "Father objected as strenuously on the grounds that it was hypocrisy to give wine to the Indians when he preached against liquor."

The missionary's tone became patronizing. "I'm convinced that if we are to accept these men and women as members of our church and worthy of baptism, we must also assume that they are capable of entering fully into the symbolic meaning of the ritual. When you or I worship, we do not think of the wine as such; it is transformed. Do you claim that the Indian cannot manage a similar feat of imagination?"

The condescension set her teeth on edge, but Kate was aware of the weakness of her position. She couldn't argue that the Haida were incapable of understanding symbolism; nearly all of their dances and ceremonies involved elaborate role-playing and the use of a symbolism that was understood by all. The so-called Cannibal Dance was one such instance. The idea of eating human flesh was certainly dreadful, but Kate was convinced that the entire thing was staged and that the "body" devoured by the dancer was actually that of an animal. Was communion, with its symbolic partaking of Christ's flesh and blood, so different?

And yet . . . she still stumbled over the fact that the missionary was condemning with the one hand and offering with the other. How odd that Richardson, who so despised all that the Haida had been, was the one most willing to credit them with an equal capacity to understand and partake of the Lord's banquet! Had she misread the depth of his dislike for the Indians, or did he give communion not as a matter of conviction, but because he believed it stirred the emotions and perhaps made his converts more willing to tithe generously?

"Mister Sims doesn't feel that the Indians do understand," she said, knowing even as she spoke that her attempt to persuade Richardson was futile. "He talked of Indians sneaking back into line for a second taste of wine."

They had reached the Mission House. Flushed with anger, Richardson stopped and faced her. "And you accepted the word of a filthy, unshaven miscreant who seldom attends the Lord's service and who undermines my every attempt to induce the Indians to habits of temperance and virtue? I wonder if it is *my* judgment we should be discussing."

Taken aback, Kate said, "I didn't intend to offend you. I listened to Sims because he is impartial. He wasn't an admirer of Father, but still he was concerned—"

"Concerned that my influence might curtail the market for the liquor he sells!" Richardson snapped. "Or does he fear that he'll no longer be able to buy a woman?"

Now she was angry, too. "Do you believe you are so much more effective than Father was? Or Mister Duncan, at Metlakatla?"

"I must proceed as my conscience dictates!" His mouth was tight, his eyes glittering. "Unlike Mister Sims, *I* admired your father, but unlike *you,* I've accepted his death. He is no longer here; I am. Rather than setting yourself up as my critic, perhaps you should go into missionary work yourself!"

Oh, dear. How had her gentle reminder of her father's views degenerated into an emotional, and very personal, conflict? She feared that she had said more than she ought to have, and to no purpose. Mr. Richardson was right; her father was dead, and his successor couldn't live by his commandments forever.

"I had no such intention," she said honestly. "I apologize if I sounded critical. I was troubled to hear of changes that are so clearly against Father's views, but he was not inflexible himself. Perhaps he, too, would have come to believe that the Indians were ready for communion. Also—" here she tried to smile "—because this is the first time I've been back, it does seem to me as though no time at all has elapsed since my father's death. The loss is fresh again, but only to me. It is time to move on, of course."

"And I apologize for reacting so violently," Richardson

said with surprising generosity. "I confess that I recently received a letter from Mister Duncan that expressed many of the same concerns you have. I suppose that made me sensitive."

"Mister Duncan's letters often had that effect on Father, too," Kate said, hoping to lighten the mood. "They didn't always see eye to eye, you know."

"To be human is to err," he said piously. "If we all knew the perfect way, we wouldn't be human. We can only strain to hear God's word . . . and to attract others to hear it, which I believe communion in part does."

"I see." She didn't like the implication, but she had said all she could.

The missionary held open the back door, to which habit had taken them. "Do you want to come in?"

"No, I believe that while I'm dressed for visiting, I shall do exactly that," Kate said.

Mr. Richardson accepted her excuse with such equanimity that she suspected he had hoped for some time alone. And no wonder! The Mission House was not large, the tension between the two men obvious. And she was clearly a reminder of . . . what? Her father? Mr. Richardson's previously subordinate position? The outside world, which could threaten his godlike powers here at Skidegate?

She wondered if that power was not what attracted men— and women—to missionary work. To be so admired, so influential, to have one's will followed to nearly any lengths, must do much to mitigate the loneliness and frustrations. Where else in the modern world could one have such omnipotence? Was that what drew Mr. Richardson, rather than any deep love for his fellow man?

She went first to the cemetery, where moss had already begun to swath the headstones. Kate found her father's stone without difficulty. His name was sharply inscribed in marble, along with the years of his life. She knelt beside it and bowed her head. Tears came easily.

"Father," she whispered, "if only I had been here . . ." But what could she have done? reason demanded. She was able to answer: At least her father would not have left for Kiusta without telling her why, and with whom.

She prayed then, longing for some sign that he was here, at peace, that a moment of violence had not wrenched his soul from his body and left it, unquiet, where the murder had happened.

But she waited in vain. She heard nothing but the forest quiet and the far-off, harsh call of a raven. This one had no message for her. If the Reverend Hewitt was here, he did not speak to her, either.

More determined than ever, her emotions mastered, Kate began her calls. As she had on the first day with Luke, she started at Grizzly Bear House. On the lower level, she found Martha with a daughter-in-law, each occupied in weaving spruce-root hats. They sat on straight-backed chairs, a table between them. The crowns of two unfinished hats were set onto stands, much like those in hat shops, so that the weavers' hands were free to twine the weft through the warp in increasingly wide circles toward what would be a wide brim.

Coals were banked in the fire pit, but still emitted enough heat to make the huge, open house comfortable. On the roomy second tier, two men talked, and children played higher yet. Another woman came to the fire and stirred something in a pot. Her glance was curious, but at the sound of a crash from above, she hurried up the steps, scolding as she went.

"Sit, sit," Martha insisted. "Do you know Yak ulsi? She is my son's wife, you remember him."

"Of course," Kate said, sitting down on a matching straight-backed chair. "How do you do?"

The girl blushed and murmured a greeting, her head shyly bowed. She couldn't be more than thirteen or fourteen, Kate thought, shocked anew. Yak ulsi's childhood had been so short! Like other girls her age, she wore no labret, the white man's idea of beauty having vanquished tradition. A baby lay in a basket beside her, wrapped in a fur. Its enormous dark eyes watched with fascination as one tiny fist opened and closed before its face.

"What a pretty baby," Kate said, her gaze drawn back to the small fist.

The girl flashed a pleased smile. "She is my first."

"And only my second grandchild," Martha said. "Sarah's boy is there—" She pointed to a handsomely decorated bent-cedar box that stood open, filled with bundles of pale roots stored until they were needed to be woven into baskets or hats. A thatch of shiny black hair gave away the presence of the child even before he peeked around the corner and then vanished again.

Kate smiled. "He will be a handsome one," she said. "What round cheeks."

"Yes, Sarah had cheeks like that." The older woman's dark eyes became unfocused as she looked sadly into the past. "She was so thin when she died. Her cheeks were like crab apples that have been dried."

Kate said softly, "I'm sorry. Was it very long ago?"

"It was last winter. I kept to myself for a long time after, but she has a headstone now, and the rest of my family needed me. The little one, already he doesn't remember his mother."

"She's in the church cemetery?"

"Yes." Martha's deft hands returned to her task. "We asked to have her Christian and birth names both on the stone. You remember the naming?"

How could she forget? Kate had been friends with Oahla and had helped her choose her Christian name. The girl had pulled her aside after church one Sunday and announced that she was to be baptized. "Your father says I am ready. But I must choose a name, like the *yetz haada* have. Like yours. Tell me some."

"You don't mind giving up your own?" Kate had asked.

Oahla gave a trill of laughter. "We have many names! Why should I give one up to have another?"

On first thought, the concept seemed strange to Kate, but after all, white women did give up their last names when they married. Maybe the new names Haida boys and girls had been given at potlatches were the same to them. Kate privately suspected that her father had insisted on Christian names because he found the Haida ones so difficult to spell and pronounce, even though he had learned the language.

At her friend's insistence, Kate began to list all the names she could think of. "Alice, Octavia, Letitia. Jane, Georgette, Agatha."

"What was your mother called?" Oahla interrupted. "Do you have her name?"

"No, she was Amy. I'm really Katherine, only Kate for short."

"Amy." Oahla tasted the name, drew it out until it sounded like two separate sounds: a mee. "Your mother might come back as your daughter and want her name. Tell me others."

"Well, there's Margaret. Or Martha. Or Emma."

"What do they mean?"

"Nothing special," Kate admitted. "At least, I don't know what they mean."

"I am a chief's daughter. I would like my name to say that."

Kate thought. "My grandmother's name was Sarah. That means 'princess,' which is what we call the daughter of a great chief. The queen across the sea has daughters who are princesses."

"Sarah." This time the sound was savored in delight, like the candy that Kate always brought back from Victoria. "Would your grandmother mind?"

Kate had never known her father's mother, but she said promptly, "No. She would be honored that you chose her name."

"Sarah." Oahla laughed and danced ahead. "Sarah! Sarah! Sarah!"

How could she forget? Kate thought again, with fresh pain. In rebellion, she wondered why, of all people, Sarah had had to die. She had been one of the rare few who lived her life with joy.

Kate's father would have said it was God's will, that He had wanted her with Him, that she was blessed to be in the Heavenly embrace, but Kate could find no comfort in the thought. She could still close her eyes and see her friend, hear her voice like a soft, far-off echo.

Though her eyes were dry of tears, Kate's throat ached with them. "I remember," she said starkly.

Martha touched her hand. "We must not think too much about people who are gone. It does no good and takes us away from those who need us."

But nobody needs *me,* Kate's heart screamed in silent protest. She had never so directly faced that reality, and now she was staggered by the emptiness left in its wake. Her aunt and uncle had given her a home, but her absence would leave no hole. Her mother had loved her, but not enough to make life worth living. Now that Kate's father was dead, too, she had no one. Perhaps it was to stave off this yawning chasm inside that she had become consumed by her quest for justice; she had known that she needed purpose.

And she was not ready to let go of that purpose. What would be left?

"I remember other things, too," she said. She nodded at the box of bundled spruce roots. "The times we gathered those, the three of us."

Martha smiled. "You were more patient than Sarah."

It had become a ritual: On fine days in May, Martha had taken the two girls to the family's traditional gathering place. Sometimes other women would come, too, sometimes not. Driftwood from the beach would provide a fire, where the roots were roasted until the bark could be pulled off. They had collected piles and piles of the roots, working until the sun began sinking to the west and they had as much as they could carry.

On those days, Kate would have dinner with her father, then hurry back to Grizzly Bear House. Martha would have already begun splitting the roots in half. She would put

Sarah and Kate to work sorting them by size, helping to bundle them, and finally packing the roots tightly into cedar boxes.

"They must be covered," Martha had said firmly, "or they turn brown. And then the painting on them would not be so beautiful."

She would not do the painting; that was the province of men. But sometimes Martha and the other women would weave patterns into the hats or baskets, using strands of cedar or grass for contrast.

Martha was one of the finest weavers among the Haida. She made baskets so tight they held water, hats with wide, graceful brims that were much sought after, and mats woven of such fine fibers, they were soft to the touch. When Kate first knew her, most of what she made was for her own household: open weave for strainers, cedar-bark baskets for gathering berries, large baskets for storage. She made baskets for her husband and son, too, to hold lengths of rope and fishing paraphernalia, to store eagle down to be scattered in ceremonies.

Now Kate saw that most of the dishes and pans were white man's, that blankets were used in place of mats. The daughter-in-law was learning the art of weaving, but were other young women? The Reverend Hewitt had admired this skill above all others possessed by the Haida and had encouraged it, but Kate doubted that Mr. Richardson felt the same. She hoped she was wrong.

The memory of her father's convictions prodded her to do what she had come here for. Her voice changed when she said, "You were as my mother, Martha. I would ask *you* to remember something for me."

Martha's hands stilled at her work; a moment ticked by. Then she lowered her hands to her lap and said, "Ask."

For the first time, the young daughter-in-law looked directly at Kate, her dark eyes grave. She had sensed the tension not yet acknowledged by words.

Kate asked quietly, "Were you here at Skit-ei-get when my father died?"

Martha looked away. "Yes. I was here."

"Did he tell anybody where he was going?"

"No." She picked up the bone implement as though to push home the weft strands, but made no move to use it. "In the morning, he was gone, nobody knew he had left. Nobody worried. Why should we? We thought he had been needed somewhere. It was not Sunday."

"Was Mister Richardson here?" Kate tried to make the question sound unimportant, even idle.

"No, he was off somewhere," Martha said. "I don't remember, maybe Masset. He was gone for days, I think."

"And Mister Durham, the other white man who is here now? Had he left?"

"He had left," she confirmed. "Your father, he made him leave. That man stole bones, and people didn't like that. Your father said it wasn't right."

Kate made herself ask the next question. "What about Sims? Was he here?"

Martha frowned. "The miner? I think he was somewhere around. I don't know. Ask someone else."

Kate nodded. She waited for a moment, searching the worn, wrinkled face of this woman who had been so kind to a motherless *yetz haada* girl, and then she asked the question that most needed an answer.

"How did my father get to Kiusta?"

Martha set down the bone tool as though she didn't remember picking it up. "Nobody saw him go."

"But a canoe must have been gone! And other men. Somebody took Father to Kiusta."

Martha picked up a fine strand and began weaving it through the fringe that surrounded the crown of the hat. Her attention seemed to be entirely on her task; her voice was flat.

"It was summer. Many people were away. Why should we notice who else had left?"

"But later." Kate leaned forward, abandoning pride in her need for an answer. "Later, you must have thought about who was here and who might have left on that day. You must have talked about it."

Part of her was aware that Sarah's son had crept from his hiding place to his aunt's side. He clutched her, staring with huge dark eyes at Kate.

When Martha did not immediately answer, Kate asked again, "Who could have taken my father to Kiusta?"

A ghost of emotion crossed the Haida woman's face, but it was completely gone when she said, "Somebody from away, we thought. Somebody had come and gotten him. How could we know who?"

She lied, and was ashamed. Kate wanted to be angry. She had loved Martha, who claimed to think of her as a daughter who had come back. Yet she chose not to tell Kate what she knew or suspected. Even to her, Kate was an outsider, a *yetz haada* who could not be trusted.

Kate stood up. "Thank you for remembering, Martha," she said, hoping only her words and not her tone were a reproach. "Killing my father was not right. Who could respect the man who did it? I want everybody to know who it was, so that he is treated the way he deserves."

Martha stood, too. The shame was still in her eyes. "It was not right," she agreed. "We do not know who killed your father."

But she knew something, something that would bring humiliation to her or to her family. For her, as for all her people, shame was more to be feared than death. The entire culture was built around the need to earn respect from others.

Kate asked one last question. "Do you remember who else was here then?"

"People were away," Martha said vaguely. "To Victoria, or at the canneries, or fishing. There were others, but I don't know who. It was a long time ago."

So Mr. Richardson had tried to tell her, Kate thought. But a year and a half was not so long past. Martha had remembered how her daughter's face had looked before she died. She would remember her grandson's birth, and which boxes she had stored huckleberries in. The Haida had no written language; they remembered the past with stories and talk.

They would have talked then, and they would remember what people had said.

All Kate had to do was to find someone who had no reason to keep this secret. Somebody who might even want to shame Samuel Frederick or his family.

Chapter Nine

Kate's question was futile, but she asked it anyway. "Nobody else left on the morning my father went away?"

Her present hostess was a young woman named Qawkuna, whom Kate had known well before Qawkuna married a man from Skedans. So many in Skedans had died, Qawkuna had told Kate, that those left felt as though they lived in a gravehouse. "We did not want to move. At Skit-ei-get we have nothing, not even a place to pick berries, but there are other people here. Other women for me to talk with about my troubles. I have family here who can give a feast and a new name to my son. So," she shrugged gracefully, "even though it is hard, we came back. There were empty houses, we had enough to pay the owner to live in this one."

Kate had heard the story many times. Those few survivors of the dying southern villages would not find life here easy. In essence, they now lived on charity. They had left behind all that they "owned"—the right to dig shellfish on certain beaches, to pick berries and dig the corms of false lady's slipper on the banks of a stream that Qawkuna's husband's family alone could fish when the salmon ran. Here, they must wait to be invited to share in someone else's riches.

Kate had followed a trail all afternoon, one that seemed like a deer track in the woods, going from here to there but leading nowhere in particular and vanishing unpredictably.

Some people had been away, she was told. The ones who were here remembered no more than Martha did. Always the answers were vague.

She had been told that Qawkuna was newly returned to Skidegate when the Reverend Hewitt died. Kate had hoped for more from her. They had been friends; her husband was from Skedans, not Skidegate. Why should they keep a secret that was not theirs? But her hope had been as futile as the question she had just asked.

"Who else was gone?" Qawkuna repeated. "It was many days before we knew your father was dead. After so many days, who could remember? We thought someone had come to get him, maybe someone from Cumshewa or Tanu. He didn't tell anybody, so we didn't know."

Wearily, Kate accepted the answer she had heard so many times, the answer that could even have been true. A knock on the door might have come in the night. If her father had been told that someone was sick, or dying and asking to learn more of the Great Chief Above, he would not have hesitated to go at once.

Kate might have believed that explanation had not the people offering it been so incurious, so unable to remember anything precise. If they had looked her in the eye as they spoke, she might have accepted that they knew nothing.

But however angry and frustrated she was, she had reached the end of this trail. It had dwindled and vanished, leaving her in an impenetrable woods. Who else could she ask? She had questioned everyone she knew. All had lied.

Defeated, she made her excuses to Qawkuna, who appeared relieved to see Kate go. She left the young woman rocking her one-year-old son, who was crying as he sucked on a balled fist. Qawkuna's soft singing followed her: *"Why does he cry as a noble cries? Why does he move around as he sits? He moves around and cries for Grandfather's house.*"

Outside the longhouse, Kate found that a fog had rolled in. The damp mist muffled sound, so that she heard only faint snatches of voice and song as she picked her way along the trail, which shifted its course according to how high above the watermark the canoes had been pulled. The jut of prows materialized from the mist and vanished behind her. The poles that did the same were like familiar friends: There was Raven's beak, the round eyes of Sea Grizzly, Killer Whale with a manlike creature on his back. Each told her where she was, how far she had to go.

And yet the familiarity was not as comforting as it might have been yesterday. Not since her first winter here had she felt as though she were an encroacher. She had been conceited enough to think she was the daughter Martha had called her, but now she knew better. In a world where kinship and lineage meant all, she was connected to the Haida by neither. They might now be Christians, they might have revered her father, but she was still an outsider.

What frightened Kate most was that along with her self-conceit, she had also lost her certainty that her father's murderer was not an Indian. Mr. Richardson had warned her; he had momentarily shaken her belief, but he had not cast it down. The barrier she had faced today, as wide and potentially dangerous as Hecate Strait, had done what he could not. Perhaps the murderer himself was not known, but Kate was increasingly sure that the entire village knew—or at least suspected—who had taken her father to Kiusta. There must have been at least two men, she thought, two men who might protest their innocence but who had not come forward to tell what they knew. They must be men from Skit-ei-get, connected by blood and marriage to the principal families here. The wrong they had done brought shame to all members of their lineage.

If the murdered man had been a high-ranking Tsimshian Indian, or even a Haida from another village, the murderer's family could atone for the wrong and satisfy the dead man's family with payment in slaves and blankets and coppers. Shame could be averted. But Christianity and exposure to white men's ways must have taught the Haida that she would not consider a heap of blankets adequate recompense for her father's life.

Her arrival must have been an unwelcome surprise. No wonder they lied! How could they admit to such shame, when it could not be assuaged?

Kate was nearly to the end of the curving beach with its single line of houses when a figure from a nightmare stepped from the oval opening in a house just in front of her. He straightened and faced her, the movement causing the claws that hung from his shaman's apron to click like the chatter of teeth. The long, tangled hair was still dark, though the beard was as white as eagle's down. He did not wear the raven headdress she remembered from that night so long ago, though charms that concentrated the powers of his spiritual helpers were suspended from a neck-ring and rattled against polished sticks. One gnarled hand clutched a Chilkat blanket wrapped around his shoulders. In the other hand, he held . . .

A small, shocked sound escaped her, and Kate took a backward step.

The medicine man's mouth twisted with satisfaction. "You know this shirt." He dangled it before her.

It was blue-and-brown checkered. Despite the fact that the checks did not quite match in front, her fourteen-year-old self had been proud of the shirt she had made for her father.

She felt cold. "Where did you get my father's shirt?"

"I have these, too." The fingers uncurled to reveal the half-moon slivers of something translucent.

Fingernail clippings. Kate fought a wave of fear and struggled to transform it into anger. "You are so poor that you must take things nobody else wants anymore?"

Hate stared at her through deep-set eyes. "You have been asking questions. You want to know what killed your father. If you really want to know, I will tell you."

"I want to know," she said, refusing to flinch even when he took another step closer and she could see the mats in his twisted locks of hair, the saliva on his lips. The mist curled around him, chilling Kate to the bone.

"He did not believe in the Supernatural Ones. He said bad words about them. They bade me find something of his and showed me how to use it. I stole his soul and sent it away, where it can't come back. He died then." The shaman opened his hand and let the fingernail silvers filter through his fingers and fall to the packed earth of the path. His bitter tone became triumphant. "The Great Chief of the Heavens that he thought was so powerful couldn't help him then, not against the Supernatural Ones."

"The Supernatural Ones were such cowards they must chase him to Kiusta? They couldn't steal his soul here?"

He leaned toward her, his eyes glittering. "He did not die right away. He had time to know that his soul was gone and that he would die. Maybe he thought he could get it back if he went there." He gestured, and the claws rattled. "Maybe he was hiding so nobody would know that his Great Chief was not strong enough to save him."

Was this why people were afraid to talk to her? Because of this old man, with his tricks and his sleight-of-hand? This grotesque creature whose only power lay in the fear he compelled others to feel?

"Why didn't he just fall down dead, then?" she demanded. "Why did he have to be hit over the head before he died?"

Her face was sprayed with spittle when the shaman hissed, "You don't believe the Supernatural Ones can make people do things, either. Keep saying bad words about them and they might make somebody hit you over the head, too!"

"You're an evil old man!" she snapped. "You've been tricking people for years, but it won't work with me. You have no more power over me than I have over the tides. Here." Kate yanked a strand of dark hair from her head. "Have it! Here's another one." The pain on her scalp was welcome as she tore out another strand, and another. The wiry, dark hairs curled into spirals as she dropped them into his arthritic hand. "Have them! Make all the spells you want. You'll see! Nothing will happen to me, nothing except that I'll find the man who killed my father. The murderer is one who at least had the courage to do a bad thing himself, instead of asking invisible spirits to do it for him!"

"You're a fool, like your father!" shouted the shaman. "You teach people that our ways are bad, and what do you give us instead? Whiskey, that makes men act stupid and throw up! The pestilence that kills everybody and leaves the empty towns to the ghosts. Are those not bad things? Do you have the courage to see a dying child and know that the evil spirit is not one you can tame?"

Even the truth in his tirade couldn't damp her fury. "My father didn't bring whiskey or pestilence here. He came to help, to save lives that you could not, to bring the people a message of peace. You should be ashamed to brag that you tried to call evil spirits to hurt him!"

He lifted his arm as though to strike her, but Kate still refused to cower. She waited unbending for a blow that didn't come. Instead, a hand grasped her arm and pulled her back. Kate turned, incensed, to face Gao.

"Kilslayoway is not one you should set against you," Gao said in a low voice. "If you come away now, he may think you are only a daughter who grieves for her father."

She wrenched her arm out of his grasp. "I may be *only* a daughter, but I won't run away from this . . . this trickster!"

The shaman stood waiting just a few feet away, but the swirling fog made the distance seem greater. His bony feet were bare, reached almost by the twisted locks of his uncombed hair. In their deep sockets, his eyes were shadowed, but his mouth was a cruel line.

Gao took her arm again. Quietly, in English, he said, "He is too old to cut off his hair and sit in your father's church. Let him keep his self-respect."

"I . . ." Kate stopped. "He claims he stole my father's soul, and that's why my father died."

"It is not always just one thing that kills a man," Gao said. "You *yetz haada* see only with your eyes."

"My eyes tell me that he plays tricks because he likes people to be afraid of him."

"How can he cure people of illness if they don't believe he has the power to do it?" Gao asked. "Don't the *yetz haada* believe their medicine men are strong?"

"We're not afraid of our medicine men!" she began hotly, before a sudden vision of her mother came to her. Amy Hewitt sitting up in bed against a heap of pillows. She was gazing nervously up at Dr. Hibbert, nodding as he pontificated. When he patted her hand and told her to be a good girl and open her mouth for a spoonful of medicine, she never questioned him, only followed his instructions docilely.

Gao saw that a memory had come to her, making her uncertain. "A medicine man must be strong," he said again. "He must have respect for his own powers."

"And my father's death gave him that again?"

Gao said nothing, only waited.

Kate sniffed and drew herself up. "Oh, very well. I'll let him think he's scared me."

She allowed Gao to take her arm again and urge her past Kilslayoway. She was grateful that Gao said nothing to the shaman, who glared at her as Gao steered her at a respectful distance around him. Her pride insisted that she hold her head high and pretend that she didn't feel his malignant gaze on her back.

They walked in silence for some distance before Kate stopped. "Why won't anybody talk to me?" she asked. "Are they afraid of the *ska-ga*?"

Gao's answer was indirect. "It would have been better if you hadn't come back."

All afternoon she had felt as if she had an invisible spear in her chest that had worked its way deeper as one old friend after another refused to meet her eyes. Now it gave a last painful twist as Gao said aloud what the others had been thinking.

But she would not let him see that he had the power to hurt her. She lifted her chin and asked tartly, "Why would it have been better? Because the truth is uncomfortable?"

His broad face showed little emotion. "Why did you come with such a man?"

Kate tried not to sound defensive. "It was the only way."

"The only way is a bad way."

"If he doesn't buy the things, somebody else will." She had almost convinced herself that Luke's justification made what she did right.

But Gao's uncompromising answer tore the smooth veneer from the raw wood that lay beneath. "Somebody else is not the one you brought, the one you talk for."

"It was the only way," she repeated. She hugged herself against the damp mist. "My father had no one else to demand what is right. You would do the same."

She had gotten to him. Kinship and honor meant more than life to the Haida. She saw even before he dipped his head that he couldn't lie. "You ask us to talk against one of ourselves."

"My government may be convinced that the murderer is one of you," Kate said. "But until today, when I heard so many lies, *I* thought my father had been killed by a white man."

"But now you believe one of us took him to his death?"

"Yes." She drew in a ragged breath. "My father was a good man. I want everybody to know who did such a thing to him."

"The other missionary, this Richardson. Do you think he is a good man, too?"

The question caught her off balance; she hesitated. "He wants you to know the white man's way, just as my father did."

"That makes him good?" Gao's tone held irony.

Kate hesitated again. "No," she finally admitted. "He could talk in one way and act in another."

"But your father always acted in a good way?"

This question was even more unsettling than the last. She had sometimes mourned what was left behind at each step forward, but had never questioned her father's motives in leading the Haida on that necessary journey. So why did she feel a shudder of anxiety, a moment of not wanting to know?

"He always tried," she insisted, recognizing her evasion only after she spoke.

"You ask us to remember," Gao said. "Do you remember?"

"Remember what?" she demanded, ignoring that moment of queasiness when she had felt as if she were in a canoe that bobbed uncertainly on water that appeared smooth. But she was talking to the fog. Gao was gone.

She turned and hurried toward the welcoming glow of lights from the Mission House. Under the cover of fog, night had crept unnoticed upon her. She was uneasy out here in the dark, where nothing was like it had always appeared, where she could not see with her eyes.

She could almost feel the unseen presence of the spirits the Haida believed were within everything material, from the great cedar trees to the salmon that struggled to return to their birthplace to lay their eggs and die. She could almost believe that the mist dampening her face and frizzling her hair was the cold breath of some supernatural being, that her soul was bound to her by only a fragile thread that could be snapped.

Luke would have preferred not to see Durham across the dinner table again, but he managed to greet him civilly. Durham claimed to be happy with his success at acquiring artifacts here in Skidegate.

"But of course," he added, "I'm hoping to find finer objects yet in the more unspoiled villages. I've put the word out that I need guides. I suppose you're doing the same yourself." He reached for another biscuit and slathered it with butter from the missionary's one cow. "Miss Hewitt, these biscuits are splendid. I believe you've missed your calling."

Luke was relieved to find that he was still a step ahead of his rival. He fully intended to have the jump on Durham, putting the other museum man in the position of trailing him down the coast, being offered for sale only what hadn't interested Luke. Nonetheless, he was alarmed by Durham's expressed intentions. If the man was fortunate enough to find a guide quickly, who knew how soon he could be ready to take off?

Setting down his knife and fork, Luke growled, "Most women make decent biscuits. Very few compose magnificent photographs."

Durham lifted a brow in his exaggerated, dandified way. "Miss Hewitt, forgive me if I gave the impression that I was belittling your photographic skill. I understand that it's considerable. In fact, I'd hoped to see you at work before we parted ways."

Miss Hewitt looked composed, as always. "You must remember that this was my home. I've taken countless photographs here at Skidegate. I can print copies of those for Mister Brennan's museum. It seemed logical to me to save my limited supply of plates for other villages. Too, I'd like to make an attempt at capturing some of the winter ceremonies, though lighting is of course a difficulty."

"I can imagine." Durham sounded genuinely interested. "How do you intend to solve the problem?"

"Surely you've seen a photographer at work before," Luke said impatiently, dismissing the subject. He strove to sound casual when he added, "How soon do you intend to depart?"

"By next week, I should think. You?"

Somewhat complacently, Luke said, "I've already found guides. In fact, we plan to leave in the morning for a short expedition to Haina and Lina."

"I saw Haina myself several days ago." Durham smiled condescendingly. "There's not much there, the village is too recent."

Luke pretended to an interest in another biscuit himself. "I've been offered a pole that stands at Haina."

"Oh?" The supercilious brow rose again. "I don't recall seeing any of particular interest. They're unwilling to sell their best, aren't they? I may be lucky, however. I believe I've persuaded a newly converted Indian to sell me a memorial pole from in front of his house at Skedans. Seems to think cutting the thing down would be a fine gesture to demonstrate his sincerity to Mister Richardson here."

The missionary smiled with satisfaction. "That must be Ni swas. Of course, I encourage them all to dispose of those wretched displays of idolatry. I shall hope to see a generous portion of the price you pay offered on the collection plate. It's gratifying to know that my efforts are at last bearing fruit."

Before Luke could counter, Miss Hewitt said mildly, "But the poles are not religious objects. Surely you wouldn't object to an English duke displaying his family crest."

"I would indeed if his crest was the devil!" Richardson said roundly. "You must admit that many of the figures on the poles are not taken from nature. The Indians think themselves to be descended from some kind of supernatural beings, which they believe in whole-heartedly. There must be only our Father in their hearts if they are to worship in a Christian church."

"But those crest figures represent their family history!" Luke said. "If you wipe out their memories of their ancestry, invaluable history will be lost!"

"Wiping out memories of their savage past is precisely my intention," Richardson said stiffly. "Think of how much prouder they can be of a magnificent church the equal of that at Metlakatla, built by their own toil! When they take Christian names, it is as though they have become blank slates, ready to be writ upon in a more civilized hand."

"If we were all blank slates, we'd have no idea of what humanity's past had been!" Luke said. "You do a disservice to those who hope to learn from the past—not to mention the disservice you do to the Indians themselves! What harm is there in allowing them to cling to some remnant of pride in their heritage?"

Richardson set down his cutlery with an audible click. "What precisely should they take pride in? Their savage attacks on other tribes? Their massacre of the crew of the

Eleanora and the assault on the *Susan Sturgis*? The polygamy, slavery, and cannibalism they have routinely practiced?"

Luke had never understood why people who despised the Indians felt compelled to "save" them. He congratulated himself on his reasonable tone when he retorted, "Do you consider the white man's history to be so virtuous?"

"The white man, at least, has advanced toward greater civilization. Our history is comprised of that march to progress! The Indians, in contrast, were sunk in depravity and seemingly contented to remain that way! Have you seen how wasteful they are when they do get ahead in the world? Rather than providing themselves and their families with a decent way of life, they give away all they have gained to some hated rival, or in payment for raising another of those wretched poles."

Luke said contemptuously, "They seem to me to have *had* decent lives until we white men determined to alter them into our own selfish image."

Richardson's normally pale cheeks fired with anger. "Do you consider me selfish? On what grounds? I give everything to my charges and take nothing!"

"Gentlemen, gentlemen!" Durham rapped on the table, then pushed his chair back so that he could lounge in more comfort, his legs stretched out. Candlelight glinted off the polish on his knee-high boots. He unwrapped a cigar and proffered it to the other men. "Would you care for a smoke? No? Miss Hewitt, would you be offended . . . ?"

"Not at all," she assured him. "You deserve a reward for averting the imminent bloodshed."

He stuck the cigar in his mouth and lit it. "Look at it this way, Brennan." He puffed out a perfect ring of smoke that rose gently before fraying. "Nearly every purchase we make is thanks to the influence of missionaries like Richardson. You don't think the Indians would part with a mask that's integral to some secret-society ritual if they weren't turning their backs on all that, do you?" He gestured extravagantly.

Ash flicked off the tip of his cigar, narrowly missing Luke. "No, we're in his debt. Come, you're an honest man. Confess it!"

Through taut lips, Luke said, "If it weren't for the influence of missionaries, we wouldn't be impelled by such urgency, either. We could take a more leisurely approach to our ethnological studies, knowing that the dances and rituals would survive for another few years. It is thanks to men like Mister Richardson that we don't have that luxury!"

The missionary leaped to his feet. "Sir, I must tell you that only my regard for Miss Hewitt keeps me from asking you to leave my house!"

"Doing so will be a pleasure," Luke said, just as stiffly. "Tomorrow morning."

He had been overly optimistic if he had imagined they could move their departure up so drastically and yet be ready to set off before noon. Doing so had probably been unnecessary, but he'd wanted to take no chance that Durham would beat him to the richest collecting grounds. This way, he could still visit Haina, see something of the inlet, and be back in Skidegate by tonight or tomorrow. Another day or two to ready supplies, and they ought to be a safe distance ahead of Durham.

He was pleased with Gao's canoe, which, at thirty-five feet long and six feet in breadth, was sturdy enough for winter travel and allowed space to carry the collection he intended to amass this winter. Gao said the craft was called *Dancing Canoe*, because it was so light on the waves. One of Gao's crest figures was the sea wolf, which was painted in typically stylized fashion on the high prow.

Luke had paid little attention to Kun taos, so now he sized him up as the young man helped load Kate's photographic supplies. He was taller and rangier than Gao, his face less broad, his features sharper, yet there was a good humor and an openness about Gao's friend that ought to make him a fine traveling companion. Like Gao, he wore European clothing; unlike him, no tattoos were visible.

Luke regretted more than ever that he didn't speak the Haida tongue. It placed him in a position where he must trust Gao. Kate's old friend had assured him that Kun taos had several times before served as guide to white men. Reading between the lines, Luke guessed that he had been hired not for his grasp of the English language—that would have been hoping for too much—but rather because he had been available. He didn't like to work in the canneries, Gao had said with a shrug. Kun taos hunted in the summer months. Otters were scarce now, but he found enough.

Gao's second shrug had made Luke uneasy. The implication was that Kun taos didn't need much to make him content. Would the salary Luke was paying be enough to motivate him when the task at hand was unpleasant?

Well, perhaps this brief excursion would show his mettle.

The sun had passed the top of its arc by the time the expedition was launched at last, with the usual cries and the send-off from a crowd of children and motley dogs. Against the pearl-gray sky, a dark V of northern geese stood out, and gulls called closer by as their white wing tips brushed the waves.

Luke had worked for the last year to bring this moment about. He was suddenly sorry that they would be coming back to Skidegate, that this was not the beginning of their long winter's journey. Yet he savored the pleasure of heading into the unknown.

"Gao, do you know what success Durham has had in finding a guide?" he asked.

Kate didn't let the Indian answer. "For goodness sake, must everything be a competition?" She looked distinctly annoyed. Her coronet of braids was slipping and her gown was crumpled. He had spent the morning urging her to greater speed in her preparations, with the result that she was now clearly exasperated with him.

"This is a race only because he's an incompetent fool,"

Luke said. "If he'd collect the stories that go with the objects he buys, if they were properly studied and labeled . . . But no, he'll purchase anything that pleases his eye, with no idea of its significance, and throw it helter-skelter into that mishmash he calls a museum. And you wonder that I'm determined to beat him to objects that could teach us a great deal about the Northwest Coast Indians?"

"Hah!" she said, clutching the side of the canoe as a swell rocked them. "You're like two little boys determined to best each other."

"You don't know what you're talking about," Luke declared. He scowled at Gao, who had allowed a flicker of amusement to show on his normally impassive face.

"Then why are you abandoning your intention to go through the inlet to Chaatl?"

"I realized that this was the more practical course," he said loftily. "We can stop at Chaatl this winter after we leave Kaisun. This way, we can take time to see the north branch of the inlet. I understand that the black slate comes from a creek just west of Lina Island?"

Gao correctly realized that he was being addressed. "Yes," he said in English. "Near there is the . . ." He cast about for a word and finally said something to Kate.

"The abandoned coal mine," she said. "I had forgotten about it."

"I didn't realize that any serious mining had been done here," Luke said with interest. "Was your friend Sims involved?"

"No, he's determined to find gold," Kate said. "Coal is beneath his notice. Besides, this wouldn't have improved his finances any. The mine was a disaster nearly from the start, I understand. The investors had given up by the time I came here. I've never seen the workings."

"They might be interesting," Luke said thoughtfully. "Gao, do you know where the mine is?"

The Indian nodded. He said something in Haida, which Kate translated. "As a youth, he went there with some friends. They rode the tram for fun and had to run away very fast after the car fell off the tracks."

"Did you get caught?"

Luke had never seen Gao smile. The effect was startling; for the first time, he looked to be the youth he was. Kate continued to translate. "The white men were too slow, he says. He and his friends dared each other to go into the tunnels, too. Gao has seen caves before, but never ones that go so far into the mountain."

"Well, why not take a look?" Luke said, his good humor restored. "I understand that this area is rich with fossils. Maybe we'll find something. Gao, do you know of any natural caves?"

After Kate had translated for Kun taos's benefit, each man shook his head. No, not here, but farther south and on the west coast in some places, like Kiusta. They were used sometimes for burials.

"Where do you put the graves for your shamans?" Luke asked.

Gao's face closed, but Kun taos spoke. Kate said, "He knows of a shaman's grave on an island that we will pass. He has seen it before. The body is not bones, but—" she listened to his rapid speech, punctuated by much hand waving—"mummified, I think. He says that the bodies of shamans do not decay like others, but dry up. If you should see only a skeleton when you look at a dead shaman, it is bad luck; you or someone close to you will soon die. If you see flesh, it is a good omen."

"You must not touch anything," Gao said fiercely in English. "I will watch you."

Somewhat ruefully, Luke said, "If I had wanted to steal from graves, I would not have hired you, Gao. I would have found a guide who would pretend not to see what I was doing."

The Indian's eyes did not leave his for a long moment. At last, as though satisfied, he gave a sharp nod and returned his attention to the powerful strokes of the paddle that, in concert with Kun taos's, drove the canoe across the choppy gray water toward their destination.

Already, Maude Island, which stood only a mile or two off Skidegate, was just ahead. It was perhaps five miles long and wooded, but less densely so than the larger islands. The north shore was strewn with strange lava rock, a stark yellow-orange that had an alien quality about it.

Haina Village consisted of eight or nine houses in a single row along the shore, with only a few poles fronting it. The finest houses and poles were clustered at one end; new construction had begun at the other end of the row. A woman who seemed to be pouring out wash water spotted them and shouted something. People came out of houses, and children ran to the water's edge, accompanied by the usual cacophony of barking dogs. Gao called a greeting that was answered cheerfully. Willing hands helped drag the canoe onto the beach.

In short order, the visitors had been invited to eat with a chief, whose name translated to "Highest Peak in a Mountain Range." An oval doorway offered entry to his house through a painted frontal pole topped by the ubiquitous Three Watchmen.

"The house is called 'House-Where-People-Always-Want-to-Go,'" Gao said.

"A popular host, I take it," Luke commented dryly. They climbed several steps to a conventional door located a few feet from the traditional opening covered with hides.

The interior, as always, was dark. They had to pause to let their eyes adjust before cautiously making their way to the central fire. Smoke floated lazily up to the large hole cut in the roof, and fillets of halibut were drying on poles braced above the fire. Corners were heaped with cedar boxes packed with surplus food for the approaching winter. The pervasive odor was fish, but it was not unpleasant.

The chief himself greeted them by the fire. He might have stepped from another century, before contact with the white man: His face was broad, with prominent cheekbones and eyes of an almost Oriental cast; he wore a conical spruce-root hat and had a particularly handsome Chilkat blanket wrapped around his shoulders. Woven of mountain-goat wool and shredded cedar bark, the blanket was painted with the owner's crest figures. Thick fringe at the bottom was snowy white and soft. Luke resisted the urge to reach out and touch it, or to allow his acquisitiveness to show.

"We're honored by your hospitality," Luke said. Kate translated, and thus began the seemingly endless round of courtesies and explanations of Luke's purpose.

The chief, of course, had nothing he wanted to sell. So he had told the other man from a museum. Still, he would have word sent around, just in case people had changed their minds. Perhaps the visitors would care to spend the night as his guests.

Luke hesitated for only a moment. They had plenty of time, and staying here tonight would allow them more leisure tomorrow. Besides, staying the night could make the difference between success or failure here. In his experience, a level of trust must be reached between purchaser and seller before the best things were offered for sale.

Like that Chilkat blanket. He was unlikely to find a finer example of the wool shawls woven by Tlingit Indian women. The Chilkat work was highly regarded up and down the Northwest Coast, and owned only by those who could afford such a luxury.

So Luke inclined his head. "Your house is well-named. We would be glad to stay the night."

They were apparently to be left to their own devices until dinnertime, so they set out for a stroll around the village.

Luke asked, "Gao, do you know where the pole Nengkwigetklals owns is?"

Gao did, though his face was the closed mask that succeeded in expressing his disapproval. Nonetheless, trailed by Kate, Luke followed the young Haida man to a house that Gao said was empty. "The people who lived here are Christians now. They moved to Skit-ei-get. This pole is the one of which Nengkwigetklals spoke."

Luke grunted and tilted his head back to study it. The

kexen, a memorial raised by the heir upon his assumption of the dead man's honors, customarily had only one principal crest figure, either on the top or the bottom, with the length of the pole plain. At the bottom of this one crouched a large beaver, complete with feet, haunches, and cross-hatched tail. A gnawing stick was held against the beaver's chest by his forepaws. The obvious incisors easily identified him. Below the stick was a small bird that Gao, when pressed, said was a hummingbird, another Eagle Clan crest figure. The upper length of the pole was divided into ten cylinders of property hat; the whole was over thirty feet high.

"Transporting something this length would be devilishly difficult. I'd prefer one with carving from top to bottom," Luke muttered. "I'd really like to find a spectacular house frontal pole. Or an *xet.*" He turned. "Like that one."

"There's a *body* in there," Kate said. Her tone was as severe as Gao's expression.

"That one" was a typical mortuary pole, short and wide, with a plaque fastened horizontally to the top, hiding the cavity wherein the body was entombed. The pole appeared to be new; the painted heron and raven, their eyes lidless and staring, had not grayed or cracked. The spiny fish depicted on the plaque was inlaid with abalone that, even on the gray day, gleamed with a milky iridescence.

"Do you know the owner?" Luke asked.

A muscle twitched in Gao's cheek. "Yes. I carved this pole."

"Really." Luke took a closer look. This mortuary wasn't as complex as some he'd seen, but it was nonetheless a fine example of the type. Raven's beak protruded several feet, while Heron's pointed down toward what appeared to be a human face. "I suppose that means you wouldn't approve of my purchasing it."

Gao spoke in Haida. "Would you sell the headstone that marks your grandmother's grave?"

When Kate translated, Luke snorted. "Hell. I've brought a moralist with me."

Beside him, she cleared her throat. "Two of them, I'm afraid."

That was hardly news, which made him wonder about his own sanity for at least the hundredth time in less than two weeks. Today she not only sounded like a female counterpart of Richardson, she looked like one. Her gown was brown, frumpy, and high-necked. Somehow she had found time to re-anchor her coronet of braids, a style that did nothing to soften her pale, strong face. She had never looked plainer.

And yet, he no longer thought her mannish. Even more disturbing, her womanliness did not depend on feminine tricks and fripperies. Nothing about her was intended for show; she was not a creature designed to live a contented life as a mere ornament.

Some part of him argued that he had never been attracted by shy glances and a deferential opinion, or by the ridiculous extremes of fashion meant to highlight a woman's softness and frailty. But those were precisely the qualities he had intended to seek out should he look for another wife. Why else would she be willing to be left behind for half of each year?

Miss Hewitt would not be. He knew that without question. Ridiculous that he was even thinking such things! Or wishing that he might see her hair unfettered, imagining that it would be magnificent. That *she* might even be magnificent, in the right circumstances. Luke preferred not to consider what those might be.

Disturbed at the tenor of his thoughts, he looked away from her, only to encounter Gao's watchful gaze. It reminded him disquietingly of the rounded, staring eyes that appeared so prominently on the poles.

His voice was louder than he had intended. "I suppose I'd better take Nengkwigetklals's pole, then. It's better than nothing. How Durham fancies he'll be able to transport one from Skedans, I can't imagine. Well?" He turned almost angrily on his companions. "Let's get moving, we have only a few hours. Gao, you come with me to translate while Kate sets up her photographic equipment to record these poles." He issued rapid-fire instructions before striding off without looking to see that Gao followed.

Blast Thompson, Luke thought again. He ought to have been working with a professional photographer who had no emotional ties to these people. And he should have hired a translator more interested in making money than in his cultural heritage.

But his largest problem was one of his own making. Back in Boston, as he'd planned the expedition, it had been easy to think of the Haida as a dying culture that was ethnologically interesting. Here, amongst the Indians, he was having the devil of a time maintaining his detachment. The Haida were a dying *people*, not just an artistic tradition or a collection of beliefs and myths.

Well, he had excavated tombs before with relish. He must convince himself that this was no different, or he would fail in his objective.

Chapter Ten

Luke required Kate to translate that evening, as Gao had vanished, perhaps to visit some acquaintance. Of necessity, she joined Luke in his male circle. The fire was dying back some, and cups of what smelled like very raw whiskey were being passed around. She saw a quickly disguised expression of distaste on Luke's face before he accepted a cup with thanks.

The company had thinned, with most of the women and children absenting themselves. A game of gambling sticks had begun on the other side of the fire, toward the front of the house. The click of the sticks was punctuated by cries of delight and hoots of derision.

The chief was the proud possessor of a sturdy European dining-room table of oak, upon which a number of items had been spread for Luke's inspection. Nothing exceptional, she saw at a glance, but he *had* expressed a desire for common, everyday tools such as these: a decorated halibut hook; a fishing float carved in the simple shape of a bird; a small box, perhaps intended to hold fishing tackle; a drill with a bone point, and a chisel with a bone blade, both no doubt supplanted today by iron tools.

The negotiating began, all participants pretending disinterest in the outcome. Nonetheless, Luke agreed too quickly to prices Kate thought were excessive. When she said so in an undertone, he barely spared her a glance. "This is only a preliminary. I must motivate them to offer more cherished pieces."

He bought everything on the table. At the end, he said with some satisfaction, "Tell them that I would like to buy more. That I especially seek ceremonial regalia and will pay high prices for it."

When she had complied, he continued, "Now tell them that I put everything I buy into a sack"—he suited action to words—"so that no one else will know what they sold to me."

"Are you suggesting—" she began with a certain amount of outrage.

He interrupted, his voice sharp. "Tell them."

Biting her tongue, she did so. At length they filed out, and the chief's wife showed the guests where they would sleep. The chief had done them the honor of allotting them sleeping spaces at the rear of the house, not in the front, where the "common mosquitoes," as the Haida called those with little status, must sleep.

Kate was relieved to be offered a mat beside two young, unmarried daughters. She had not been certain of how her relationship with Luke would be interpreted and had braced herself for the inevitable awkwardness of explanations.

This was not the first time she had shared a huge communal space; in the past, she had traveled with her father as far as Cumshewa and Tanu, where they had necessarily stayed as guests in the houses of their Haida hosts. There might be as many as forty people living in this house, all rather loosely considered to be family but for the slaves, if there were any. Of course the sleeping areas were partitioned from each other by screens or stacked cedar boxes. Nonetheless, one could *hear* others: giggles from the two girls, who were too shy to speak to her; whispers from farther away; a cough; a peculiar rhythmic thumping that ended with the sound of a deep grunt. Luke's mat was not far away; several times she thought she heard the scrape of wood, as though a board were being pried loose, then the sound of soft voices. She lay wondering if he had scheduled some sort of tryst—but how could he have? And with whom? The chief's plump wife with an enormous bone labret in her lower lip?

The packed-earth floor beneath the mat was very hard. Turning to her side and finding that no better, she reminded herself sternly that she must get used to sleeping under such conditions. Except for one more night in Skidegate, she wouldn't see a feather bed again for many months. She was weary enough that her eyelids were heavy, but there were the voices again—or were they different ones?

It wasn't the voices that were keeping her awake, she realized at last. It was the odor. Not of grease or smoke or anything fishy, but more as though something was rotting. Something that had been alive.

With the horror of her thought, she was jolted awake. She *knew* what she was smelling.

Her stomach roiled, and sleep became impossible. Could she move her mat to the front of the house? But that would insult their host. No, she must stick it out, block from her mind the source of her disturbance.

Eventually she did doze, though her dreams were part and parcel of her waking knowledge. She had once seen the mummified remains of a *ska-ga,* and now as she walked in her dream through an otherwise deserted village, he continually sprang out of hiding places to frighten and taunt her. Even though the flesh on his face had withered to a yellowish, skeletal mask, he smelled as though he were rotting, and when he stretched out a hand to her, she saw maggots on it.

As soon as she heard the first stirrings by the fire pit, Kate dressed in the gown she had laid over a screen. She knew she must look ghastly: hollow-eyed and wan, like a corpse herself. Though most of the inhabitants still slept, Luke appeared shortly thereafter, his features drawn and his clothes so wrinkled that she assumed he had slept in them.

He accepted a cup of Haida tea and sat down heavily beside Kate on a crude bench. "How did you sleep?"

"Not well," she admitted. "You?"

"How could I?" he said in an undertone. "Did you notice that disagreeable odor? I suppose some kind of foodstuff has turned, but wouldn't you think they'd throw it out?"

"I doubt that it was food." She set down her cup of tea, suddenly unsure that her stomach would tolerate it.

Luke paused in the act of drinking. "Then what the devil . . . ?"

"I believe it originated from a decomposing body. The gravehouses are right outside the back wall, you know." Acid rose in her throat. "They are often in poor repair. I've seen dogs dragging away a human leg."

"Gad!" He set down his cup as well, tea untouched. "I assumed that the bodies were at least placed in boxes."

"Most often they are, but the Indians don't seem to have our abhorrence of corpses. When a man dies, they set the body up at the rear of the house, paint his face, and place a dancing-hat on his head. Then they sing mourning songs, and dance, and put tobacco in the fire, by which means it supposedly goes to the dead one in the Land of Souls."

"Not so different from our practice of laying out the body," he suggested.

She shuddered. "Yes, but then they carry the corpse out the rear of the house in a grave box and leave it as though it had no more significance. Nobody seems to give it another thought, unless the man was a chief or a medicine man. But even when a chief's body is transferred to the *xet*, it's often only a few steps from the house. You've seen many of them. Father worked to convince the Indians that the practice was unsanitary, and in Skidegate, most of those who die are buried in the cemetery now."

"Then the missionaries accomplished one worthwhile purpose." They sat in silence for a moment before he added, "Just as well we don't spend another night here."

She uttered a fervent, "Amen."

A moment passed; then he said meditatively, "I suppose the deserted villages have similar gravehouses. I wouldn't mind collecting a few skulls. If I can escape our worthy guide's sharp eye . . ."

"Why do you want skulls?" she asked with distaste.

"Mmm?" He roused from his reverie. "Physical anthropology is nearly as interesting and useful as cultural, you know. We can learn quite a lot from measuring and examining skeletons. For example, how are we to discover which racial groups are related? Are the Haida necessarily of the same stock as the Nootka down south, or even the Tsimshian? They are certainly taller and fairer-complected than other Northwest Coast Indians. I should like to measure a number of crania. I must remember to do so with each stop."

More people were appearing; breakfast in a number of forms was being cooked on the fire. Kate was annoyed at herself for her squeamishness, but she could not bring herself to eat at all, far less the *k'aw*—preserved herring spawn—she was offered.

Luke, too, declined the *k'aw,* though he at least was sipping his tea. She had given him food for thought, which apparently supplanted the need for the more usual kind intended for the stomach. His contemplative expression no doubt indicated his intentions to take part in ghoulish activities that she hoped she would not be required to photograph.

When the chief at length made his appearance, Luke opened negotiations for the coveted Chilkat blanket. As they seemed to be managing well enough in Chinook, Kate returned to her sleeping area long enough to brush and braid her hair. The odor was less noticeable this morning, either because it competed with the smell of food cooking or because her thoughts were less fanciful. Or perhaps "nightmarish" was the right word.

She felt more herself when she returned to the fray. Luke's offer had risen to thirty-five dollars, which the chief was seriously considering, though he pretended to wave it off.

Luke glanced at her with relief. "Tell him I can buy one elsewhere if he is adamantly against selling."

The main obstacle, it developed, was that the chief was reluctant to part with his blanket right before the winter ceremonies. It was part of his costume; he would be ashamed to speak at a potlatch or to dance in a ceremony without it. Perhaps in the spring . . .

"Is that a firm commitment?" Luke demanded. "He'll sell it to me in the spring?"

"Apparently," Kate replied. She listened again to the chief. "For forty dollars, he says."

"That's highway robbery!" Luke shot to his feet. "Blast it, thirty-five is my top price!"

The chief appeared gratified by such a show of emotion. He might take thirty-seven or thirty-eight. In the spring.

Luke had to be content with the vague promise.

Kate suggested, "Let me see if he'll allow me to photograph him wearing his regalia out in the daylight."

Their host agreed with alacrity. While Gao and Luke loaded the canoe with Luke's purchases and some foodstuffs that were urged upon them, Kate set up her camera on the beach. She positioned the chief before his house, so that the fine frontal pole and a memorial pole crowned by a black-painted raven were in the photograph. He had donned not only his Chilkat blanket, but a conical hat handsomely painted with his crest figures, and he held two prized coppers.

Kate had come to rely on Wynne's Infallible Exposure Meter, which used sensitized paper to measure light. She had just determined the proper exposure when she was startled by Luke's voice from behind her.

"I don't suppose he would sell one of those."

"Why do you always sneak up on me?" she asked in exasperation. She ducked under the cloth and peered through the camera's aperture at the upside-down image of the chief to check her focal point. "If you mean the coppers, I doubt that you could afford them. Each may be worth a thousand blankets or more."

Even that price didn't convey the value the Indians placed on the shieldlike sheets of beaten copper, engraved with crest designs through a coating of black lead. The copper enhanced, even symbolized, a chief's status; its name, such as "Making-the-House-Empty-of-Blankets," glorified him.

Luke grumbled something, a snatch of which she caught: "If only the trustees understood how rapidly the fine artifacts are vanishing."

She had finished her photographing when shortly thereafter, Gao hunted down Kun taos and they made their goodbyes, which involved dragging the canoe over a beach exposed by a low tide. Tiny crabs scuttled out of the way and Kate stepped warily on the slick seaweed.

Birds were everywhere, feeding on the tidbits left behind by the tide. Flocks of crows mingled with gulls, and as two boys ran down the beach waving sticks and shouting, the air whistled with the wing beats of escaping goldeneyes and geese that settled back down in the boys' wake. Near the water's edge, a blue heron took ponderously to the air.

Once *Dancing Canoe* was afloat, they followed the shore for some distance. Kate was delighted to see a bald eagle, tempted by the rich fare, in the undignified position of quarreling with a raucous gull over some prize.

For the first time, snow could be seen on the upper reaches of the mountains. Moresby Island, to the south, was little more than a mountain range rising from the water; the rocky slopes plunged into the strait, with few safe landfalls. It was no wonder the Haida knew little about the interior of their islands, when so much of the land was inhospitable.

Yet the shores of Skidegate Inlet were less bold, the land heavily wooded with spruce and cedar trees of remarkable size. Many tiny islands dotted the inlet, most of them little more than a tumble of rocks with a few stunted trees clinging for purchase.

It was mid-morning before they neared the small, rocky islet that contained the burial of a Skidegate medicine man. The short trip had been passed in near silence, the others seemingly as content as Kate to enjoy the chill sunshine and the sight of dark V's of geese passing overhead to warmer climes. As they approached this particular isle, Kun taos gestured. A building of some sort could be seen perched near the water's edge. The young Haida man's cheerfulness of yesterday was now gone; Kate thought that he looked fearful, and perhaps regretted his mention of this place.

"Did you know this medicine man?" Luke asked Gao.

The strokes of Gao's paddle varied not at all, their regularity nearly machine-like. The paddle dipped, pulled, rose and returned to the beginning. Droplets shimmered on its length, as though they were tears shed by the creatures painted thereon.

"Yes," Gao said. "He died ten, or maybe it was twelve, years ago. He was strong and much feared. He chose this place for his body."

Seen closer, the building was an unimpressive, boxlike hovel perhaps five feet square. It was constructed of split cedar boards, neatly joined, with a roof similarly made, on which large stones had been piled to keep the whole firm. A board on the water's side could be seen to have fallen out. Atop the structure sat two glossy ravens, so still they might have been carved and painted decoration. Their presence made Kate wonder; had the *ska-ga*'s spirit helper been Raven?

Though there was no beach, Gao and Kun taos were able to bring the canoe alongside a slanted gray boulder. Luke leaped out and turned to reach back for Kate, who gathered her skirt and followed. For a second, she felt herself falling back and was grateful for the warm strength of Luke's hand. Although she wore a pair of sturdy, laced boots, the high, narrow heels were still a distinct disadvantage. Behind her, Gao leaped nimbly out after a few words with Kun taos, who showed no inclination to follow, even had he not been required to stay with the canoe.

The moment she and the two men turned to face the crude shelter, the two ravens rose with a heavy beat of powerful wings. Yet they were otherwise silent as they retreated only as far as the branch of a stunted tree, where they settled to watch the human intruders.

Despite their presence, Kate felt no superstitious dread, but neither did she share Luke's eagerness. Her dream of the night before was too vivid in her recollections. Nonetheless, her curiosity insisted that she stoop beside Luke to see into the gravehouse.

Light fell through the opening in the front left by the wide plank, enabling them to see that the wall farthest from the water was covered by a cedar-bark mat. Wrapped in a large red blanket, the body leaned against this, having been placed in a sitting position. The long black hair, still glossy, was wound into a knot atop the head, with bone pins stuck through. In one corner was propped a carved stick, such as a chief or a dignitary carried on ceremonial occasions, and in front of the *ska'ga*'s knees sat a square cedar box that no doubt held the tools of his trade.

The face sent a shudder through Kate. Despite the damp climate and the many years since the medicine man had died, it was not a skull that gazed sightlessly toward them. Instead, the flesh had partly dried on the bones, giving the countenance a mummy-like aspect. It was not often that one gazed at the dead, and she felt the need for some sort of gesture to ward off evil, or to offer benediction. Had she been Catholic, she would have crossed herself.

"Interesting." Luke shifted to get a look into all the corners. He kept his voice low. "I'd give a great deal to see what's in that box. If you could distract Gao . . ."

"You promised," Kate reminded him.

He gave a hunted look over his shoulder at the Indian, who watched implacably. "Devil take it," he muttered. "What was I thinking of to hire him? Another one like Kun taos, docile and anxious to please . . ."

"But Gao is intelligent, speaks English, and understands what you want."

"And is determined to prevent me from *having* what I want."

She countered, "Is it so unreasonable to ask that you not desecrate the graves of their dead?"

He grunted. "You told me yourself that they don't care a tinker's damn about their graves."

"I believe," she said thoughtfully, "that a medicine man's grave is different. Kun taos looked frightened."

Luke made another, noncommittal noise, but she had restored him to reason. He straightened and said to Gao, "Have you seen the bodies of other medicine men? Is it true that none decay?"

"It would be bad luck if you saw a skeleton only."

"Are there any other beliefs connected with graves such as this?"

There was generally a brief pause before Gao answered a question; Kate was never sure whether translating was a laborious business for him or whether he was considering how much he wanted to reveal. This time, he replied in Haida, and Kate rendered his words into English even as he continued to speak.

"I have heard a story. There is another *ska-ga* entombed near Skit-ei-get Village. A man was coming home just as the sky was closing—at twilight," she amended. "He looked toward where he knew the gravehouse to be, and he saw the *ska-ga* himself, standing outside with his rattle in his hand. The man ran home very frightened and told people what he saw. He knew it to be an evil omen. That same year, his wife, brother, brother's wife, and two sisters went to Victoria. All died of the smallpox there."

A chill feathered Kate's spine. The tale seemed to have no such effect on Luke, who only inquired, "Do you believe that the two events were connected?"

Gao hesitated, shrugged. "Who knows what to believe? Supernatural beings can show themselves in many ways. I do not make them small by my thoughts, any more than you would do to your Great Chief Above."

Luke gave one of his interested noises. "Have yourself ever seen a supernatural being? Or had a vision?"

This silence was even longer than usual. A breeze

wrapped Kate's skirt around her legs and she cast an uneasy glance over her shoulder at the bar of sunlight that lay across the shriveled face. For a second, she thought she saw movement, as though the *ska-ga* had turned his head, but of course that was impossible. Wind found its way through the cracks between planks, the red blanket might have been stirred.

She spoke up. "Oughtn't we . . ."

But Gao did not seem to hear her. He spoke as though the remembering had gripped him. "I was ill once, so that I could not eat for days. The spirits found me because I was clean. People told me later that I was near death, so cleaned of bad things that you could see through me like glass. I didn't know that; I felt good, better than I had ever felt before. I saw a circle of shamans around a big crab in the sea. They tried to throw the crab on me. If they had made that crab go over my shoulders, I would have become a shaman, too. I was afraid, because I didn't want to be one." He broke off abruptly and looked past Kate to the medicine man's tomb with the first hint of fear she had seen on his face. "I should not have talked so here. It is not respectful. A *ska-ga* is a powerful thing to be, but I did not feel as if I were that strong. I am strong only when I carve in wood or on the soft stone."

Luke had the expression of a keen hunter who had cornered a deer. "Is that how one brings on a vision deliberately? By going hungry?"

"It is good to clean yourself thus," Gao said. "You will have better luck hunting if you fast. Now we should go."

"Wait! Kate, can you photograph the interior of the tomb?"

She didn't want to. Her reaction was one of utter abhorrence. To matter-of-factly set up her equipment, fussing about the composition just as she would when taking a portrait, seemed horrible to her. And to have to see the face again and again when she developed the plates, hung the results up to dry like laundry, checked their progress!

One of the few times she'd had a commission, it had

come from a young woman whose infant was stillborn. The bereaved mother had wanted, in the style of the day, to have a sentimental portrait of the babe, an aim that Aunt Grace had thought proper.

"But surely it's better to forget!" Kate had protested in her innocence. "No photographer has the skill to prettify death! I know I do not!"

"She doesn't ask you for a miracle. She seeks only to ensure that her memory does not play her false someday. It is so easy to forget . . ." Aunt Grace broke off.

Kate could not deny the young woman's request after that, for she had seen the pain that her aunt—who had miscarried several times and lost two infants within days of their birth—could not hide. But the doing had been nightmarish; Kate had done her best to block from her mind the pathos she photographed, concentrating only on the technical details, taking care not to expose the same plate twice . . . for it was one portrait that could not be retaken if she later discovered she had erred.

Now Kate rebuked herself. This was hardly the same thing. She didn't have to deal with the mother's grief or her own deep pity for an innocent who, through some cruel twist of fate, would never suckle at its mother's breast, or smile, or walk. This had been a grown man, perhaps even one who had died of old age. She did not believe in the powers a medicine man claimed to control. Why should she fear a corpse, or be in awe of it?

Nonetheless, she worked hastily. The only difficulty was in keeping lit the two candles required for her flash device. However Luke shaded them with his hand, they persisted in flickering out. At last he hung halfway into the gravehouse, one arm wrapped around the candles and his shoulders hunched over them like a protective father.

"Hurry!" he exclaimed.

"You must remove your arm," she reminded him.

"Yes, yes, don't delay."

She signaled him, the white light flared, and she released the shutter. It was done, whether successfully or not, she wouldn't know until tomorrow. There was no point in using a second plate; she had calculated the correct exposure to the best of her ability, taken equal care to ensure a sharp focus.

As she packed up her camera, Luke bent for a last, lingering look into the gravehouse. She ignored the question she assumed was directed at Gao, who had hovered anxiously in the background.

"Do you know what's in the box?"

"Only another shaman can take something," Gao said flatly. "No one else. We should go."

Kate handed Luke her camera, safely enclosed in its case. In a low voice, she said, "He won't trust you again if you don't cooperate now."

He snatched the tripod from her. "Some private collector is sure to find this place and ransack it! If I could just look . . . Blast it, I'm coming."

Kun taos shoved them off from the isle even before Luke, the last to leap into the canoe, had found his seat on the thwart. Kate grabbed her camera as it tipped when the canoe rolled in the first swell. She did not remonstrate, however, as she shared the Haida man's eagerness. Thank goodness they were not spending the night in this locale! Last night's dreams had been ghastly enough. Before she slept again, she wanted to be far away from here.

He had been foolish to think he could keep the man from taking things, Gao thought. If Luke wanted, he would just go back. If he didn't, somebody else would take it all. Gao was beginning to wonder why he should care, when no one else did. He had talked to people at Haina and told them not to sell to this man, but he saw how full were the bags Luke put in the canoe that morning. People didn't think it mattered how much they sold. They liked the *yetz haada* things better anyway.

Luke wasn't a bad man, Gao thought. When Gao said something, Luke listened without scoffing. He wanted to learn about the Haida, not to just buy their things, but in the end, what did it matter? He would go away in the spring, taking the stories and songs and masks with him. People would never see any of their things again, and when next winter came, they would be sorry not to have the masks and blankets and rattles that showed how the spirits came into them when they danced.

He took Luke and Kate to Lina Village, on the east end of Lina Island. He knew they would find nothing there but some poles that had begun to lean, and the gravehouses behind the main row. It had never been a big village. When people left, they took the planks off the houses to use on the new ones they built wherever they went. Only the supporting timbers remained behind, except in a few places where bark shelters had been made by fishermen. Nobody had lived here in Gao's memory, though the place was sheltered from the sea and storms by small islands and the arm of the bay. Salal and spruce seedlings were growing from cracks in the beams and poles. He saw a weasel glare at them from beneath a grave box that had fallen from its base and split open.

He didn't like such places. In not so many more years, the last poles here would have fallen and even the timbers would have split and rotted. The forest would have grown over this town and nobody would remember where it had been. Would Skit-ei-get be as empty soon? With so many still dying, and so few babies being born, more towns would be left to the ghosts. Maybe the time would come when no people were left on Haida Gwai, when the dark, secretive forests crept down to the shore and the great cedar trees thrust their roots through the last carved faces of Grizzly Bear and Raven.

He shook his head, ashamed that only a few deserted houses could make him see ghosts everywhere. He was still alive, wasn't he? The smallpox might have killed everybody if Hewitt had not come, bringing with him the scratch on the arm that kept one safe from the disease that was said to sail in a canoe with huge white wings. Gao's grandfather claimed that when the first *yetz haada* anchored offshore, people believed their ships to be the canoes of Pestilence, which legend said would arrive so. At first they changed their minds and thought the coming of these strange people who paid so much for sea-otter skins was good; but then they found that, after all, Pestilence had traveled in the ships with wings. Gao had not liked the missionary, but he could not hate him as he would have liked, because his medicine had saved the people who were left. Instead of saying that here it comes to a stop, they could now think that they might make a knot, like a storyteller does when the story is too long to finish in one night. People could know that tomorrow would still come. Who knew what it might bring?

Gao started a small fire and roasted some potatoes for them to eat. He let Kate and Luke wander all they wanted. There was nothing here to take but bones, and he would see those if Luke tried to put them in the canoe. Kun taos sat in the sun and didn't do anything useful. He was like that, lazy, but Gao never minded. Kun taos's parents were nobodys, they couldn't even potlatch for him. Maybe that was where he got his laziness. But he could be trusted in the canoe, and he always had luck at hunting and fishing, so he was a good one to be with.

But it wasn't Kun taos he wanted to think about. Gao had noticed something today. It was the way that Kate looked at Luke when Luke couldn't see, as though she would like to lie with him. Did white people lie together if they were not husband and wife? Gao remembered his sister telling him that Kate had said the *yetz haada* married later than the Haida did. He wondered whether Kate's parents had promised her to somebody.

Gao himself would have been married by now if the girl had not died. Her name had been Sit kwuns—Red Moon. When Sit kwuns was born, her mother had given Gao's mother many blankets. After that, he could not marry anybody else without paying the blankets back. Sit kwuns would have made a good wife, he thought; she was not pretty, but she was graceful and shy, not one to talk too much. She had died of the smallpox just before the missionary came and gave the scratch—he called it a "vaccination"—against the sickness. Gao's own parents had died near the same time, and he quit thinking about marrying.

This last year, he had taken notice of a girl named Jadal, whose family had not chosen a husband for her. They were noble, and in other times, they could have looked higher than Gao for their daughter. But today there were not so many young men to choose from.

She was young, only now becoming a woman. He had not seen her for some time, because she had reached the age where she must sit behind a screen and stay to herself for twenty or thirty days, and even after that, she must be careful where she went and what she did. She could not eat salmon, or else they might become scarce. If she walked on the beach below the highwater mark, she would make the tide come in, and then the other women could not dig clams or pry chitons off the rocks.

When these things happened to a girl, everybody knew she was ready to be married. Gao had sent his aunt to talk to Jadal's mother, but her family was not sure. They had not let their daughter do much work and had told her to lie in bed late, so that she would marry a chief and never have to work hard. Gao might be a good husband, they said, but would their daughter be a chief-woman or more like a slave?

Gao would have liked to have many blankets and other things to show them, but without working in the cannery this year, he had not been able to save very much. But if he could hold a great potlatch in the spring and give away enough to earn respect, maybe her family would see that he could take care of her well.

When Kate and Luke came back from looking around, Gao was still thinking about Jadal, about the way she smiled bashfully when she saw him, as though she thought more of him than she should of a man of whom her family had not approved.

Kate smiled at Gao and said, "Bless you, I'm starved. Don't we have some berry cakes, too?"

"Here," Gao said, shaking away thoughts as foolish as his

earlier ones. Her family had not promised; he might find in
the spring that Jadal was already married to someone else.
He opened a cedar box that was packed to the top with
berries and roots put up in cakes. There was seaweed, too,
and smoked salmon. Their host last night had been generous.

"Gao, do you know the history of this village?" Luke
asked. "Is it the only one on this island?"

"No, there were others a long time ago. Some people at
Skit-ei-get were always fighting with their neighbors, so
they came here to get away from it. They made Gambling-
Sticks Village, around that way." He gestured to the south.
"And Drum Village was another that was not far away. I
heard a story that the chief there had so much food that when
everyone was going hungry, he invited them to a potlatch
and fed them all until they were well again.

"That was so long ago, I don't know any more. People
lived here at this village since then, but they all died or else
they went to Skit-ei-get, I don't know."

Luke gave the grunt that meant he was pleased by what he
heard. "Do we still have time to take a look at the coal mine?"

Gao glanced at the sun, which was never high in the sky
in this digging month, when the bears were getting ready to
hibernate. "Yes, but we should go now."

"I'm ready," Luke said.

Kate nodded, and Kun taos kicked dirt onto the small fire.

It was nearly as far to that old mine as it was in the other
direction to Skit-ei-get, but the tide was still sweeping in.
That made paddling easy. If they timed it right, the outgoing
tide would help them return to Skit-ei-get, too.

The water was blue and choppy, and The One-in-the-Sea
was dressed up in fluffy white clouds that the wind pulled
into long, thin pieces, like a blanket torn into strips. Northwest Wind always brought clear skies and cold. The weather
would be good for travel for a few days, at least.

Gao pointed to the north and said, "There is a stream over
there that comes from that mountain. It is where we get the
black stone to carve."

"Do you do any carving in argillite?" Luke asked.

"Sometimes to sell," Gao said.

This *yetz haada* had a way of almost looking through you, as though he knew your thoughts just like Power-of-the-Shining-Heavens did.

"Could you carve a model of a totem pole in argillite?"

Something hopeful lifted its head in Gao's breast. What could it hurt, making a copy? He had too much respect for himself to carve things to sell from a blanket when the steamboats tied up at Skit-ei-get. Those were trinkets bought by people who didn't care what the carved faces meant. Luke did care about the stories. Many people would see Gao's carving in the museum.

"Yes," Gao said, "if you told me which one you wanted. It would take a few weeks."

"Splendid!" Luke exclaimed. "Can you work as we travel this winter?"

Gao thought. "I have some of the slate. I could bring it."

"Good."

A salmon, long and fat still, jumped not far away. Then there was another, and another. An eagle screamed and circled overhead, choosing its meal.

The sun had crawled only a little farther before Gao saw the wharf ahead, which he remembered. It was long and still solid, with barnacles crusting the part that was down in the water. Even with the tide in, the wharf was too high for them to use. It had been built for steamboats. They beached *Dancing Canoe* in the cove to the north and walked back. Even Kun taos was curious.

"They must have poured money into this place," Luke said. "That dock is a good six hundred feet long. And you say they never got any decent coal out?"

"Years of work, and I believe they finally sent half a shipload to Victoria." Kate veered toward the buildings. "These are still in good repair." She rubbed a spot clean on a small window to look inside.

"Men slept there," Gao said. "They ate in a different building."

Kun taos cleared another place in the glass and gazed in

wonderingly at the rows of bunks and the round black stove in which they had built fires to stay warm. "Why would you need two houses, one for sleeping and one for eating?" he asked. Gao had no answer, and Kate had moved on and didn't hear him.

Big stumps showed where giant trees had been cut down for the lumber, but the tram rails disappeared into the forest. Gao followed almost reluctantly when Luke, carrying a hurricane lamp, began striding along the tracks. The rails were laid on a trail that had been built up to make the ride smooth. In places, they were twisted where the ground had sunk. Moss, as soft as an otter's coat, grew over everything, making even their footsteps silent. Ghosts lived in places like this, or wild men. Gao thought that he had been both brave and foolish when he was younger.

The rail line crossed a small creek and then a larger one. Both murmured softly. Gao could feel the eyes of the Creek Woman. All was a deep green here. Moss clung in the shape of balls to the branches of the trees. They would not have been able to walk had the rail line not been here. Undergrowth grew too thickly, and beneath it were trees that had fallen and were rotting as others grew atop them.

At last they saw the dark opening of a tunnel ahead. It was just a glimpse; the entrance was screened by salal and huckleberry and ferns. Luke's voice sounded very loud when he said, "The line continues. Are there other shafts?"

Kate sounded hushed in contrast, as though she felt the secretive presence around them as Gao did. "Yes, I think there were several. Shall we go on?"

Luke was poking around. "Hmm. Yes, these beams look rotten. I wouldn't care to go far in here." He shoved aside greenery and stepped in, swallowed by the darkness.

Kate began, "Then don't—"

He reappeared, shaking his head to rid it of twigs. "I wonder if they found any fossils as they excavated."

Gao didn't know what fossils were, or understand "excavated," but he didn't ask. He was too uneasy. Even the air was heavy, redolent with things he couldn't comprehend.

When they started again, Kun taos stepped on Gao's heels, so closely did he follow him, but Gao didn't say anything. They had gone only a few more feet anyway when a dark hole opened ahead of them. Gao knew that men had blasted it out, but it made him think that Sacred-One-Standing-and-Moving was yawning. Or maybe this was a way of getting down to a killer-whale town.

They had all stopped, though Luke was lighting the lantern. "Geology is an interest of mine. I wouldn't mind getting a look at the layers of sediment here."

The rest of them hesitated when he disappeared into the tunnel. Kate finally said reluctantly, "I suppose . . ."

Gao made himself take a few steps, passing her. He could smell the pungent earth and the rock, undisturbed for so long.

Luke's voice ahead echoed, making him sound farther away than he could be this soon. Gao couldn't understand him at first, until he said, "Now this is looking like slate. Gao, is this what you use for carving . . . Damnation!" A clatter, and then silence.

"Luke?" Kate called. She was right behind Gao. "Did you fall?"

"I tripped over something. Let me see." Another small silence, then, "Gao!" he roared.

Gao went, even though he didn't like the dark hole. Somebody stepped on his heel again, but this time, it was Kate. He kept his eyes fixed on the small beam of light from the lantern. It seemed far away, but wasn't. It had been partly shielded from their sight by Luke, who was kneeling beside something that lay at his feet.

A strangled sound came from Kate. Gao felt cold. It was a skeleton that Luke had stumbled over, a human skeleton lying facedown. There was no flesh on these bones, only the tattered remnants of clothes and some black hair clinging to the skull—a skull that had been smashed in from behind.

Chapter Eleven

D amnation!" Luke was the first to speak. "Kate, send
Kun taos back to the canoe to fetch torches. We'd best
conduct a further search of the tunnel."

Kate translated; Kun taos nodded and made his way back
to the entrance. The others waited in silence, staring at the
grisly remains. What was saddest and most frightening to
Kate was how little these bones and bits of clothing had to
tell. Only one fact was clear: He, or she, had been murdered.

Kun taos must have run, because he returned before the
wait became unbearable. He had lit both of the branches,
which were dipped in pitch to burn with a high, hot fire.
Luke gave the hurricane lamp to Kate, and he and Gao carried the torches. Leaving Kun taos with the remains, the
three advanced deeper into the earth. The firelight danced
unevenly off the rough walls and the beams that supported
the roof. Kate found it hard to draw a breath, and she longed
to turn and run out of the place. Her companions looked no
happier. In the shifting light of the torches, the two men's
faces were tight.

Not twenty yards farther, they came upon a second skeleton. The dampness and the worms and the crawling insects had ensured that again only bones and some few fragments of clothing were left. This skull, too, had been shattered.

Gao knelt beside the remains. Luke lifted his torch high and said, "There's a box over here. No, two."

Kate followed the few steps to the bent-cedar boxes piled one atop the other on one side of the tunnel. The painted figures that decorated the lid of the top box seemed to shiver and move in the flickering light. Luke passed her the torch and used both hands to unwedge the lid, stuck tight perhaps because the wood had swelled and warped in the dampness. Even as he lifted it, Kate gave a cry.

"Skulls."

Gao stood. Despite the shadows, she could see how closed and angry was his expression.

"We'd better see what's in the other one," Luke said. "Gao, give me a hand."

The men carefully lifted the first box off the other. Its lid, similarly pried off, revealed more of the same. Skulls were stacked in a jumble within, empty eye sockets staring up beside the smooth bones of other skulls that lay upside down or sideways.

"Somebody didn't dare come back once murder had been done," Luke said grimly. "Gao, is there anything left on either body that will give us a clue as to their identity?"

"I found a bracelet," the Indian said. "It was underneath the second one. He might have had it in a pocket, so it was not seen."

He held it up, the sheen of silver evident through the tarnish despite the poor lighting.

"We'll take a look at it outside. In the meantime, I suppose we'd best go on and see what else is to be found." Luke sounded no happier than Kate felt, but of course it had to be done. "Kate, it looks to me like the tunnel narrows ahead. You wait here, and keep the bracelet."

Gao handed it over without protest, and he and Luke continued, leaving her to the macabre companionship of a skeleton and what must be two dozen human skulls. To stave off her fear of the dark and the heavy earth above, Kate held up the lantern and studied the boxes of skulls more closely.

She didn't know enough about the decomposition that follows death to hazard even a guess at how long had passed since the double murder. Months? Years? But the skulls were clearly of great antiquity. The bone had darkened; there were cracks, and places where sharp edges had crumbled. They had been removed from gravehouses, she supposed, presumably to sell to someone such as Luke.

Had the two murdered men been hired to help hide pilfered items here deep in the earth until a purchaser could be found? Perhaps there had been other things of more value, things worth the risk of retrieval even after the dreadful deed had been done. She made a careful search and found scrapes on the earthen ground indicating that something had been dragged, something with a flat bottom and clean edges. Another box. And another over there, she saw.

How much were the skulls worth? She would have to ask Luke. A few dollars apiece? Even at five dollars, the whole cache would be worth only a hundred and twenty-five dollars or so. Surely not enough to justify murder!

No, she wasn't thinking straight. The skulls had been abandoned. Had they been the cause of the killings, they would be gone. The two men had been bludgeoned from behind, one at a time, for another reason: because of a betrayal, or to ensure their silence.

She knew of only one crime of such severity that might compel a desperate man to murder in order to hide it. Another murder. Her father's? Could these be the men who had taken her father to his death? Who might not have killed him themselves, but knew who had?

She was conjecturing only, but her speculation made sense. A second crime to cover the first, and a reason, possibly, for her father's murder: stolen Indian artifacts, and even skeletons. Had her father in outrage discovered some part of the scheme and thus become a threat to it?

If so, the disappearance of a portion of his collection might be linked. It had probably long since been sold! Might Luke himself, or James Durham, unknowingly have bought some part of it?

Kate felt cold, and was grateful to see the returning flare of torches. When they neared, she called, "Did you find any more?"

"No, thank God," Luke answered. Rather than his voice echoing, it seemed to be swallowed, muffled by the soft material from which the walls had been gouged out. "The tunnel curves—it must be six hundred feet or more long—but we found nothing else to suggest recent occupancy."

"It looks to me," Kate said, "as though other boxes have come and gone. See here—" she directed the flickering light of her lamp "—and here."

Luke made an unhappy sound. "I suggest we leave all as it is, save for the bracelet. Gao, before we go, can you tell anything from the designs painted on the cedar boxes to suggest who made them or where they came from?"

Gao looked, but seemed unsure. One drawing depicted a bird that he thought was Hawk, but might be Horned Owl. On the other box, there was an upside-down creature between the ears of a human-like face.

"It might be Dzelaqons. She married a chief of the Grizzly Bear People. But it is hard to know." Gao stepped back and shrugged. "Both figures are common. They do not tell me who owned these boxes."

"I suppose that was hoping for too much," Luke said heavily. "Well, I suggest we depart."

The minute Kun taos saw them, he uttered a spate of Haida. Where had they been? What had they found? He had looked at the bits of clothes and thought he recognized them.

Gao made a sharp gesture, as though to silence his friend, but it came too late.

"Ah," Luke said. "I thought you might know. Kate, the bracelet?"

She handed it over. Outside in the daylight, Gao and Kun taos huddled over the wide silver band. Even she could see that the central motif was Raven, but the highly stylized creatures that would wrap around the wrist of the wearer were less easily identified.

If the bracelet had actually belonged to the dead man, finding it was a piece of tremendous good fortune. The crest figures that were carved or incised on nearly every object a Haida used, from the mortuary poles to a simple dish, were specific to certain groups. An entire lineage might use the cormorant, while one family alone had the right to display the mountain goat, and a chief might jealously guard his prerogative to the starfish motif. Thus the sum of an individual's crest figures told of his ancestry and family in a way that identified him quite specifically.

Silver bracelets, however, were customarily worn not by men, but by women. Could the skeleton have belonged to a woman? Queasily, Kate thought not. The bones had been thick, the pelvis not as wide as she would expect of a woman.

Kun taos and Gao seemed to have reached a decision. They faced Luke, who casually crossed his arms. "What can you tell me?"

Gao looked at Kate for a moment, then at Luke. "We think these were two men from Skidegate. They have not been seen in a long time. People said they had gone to live up north, with the Kaigani Haida. But nobody was sure."

"You knew them well?"

Gao's gaze dropped, revealing shame that must be painful to him. "They were ones who sometimes caused trouble. Iyea was close to me, a son of one of my mother's sisters. This bracelet, I think, was my aunt's. Xaosti was Eagle. Him I didn't know so well."

"Iyea," Kate repeated slowly. "I believe I remember him. He worked for Sims one season, and he stole some tools."

"Sometimes he did not show respect for himself," Gao said impassively.

"When did these men leave Skidegate?" Luke asked.

Kate almost held her breath as she waited for the answer. Unable to understand what was being said, Kun taos looked from one to the other of them, his anxiety plain.

"I was not here when the missionary disappeared." Gao's answer was reluctant. "But it is said that they went away about the same time. I did not know that the two things went together, but I thought sometimes that they might."

"Why didn't you tell me?" Kate asked.

"I didn't know," he said stubbornly.

So. Here, at last, was the explanation for the peculiar reception she had received in Skidegate. All Haida were born members of one of two groups, Raven or Eagle. Iyea was a Raven and a member of a prominent family, though a black sheep. His compatriot, Xaosti, was Eagle, and therefore related to everyone in Skidegate who was *not* related to Iyea. Thus all had guessed, and no one had wanted to speak.

It was good to know this much, at least. Unfortunately, Kate couldn't see that this new knowledge brought her any closer to discovering the Reverend Hewitt's murderer. Any white man in the Queen Charlottes might have been involved in selling Indian artifacts. But so, too, might a Haida. In either case, her father would have disapproved, and most certainly been outraged at the robbing of graves to sell the bones. If she had found Iyea or Xaosti alive . . . But it was not to be. The murderer had seen to that.

Durham is gone."

Luke had tracked Kate down to her darkroom, set up in a storage shed behind the Mission House. To protect her work from possible damage by light, she had hung two blankets a few feet inside the small building's one door, thus forming a sort of vestibule. One could enter, shut the door, then push aside one of the blankets and proceed the rest of the way in. It was fortunate that she had done so; Luke had come stomping in with a heedlessness soon explained.

"Blast it, Durham couldn't have properly prepared so quickly! But he was determined to beat me to the southern villages, and I was foolish enough to give him the opportunity!" He paced the small space, his gestures extravagant enough to express the emotions she couldn't see on his face in the dim lighting provided by the one candle encased in a red glass jar.

"Do be careful!" she remonstrated. "This table is not very sturdy. You'll spill my chemicals."

His pacing slowed, although he otherwise ignored her. "How soon can you be ready to depart? We must make haste; I refuse to spend the winter ignominiously trailing that scoundrel around the islands!"

She carefully lifted a plate from the tub containing a pyro-gallic acid solution and examined it. From the front, its highlights were strong and distinct; from the back, the broad outlines of the darkest parts were visible. Satisfied, she rinsed the plate in water, then placed it in the fixing bath.

"I should be finished with developing these negatives today," she said thoughtfully. "It would be tomorrow before I could print them, but unless you're anxious to see the results, the printing could be delayed until our return."

"They would be safe for some months?"

"Yes, certainly. And even at this stage, it's possible with a little imagination to see how they'll come out. Look at these, for example." She indicated the plates that had already been fixed and thoroughly washed and now were drying in the crude rack she had devised for the purpose.

The images were reversed in coloration, the dark portions light and vice versa, but the outlines of a house, two poles, and the man who stood in the foreground were clear.

"Haina." Luke's tone had changed. In his mercurial fashion, he had entered fully into the pleasure of studying the results of her work. "It's possible to see all the detail I had hoped for! What about the shaman's burial? Have you come to that one yet?"

"Yes, right here." Kate lifted a plate from the bath of water she had changed innumerable times today. "It took somewhat longer because I feared it might be underexposed, but I believe the result is satisfactory."

Indeed, the lines on this plate, too, were sharply defined. Because the color was reversed, the features of the skeletal face would not be clear until the negative was printed, but she had confidence that this photograph would be the equal of her best work. She would not care to keep a print of this image for her own collection, however.

"Hah!" Luke exclaimed. "Thompson couldn't have done any better."

"Thompson?"

"The photographer whom I had hired, the one who failed to show up."

"Umm." Her hands were occupied by rinsing another plate, but her thoughts had moved on. "When did Mister Durham depart? Wasn't he in the crowd yesterday?"

"He left early this morning." Luke scowled again and resumed his pacing. "Before first light even. It's just like him to skulk away in this cowardly fashion."

"Surely an early departure was only common sense," Kate suggested.

To no avail. "He might have mentioned his intentions! He knew mine!"

Kate opened her mouth to argue, but gave up when a knock sounded at the door. "Can you see to that?" she asked Luke.

He was gone for some time, so long in fact that she thought he had proceeded to set in train their preparations for an early departure of their own. She was relieved, or at least she told herself that relief was what she felt. The alternative was to admit that she was so physically aware of him, she couldn't be comfortable when locked with him in such close quarters.

Ridiculous! she decided firmly. It was only that he was a large man whose vitality and intelligence fairly vibrated in the air around him, with the result that he was difficult to ignore. He had been distracting, and she didn't like to be pulled two ways. Back in Victoria, she had been secretly annoyed when Alice visited her darkroom, too, and relieved when her cousin left.

Kate became occupied again by her work, as enthralling in its own way, and requiring as great a skill, as the actual taking of the photographs in the first place. The solutions could be varied to achieve different purposes, alleviating under- or overexposure, enhancing the natural appearance of features that did not photograph well, such as the sky. The fumes in here were strong, but she had long ago become accustomed to them, and to working in the dim red light.

Luke entered somewhat more cautiously this time. "That was Gao. We've been invited to a ceremony of some kind. I gather that it takes several days. I don't know if we'll want to linger so long, but it ought to be interesting."

"Did he say what the occasion is?"

"Company is expected this afternoon—from Masset, I believe. The ceremony is to initiate some young men into a dancing society. He said there would be tattoos and new names given. I'd like you to translate, so that I can get down the words to some of the songs."

"Very well," Kate said. "I should be finished here in an hour or so."

The evening's festivities were really rather tame, showing how much the Skidegate Haida had changed in a very few years.

Luke grasped Kate's arm to keep her firmly at his side when they joined the crowd on the beach to greet the visitors. She stiffened under his hand, but made no attempt to pull away. Those on the shore sang about brave deeds of the past, which Kate translated in an undertone. It was answered in a similar vein from the canoes. A cedar box with a hide stretched across the top was used as a drum to keep time, by which dancers swayed and gracefully waved their hands.

Suddenly two men rushed through the crowd and into the sea. Both were completely naked, their bodies blackened by charcoal. They carried something that they cast into the water in front of the canoes.

Kate's voice became constrained, reminding Luke of what an extraordinary sight this would be to most young women of her class. "They are slaves, throwing coppers away as a mark of honor to the guests," she told him.

"They throw away something so valuable?"

"Well, not exactly. As soon as the tide goes out, they will recover them."

"Ah." He returned his attention to the activities. The visitors were being assisted from their canoes; dancers with painted faces led the way in a procession to Nengkwigetklals's house.

Kate said, "Traditionally, the dancers would have been in costume. I suppose most of them have sold theirs."

He glanced sharply at her, but she was watching the last of the dancers vanish into the large house, followed by the small crowd. She looked sad, and he thought her observation had not been intended as a barb.

They, too, pushed their way into the crowded house and found a vantage point that allowed them a view of the rear, where Nengkwigetklals waited. Already sweating, Luke muttered, "This is worse than an overcrowded theater. Is the whole village here?"

"Probably." That note of sadness was in her voice again. "There was a time when not a tenth of the Skidegate Haida could have fit into one house. Samuel Frederick said that when he was a child, there was not room, even with the whole length of the beach, to launch all the canoes of the village in a single row. Now see how few they are."

Chastened by her observation, he looked around with a new eye, seeing how many of the faces were familiar. Beyond the fire, Nengkwigetklals was greeting the guests. He wore a handsome caribou robe, similar in effect to the Chilkat blanket. In his hand was a tall, intricately carved staff.

Kate whispered, "The staff is called the 'Chief's Talking Stick.' "

The garb of the visitors was in contrast. Most wore European clothing. One had a Chilkat blanket, not a particularly fine specimen, over his trousers and high-necked shirt.

Another wore a crimson-brocade smoking jacket. Navy uniforms seemed to be popular. The overall effect detracted from the atmosphere of primitive drama.

The incessantly gray daylight filtered through cracks in the plank walls and roof. The fire below was leaping high, the crowd within giving off body heat. The drumbeat distracted Luke from the chief's lengthy speech.

"What's he saying?"

"That his son goes to live with his mother's brother, to whom he will be heir, and that the boy's mother and father now wish to do him honor." Kate paused, adding, "What's happening is that he and his wife, who is technically the hostess, seek to have everyone here acknowledge that their son is entitled to be the heir to Nengkwigetklals's brother-in-law. It's like an election without a second candidate." She listened for a moment. "Now he's thanking the guests for coming, saying that he and his son are as mosquitoes that the guests could slap down, but instead permit to fly."

They were forced by the overcrowded room to stand, and even Luke began to weary of the speechifying. The visiting chiefs each spoke, the tone similar; eventually, singing began, in which Nengkwigetklals and his son were glorified.

Finally, their host announced that they would eat. Tomorrow his son would be initiated into the Hamatsa Dance Society. He had been taken away by the spirits, but those who were inspired—that is, Kate whispered, already members of the Society—would dance tomorrow to call him back.

"I'm almost tempted to say," Luke muttered as the pressure of the crowd pushed them through the oval doorway. Fires burned on the beach, where seal was roasting. In much the way of white people's society, many of the women had skipped the talking to prepare the feast. He looked down at Kate. "What do you advise?"

"I believe you would be disappointed," she said frankly. "And also that we will get our fill of similar ceremonies everywhere we go."

He considered for a moment before nodding reluctantly. "Then we will aim for the morning departure I had intended. I must speak to Gao. Have you seen him?"

"He'll be here somewhere." She didn't even glance around. "I didn't quite finish up in my darkroom. If you can do without me, I shall go back to work."

"Very well." He stayed Kate with a hand on her arm. "Do you need help in packing photographic supplies?"

"No, I haven't unpacked what I didn't need," she said. "I don't intend to take any developing supplies."

"Then I'll see you later."

Luke watched her purposeful retreat and wondered if it was more in the nature of an escape. Did Kate regret their decision not to hire a native woman to accompany her as chaperone? Loaded with her photographic supplies, as well as with food for the winter and Luke's purchases along the way, *Dancing Canoe* would have been cramped had another passenger with personal effects been added to the expedition. Even the short trip to Haina had made Luke grateful that Annie hadn't been able to come. But perhaps Kate was becoming apprehensive about the weeks and months ahead, the sole woman traveling with three men.

But the decision was made, he reminded himself in some irritation. He was wasting precious time speculating about a woman's state of mind, something that was rarely interesting enough to be worth the effort.

Darkness was falling without the glory of a sunset, thanks to the dismal mist. Luke made no attempt to join a line for food. Instead, within the limitations of the language barrier, he made small talk with individuals he'd already met and patiently explained his purpose here to those he hadn't. He was already picking up some Haida, and many of the Skidegate band spoke a little English.

All the while, he wondered if anyone here was mourning Iyea and Xaosti. There must be family left who still cared. Yet there had been astonishingly little reaction to the news he and the others had carried back from the Cowgitz coal mine. There was no magistrate here to inform, and Gao had volunteered to let the respective families know. Kate told the missionary about the skeletons, but Richardson hadn't known either man and could see nothing to be gained by attempting to contact the authorities in Victoria.

"You can certainly notify them when you return in the spring," he had suggested. "Though quite honestly, I doubt that it will accomplish anything. What *can* be done, so late? Certainly no more than you did, and you found no real clues."

Luke didn't like the man, but he couldn't argue. Even assuming there had been a magistrate closer than Duncan at Metklakatla, how interested would he have been in the killing of two Indians as little-liked as Iyea and Xaosti seemed to have been? At that, murders that had taken place a year and a half ago!

He noticed that Kate made no mention of her suspicion that the two victims had been involved in her father's murder. Did she fear that Richardson would point out how shakily founded was her belief? Or did she not trust the missionary?

Tonight Luke at last came face to face with Nengkwigetklals, fortunately while in the company of Samuel Frederick, who, to Luke's surprise, spoke serviceable English.

With seeming cordiality, his host asked whether Luke had eaten.

Following Samuel's translation, Luke said, "Not yet, but I'm grateful for the invitation."

The chief tapped him on the shoulder and said in Chinook, "*Kloshe, kloshe.* Good, Good. You will see the dancing tomorrow?"

"I'm afraid not," Luke said. "I leave in the morning. I wanted to thank you for arranging to have your kinsman guide us."

No trouble at all, he was assured.

"Have you thought more about selling the pole at Haina?" Luke asked. "I might be able to pay a dollar and twenty-five cents a foot."

Nengkwigetklals affected a look of surprise. "Sell the

pole? I would be ashamed to sell something made in memory of an important man of my family. I thought you wanted only to look at it."

"You said you never get over there," Luke reminded him. "That it's no good to you."

"I can't sell it," the chief said, his eyes opaque. "I don't know why you thought I would."

Watching Nengkwigetklals continue through the crowd, pausing to speak amiably to his guests, Luke pondered the chief's change of mind. Had he discovered that relatives were opposed to the sale? Or had Samuel's presence made him ashamed? His ownership of it might even be in dispute, as sometimes happened, or Luke's standing had sunk in the chief's eyes for some unimagined reason.

Devil take it, he refused to leave in the spring without having purchased at least one pole! Fortunately, his heart hadn't been set on Nengkwigetklals's, but where was he to find another? Well, that was a question that must be left for spring, but it was in a state of some disgruntlement that Luke began looking for Gao.

Strangely, he was unable to find him. He did see Kun taos disappear down the beach with a plump young woman. Ah well, Luke thought philosophically, perhaps Gao was similarly occupied. After all, it might be their last chance for dalliance until spring.

Perhaps inevitably, that brought his thoughts back to Kate. He felt uneasy about her for no reason that he could pinpoint. Would she remember to eat without urging?

He realized that he had no appetite himself, that his interest in the now-fragmented, casual festivities was not sufficient to keep him from the preparations he ought to be making for tomorrow. Starting back to the Mission House, he decided to check up on Kate before finishing his own packing.

Behind him, the fires crackled orange, sending sparks into the damp sky. Sounds of voices and drums and singing receded. Several times he had to step aside to let people pass. He heard giggles from the deeper shadows between canoes, and passed a group of men absorbed in a gambling game on the platform before one of the large houses.

The church was closer to the village than was the Mission House, so Luke circled its dark bulk and felt his way through the foggy night to the shed behind. He didn't expect to see any light emanating from it, of course; Kate had blanketed not only the window and door, but any possible cracks in the structure.

He thought he heard a sound from within. "Kate!" he called, hammering on the flimsy door. A moment of utter stillness followed. Frowning, he reached for the latch.

Without warning, the door slammed open. As Luke stumbled back, a dark figure hurtled out and shouldered him aside. Swearing, Luke regained his balance and sprinted after his assailant, who had disappeared into the night but whose running footsteps could be heard.

There was no time for caution. Luke guessed at the turn of the path and picked up speed. He heard a thump; the bastard had miscalculated. Luke felt triumph, but too soon. His shoulder slammed against the corner of the church and he was flung to his knees.

"Damn it!" One hand against the rough clapboard, he dragged himself to his feet and listened intently.

Nothing. Either the intruder had the sense to hold still, using the night and the fog as allies, or he was long gone. Luke's sense of urgency didn't allow for further pursuit or an undoubtedly fruitless search. He turned and stumbled back toward the shed, his pace nearly as foolhardy as it had been a moment ago.

The door stood open; he wrenched the blanket aside, praying that Kate was not here, that the intruder had been an Indian, curious at what she did inside this small shed. But in the flickering light of several candles, he saw her immediately, sprawled on the floor. She was frighteningly still, her face slack. Blood flowed, dark and sticky, across her forehead.

* * *

Knowing she must, Kate struggled out of her cloudy nightmare. Why was it so hard to wake up? Why did her head ache? Why couldn't she remember going to bed?

Her lids felt weighted by stones, but she lifted them anyway. She heard a sound—a groan—and realized that she herself had made it.

"At last!"

It took Kate a tortured moment to understand that it was Luke who had exclaimed so, almost prayerfully, that it was his strained face she saw hovering over her.

"How do you feel?"

Kate moved her hand on the coverlet. Turning her head slightly, she found that she was not mistaken, she was on her own bed. "Feel?" Her dull-witted echo came out as a croak. "Wretched."

"You're yourself." He sounded relieved.

"Who else should I be?" she asked pettishly.

A sigh; the bed gave as he sat down beside her and gently brushed her hair back from her face. He looked awkward, as though the tenderness that touched his mouth was new to him. "Do you remember what happened?" he inquired.

"Remember?" There she went again, repeating his words to no good purpose. What should she remember? She raised her hand and touched the thick pad of cloth that wrapped around her head. In near panic, she asked, "How did I get here?"

"I carried you. While I bandaged your wound, Richardson has gone to fetch Martha. I thought you would want her."

"I don't understand."

"You were assaulted," Luke said bluntly. "In your darkroom. Fortunately, I had come looking for you and interrupted your attacker. I was unable to catch him. I hoped that you remembered who . . ." He stopped. "But this isn't the time to tire yourself. Tomorrow will be soon enough."

"Aren't we leaving tomorrow?"

He sounded grim. "We can't go anywhere until you're recovered. Though I begin to think your safety depends on getting you away from here."

Her head hurt even worse, but she tried to concentrate. She had gone to her darkroom and checked the plates she had left out to dry. She remembered that much. Then she had begun replacing the bottles of developing solution and chemicals in the boxes that would hold them safely in storage.

Kate frowned. "I heard something," she said slowly. "I turned . . . But I can't remember any more. Oh!" Her voice rose in frustration. "It could well have been Father's murderer! If I had just *seen* him . . ."

Luke's large hand closed around her clenched fist. "It might have been something else altogether, you know." Lines were drawn between his brows, his mouth was tight. "An Indian who thought you had something worth stealing in the shed and didn't expect to find you there . . ."

"But everyone knew we were to leave soon," Kate said. "Why take such a risk now?"

"Because you might store everything here in the Mission House."

"Do you believe that?" she demanded. Her fingers uncurled, met the strength of his.

"No." His blue eyes were steady, clear. Angry. "I think you flushed the murderer out of hiding. If I had only been a little quicker . . . Blast it!"

She held tightly to his hand. "You saved my life. If you hadn't come looking for me . . ." Her head throbbed unmercifully. "Why did you?"

"I don't know." He was frowning again. "I began to worry, thought I should get on with my own preparations. Thank God."

She was aware of a warm current that seemed to flow from the joining of their hands. "You must wish you hadn't brought me."

The lines that carved his face from nose to mouth deepened. "There have been moments, I confess, when I've wondered whether I was a fool. Finding you unconscious on the floor was not one of them. Then I regretted bringing you only because the fact that I did so has put you in danger."

"I used you," she whispered, tears stinging her eyes. Oh, why did she feel so weak? She was becoming positively mawkish!

"No more than I did you." He released her hand and stood abruptly, his expression almost angry again. "I knew you had complicated motives for wanting to come back here, and I took advantage of them. You were my only remaining hope if I was to have photographs to include in the exhibit. My wife . . ." The words stuck in his throat. "My wife accused me once of putting my passion for the past before all else. Now you, too, have been the victim of my zeal."

"Too?" Kate echoed. "What happened to your wife?"

The regret, the pain, the bleak honesty she saw in his eyes were abruptly masked as the bedroom door opened behind him. Martha bustled in, the missionary at her heels.

"Kate!" She hurried across the room and sank down in Luke's place. In her agitation, she spoke Haida. "Mister Richardson says you are hurt!"

Kate touched her bandage with a tentative hand, looking only at the woman who had loved her like a daughter. "Somebody hit me over the head."

"But why?"

"I don't know." Tears threatened again, and she held them back by force of will. "Something to do with Father . . ."

"You think whoever killed him . . ." Martha stopped, too, and cast a glance at the two men waiting silently by the door. She drew a breath. "Gao told us what you found. Those two men, they were always trouble. My husband, he had to potlatch to make up for what Xaosti did to a girl at Skedans. You remember? Everybody wished those two would go away. When they did, we would have been happy, except—" her eyes were downcast, her fingers twisted together "—except we thought maybe they had done something bad to your father. But nobody knew. How can we talk about something we don't know anything about?"

"I shouldn't have asked you to," Kate said and gently covered Martha's rough knuckles with her own stained hand. "We *yetz haada* talk about things we don't know are true. I wanted you to do that so I could find out what happened to my father. The way he died wasn't right, but it wasn't right for me to ask you to say bad things about those who are close to you, either. I have been away in Victoria too long. I forgot things I should have remembered."

The wrinkles on Martha's face had grown deeper these last two years; set amongst them, her brown eyes were sadder and older than formerly. "I forgot things, too. Xaosti," she shrugged, "he was always trouble. You were my daughter. You brought me joy, not trouble."

Kate's smile felt as painful as it must look. "But I am not Haida," she said softly. "I can never be. In the spring, I will have to go away again."

"You will always be my daughter."

This time, Kate could not stop the tears. Through them she saw Luke take a quick step forward, then stop. A moment later, he was gone, taking Richardson with him. In Martha's arms, Kate could at last cry for her father, cry for the dreams she now knew to be childish. At last she could begin to say good-bye.

Chapter Twelve

The moon was at its fullest, casting a silver path across the water. Since the canoe had rounded Cumshewa Head, deep swells had quieted to long, slow rolls of sea. Behind the canoe lay tiny Kin-gui Island, the bristle of dead trees an eerie silhouette. Ahead was the shoreline, heavily forested, the tips of enormous trees a jagged line against the velvet-blue, darkening sky.

The sails had been taken down. Now the paddles slipped into the water, rose shimmering to dip again. The canoe passed a deep bay to the right, wherein Kate knew that a trading post had once stood. All was so still; only the silvery lap of ripples against the rocky shore disturbed the night. And then, far off in the darkness, came a metallic, trumpet-like note, becoming louder as it neared until it sounded overhead. Then gradually the call faded, becoming fainter and fainter, until it died away in the distance.

"What was that?" Luke asked in a low voice.

"Swans," Kate said softly.

They fell silent again, for the village ahead appeared in

the moonlight. The houses were hidden in the shadow of the forested bluff behind, but the tops of the poles were picked out by silvery light, as mysterious and exotic as the columns in an ancient Greek city.

Another tiny island lay just off the village. As they neared and passed the rocky islet, Kate could discern the angular lines of a gravehouse. Still no dog barked, no voice called out greeting or warning. It was as though the village ahead was deserted.

White men called it Cumshewa, after the hereditary name of its chiefs, which meant "Rich-at-the-Mouth-of-the-River," but to the Haida, this was Hlkenul, an Eagle village. It formed a ragged line along the shallow, curved shore of the bay; several houses had been built in front of others, and one house stood alone on a jut of land across a creek, separated from the rest of the village.

Kun taos and Gao turned the canoe and drove it with a few last hard strokes of the paddle stern-first onto the rocky beach. The scrape of the hull and the crunch of boots on gravel as Gao and Luke pulled the craft higher seemed unnaturally loud. The massive bulk of the houses was now clear, the faces of some of the creatures atop the poles eerily lifelike. Still there was silence and the dark.

Luke was the first to speak—firmly, as though he refused to allow moonlight and silence to intimidate him. Yet the way he searched the dark line of houses was uneasy. "I understood this village to be inhabited. Can it have been abandoned so recently?"

"No," Gao said positively. "There are people here. I smell smoke."

Kate had smelled it, too, she realized with relief, the scent of burning wood that lingered in the chilly night air so familiar as not to be noticed.

"Are there empty houses?" Luke asked.

"Many," Gao said, his voice unemotional.

"If you know which, let's choose one and carry enough of our possessions in to get us through the night. Then, before we settle in, perhaps we can stumble around until we find some inhabitants, so our arrival isn't too much of a surprise come morning."

Gao nodded without comment, speaking briefly to Kun taos. Kate collected her traveling bag and the leather case that held her dressing items. Luke took his own bag, while Gao and Kun taos, who had fewer possessions, were free to carry Kate's camera, tripod, and lenses, which she was reluctant to let out of her sight.

From a distance and veiled by darkness, the village had appeared to be solid and substantial. But now, even in the moonlight, closer inspection showed the truth. Gaps between houses, empty but for forlorn poles and salal and spruce saplings, showed where other houses must have once stood. Some were skeletons only, the planks and roof gone, exposing the beams. Canoes were pulled high on the beach, but they were few, as were other signs of habitation such as halibut-drying racks and stacks of firewood.

Gao knew that Hair Seal House was empty but still sound against the elements. Luke lit a lantern so that they could find their way around the canoes, drifted logs, and poles.

"Listen," Gao said suddenly as they neared the center of the village.

They paused and heard the muted, monotonous sound of drums. At last they saw a dim glow, too, from a house at the end.

"Is the entire village there?" Luke asked incredulously, not expecting an answer.

But Kate gave one anyway. "Skidegate may be the most populous of the villages, and its inhabitants could nearly fit into one house."

He made no comment, only hunched his shoulders and ducked to enter through the uncovered door—the house had no frontal pole—that Gao led them to. Inside, the air was dank and cold. The interior had two levels only, but it still seemed cavernous and dark. Stacks of cedar boxes that had been left behind filled shadowy corners. One pressed-back oak chair stood alone by the fire pit, empty but for charred rocks.

"Well." A false note of confidence rang in Luke's voice. "Shall we set up housekeeping?"

Kate shivered. "I suppose it will be impossible to find wood for a fire tonight."

"Kun taos can look," Gao said, "while we go to talk to the people."

Luke nodded, then said brusquely to Kate, "Have you something warmer?"

Kate wore a full-length cloth reglan already, but wordlessly she dug into her bag and found a shawl. The winter would get far colder; she had shivered not so much from the chill air as from the circumstances. But she didn't like to say that she was made apprehensive by her suddenly unavoidable realization that she was a woman alone with three men, that tonight they would all sleep together in this open space that permitted no privacy. That she must become accustomed to the intimacy of close living with near strangers! Perhaps, too, she shivered from exhaustion and the headache that had begun to throb this last hour.

She had insisted that they depart today despite her misadventure. Preparation took longer than it would have had they packed as intended the night before. Nonetheless, there had been no talk of waiting. What more might happen if they did?

They had eaten lunch before the canoe was ready to launch. Except for places to sit, every space was filled with trunks and cedar boxes. Some of them contained Kate's photographic plates and apparatus. Those that were packed with foodstuffs would be used to carry Luke's purchases as the food was used up. Though they would most likely be guests some of the time, and able to catch halibut and dig for clams, they must be prepared with all they needed to survive the winter.

Kate had wished suddenly, passionately, that Annie were here and would be a member of the expedition. Without warning, she felt that she must have been mad to agree to set off for months with a man she scarcely knew, and to such a destination: abandoned Indian villages, the almost entirely unknown west coast of these misty, barbarous islands! And to what purpose? Had she really imagined that she could find her father's murderer when the trail had grown so cold?

Nonetheless, she had been given the chance; now she must pay the price.

Thus she found herself following Gao tonight, aware of Luke at her heels, as they made their way as best they could along the zigzagging path that wound between houses and around obstructions. The glow ahead became brighter, the thump of drums louder.

Kate stumbled and nearly went down; Luke's strong hand caught her and set her back on her feet.

"Slow down!" he called to Gao, who had drawn ahead with the only lantern.

Gao stopped and held the lamp higher so that it cast its feeble light more usefully. He nodded at their destination. "Grease House."

Now orange light could be seen through the cracks between planks, and a few sparks leaped upward from the smoke hole. They reached the door, covered by hides and located to one side of a frontal pole that had no opening. Gao pushed aside the hides and stepped in, Kate and Luke close behind.

They found themselves behind a row of dancers who faced the rear of the house and the audience. It was disconcerting, a little as though one had stepped unexpectedly from the wings onto the stage during a production at the Theatre Royal to become the object of astonished stares. Kate knew her color to be high as they edged around the dancers, who ignored them, and found a clear place to stand to one side amongst the crowd of men, women, and children who squatted in various poses on the cedar-plank floor.

Nobody moved to speak to them, though some stared openly and a few nodded to Gao. The drummer sat near the fire, holding a tambourine-like instrument, formed of hide stretched on a hoop. He beat the drum with double taps— *dum dum, dum dum, dum dum*. The dancers, stretched in a line at the front of the house, kept time with a chant that sometimes died away altogether and at other times swelled to a chorus. Kate did not understand the words; many of the songs used in the winter ceremonies were sung in Tsimshian, or even in Kwakiutl, evidence of the borrowing among tribes.

The performers were magnificently attired and their faces painted in bold colors. Here, their customs were not yet so diluted. Change had found them most obviously in the diminution of numbers. All wore hats or headdresses adorned with feathers or the whiskers of sea lions. The closest to Kate wore a handsomely carved wooden hat that depicted a wolf baring its teeth. Between the creature's ears sat a tower of property rings that leaned and tilted with the movements of the dance. From it, and from similar conceal-ment in other headdresses, was cast the sacred white eagle down, which floated around them and into the audience. When some tickled her nose, Kate sneezed.

Shoulder girdles, dyed and decorated with tassels, were common. Two men wore leggings covered with fringes of puffin beaks strung together, which rattled as they moved in the shuffling, jerking fashion of their dance. Amongst the performers were women dressed in traditional bark skirts and Chilkat shawls, their faces covered by masks inlaid with abalone, from which dangled ermine skins.

Some dancers carried cuttings of fresh spruce, while oth-ers shook rattles to punctuate moments in the chant. The movements themselves were as far from a waltz or a country dance as could be imagined. Feet were scarcely lifted from the floor; rather, each beat of the drum sent a sort of shudder through the performers, who moved by jerks, sliding their feet at the same time. Kate could not have captured in words the effect of the whole, and yet in the firelight, it was myste-rious and dramatic. Here was the setting that gave life to the inanimate objects in her father's collection. Here the like-ness of Grizzly Bear was not a carving alone, but a presence. Who knew when one of the Grizzly Bear People might choose to take on a human shape and slip unnoticed into the crowd?

Sweat dripped from the dancers' faces. Kate was already flushed; now, with the heat from the fire and the press of so many bodies, she began to divest herself of garments, though she supposed she and the two men wouldn't stay long. She hoped they wouldn't. The throb in her temples was becoming fiercer; now that she was warm, her body was crying out for rest. Nervous as she was about the sleeping arrangements, she longed to lay herself down and close her eyes, even if it was on a hard mat.

Fortunately, some sort of signal was given and the drumbeat and the dancers stopped at the same moment with an audible gasp. A hum of talk rose in the audience, and people stood to stretch and to lay sleepy children more comfortably beside them. It was obvious who were the prominent men of the village, as they had front-row seats, where they could lounge in the greatest comfort. Gao went to speak to them, returning after a moment.

"They say we can stay if you like. The chief of this house invites us to be his guests tomorrow night, when he gives out things to those of his daughter's husband's family."

"Tell him we will be honored to be his guests then," Luke said. "But I'll head back with Kate now. She looks as if she'll collapse at any minute if she doesn't get some rest."

Gao agreed, and Kate allowed herself to be hustled out before the dancing resumed, as it obviously would since the performers were again lining up. Outside in the darkness, Luke waited while she put on her coat and rewrapped the shawl. Then he transferred the lantern to his left hand and with his right, gripped her arm.

"You needn't hold me up." She hoped she sounded tart, self-sufficient; that he couldn't tell how desperately weary she was, how much she would have liked to lay her head against his chest and rest, just for a moment.

"If I don't, you'll fall and break an ankle," he said curtly. "Why are you always so reluctant to accept help?"

She stumbled a little and would have fallen but for his hand. Pain stabbed through her head. Through its fog, she said, "I suppose I'm not used to it."

He snorted. "Come, you can't be more than twenty, twenty-one. You went straight from your father's home to your aunt and uncle's. Hardly the life of somebody who has had only herself to depend on."

Kate was stung by the need to justify herself, though why she cared enough to bother, she didn't know. "My mother was an invalid. It was I who shopped, cooked, cleaned, and fetched. I have no memory of playing, of being held while I cried. I was the mother, she the child. And my father . . ." It hurt to say, but she made herself go on: "He took me with him because he must, kept me with him because I was useful. I have had great experience at being needed, and none whatsoever at needing someone else."

She felt his frowning regard, though she kept her gaze on the ground ahead so that she could avoid the ignominious fate of being supported by a man irritated at the necessity.

"That explains much about you," he said at last, thoughtfully. "I beg your pardon. I am often exasperated with those who leap to ungrounded conclusions, and here I have done so myself."

"No, I should ask your pardon," she said with difficulty. "You have been kind to me, and I fear I am often snappish."

"Good Lord, we'll become mired in sentiment if we're not careful!" Luke exclaimed. Yet it seemed to her that his hand was gentler. "I suggest we drop the entire subject. Ah, here we are."

The front of the house was familiar, though in her weariness, she would have stumbled on by if left to her own resources. She felt so odd. Was a blow to the head enough to explain her peculiar sense of distance from her surroundings?

She allowed herself to be steered through the open doorway. Inside, a fire flickered bravely, leaving much of the space shadowed and cold, but achieving a circle of warmth around it.

"That feels good," she said to Kun taos in Haida. "Thank you."

"Tell him that he can join the festivities, too, if he'd like," Luke suggested.

She did so, and Kun taos departed with every appearance of delight.

"Wouldn't you prefer to go back also?" she asked Luke. "I promise I'll be content on my own, and no doubt asleep in ten minutes."

"I don't want to leave you alone." He shrugged out of his coat, tossed it carelessly aside. "No, don't argue. Have you forgotten yesterday so quickly?"

"Are you implying that the assailant might have followed us?" She laid aside her outer clothing reluctantly. Now what? Did she unbutton her dress in front of him?

"You must have thought of the possibilities, as I have." His expression was one of impatience as he frowned at her across the fire. He seemed very large and very male at this moment. "We could easily have been followed, though I admit it's unlikely. But we might have been preceded as well. I expected to encounter Durham here, for example. Has he never arrived? Or did he conveniently leave yesterday, ostensibly to the south? His supposed departure from Skidegate doesn't remove him from a list of possible suspects, you know. And God knows where Sims took himself to. Devil take it, we might have brought the assailant with us! Gao is remarkably helpful for a man who detests my entire purpose here—and yours by extension."

Kate sank down on a trunk. Slowly, she said, "I didn't realize that you, too, were thinking that way."

He glowered at her. "Your opinion of me is so low, I wonder that you trusted me enough to accept my offer!"

She bit her lip. "My opinion of you is not low. It's only that you had no way of knowing why I came. How could you have, when I didn't tell you?"

In an abrupt movement, he swung away to present his back to the fire, and to her. Over his shoulder, he tossed, "I knew well what you intended from the moment you began to bait Sims and Durham on the *Skeena*."

Kate looked down at her hands. "I didn't realize I was so transparent."

He grunted. "You were surely intending to be transparent to the murderer. Wasn't that your plan? To frighten him enough to drive him into some kind of action?"

"You make me sound like a fool."

"Do I?" Still his back was to her. "You succeeded, after all."

"If getting hit over the head without seeing my attacker can be called success."

He seemed to sigh; she felt some tension leave him. Turning, he looked at her directly, his gaze intent. "Who do you suspect?"

"Everyone! I can eliminate nobody!"

Luke rubbed the muscles at the back of his neck, as though they were tight. "I wish I could do so for you, but unfortunately, the assailant had ample time to present an appearance of innocence before I had a chance to make inquiries. Gao was nowhere to be found, which might be in his defense; if he had just attacked you, surely he would have tried to provide himself with an alibi. Richardson was at the Mission House when I carried you there, which proves nothing." He shrugged. "I don't know which Indians you suspect . . ."

She gave a laugh that was far from amused. "I meant it when I said everyone. Father had many enemies. One of the medicine men even tried to claim credit for his death, because Father had 'cursed' him. But it was obvious to me that his hand wasn't the one that struck Father down. Though I suppose he might have attacked me. I know I angered him. Father's murder might easily have been cold-blooded, with no feeling behind it at all. If he interfered in a profitable sale of stolen antiquities, mightn't that be reason enough?"

"Unfortunately, yes."

Kate swayed slightly and gave her head a shake to clear it. "I suppose I've lost my chance now . . ."

He moved so quickly that he was at her side before she realized he was coming. "Not necessarily," he said. "But for now, you're going to bed before you collapse. Where would you like to sleep?"

"I don't know." She looked around helplessly. "I suppose I could screen off an area . . ."

"And freeze," Luke pointed out unsympathetically. "I'd rather have you where I can see you."

She was too tired to think about it, too tired to protest. What did it matter if he or Gao or Kun taos saw her sleeping, her hair tangled and her mouth hanging open? If she ever married, some man would be privileged to behold her thus. And as far as she knew, she didn't snore.

"I don't care," she said.

He nodded brusquely. "As soon as I spread the mats and blankets, I'll find some water and give you privacy so you can change. In the meantime, if you need to go out—" he cleared his throat "—there seems to be a back door. You can take the lantern. If you require assistance . . ."

"Thank you, but no," she said hurriedly, hot blood mounting in her cheeks. She seized the lantern and went in the direction he had nodded, horribly conscious of his gaze following her.

With the aid of the lamp, she quickly found a spot not too overgrown and answered the call of nature. It was unpleasantly dark back here, with the silence of the forest behind her and the bulk of the houses ahead. There were several smaller structures to each side, undoubtedly gravehouses. Thank heavens, her nose gave no indication that any had gained a recent occupant. Kate nearly bumped into a pole as she hastened back toward the house, shivering.

In her absence, Luke had laid out the thin woven mats and dropped several blankets on each. When she handed over the lantern, he departed without comment, carrying a bucket. Kate had never undressed so quickly. With some vague notion of modesty, she left her chemise on beneath her high-necked flannel nightgown.

Luke returned with such dispatch, she had barely time to

snatch up a blanket. His glance was quick and comprehensive, but he said nothing, for which she was grateful. Swaddled like an infant in the scratchy wool blanket, she took a cup of water and with her back to Luke, self-consciously brushed her teeth. When she turned around, she saw that he had done the same and was just returning his toothbrush and tin of powder to its case. Following his example, she poured out the water in her cup to soak into the hard-packed earth floor beside the fire pit.

Kate knew she was blushing. This was all so very awkward! Luke had shed his boots and was unbuttoning his shirt. She had just a glimpse of his strong brown throat and an undershirt before she looked away.

Sitting on the mat, she attacked her curly mass of hair with a brush. Freed from the braids, the locks wanted to spring in every direction. Should she braid it again? But when she lifted her arms, the blanket persisted in slipping, and she wasn't fond of laying her head on thick braids anyway, so at last she gave up and set the brush to one side. She reached for a blanket to fold into some semblance of a pillow. As she did, she glanced over to find Luke's gaze fixed on her. His eyes seemed to have darkened, though perhaps it was just the shadows. Yet there was something in his stillness that caught her breath in her throat, something in the way his eyes moved from her hair to her breasts and at last to her face that left her shaken without knowing why. She sat there frozen, knowing that she should say something or turn away, yet she was unable to do either.

It was only an instant that seemed an eternity before he was the one to wheel around, leaving her dry-mouthed, staring at his broad shoulders, bare and rigid. Surely she was imagining the tension, transmuting mere embarrassment into something more meaningful.

And yet it was not so easy to quell her physical reaction to . . . what? A man seeing her in her nightgown? As she lay down, her pulse bounced like a child impudently skipping to some imagined tune that she couldn't hear. Her posture was stiff; even after Luke blew out the lantern and wrapped himself in blankets, Kate remained conscious of the firelight playing over her, and of Luke's nearness. Sleep seemed an impossibility.

Time crept by, rest eluded her. The low fire crackled, Luke rose once to feed it. She lay very still, listening to his movements, breathing silently. Eventually she had to roll over, her hip already tender from the hard floor, but she wouldn't let herself toss and turn. She stayed as still as possible, hoping that Luke would believe her to be asleep.

When she pressed grainy eyelids shut, Kate wondered: In a week or two, would she laugh at tonight's discomfiture? Would the awkward aspects of living with a man to whom she wasn't bound by ties of affection ease into the commonplace, the unnoticed? Or would she discover that the strict regulations imposed by society on unmarried men and women—regulations she had always scorned—existed for a sound reason?

The answer was somewhere in between. The acute awkwardness abated; the tension did not.

The very next day, Luke arranged a sort of dressing room for her, its walls comprised of stacked boxes set amidst mats suspended with cords. Had it been summer, or even early fall, she would have slept there. Despite his professed desire to have her where he could see her, she would have been perfectly safe in her cubicle, which allowed no ingress except through the central room. It was now late November, however, and the weather continued cold. Kate could not bring herself to sleep in the dark, cold corner removed from the fire. It was all she could do to make herself remove her clothing there and change into night garments!

By the third night, Kate had pinpointed the exact moment when Luke fell silent, or seemed to look at her with unusual intensity. It was when she let her hair down. Something about her loose hair disturbed him.

But what could she do, she asked herself defensively. Sleep with pins stabbing her scalp? Besides, she *enjoyed* those peaceful moments sitting by the fire, pulling the brush through her curls. She even took guilty pleasure in her awareness that he watched every stroke she made. Unlike most women—pretty women—she had never before seen that peculiar kind of hunger in a man's eyes when he looked at her. Why not luxuriate in the illusion that he wanted her? It would be stripped from her soon enough, when the winter ended and brought her harshly up against the spinsterish, penurious existence that would be her lot.

Aside from those moments as they readied for sleep, Kate sometimes wondered if Luke thought of her as a woman at all, or even as an individual. He had retreated after that first night, becoming distant and businesslike. His tone was sometimes sharp when he snapped orders to her. He seemed reluctant even to look at her.

Typical was the third morning, when they awakened to find a delicate dust of white over everything, even their blankets. Snow had filtered through cracks and the open smoke hole to cover them as they slept.

Kun taos was still shaking the fluffy stuff from his hair when he came to the banked fire. He and Gao had set up their sleeping quarters somewhat removed from Luke and Kate. Good-naturedly, Kun taos said, "Somebody threw a stone at the duck."

Luke swore as he hastily drew on his boots and thrust his arms into his coat. He grumbled, "I suppose some supernatural being was in the mood to shake out his rug."

"Well, something similar," Kate said. She decided to stay cozily under her blankets until the fire was built up. "It's said that there is a pole holding up the sky, with a string hanging from it. If somebody throws a rock at a buffle-headed duck, the duck pulls the string and the mallard feathers come down from on top of the pole. They are the snow."

He grunted without looking at her. She supposed he hadn't really wanted an answer. At least not one from a woman still in her bedclothes.

She tried to match his demeanor and efface her personality, especially her femininity. How could she do else, given her choice of wrinkled muslin and heavy wool skirts with jackets? She couldn't even iron them! And of course she had brought no bustle, no corset, no jewelry, only the bare necessities. In truth, even with those trappings, she had few feminine graces.

In all fairness, she sometimes suspected that he wouldn't have noticed if she *had* been beautiful, so wrapped up was he in the exhilaration of collecting artifacts and stories.

More dances had accompanied the potlatch they attended. Luke was especially delighted with a warrior's dance in which a raven was depicted. The dancer wore a shredded-bark costume that in the firelight simulated feathers. He moved in a low crouch, turning his head sharply to the right and the left, snapping the long beak of the mask open and shut. The beak made a clattering sound that had children in the audience shrinking back wide-eyed into the protective arms of their mothers. His arms were hidden beneath the costume; Kate guessed that somehow he was manipulating the beak by strings or wooden rods.

The song, sung by the other men in his secret society, was one suitable to a warrior:

> *Wa! everyone is frightened by his winter mask!*
> *Wa! everyone is frightened by his cannibal mask!*
> *His hooked beak makes us tremble.*
> *His Hohok mask makes us tremble.*

The deep beat of drums seemed to vibrate through Kate's very bones. Sacred white-eagle down floated in the air, dancing with sparks from the fire and obscuring Kate's already inadequate view through the camera's aperture. The interior of the house was hot enough; under the black cloth that enveloped her and the camera mounted on its tripod, she was suffocating. Sweat trickled between her breasts and made patches of wetness under her arms.

Kate had set up her photographic apparatus in advance with the permission of the house-chief and, presumably, tonight's performers. She had never been denied the opportunity to photograph the Haida under any circumstances. She had discovered that they viewed both photographs and the written word in much the way they did their oral histories: as a way of legitimizing their claims to crests, stories, and dances. A dance might be done to show the guests that one has the right to do it; how much better, then, was a photograph! Not ephemeral, as was the performance itself, the photograph, by virtue of its permanent nature, was highly prized because it recorded something that was claimed to be a truth—and now could be proven as such.

She had high hopes of capturing a reasonable likeness of the Raven Dancer; with nearly the entire village in attendance, the fire had been built so high that it leaped through the smoke hole. When it showed signs of dying back, someone poured grease on it, to immediate, impressive effect. Surely it would make the difference, providing the brilliant light missing from most night scenes. Nighttime photographs were being taken these days; she had succeeded with some herself, although not when she was also trying to stop motion at the same time. The two difficulties were normally combated by opposite tactics: freezing motion required a quick shutter, while poor lighting demanded a long exposure.

The Indians here had rarely before seen a photographer at work. They maintained a wary distance from Kate, who had set up two separate flash devices. Now she checked her focal point again, estimating the dancer's path. When she signaled Gao, who had been drafted as her assistant, he simultaneously squeezed the two rubber orbs, sending puffs of magnesium powder to four separate candles to ignite the flash. Gasps and cries came from the audience, audible through the black cloth enveloping Kate. Even the dancer, she saw a split second after releasing the shutter, had faltered. She hoped that in the blinding instant of white light, nobody had noticed, else she would be responsible for his shame. The steps to many dances were rigidly prescribed, with the consequences for error dire.

Not until she removed the magazine of plates from their

holder and safely returned them to light-tight boxes did she emerge from under the dark cloth. She wouldn't know whether she had succeeded tonight until she developed the plates several months from now. She would have other opportunities, but what more could she do? The fire had been built to crackling heights; nobody had objected to the white flashes or the cloud of acrid smoke. She would not find a more agreeable subject.

She continued to ponder the problems of nighttime photography all the while she dismantled her camera, carefully placing the lens in its box and collapsing the bellows before removing the camera from the tripod, which she then folded.

Surely there was a way to get better effects!

Advances in photography were being made every day. Look at the gelatine-bromide dry plates, such an improvement over the wet collodion plates she had been forced to work with until recently. The quality of the finished product had been as good, but with the wet plates, she could take a picture only if she could instantly develop it; not only had she needed a portable darkroom, she had needed a nearby source of water. Most frustrating of all, people and events rarely waited while she developed the first plate before she could return to take another.

At last she was free from the shackles of the darkroom. If that could be accomplished, what other miracles might follow! She had seen some of the work done on freezing motion, the most famous of which was a series of sensational photographs taken by Eadweard Muybridge of a galloping horse, which showed that at one point in the horse's stride, all four hooves left the ground. Of course, *he* had used a calibrated backdrop and trip wires that operated the shutters of no fewer than *twelve* cameras equipped with Dallmeyer stereographic lenses, besides having had the advantage of daylight.

When Kate joined Luke, he furiously scribbled down the words as she distractedly translated them. His handwriting was a crude scrawl because he could scarcely tear his gaze from the picturesque performance.

That night was one of those when Gao and Kun taos did not returned to Hair Seal House with them. Kun taos in particular kept late hours. Gao was more scrupulous in asking whether he would be needed before he vanished.

On the dark walk back to Hair Seal House, Kate asked Luke, "Have you discovered whether Mister Durham was ever here?"

"He did visit, but stayed only two nights. He apparently found little to buy. My informant said that he wasn't a very patient man."

Kate tried to decipher why Luke didn't sound jubilant at having bested his rival; she knew *he* was finding things to buy, as she had translated some of the transactions. Already, he had nearly filled a large, bent-cedar box.

"I suppose he left here the day I was attacked," she said slowly.

"So I am told," Luke said, sounding grim. "The coincidence is an unhappy one."

"Yes." What else was there to say? She didn't really believe that James Durham had killed her father. What could his motive possibly have been? How would he have returned to Skidegate, accompanied her father to Kiusta, and then made another departure from the Queen Charlotte Islands—all without having been seen by other eyes?

Of course Iyea and Xaosti *had* seen the murderer, she reminded herself; thus they in turn had been silenced. But their murders had occurred close to Skidegate, implying that the killer had returned there. Among the few straight answers Kate had gotten from the Skidegate Haida were assurances that Durham had indeed left on a steamer before the Reverend Hewitt disappeared, and that he had not come back.

The walk was completed in silence; preparing to retire, she and Luke conversed minimally. And yet Luke watched as Kate unbound her hair from the severe braids. His eyes seemed to burn a hole in her as she brushed it until the curls crackled and formed a wiry cloud that tumbled over her shoulders and down her back.

For the first time that night, as she pursued sleep, she

wondered not about her father's fate, but about Luke's wife. What had she looked like? What had happened to her, and why did Luke hold himself responsible?

His awareness of Kate as a woman had become more than annoying; it was distracting, even nerve-racking. Why the devil couldn't she leave her hair in braids when she slept? She must know how she appeared to him in a nightgown, with her hair in a dark cloud around her shoulders and breasts! Yet, infuriatingly, she sat there and ran her brush through the locks, over and over, until static electricity made the dark mass crackle as though it had a life of its own. Luke's nerves would stretch tighter and tighter, until they quivered with each stroke of her brush—and then she would lie down, giving a soft sigh as she nestled into the blankets an arm's reach from him.

How could he sleep, after she had tormented him so? He felt as though he was becoming more haggard each day, shorter with their two guides, more desperate to avoid Kate. And the entire winter lay ahead, night after night, while he wasted away until he would have so little substance that people would see right through him, in the way of the Haida who sought a visitation from the spirits.

What could he do? Sleep elsewhere? But he hadn't forgotten the sight of her body crumpled on the floor of her darkroom, or of her face afterward, bleached of color. He would rest no better if he couldn't reassure himself of her safety with a glance.

For the first time in his life, he considered visiting a prostitute. These wretched feelings were sexual, and perhaps if he once assuaged them, they wouldn't return. But it would be effective only if the woman he hired could arouse the same feelings, and he saw no one who did. Dark eyes, however soft, could not replace mist-gray ones in his fantasies; the plumper curves of the Haida women did not hold the dangerous appeal of a straight, narrow back, of breasts that did not beg to be touched, but held themselves aloof.

A visit to a prostitute held potentially ruinous consequences in any case. Kate wanted to despise him; it would
take only that to accommodate her. She wouldn't be alone,
either. Gao, moralist that he was, would be angry. Luke
thought he had made some progress in gaining Gao's
respect, and he dared not risk losing it. If Gao was not yet an
ally, neither was he an enemy—but how easily that could be
changed!

Fortunately, Luke's days were well occupied, which kept
him from dwelling on the misery that awaited him each
night. Many of the Indians were eager to sell possessions
they regarded as inferior to the European manufactures.
Although there was no mission here, the Reverend Hewitt
and his replacement had gained some influence. Even poles
were available for purchase, had there been any way of
transporting them.

Luke's one source of dissatisfaction with his collecting at
Cumshewa was his failure to find any ceremonial items
available for sale. He would have had better luck in the
spring, he suspected, when the winter ceremonies were over
and the next ones comfortably in the future. But right now,
the masks and robes were wanted; anything sold would
leave a noticeable gap in the next performance, shaming the
one who had been responsible for its safekeeping.

So when a young chief indicated his willingness to show
Luke his hidden cache of secret society masks and whistles,
Luke had difficulty in hiding his jubilation.

In Chinook, he succeeded in conveying his intention of
bringing a translator, so that he could understand the stories
that went with the masks. Dagas's alarm was immediately
obvious.

"*Wake, wake!*" he exclaimed. "No, no! *Mesika, wake
huloima.* You, no other."

Luke agreed only because he might not be allowed to see
the objects otherwise. "Now?" he asked.

"No," Dagas said vehemently. "Tonight, when others are
at Sky House."

Kate was to photograph again that evening; Luke helped

carry and set up her equipment. The dance and chanting began, and he waited until he saw the young chief slip out before he followed suit.

He had grabbed a lantern; now, outside in the dark and drizzle, he fumbled to light it. He succeeded, but the feeble rays were inadequate against the mist. Stumbling, twice almost falling, he made his way north along the beach.

Dagas was awaiting him. The Indian held open the hide door covering, then motioned him toward the back wall, upon which was a painted design of a hawk, or an eagle. The house appeared to be entirely deserted but for the two men. The banked fire was still burning, the odor of cooking lingered.

Luke expected Dagas to go to one of the boxes heaped about. Instead, the chief approached the wall itself. His back was to Luke, his shoulders hunched as though to hide what he did. When he turned back, he had opened a narrow door, revealing a small room within. The door itself had been so skillfully framed and disguised by the painted design that it would never have been discovered had an observer not known what lay concealed behind.

Luke stepped in, lantern held high. He felt triumph mixed with wonder as he beheld the ceremonial trappings of a Haida chief: masks, a splendidly carved speaking staff, used to rap on the floor to gain an audience's attention, small whistles that must be concealed in the mouth to make the mysterious noises that indicated spirit possession during a dance, a splendid Chilkat shawl, and a hat with Killer Whale painted in broad strokes of black. It was a treasure house. There was a box that held nothing but rattles; three coppers leaned against a wall; dancing headdresses lay atop a box, their attached ermine pelts looking as though they might regain life and scamper away if he moved too suddenly.

The masks drew Luke. A woven mat covered one wall, and from it hung a number of them. In the flickering light, they were lifelike despite their immobility. There were realistic human faces, surrounded by long, glossy black hair. One represented an old man, the wrinkles radiating from the eye sockets and from the mouth set in a grimace; this one's hair was gray. A raven, or an eagle, had a beak as long as Luke's arm; he guessed that it would open and close much as the beak they had seen the other night. Most fascinating were the transformation masks. The human face within was transformed when the spirit of Raven or Mosquito or Grizzly Bear took over the dancer; this possession was graphically illustrated by the face of the spirit animal that closed over the human face.

Inwardly cursing the language barrier, Luke asked, "Will you sell me some of these things?"

"The spirits would be angry," Dagas answered. He stiffened in alarm. "Wait. I hear something." He disappeared, leaving the door open. When he returned a moment later, he appeared only partially reassured. He kept casting glances toward the opening. "I should not have shown you this."

"You have many . . ." Luke motioned to indicate the masks. "Will you sell one of these?"

He could feel the young chief's tension. It might even be called fear. Yet, in a low voice, he asked, "Which do you want?"

"This one interests me," Luke said in an understatement calculated to keep the price within his means. "This one" was more than a mask; it represented Killer Whale, the most powerful and feared of the supernatural beings who lived beneath the sea. The carved and painted headpiece was attached to a black cloth that would cover the dancer's upper torso; appended to it was a wooden tail. The whole must be four feet long and nearly as wide. Luke experimentally pulled a string that dangled, and the flukes moved in a swimming motion that clattered loudly in the silence. Dagas jerked.

"I should not sell that one," he said.

"I'll pay you eighteen dollars for it," Luke said rashly. So much for disguising his avidity; a chance like this might not come again.

Dagas took more furtive looks around the door. He was sweating. "I might sell it for twenty-five."

"Very well," Luke said, not even making a pretence of bargaining further. "I would like more things, too. One of these whistles, and a rattle. Another mask, perhaps this one . . ." He indicated a transformation mask.

"No, no," Dagas said strongly. "This, maybe." He lifted a dance hat of blue-painted wood inlaid with copper to represent the eyes, nostrils, and teeth of some fierce creature. Atop the hat were basketry property rings that swayed.

More negotiating followed. Luke had the advantage, if only because Dagas was so anxious to be done with this, to have the door safely closed again on these sacred objects. How he intended to explain the disappearance of the things he sold, Luke had no idea. Perhaps he had so recently inherited that he could pretend the old chief was responsible for any losses. He wouldn't be able to get away with that, of course, if tonight's transaction were witnessed, or even heard. Thus his uneasiness, which became contagious. Twice, Luke would have sworn he heard a creak, as though someone moved just outside the secret room. Both times, Dagas looked but saw no one, though his anxiety level rose.

When they had agreed upon prices, Dagas said, "We must go. You will not show anyone what you have?"

"I will put what I bought in these bags . . ." Luke carefully stowed the killer-whale mask in the first, a huge burlap sack, which it nearly filled. Then he placed the dance hat and the smaller items in a second bag. "No one will see."

They hurried through the still-deserted house and parted outside. Luke, heavily loaded, returned to Hair Seal House, where he secreted his purchases inside boxes, wrapping each item in the cotton batting he had brought for the purpose.

Afterward, he followed the muted beat of drums back to Sky House. He slipped in as casually as though he had just stepped out for a breath of air. Immediately, he spotted Dagas, who didn't even glance his way. Luke was reassured further when he saw that there was a momentary break in the performance; the audience was moving around and talking, the dancers wiping sweat from their faces. Why would anybody have noticed his brief withdrawal, or connected it to the young chief's?

Kate stood beside her camera looking annoyed. *She* had noticed his absence. When she saw him, she waved him over imperiously.

"Where were you?" she demanded. "I can't find Gao—he was to operate the flash. How can I take photographs if you two both disappear?"

Luke suffered a momentary disquiet. Could Gao have followed him? But why would he have done so and then not shown himself? If he had wanted to prevent tonight's transaction, he could easily have accomplished that by interrupting. Dagas would have been too ashamed to sell sacred objects in front of a witness.

Somewhat callously, Luke reflected that the problem was not his in any case. He had bought in good faith and paid fair—even escalated!—prices. Why should he worry?

Stepping toward Kate, he said practically, "Tell me what to do."

Kate had begun to do so when a stir passed through the crowd. Luke followed the direction of the stares to see that Gao had reappeared, and in the company of another newcomer to Cumshewa.

Less than happily, Luke interrupted Kate. "It would seem that your old friend Sims is paying us a call."

Chapter Thirteen

I don't like wasting time, but I'm short of funds," Sims said. He took a deep swallow of the whiskey he had offered to Luke. He added gloomily, "If I could just find a vein! I know the gold is there somewhere, why else the flakes, and even the nuggets? But I can't keep looking forever without return. So now it's copper I'm after. I told you I had some investors."

"Yes, but you didn't say you were coming this way," Kate pointed out. The three of them had retired to Hair Seal House. Kate was grateful for Luke's presence. She had never thought the day would come when she was frightened of the big, bluff man who had befriended her when she was most vulnerable, yet since that night on the *Skeena,* she had realized how little she knew of him. Where had he come from, for instance? His accent was American; beyond that, she had no idea of his background.

The bushy beard made reading his expressions difficult. Even now, had it not been for his tone, she could not have guessed what he was thinking. It went to show how self-centered she had been when she first knew him that she had apparently not cared enough to wonder what he felt or thought!

"There are copper signs all along this coast. I heard that a shaft had been sunk years ago just north of here, near the Kaste River. Thought I'd take a look; fellow just might've given up too soon." His gloomy tone hadn't moderated. "Found the damn hole full of water. Pumping it out would cost too much."

"So are you giving up?" Luke asked.

Sims shook his shaggy head. "Figured I'd keep going south. Indians found virgin copper somewhere. How else could they have made those plaques they set such store by?"

"I wonder if many of them weren't traded from other tribes," Kate said.

The miner grunted. "It's possible. Well, I'm being paid to take a look."

"Do you leave tomorrow, then?" Luke asked evenly.

"If I can rouse those Indians I hired." He tilted his head back for another long swallow. The warm, shifting light of the low fire cast odd shadows, making the darkness beyond its small circle seem deeper.

"What will you do if you don't find copper?" Kate asked. "Will you give up and go home?"

"Home?" He choked on the liquor burning his throat and uttered a harsh laugh. "This is it." Sims gestured with the hand that held the small bottle. Whiskey splashed out. He seemed to sway slightly. "Home sweet home."

"But you must have come from someplace . . ."

"Killed a man," he said baldly. "Can't go back."

Kate felt Luke stir, but he remained silent. She bit her lip. "Was it . . . was it very long ago? Are you still wanted?"

He looked past her, his eyes bleak. "Twelve years. Don't suppose they're looking very hard, but I'm not going back to offer my neck to the noose, either."

"If you pleaded innocence . . ."

Even Luke gave her a sardonic look. She sounded at best naive, when in fact, she was only shocked. Sims, a murderer!

His muddy eyes were shrewd. "A dozen men saw me kill the bastard." He downed some more whiskey, then wiped his mouth on his sleeve. "Deserved it, but I'd hang anyway."

She looked steadily at him. "Why did you tell me now?"

Beefy shoulders lifted in a shrug. "Never tried to hide it. Except maybe from the Reverend."

"He didn't like me spending time with you," she admitted.

"Wouldn't have stood for it if he'd known."

"No, I don't suppose he would have," Kate said slowly.

Sims, a murderer, she thought again. And yet, why was she so shaken by the notion? She should have guessed that he had run from something. Why else come here, to the ends of the earth? He could just as well have followed another gold strike to a place that had saloons, fancy women, and other miners to drink with. Here, there was nothing but rain and dark forests and Indians. He had found the occasional nugget and some flakes of gold, but never enough to explain the years he had spent hunting the illusory vein. But what better place to hide out?

"I suppose you'll be thinking now that if I could kill one man, I could just as well kill another." His voice was belligerent.

Kate's throat seemed to have a lump in it. "Do you believe my father deserved it, too?"

"We didn't get along." He glared at her.

"There is a vast difference between hating someone enough to kill and not getting along."

Sims tried to take another drink and discovered that he had drained the bottle. In disgust, he tossed it over his shoulder without tearing his bellicose gaze from her. "So you think I killed him."

A strange calm came over her. "No," she said collectedly. "I have never thought such a thing. You were too kind to me. No matter how you felt about him, he was my father. You wouldn't have hurt me."

The miner cursed and staggered to his feet. "You're a fool to trust someone like me," he said in a tone of self-loathing. "Can't trust myself." With that, he turned and stumbled in the general direction of the front door. A crash was followed by bitter swearing.

Without comment, Luke followed him, presumably to be certain he made it safely to wherever he stayed tonight. Kate discovered that under the force of her emotions, she had risen to her feet and pressed her fingers to her mouth. Part of her wanted to follow Sims and demand an explanation. Was he only drunk? Or had he some guilty secret that would corrode his soul until he went to his grave?

How could she find out? Did she dare to press him further, until he exploded with the rage and fear she had seen in him so starkly tonight?

Gao stood out in the darkness where he would not be seen and watched the miner blunder away. Luke was beside Sims, although not with him, Gao thought. He had heard the raised voice, but not understood the words. He could tell that the miner had been drinking so much *hoochino,* it had made him stupid. But even animals that were not very smart could be dangerous.

Gao knew that Kate was alone in the house, and for her safety, he would stay here until Luke returned. After that, there was something he must do. There had been other words spoken tonight that he had heard, words about selling things that should not even have been shown to a *yetz haada.* He would repeat those words to the foolish one's aunt, an old woman who would know how best to shame one unworthy of his inheritance.

Thus it was that Gao was not surprised the next day when the young chief and his father's sister came to Hair Seal House. Gao was carving in the soft black stone, copying a Skidegate pole that he saw in his mind's eye as clearly as though one of Kate's photographs lay in front of him.

Kate had gone to the part of the house where she dressed, saying that she must mend something. Luke sat beside Gao, writing down the stories that Gao told as he worked. Some stories could not be told of course; they belonged to just one family. But he had let himself be talked into telling those that were common knowledge.

During these last days, Gao had felt pulled two ways, like bait on a fish hook that was being eaten at the same time it was being yanked to the surface. He had said he would help Luke, though he had intended to talk against him. Gao had done what he meant to do; Nengkwigetklals would not sell the pole at Haina now, and Dagas would demand back what he had sold. There were other objects people had thought to sell, until Gao spoke against it. But Gao sometimes did not like the way he had acted, taking money from Luke and then not doing the things he had promised to do. Two things he could do: Stories could be shared without loss to Gao's own people, and the Haida words could be explained so that Luke learned the language.

Thus, as he carved, Gao talked about Raven, who had thrown stones into the water to create the islands and spilled drops of fresh water that formed lakes and rivers. He had heard the first humans crying out and had released them from cockleshells. Raven himself could be bird or man whenever he wanted. Sometimes he took off his bird skin to mingle with men, especially if he could trick someone by not looking like himself.

Gao was telling about the days when the world was dark, back when a chief in the Sky World owned the sun and the moon. The chief's daughter was guarded carefully, but Raven turned himself into a hemlock needle floating in the water she drank. She became pregnant, and eventually Raven was born of her. Though the chief had been angry at his daughter, he came to love his grandchild. Soon Raven began to cry and begged to play with the moon, but when the chief allowed him to, Raven threw it up through the smoke hole, where it could not be recovered. Still Raven cried and asked to play with the other bright ball. When he was given it, he flew out through the smoke hole himself, carrying the sun with him.

Always, Raven was greedy, doing what he did for himself, not for others. Thus the Haida did not hold him in great respect, even if so many good things had come from him.

"Does he still try to trick people?" Luke asked. He sat on an empty cedar box, his elbows on his knees and the glass jar of ink on the floor in front of him. Little droplets of the ink had splattered his trousers and the paper with the words written on it; he didn't seem to notice, or to care. Gao would rather not have liked this white man, but it was hard not to. He acted as though he really wanted to hear the stories and to know why the Haida believed the things they did.

Sometimes Gao let himself hope that this white man did not talk out of the other side of his mouth. Luke said that he wanted to show the *yetz haada* what the Haida were really like, so they wouldn't believe the things that were untrue, that made the Haida sound bad. Maybe Gao should have let Luke take the objects he wanted, if his museum was so powerful.

Gao was about to answer Luke's question when they were interrupted. The old woman had come as she said she would, with her nephew trailing behind like a dog that had been kicked.

Luke set aside his paper and pen and slowly stood. "Dagas. *Clahhow-ya.*"

Dagas stood shamefaced. He did not want to meet anybody's eyes. "I would talk to the *yetz haada.*"

"If you want, I will stay to put your words into the white man's language," Gao said. He was careful not to look at the old woman.

Kate appeared around the screen from where she had been working. Gao saw her bend and break a thread with her teeth before she came closer to hear what the visitors wanted.

Dagas looked not so much like a dog now, as like a rabbit being hunted by a hawk. Gao knew that the chief didn't want anybody to hear what he had come here to say, but neither Dagas nor the old woman spoke the white man's language. How could he tell Gao no? All the while, the old woman looked at him and waited, her arms crossed.

"Yesterday something bad came over me." The foolish one was sweating. He spoke very fast. "I talked as if I would sell things. I let the white man take them to look at and decide which he wanted to buy."

Gao did not let his expression change. He put the words into English.

Luke said, "Yesterday I bought some things. We agreed on a price. I paid the money to Dagas and in return, he gave me the things. They are mine now."

Dagas gave a fleeting, desperate look at his aunt. "I have the money," he said loudly. "I want to buy them back."

Gao translated; Luke said, "Ask him if the price was an unfair one."

"When I was not myself, I thought the price was fair. I owe a man money, and I thought that I could pay it. But today I am ashamed of the way I got the money."

Scathingly, Luke said, "Ask him if he is a chief or a little boy who must ask his mother before he does anything."

The old woman waited without comprehension. Before Gao could translate, Kate stepped forward. "What a despicable thing to say! I suppose you cozened him into secretly selling you things, and now you claim he is weak-willed only because he changed his mind!"

Luke snapped, "He approached me, not the other way around! I am not in the habit of tricking anybody! He offered some items for sale, and we agreed on a generous price for each. The matter was straightforward."

She crossed her arms, her expression much like the old woman's. "What did you buy?"

"That's hardly the issue . . ."

"What was it?"

"Masks," he said shortly. "A dance headdress and rattle. What difference does it make? How would you feel if you had paid on outrageous price for some fine fabric from a merchant in Victoria and then he chased you down the street demanding it back?"

"If he had sold it to me in error, I would agree without hesitation," Kate said.

Luke's voice rose to a near howl. "In error? He knew perfectly well what he was selling! Now, because some old biddy doesn't approve, he wants them back! Well, he can't have them! Blast it, Gao, tell him what I said!"

When Gao did, there was so much noise that it was as if the wind called Pebble Rattler had become trapped inside the house with them. The old woman began screaming at Luke. Dagas acted as if he were angry, to cover his shame. Kate and Luke continued to argue. Only Gao said nothing.

Finally, Luke roared, "Devil take it, he can have the damn things back, if that will shut you all up!"

Pebble Rattler swirled out through the cracks of the house and left silence in its wake. Luke stomped over to a cedar box and lifted the lid. One by one, he thrust the things inside at Dagas and the old woman. When Gao saw the killer-whale mask, he was glad he had gone to the foolish one's aunt. He had seen the mask once before, in a dance. It was used to act out the story of how the chief's family first became looked up to, noble. Without the mask, how could they keep their respect?

Dagas and the old woman returned the money and took their things, hurrying away as if they thought Luke might snatch them back. Only in the doorway did the aunt stop. She turned as fiercely as someone acting out Oolalla, the demon who came from the mountains to devour men.

"That one—" her voice shook when she pointed at Luke "—is a maggot that feasts on a carcass." Then she was gone.

Glowering after her, Luke demanded, "What did she say?"

Gao would not have told him. Kate did.

"I gave them back what they wanted, didn't I?"

"Reluctantly." Her voice stung like a jellyfish.

"How was I to know that buying those particular things would stir up trouble?" In a fit of temper, Luke kicked the log that had been his seat. It jolted sideways and knocked over the ink bottle. He swore and hastily snatched it up, but the black ink smeared his fingers. "The devil with it! What I'd like to know is how that old crone found out what her nephew had sold me."

"You were obviously overheard," Kate said.

"Indeed." He narrowed his eyes to slits and looked straight at Gao. "By somebody who skulked around eavesdropping, too cowardly to show himself!"

It seemed to Gao that this would be a wise time to think of someplace else he ought to be.

"You wouldn't happen to have had anything to do with this, would you?" Luke demanded.

Gao took a step back.

Kate said, "Why accuse Gao? It could as well have been me."

Luke's narrowed, glittering eyes stayed fixed on Gao's face. "You," he said, "would never have left your photographic equipment untended. I seem to recall, however, that your assistant, who had promised to be there, was missing. Why don't you ask him where he was?"

Gao told himself that he had done what was right. Why should he lie, as though he had reason to feel shame?

"I heard you and that one talk about buying and selling," he said, holding his head high. "I heard you say you would meet him when nobody would see. I followed you to find out what he wanted to sell."

"And then told his aunt."

"Yes."

Luke paused and took a deep breath. "Why didn't you just stop him?"

"Because then he might have met you at a different time, when I was not there. Now he will not sell anything."

"The old biddy'll have him under her thumb," Luke said sourly. He set down the ink bottle and absentmindedly wiped his fingers on his trousers. "Well, what's done is done. I suppose there's no use in asking you not to interfere again."

"No."

"I didn't think so." He raised an eyebrow and looked from Gao to Kate. "I have no doubt that my reputation here is shot. I was going to put on a potlatch of my own, but now I suppose the effort would be wasted. I might as well save my goods for another stop. Tomorrow why don't we take a look at that ruined village Gao says is here in the inlet and see any other local sights, then move on the next day."

Gao nodded, in his usual way showing no approval or disapproval. "I will tell Kun taos."

"Gao."

He stopped.

Luke nodded at the slate carving, which still lay where Gao had set it. "I may occasionally wish you to the devil, but your carving is fine enough to make it worth putting up with you."

The words were not completely clear to Gao, but he understood the sense of them. He would not have cared what most white men thought of his skill, but this one admired the things the Haida carved of cedar and the soft slate. Gao was glad to know that Luke thought his carving was good.

He spoke before he thought. "I could carve you a mask like the one with the killer whale."

"Nobody would object to that?"

Gao shook his head. "That mask goes with the stories and has been used in dances. I can carve one that is like it, but it will not be the same." He struggled to explain. "It will be like the images on paper that you call photographs. The one of me is like me, but not me. It cannot move or sing or eat."

"It has no spirit to animate it," Kate said softly.

Gao did not know what "animate" was, so he only waited.

After a moment, Luke nodded. "I understand. In the museum, it will not matter. The people who look would not see the difference between that mask and the one that is only a copy, anyway. If you can carve so skillfully, I will buy what you make."

Gao nodded again, and the hope in his chest unfurled leaves that reached for the sun. It might be that there was a way after all to stop people like Luke from taking so many things that could never be replaced. Families might care someday about what they had lost, even though they didn't care right now. They used what they still owned, but they would like to have European things instead.

That way would also allow him to carve, and to gain greater skill. It might be that as soon as next winter, he could raise a pole to remember his father. If he showed that he could do that, Jadal's parents might consider him worthy enough to be their son-in-law.

Now Gao wondered whether this white man was so different from others like him, or if the others might also have bought things he carved had he said he was willing to sell. Perhaps he too had been foolish.

But he would not be so foolish as to trust the white man completely. He would still watch him.

The village of Grizzly Bear Town, or Skedans, was sheltered by a long, narrow peninsula thrusting out from the mountainous island that was the third largest in the Queen Charlotte chain. Their arrival there was greeted by the usual reception from children and barking dogs.

They had moved their possessions into one of the houses that Gao thought was called Peaceful House, and Gao and Luke were about to go officially to announce their arrival to the town-chief when the sound of pounding came from the front of the house. A voice raised a cry. *"Huuu!"*

It was usually a summons to gamble, or sometimes to wrestle, neither of which seemed likely so soon after their appearance. Kate's curiosity insisted that she follow the men, who were hastening to the oval entry, over which Luke had tacked a blanket.

Outside were six men, each dressed in a dancing skirt, leggings, a hat, and cedar-bark rings. Their faces were painted, and one beat time with a stick. It was he who said something in a language Kate did not know, perhaps Tsimshian, commonly used on ceremonial occasions.

Gao translated, "The spirits will stand up today. They invite you all, and you must wear good clothing."

A potlatch, then, Kate thought, and wistfully contemplated the meager contents of her trunk. Nothing therein qualified as "good clothing." The only alternative to crumpled muslin was the heavier woolens brought for winter wear: skirts, thick chemise and stockings, and a gray wool mantle with fur trimming. In Skidegate, her wardrobe's lacks would have been obvious, as many of the women regularly replenished their own wardrobes in Victoria. Here, she might be lucky enough to find that the women dressed more traditionally, rather than in European clothing that would put her attire to shame.

Which begged the question of why she cared.

On the heels of the six men, who progressed to the next house, came a familiar figure. Durham bounded over a log that intruded on the path and waved vigorously, calling, "I heard that you were here. At last!"

Luke grumbled, "I don't know whether to be glad to see him or not."

"You knew we would catch up with him sooner or later. Surely sooner is better, so that he doesn't beat you to Tanu and Ninstints as well."

Despite the truth of her words, he continued in a similar train under his breath, but Kate ceased to attend. The sight of another white man, similarly dressed to Luke, made inevitable her fresh awareness of the contrast between the two men.

Mr. Durham undoubtedly considered that he was roughing it, because his boots had lost their high shine and his frock coat was wrinkled. Luke, of course, had started out that way. He had stayed clean-shaven, however, and had bathed more often than she. Kate knew he had plunged at least once into the cold stream that emptied into Cumshewa Inlet, as well as partaking of the sponge baths she had been forced by modesty to consider adequate.

Somehow, despite the primitive conditions, Durham still boasted a starched collar. Luke, in contrast, had shed his coat and rolled up the sleeves of his rumpled flannel shirt, which was open to expose a strong brown throat. Waiting with crossed arms and a shoulder braced against the frontal pole, he had an animal magnetism that was at home here in this wild setting, where Durham's urbanity and refinement sat ill.

"You're just in time for the celebration!" Durham had come up to them while she was indulging in the sort of treacle suitable to a young lady overcome by her first romantic feelings. Thank heavens Luke's attention had not been on her as she admired his brawny chest and muscular forearms!

Flustered, she said the first thing that came into her mind. "Have you been here long?"

Luke gave her a sharp look, and she realized that he, at least, would assume her to be probing Durham's whereabouts when she had been attacked.

Durham, however, said blithely, "Oh, for a week or more. I found little worth pursuing in Cumshewa, and heard that a dance and potlatch were to be given here. Not much has happened yet; several days ago, a number of young men headed down the beach and into the woods, uttering strange whistling sounds all the way. I don't think they came back that day, anyway. Some guests have arrived from Tanu. The greeting was odd; the hosts went down to the beach and laid out gambling mats and sticks, which my guide tells me is a form of invitation that meant the guests were being asked to stay until after the potlatch. Sounds as though it's to be tonight."

"So I understand," Luke said with reasonable civility, considering how he felt about Durham, who followed them uninvited into the house.

He looked around at its shadowy corners. "These places aren't exactly cosy, are they?"

"No," Kate agreed, "but we've been fortunate in the weather thus far. The one snowfall was a mere dusting."

"I hope it doesn't rain tonight. The Indians are no doubt accustomed to it, but when they all crowd into the house to see the spectacle, the odor of unwashed savages gently steaming themselves dry must be nigh on unbearable!"

Fortunately, Gao was presently out of earshot, but Kun taos was near enough to hear, though unable to understand. Kate said sharply, "I believe they are as clean as most white men in similar circumstances."

"I offended you."

"*I* am not the one you might have offended."

"You're worried about one of the Indians understanding me?" He smiled with condescension. "Even those who claim to speak English understand only one word in ten, you know. They haven't your sensibilities, anyway."

Kate was momentarily speechless.

He continued, "Ah, well, I'd best let you change out of your traveling costume. I suppose I'll see you later?"

"Yes, yes, how can we help it?" Luke said.

Durham apparently didn't recognize the insult, and he went away repeating his delight at their arrival.

Kate gazed after him. Of nobody in particular, she inquired, "How is it that a man with such excellent manners and a great deal of charm is so unlikable?"

Luke's eyes met hers. A faint smile curved his mouth. He said quietly, "What's most remarkable is how few people notice."

She was unreasonably warmed by his approbation. Or perhaps it was not the words at all, but the look in his eyes, so blue that for an instant she saw nothing and no one else.

But inevitably he turned away to speak to Gao, who was just arriving from his visit to the town-chief, and Kate tried to ignore her strangely accelerated heartbeat. Repairing to her trunk once more, she gazed at its contents without much hope.

The evening's festivities turned out to be the most elaborate and expertly choreographed that Kate had seen in many years, though according to Gao, others at Skedans in the old days were more impressive. Kate was sorry she hadn't yet asked permission to photograph.

"Once they made thunder and lightning," he said. "They used dynamite, I think."

A novice of the Eagle crest was being initiated as one of those whom the gambling spirit spoke through. A huge fire had been kindled in the host's house. When the guests filed in, those at the back of the house, who were Ravens, began the singing. All put out their hands as they would if they were gambling. Behind them stretched a curtain, above which the tops of two trees could be seen.

Kate, Kun taos, Gao, and Luke were squeezed amongst the crowd on the second level, where the men had a good view and Kate had to stand on tiptoes to see around a woman who stood in front of her. Kate had tried to avoid treading on toes or being plastered against Luke, but it was a battle she lost when a child wormed her way through the crowd to the woman's side. At the strangled sound Kate made as she was shoved back, Luke reached out a long arm and wrapped it around her, gently propelling her to a place in front of him. He kept a hand on her shoulder, firmly anchoring her so closely before him that she could feel the rise and fall of his chest when he breathed. There was no escape without betraying her self-consciousness.

In front of the curtain, the main event played itself out. The novice, a boy of perhaps fifteen, laid out a mat and sticks. From behind the curtain came a man who sat down to gamble, bringing with him his own bundle of sticks. As the two played, he guessed each stick when it was drawn from the bundle, and the audience repeated its name. At last it appeared that he had won. He took both sets of sticks and began dancing, singing what Kate interpreted as a spirit song.

As he danced, he threw one set of sticks at each treetop. The result was startling; quite magically, the sticks became birds, which, with a panicky flutter of wings, swirled above the audience and one by one escaped through the smoke hole.

More dancing took place, accompanied by songs in Tsimshian. In the grand finale, a small pole was brought out from behind the curtain. The pole was laid across the shoulders of a man, attired in a magnificent Chilkat shawl, who stood to receive it.

"He is the chief of Those-Born-at-Skedans," Gao murmured. "Watch."

Two other men stood and simultaneously sat upon the

ends of the pole forming a sort of seesaw with the chief as the fulcrum.

"What the devil does that mean?" Luke asked as the pole was lowered and the murmurings amongst the crowd turned to chatter as people headed for the food steaming outside on huge fires.

"He is the town-chief, and by this, he says that he is the greatest chief of the Haida. The weight of other chiefs is as nothing to him."

"Interesting," Luke said later as he and Kate walked alone though the darkness back to their current home away from home. "They can't seem to make up their mind whether to be self-deprecating or vainglorious. You'd think that one or the other would be considered good manners."

"Of course the deprecation is universally known to be insincere," she pointed out. "It is not unlike the hostess in Victoria who knows her dinner to be a triumph of culinary achievement, all the while assuring her guests that it's nothing unusual, their compliments are too, too kind."

"But you must admit that subtlety is somewhat lacking here."

"Because we value subtlety, it doesn't mean that it's admired by all, you know."

"Ah," he said with faint amusement, "an ethnologist in spirit." As though it were a matter of course, he took her arm to steer her around a stack of cordwood.

Her voice was slightly breathless as she answered, "No, I haven't the ability to become clinically detached. My interests are more inclined to people than to cultures."

"People *are* the culture, and vice versa," Luke argued. He pushed aside the blanket and stepped back for her to enter the house ahead of him. Inside, it was very dark; until he came up behind her with the lantern, Kate's feet were guided only by the orange glow of coals in the fire pit one level down. He continued: "It is rare to be willing to see people within *their* context rather than your own."

"Why, I do believe that's a compliment." Striving for

lightness, she instead achieved a tone that she realized with horror might be taken for flirtation.

His voice from behind her sounded oddly rough. "Do I give you so few?"

She deliberately didn't turn, which would have revealed her expression in the lamplight. "Not at all! Why, you defended my prowess as a photographer quite admirably when Mister Durham tried to return me to the kitchen."

"To the kitchen?" He set down the lamp on a conveniently placed trunk as she warmed her hands on the banked fire. "Ah yes. I recall that he thought your biscuits were a greater achievement than is your photography."

"His view is held by more than not," she said, a hint of bitterness escaping. "Particularly by men."

"There are those of us who are exceptions."

She turned her head to meet his gaze, but found his face shadowed. She knew that she ought to agree, ought to put into words her deep sense of gratitude. Yet some need for greater honesty compelled her to say, "Can you tell me truthfully that my gender didn't give you cause to hesitate about hiring me?"

After a moment of silence, he said, "I cannot. But my reasons were more . . . personal than societal."

Kate supposed he was referring to his wife. She found herself strangely reluctant to ask questions. Her relationship with Luke was a peculiar and delicate balance between the intimate and the businesslike. The idea of upsetting that balance was frightening. How would they manage in the long weeks of winter to come if the ground became so shaky underfoot?

And yet . . . and yet a part of her wanted nothing more than to experience life at its most uncertain. Part of her wanted very badly to know whether the look she sometimes saw in his eyes was for her, or whether she only made him think of another woman, patiently waiting back in Boston.

And so she said, "Your wife . . . Did she . . . does she . . . travel with you?"

She heard a long sigh. "She did, and died because of it."

"I'm sorry," Kate said softly after a pause. "I didn't mean to pry." But, of course, she had meant to do just that.

"Her name was Mary." He sat on a turned-up tree stump, elbows braced on his knees, and stared into the low fire. "She was a pretty, delicate creature, as talented as you but in a different art. Mary could draw and paint in a way that was more than representational. She saw the spirit that lay beneath the surface. Gao would not have wanted her to draw a mask and then take the drawing away when we left; he would have thought she had stolen the spirit." His voice became harsh. "I saw only her talent, not her frailty. Selfishly, I wanted her with me, and I wanted to make use of her for the sake of ethnology. I knew she was frightened when we departed on our second expedition, but I laughed at her fears. I thought I could protect her; I thought she merely suffered from nervous excitement." Even in profile, his face betrayed his anguish.

"Surely she could have refused to go."

"She wanted to please me." He turned to look at her. His mouth was twisted, his fingers knotted into fists. "Even though I offered to leave her behind, she knew me too well. The entire damnable tragedy came about because she couldn't bear to disappoint me."

Kate's fingernails bit into her palms. "What happened?"

"We went to the Yucatan Peninsula to excavate Mayan ruins. Mary was following me up a pyramid when she stepped on a poisonous snake."

"I suppose no medical help was near . . ."

His raw voice cut her off. "If it had bitten her, at worst she would have been vilely ill. But she wore high boots. I doubt the adder could have struck her through the leather. No, she had lain awake nights, terrified, listening to the sounds of the jungle. Now when she saw the snake, she reacted with fear rather than intelligence. She stepped back . . ." He could not continue.

And fell. The words did not need to be said. She saw the scene, Luke turning, reaching desperately for the woman who tumbled back, her pretty face contorted with terror.

She ached to touch him in comfort, but hadn't the courage. "I'm sorry," she whispered.

He hunched his shoulders in a shrug and didn't answer. The fire popped, sending a burst of sparks that briefly illuminated the deeply carved lines on his face.

How had he been able to bear the guilt that still tore at him with such sharp claws? she wondered. "And yet . . ." Kate scarcely knew she was speaking aloud, "you hired me."

He gave a laugh not unlike the sound of a canoe being scraped across gravel. "I swore I would never take a woman on my travels again. Yet little more than four years later, I find myself breaking my own vow. I suppose it was selfishness again. Selfishness and . . ." He abruptly broke off.

"And?" she pressed.

His voice was odd, as was the way he looked at her. "I didn't see Mary in you. I thought you were stronger."

Why did the words hurt so badly? She had always known that she was not a woman who attracted men. But to be told so bluntly that she was nothing like his delicate, pretty wife, to know that he had hired her precisely because she possessed an unwomanly strength . . . !

"You have a directness, a determination, an understanding of yourself that Mary lacked. And no wonder! She was a girl, not a woman." He seemed to be talking to himself. "I wonder now if I loved her at all, or whether it was her talent."

Above all, Kate thought, she must hide how she felt. He must never know.

"You speak as though they are separate entities. Your wife was not just a woman, but an artist as well. How could you *not* love that part of her?"

"You are not like her, and yet you are. I must be mad." He shook his head and lurched to his feet, as though he had drunk too much of the whiskey Kate knew he had not touched. "Why can't I be content with the kind of woman other men admire? Why am I so damnably tempted to take the same kind of risk again?"

Her mouth dry, Kate rose to her feet. Her heart beat so loudly, it was as though she heard the drums again, as though the dancers moved like ghosts in this dark house. Did she understand him right?

"Sims is not the only one you shouldn't trust," he said roughly. "You are not safe with me."

She didn't want to be safe, she saw suddenly. She could not have been less like her mother. What an odd moment to feel pity for one's own parent!

Kate opened her mouth to speak, to say what, she knew not, but she had hesitated too long.

"Go to bed." He turned away, leaving the lamp near her, his strides taking him to the foot of the ladder that led up to ground level. "God knows what you must be thinking. I sound like one of Gao's wild men. You are perfectly safe, insofar as it is within my power to protect you."

"I chose to come. You are not my custodian." Some instinct told her she must convince him of that, before all else.

"Go to bed." He sounded weary this time. "I'll be outside, you keep the lamp. I will no doubt seem saner come morning." He didn't wait for a reply, for reassurances he didn't want. He was gone, leaving her alone, filled with trepidation and joy.

She had wanted the ground to move beneath her, and now it had. But did she have the courage her mother had not, the courage that would allow her to seek her own happiness, rather than wait for it to come to her?

For Luke's terrible guilt would not let him take the next step. No, if she were to discover what he meant, to experience real passion, it would be up to her to press Luke until he could not contain his emotions.

The idea was unnerving, for he would not be the only one taking a risk. The loss of his respect, the potential humiliation . . . She tried to close her mind to these possibilities, but could not do so entirely, just as she could not be sure that she hadn't misinterpreted him.

Did she have the courage to find out?

Chapter Fourteen

The next day dawned clear and cold. Kate awakened late to find all three men gone—assuming they had slept at all. She had heard none of them come in.

She emerged through the blanket-covered front door to find the tide low, exposing jagged, barnacle-covered rocks and brightly colored denizens of the pools and rivulets. Several varieties of starfish were visible even from a distance, their gaudy orange colors shining wetly. Children picked their way along, squatting occasionally to watch a crab or poke a mussel. Women with digging sticks were more purposeful, wearing hiked-up skirts lest they become soggy from the beach puddles, and sturdy boots that might have been their husbands', but were needed now to protect even callused soles from the rocks. Gulls fluttered and squawked as they fed on the riches.

Mist floated ghostlike above the kelp-covered water that rose and fell in swells to break into white foam on the shore. The steep, spruce-mantled mountain behind the village reached the pale blue sky without its usual shroud of clouds.

Kate's gaze followed the curve of the bay in the other direction, toward the point with its two peculiarly shaped protuberances that reminded her privately of nothing so much as a woman's nipples. If she could find a path that would take her to the end of the point, which dropped steeply into the sea, she might have an excellent vantage place for photographs.

She decided that for the moment, she would begin by photographing the poles and house fronts as Luke had requested she do. He hoped to discover the family and house names to go with each photograph, thus having an accurate record for posterity; already the people had forgotten who had owned a few of the houses that had been long abandoned. What had been a populous village had been shrinking since the 1850s, when the first smallpox epidemic had struck the Haida.

Where was Luke? she wondered, in part relieved that she didn't have to face him again just yet. When they did meet, would he mention their previous conversation, or would he pretend that it had never taken place? Ought she follow his lead?

Her nervousness seemed to be swamping last night's sense of feminine triumph. She had read so much into so few words! Even if Luke *had* been indicating a certain interest in her, she could not assume it to be other than physical. He was a man; she was the only white woman he had seen since the *Skeena* left them at Metlakatla, the only white woman he *would* see for the next three months. He might be fighting some desire to touch her, to hold her—even to possess her—but that didn't mean his emotions were meaningfully engaged. He had vowed never to take a woman on his travels again, and though he had made an exception this time, he might well regard it as an unpleasant experience he preferred not to repeat. There was no denying the tension between them that seemed always to stand in the way of the kind of camaraderie he must be accustomed to.

In the years to come, she might regret it if he never kissed her; her previous experiences, embarrassingly few, had left her disappointed. Surely there was more to the whole business, else why did women in love blush and simper and giggle? Why did they so willingly hand over their lives and fortunes to men?

Kate had always assumed that she would never find out. Last night had taught her differently. She had felt something mysterious, something that sent warmth through her bloodstream and weakened her knees. She had wanted very badly to know what came next. Still, it was ridiculous to suppose that even were she brave enough, she could tempt him with some kind of feminine wile. As if she had ever possessed any such thing!

A child's shout brought her abruptly back to herself. She realized that she had been staring into the distance for some time. She should get her camera and begin work, if only to give herself something else to think about.

Another shout joined the first, and Kate shaded her eyes to see what the boys were pointing at. A small coastal canoe was approaching from the south, poking its way through the thick kelp. Children were gathering, just as they had when she and Luke arrived yesterday. More visitors?

Her curiosity aroused, Kate strolled down the curve of shore, staying well above the rocky beach. She was passing the enormous house called "The-Clouds-Sound-Against-It-as-They-Pass-Over" when Luke ducked through the hide-covered doorway just ahead of her. He was straightening when his eyes met hers. For an instant, he froze as they looked at each other. She had the sense that he was searching for something on her face, some hint of . . . what? And then he stood upright, his expression so much as usual that she wondered if she had imagined what had gone before.

"Good morning," he said, inclining his head. "I hope you slept well."

What could she do but agree that she had? "And you?"

"If Kun taos didn't snore . . ." His gaze had gone past her. "Surely that's not Sims. Damn!"

The last was so heartfelt that she turned to stare at the men stepping out of the canoe. Two of them were obviously white men; they were allowing the Indians who had wielded the paddles to do all the work in dragging the canoe above the tide mark.

One she recognized immediately: Mr. Richardson. She felt a thrill of alarm. What was he doing here?

The other man she didn't know. Tall and raw-boned, he strode confidently beside the slighter missionary. Dark hair and a close-cropped beard gave him a saturnine aspect that went with a long face. As he came nearer, she saw that he was the kind of man who must shave his neck every day, whose fingers would be covered with curly dark hairs.

They were approaching, already hailing her and Luke. She stole a glance at Luke, to see that his face was unexpectedly grim. He and Mr. Richardson had conceived a cordial—and mutual—dislike for one another, but surely that wasn't enough to explain his inimical stare now. Then she saw that it was not the missionary he was looking at, but the other man.

The bearded man was smiling, but with a certain wryness. He held out his hand to Luke. "Richardson told me you were wintering here. It's been a while."

Luke ignored the extended hand. "Not long enough, Jarvis."

"You're still holding a grudge." The stranger dropped his hand, and the smile became, if anything, more rueful. "Merely because I bested you in a game that we both play quite well."

"A game to you," Luke said stiffly. "I consider preservation of the Indians' past anything but a game."

Kate looked in bewilderment from one face to the next. Luke had made plain his dislike of Durham, but this was something else again. His arm brushed hers, every muscle rigid, and the animosity in his eyes was deadly.

Richardson appeared oblivious. With one hand, he drew her aside. "Kate! What luck to come upon you so soon!"

"You came in search of me?" she asked in astonishment.

"No, no, merely I felt uneasy in my mind about you, and thought to reassure myself. I'm here to bring God's word to these isolated villages, and to continue to persuade their inhabitants to move to Skidegate, where they will be near the Mission, but I must confess that I timed this particular journey in hopes of overtaking you."

"I'm grateful for your concern," she said. "But as you see, I'm in one piece, none the worse for my travels. I flatter myself that I have taken some excellent photographs—"

It was his turn to sound rueful when he interrupted. "And I know well how absorbed you become in your hobby. Here I was, determined to persuade you to return to Skidegate with me. To continue around to the west coast, battling winter seas, is madness!"

She couldn't decide whether to be irritated at his officiousness, or touched by his concern. Half of her attention was on the other two men. Jarvis was talking with every appearance of amiability, but Luke's face was set in granite. In the meantime, the missionary continued, saying something about Mr. Jarvis's kindness in offering transportation on his steamboat.

Kate contented herself with a cool, "I cannot back out on my agreement now. But tell me, you did say 'steamboat'? Is Mister Jarvis the captain? It's fortunate that he knew the coast well enough not to attempt to bring a ship in here."

Richardson's brown eyes remained grave, but he accepted, at least temporarily, her sidetrack. "No, Jarvis is here on much the same mission as Mister Brennan, though I understand that he collects not for museums, but for private interests. Thus he is able to travel in greater comfort."

Aha! Kate thought. No wonder Luke despised him!

"We left the steamboat several miles to the south," the missionary continued, "where the captain deemed the anchorage to be safe. He's an experienced hand on this coast." He glanced to the private collector. "We'd best be settling in. Can you recommend an empty house? I prefer that to being a guest."

The Reverend Hewitt had felt the opposite; his time spent as a member of Haida households had allowed him to know the people in a way he could not have known them otherwise. He had sought to influence his charges in more than the spiritual realm, and how could he do that if he didn't see them at work cooking, laundering, and parenting?

But in all fairness, her father was unusual in his aims and in the means he had employed to accomplish them. He had not liked the idea of tearing children from their parents to rear them as good Christians, though such boarding schools were becoming increasingly common. He had believed that the family as a whole could be taught the arts of civilized life, could grow in their faith together. Kate knew without asking that her father's successor would not feel the same.

"Over half the houses are abandoned," she said. "You have a wide choice. Do you stay long?"

"Only for two nights. I will arrange to hold a service this evening. Mister Jarvis feels that he can buy sufficient articles once the word spreads that he pays top prices."

Was that what he and Luke had been arguing about? Luke would hardly be happy to have another competitor arrive, and at that, one who could outbid him on all fronts.

The two newcomers departed to set up housekeeping. With Luke stalking at her side, Kate returned to Peaceful House to collect her photographic equipment.

She said dryly, "I take it you and Mister Jarvis are acquainted."

"Regrettably," Luke said through taut lips. "He's an unprincipled, unscrupulous . . ." Words failed him. "Jarvis is what Gao imagines me to be. Wherever he travels, he leaves behind a trail of outrage that hampers the efforts of legitimate collectors such as myself. The Haida are so vulnerable. He will take unmerciful advantage of them."

Surprised that his thoughts were not entirely selfish, she commented, "Mister Richardson said he pays top prices."

Luke growled. "Only when he can't steal whatever it is he covets."

"Perhaps if Gao warned people . . ."

"It's worth a try." Gloomily, he added, "I suppose Jarvis, too, assumes that Masset will have been stripped of anything worth collecting and thus must come this way, even if it means dogging my footsteps. No, blast it, he probably came just for that reason! Assumes he can outbid me, and with the steamboat, he can get ahead of us as well. He's probably relishing the chance to pay me back for past disagreements."

"Do you know," Kate said thoughtfully, "I wonder if Mister Richardson didn't persuade him to come here first. He says he is determined to take me back with him."

"You are not so trusting . . . ?"

"Of course not."

Shortly thereafter, she set up her tripod outside Peaceful House to begin her day's work, Luke's last words ringing in her ears: "Photograph as many poles as possible, before Jarvis and his kind cart them off. With a steamboat, he can buy the monumental pieces Durham and I are forced to pass by."

This particular house frontal pole illustrated a story that had interested her father because of its resemblance to the biblical flood. Supposedly, when the world was incomplete, Raven had quarreled with a chief named Qingi. To punish the chief, Raven called a flood upon Qingi's village. The chief had supernatural powers of his own, so he caused his segmented dance hat to grow so tall that the villagers were able to climb above the floodwater and so were saved.

At the foot of the pole, a man in a squatting position was portrayed. Eight tiny humans were depicted climbing the hat. On top was an eagle, seemingly sheltering the people with its wings.

"Stories of cataclysmic floods are common," the Reverend Hewitt had said thoughtfully. "I've talked with other missionaries who have collected similar stories from China to Africa. It makes one wonder . . ."

Now Kate released the shutter, only to realize a fraction of a second too late that her own shadow would lie across the developed image. The error was so amateurish that she was disgusted with herself. She didn't have enough plates to waste one merely because her concentration was inadequate to the task. Nor did she know why she felt so unsettled.

Richardson and Jarvis would soon be gone; she and Luke were unlikely to encounter them again. Why had she been so surprised to see the missionary? The Reverend Hewitt had made a practice of traveling to these southern villages several times a year. He had not usually come in the winter, when the weather could change unpredictably, but he, too, might have seized the chance of traveling by steamboat. Except, of course, that he would not have come with a man like Mr. Jarvis.

She ought to be grateful that their arrival had been so timely, saving her from the awkwardness of this morning's encounter with Luke. He had certainly forgotten her quickly enough in his agitation over Jarvis's presence.

Sighing, Kate moved the camera to a better position for a second exposure.

Kate had thought to attend Mr. Richardson's evening service, to be held at Grizzly Bear Mouth House, the residence of a Raven family belonging to the Peninsula People. When she asked if Luke cared to join her, he shook his head in some irritation.

"I don't trust myself not to speak out in defense of all he is denouncing. Since that would be useless, I'll simply stay away."

Once again he was thinking of the Haida, not of himself. After all, the missionary's presence might actually work to Luke's advantage, persuading someone to sell objects he wouldn't otherwise part with. Yet Luke didn't seem to regard that potential advantage.

"Would you rather I don't go?"

A forkful of flaky white halibut meat halfway to his mouth, he looked at her in seeming astonishment. "Do you imagine that because I'm your employer, I have some say in your private convictions? Don't be ridiculous."

His indifference stung after last night's fantasies and her more recent charitable thoughts. "I wasn't implying any such thing," she said stiffly. "I thought only that you might be needing me to translate."

"No, I'll do very well with Gao," he said, sounding distracted.

After that, pride alone would have motivated her to go, even had it not been allied with a sense of duty. She carried a lamp but did not light it, for the half-moon lit the village with its pale, silvery glow. Kate proceeded cautiously, passed by others going in family groups, all knowing the trail well enough to move with confidence.

Thus she was alone by the time she reached the house. It was entered by an oval doorway just below Grizzly Bear's mouth on the frontal pole. No, not totally alone, for two others stood in front, the smaller and slighter of the figures speaking earnestly.

Kate hesitated when she realized that the language was English. With no intention of eavesdropping, still she heard the young woman.

"Will you marry us? Tomorrow, before you go?"

"You dare to ask?" The voice was familiar, but so cold. "Marriage is a sacrament that demands purity. I cannot accommodate the Gospel to your thoughtless sin."

"Please!" The slight figure raised her hands in supplication. "We could not come to Skidegate. I was at the cannery, and Gitajung, he was hurt when fishing. But now that you are here . . ."

"You have given way to gross appetites, despite having been shown the light of the Gospel. His Lord Jesus Christ is all-forgiving, but as His agent, I cannot sanction sin by wrapping you in His grace."

The girl's voice rose in a piteous cry, but the missionary turned away abruptly and ducked through the doorway. The hide swung into place behind him.

Kate's hand was pressed to her mouth. Momentarily, she was frozen, made dizzy by a memory that seemed to overlay the present, like a stereoscopic picture in which the two sides showed different scenes. By the time she was capable of movement, the girl had hurried past her. Kate would not know her tomorrow in the daylight, her features were not clear, but in silhouette, the moonlight revealed her "sin." The slight body was not so slight after all; rather, her waist was swelled with child.

There had been another time, when Kate was no more than fifteen. That young woman had not wanted to be married; she didn't even know who the father of her unborn babe was. Her own father had taken her to Victoria, where he prostituted both her and her mother. She alone returned to Skidegate. The misery of that life showed on her face, swollen and misshapen, and in the desperation in her eyes.

She asked the Reverend Hewitt for forgiveness, for the healing embrace of the church. He considered that she had given herself in sin willfully.

"She does not return to us in true repentance, but rather because she is disillusioned by the path she thought was paved with riches." Though his face held compassion, his voice was unwavering. "God is just, but demanding. She knew the price to be paid for rejecting Him."

The young woman could not seem to believe that the missionary—who had always been kind to her, leading her by the hand into the light—would turn his back now. And so she had come into the small, crude church that Sunday.

She stood in the doorway, blocking the sunlight, her body ripe to near fruition, yet her face childish and scared. The Reverend Hewitt stood already behind the pulpit, the Bible open before him. As an unnatural silence fell over the gathering congregation, he lifted his head. With all her being, Kate prayed to see his face soften.

Instead, she saw only distaste that hardened into anger. His voice thundered over the silent crowd of witnesses. "Begone, child of sin! You, who were welcomed within these doors, rejected the Lord God's teachings. There are only two choices: His eternal grace, or Hell for all eternity! You have chosen the last! Begone!"

The young woman's face had been utterly stricken, her

eyes huge and dark. Her arms were wrapped protectively about her swollen belly when she turned and rushed out.

Kate had convinced herself that she didn't know the young woman's fate, though there were whispers, hushed when she came near. It was easy to pretend ignorance, for there was no new gravestone in the churchyard, no earth rich and dark from fresh turning. Her name was never uttered again by Kate's father, and Kate could not remember it now. She had even forgotten the face, the occasion. It had been less painful to forget.

How could she have allowed herself? she wondered now in horror. At the time, she had been shocked. Before then, she had thought she was coming to know her father, who had been a stranger until the last year. She had begun to admire him, even if she didn't understand his dedication. Now, suddenly, she saw the man her mother had described: one so rigid that he could not, and would not, bend.

By his own lights, he was right. The young woman might well have gone willingly to Victoria, imagining the pretty clothes she could buy herself, the admiration of white men, the freedom from a life that was near drudgery for women. Was that so wrong? How could she have known what her choice meant? Were not children taught to accept the guidance of their parents?

Would it have been so wrong in turn to extend to her the forgiveness that Christ had offered to all?

Kate suddenly heard Gao's words. *You ask us to remember.* Do you *remember*? Was this memory the one he had asked her to recall?

Sitting attentively through the service had become an impossibility. Kate hurried back the way she had come, her pace heedless until she stumbled over an obstacle and fell painfully to her knees. The stinging in one shin brought tears to her eyes. She slumped there, each ragged breath teetering just shy of a sob. She was grateful that the nearest house was a skeleton in the process of being reclaimed by the forest; she didn't want to be overheard, to be forced to accept solicitous hands helping her to her feet, outcries—in whatever language—over a wound no worse than a child's scraped knee. She wanted only solitude in which to wallow in guilt.

The guilt was not hers, of course, but had she not turned her eyes away? Allowed herself to forget? What else had she forgotten in her complacency? she wondered bitterly.

At last she struggled to her feet, one hand on the log that had tripped her. She went more slowly now, hobbling, determined to regain her composure. She thought she had, until she came within the circle of firelight in Peaceful House.

Luke sat writing in deep concentration, surrounded by a semicircle of assorted objects he had purchased. It was his practice to take some time every few days to expand on his brief notes, before his recollection of what the previous owner told him had faded.

Kun taos was nowhere in evidence, but Gao was at work putting the finishing touches on the miniature pole that Luke so admired. Silence reigned but for an occasional pop from the fire and Luke's mumbled comments to himself.

She didn't know whether she had made a sound, but suddenly he looked up. With an exclamation, he was on his feet and at her side.

"What is it?"

Gao, too, sprang up as Luke helped Kate to a seat by the fire with all the solicitude she had dreaded. He crouched at her feet, his blue eyes seeing effortlessly through her defenses.

"Were you attacked?"

"No, no, of course not." She evaded the gaze of both men and stabbed pins back in her hair, where touch told her that it was slipping from its constraints. "I saw something that . . . that upset me. And then I stumbled. Of course I wasn't sensible enough to light the lantern. No, you needn't fuss. I'm perfectly fine."

He hadn't fussed at all, only waited impatiently while she babbled. "Where did you hurt yourself?"

Kate bent and lifted her skirt. Her thick stocking was ripped and her shin beneath it scraped raw.

Luke frowned. "Don't you know how easily even a minor

wound can become infected? Gao, do we still have boiling water on the fire?"

Kate said nothing more while he gently cleansed the scrape and covered it with a clean cloth, tied in place with thongs supplied by Gao. The Haida's presence was all that saved her from dwelling on the deft touch of Luke's long fingers.

He had not quite finished when he said, "What did you see?"

Gao waited, still standing.

"I . . ." She didn't want to tell them, but she knew that Gao's auspices were her only practical means of assisting the young woman. And so she told the two men of what she had overheard. "Do you know Gitajung?" she asked Gao.

"Yes. I did not know he was to marry, but it is true that he was hurt when he hunted sea lions with the other men."

"Will you tell him to take her somewhere else? Another missionary would marry them, especially if he thought them new converts and baptized them first."

Gao's dark, fathomless gaze rested on her face. "I will tell them."

"She sounded so . . . despairing." Kate pressed her lips together. "I don't like to think . . ." She couldn't finish.

Luke rose to his feet, his brows drawn, though his expression was thoughtful.

It was to Gao she looked, however. "Tonight reminded me of that young woman Father denied. She killed herself, didn't she?"

"She chose not to live," he said steadily. "She would not eat or drink. Her shame was great."

"It was my father who shamed her," Kate declared with undiluted bitterness.

"She does not hang her head now. We sang crying songs for her, so that she could have a good name in the Land of the Souls. We send her food and drink, so that she is not poor. Who knows when she might come back?"

"I wish I could believe that she would have another chance."

"Would your Great Chief of the Heavens think her so bad only because she was pregnant and not married?"

"No," Kate said, suddenly calm. "I don't believe he would think her bad. I believe it was my father who could not accept rejection. Do you know, he was infinitely patient with those who were not sure of their faith and had trouble letting go of their old ways. But once he had enough confidence to baptize a convert, he felt no sympathy at all for backsliding. He took it very personally."

Seeing Gao's puzzlement, Kate translated her reflections into his language, insofar as it was possible.

He nodded. "Our medicine men, too, are angry for themselves when someone does not believe in their power. It is as I said once about Kilslayoway. To make others believe, men like that must be strong. They must not let anyone say bad words about them."

"Men of God should have compassion above all else," Kate said. "Jesus would not have turned away a soul in need, whatever the cause of that need. My father was wrong to do so."

Luke spoke for the first time. "But we mortals are invariably flawed. Are you expecting more of your father than you do of other men?"

Her eyelids stung, and she blinked furiously. "I don't know!"

He produced a handkerchief that was none too clean. Kate had seen him use it for wiping accumulations of dirt and grease from the narrow, incised lines of carved objects. Still, it was better than nothing. She firmly blew her nose.

"Well, I missed the service," she said. "Gao, are most of the Skedans people Christian now?"

"Not yet." The mask he so often wore could not quite hide his bitterness. "But most people think the one you worship must be stronger even than Shining Heavens, else why are your people so many that you need new lands, when my people are dying from your diseases? They think that if they go to your church, they can have the things you have. They think that maybe your Great Chief of the Heavens can protect them. They close their ears to anyone who says we should remember our ancestors. They ask me what good remembering does. Soon they will all go to the Mission."

It was the longest speech Kate had heard Gao make. She had no answer, nor apparently did Luke. After a moment, Gao's mouth twisted and he turned abruptly and left, ducking through the doorway.

Kate's guilt was not assuaged, but rather many times multiplied, for Gao was right that the missionaries—even her father—took advantage of the Indians' fear of the unknown forces that had so changed their lives and taken away so many of their loved ones. Of course it was not salvation in this world that her father had promised, or believed in, but rather, in the next. But did the Indians truly understand, or did they expect that they could don the white man's religion as a sort of suit of armor, or perhaps as a new crest figure that would give them the *yetz haada*'s privileges and status?

Feeling unpleasantly melancholic herself, she saw that Luke had sunk down in his former place, but had picked up neither paper nor pen. His elbows were braced on his knees, his shoulders were slumped, and he appeared to be brooding over the objects he had earlier arranged around him—a mask, a woven fish trap, a carved wooden food vessel, and a doll that he had shown her the previous day; it had been chiseled from a stalagmite, and hair had been glued to its head.

He looked up to meet Kate's eyes, his own dark, his mouth set. "The old woman was right," he said wearily. "If I'm not a maggot feeding on the carcass, I'm at least a vulture circling above a dying creature. I talk of salvation, but my form of it is no more real to these people than your father's talk of the hereafter. Neither of us offer them anything here and now, not even hope."

"That's not altogether true," she protested, surprised to find that his despondency had begun to effect a cure of her own. "Father had a great deal that was useful to offer: a vaccination for the smallpox, his knowledge of medicine and sanitation, his experience in dealing with the authorities. He wrote letters and spoke in favor of the Indians' right to their land and to the minerals found under it. I told you he hoped to buy a steamboat so they could transport the furs to Victoria and thereby sell them for a fairer price than they get from the Hudson Bay Company. If only he had lived . . ." She stopped.

His eyebrow quirked up. "You've remembered his virtues, at least. Tell me, have I any?"

"You will provide a storehouse for their culture. How many times have you told me that? Who knows—" she said, only half-serious "—perhaps a hundred years from now, Haida who have forgotten the ways of their ancestors will be able to travel to Boston and find those ways carefully recorded in lined journals, the pages faded, the hand somewhat careless, but the content exact."

He grimaced. "Ah, but we're back to the unknown hereafter. Gao would be unlikely to see my storehouse as a point in my favor. If the things I collect were not sold in the first place, no storehouse would be needed."

She said bracingly, "But then Mister Jarvis and his kind would buy everything instead."

"Don't remind me."

She was actually enjoying herself. "Surely it's unwise to be in less than fighting fettle when the enemy is so near. Why, even as we speak, he is abroad doing his worst!"

A glimmer of humor showed in his eyes, though his tone remained gloomy. "What can I do? He can outbid me every time. I've even primed the pump for him, so to speak. When I think about the hours I've spent persuading the Indians to offer their best things for sale . . . And all for his benefit!"

At last they had arrived at the true source of his depression: He was sulking over Jarvis's inopportune arrival. Or was he? Something in the way he watched her made Kate wonder if, instead, he had assumed a part played for her benefit. Think of how he abhorred any accusation of altruism! Clearly, he would rather she thought him selfish.

"Well, *I* am going to bed," she announced. "You may do as you please. If I were you, however, I believe I'd be conspicuously about when that service ends, just in case Mister

Richardson has gained some new converts eager to be rid of all the idolatrous trappings of their old life."

"Do you think that hadn't occurred to me?" he inquired, less than graciously.

Kate smiled. "I'm nagging you. Isn't that a woman's role?"

"I wouldn't know. I haven't had one around long enough to find out."

She opened her mouth to riposte, but collected herself in time. She had never flirted in her life, but it would appear that she had been unconsciously studying the technique. She would *not* indulge that particular desire, which could pay humiliating dividends.

Instead, she said meekly, "Do you need me to accompany you?"

"To translate?" His eyes were unreadable. "No. I'll do well enough in Chinook. Will you feel safe here alone?"

"Yes, of course. Do you imagine that Mister Richardson will assault me with his Bible?"

He rose to his feet. The fire, which had been burning low, hissed and snapped unexpectedly. "Don't forget for a minute that somebody did assault you," he said grimly. "It cannot have escaped your notice that we seem to have reassembled the original cast."

"Are you so certain the murderer is not an Indian?"

"*I* am not the one who has dismissed the Skidegate Haida as suspects. That medicine man who confronted you sounds cold-blooded enough to me to have committed the crime. And as you know, I don't altogether trust Gao, though I find myself inclined to despite his confounded predilection for getting between me and the most desirable purchases."

"I cannot imagine Gao . . ."

"No, I can't either," Luke admitted. His dark brows were drawn together in one of his frowns that seemed to indicate troubling thoughts rather than actual irritation. "Besides, something about the crime suggests a white man to me. Perhaps it's only the planning . . . No, I keep coming back to Kiusta. Why there? Did the town mean something to your

father? Had he ever spoken of it in connection with anybody? Did he have some knowledge of the place that must
be coaxed out of him before he died?"

"I believe he had been there only once or twice," Kate
said slowly. "It's deserted, you know. The town's inhabitants moved to Masset, not to Skidegate. I cannot recall . . ."
Her words trailed away.

Luke's eyes narrowed. "You do remember something."

Flustered, she said, "No. I had a fleeting thought, but it
seems to have fled."

"In other words, you prefer not to tell me." He snatched
up his coat and thrust his arms into it. Then he dug into his
gladstone and produced a revolver. "Here. It's loaded, keep
this by you."

Kate regarded it with revulsion. "I didn't know you had
that. If I must have a weapon, I'd prefer a sturdy stick."

Now he was scowling at her. "Must you always be so
blasted independent? Whether you like it or not, you're a
woman and therefore given to some of your sex's weak-
nesses. Do you imagine that you could win a duel to the
death with the man who has already bashed in the heads of
at least three victims?"

"Who were surely taken by surprise . . ."

He spoke scathingly. "What if Gao returns tonight before
I do? What if Richardson calls to find out why you didn't
attend the service? Or your tame miner decides to visit,
whiskey bottle in hand, to reminisce? Any of them could
easily take you by surprise!"

Her protest was weak. "Sims is not here—"

"But will be so imminently. I think we can assume that he
will dog our footsteps from now on, at least until we pass
Ninstints."

She let out a long breath. "Very well," she said reluctantly, and accepted the revolver. It was considerably heavier than she had anticipated, and she nearly dropped it.

"Take care!"

"Now you worry about me shooting a foot off!"

"That's the least of my worries." His voice was rough.

"Kate . . . Hell." He closed his eyes momentarily, opened them. "Never mind. I won't be gone long."

He took his departure, having ruined any chance that she might actually get a good night's sleep. Instead, she shied at shadows and quivered at the faintest sound all the while she readied herself for bed. This was one night she would not undo her braid and leisurely brush out her hair! At last she blew out the lamp and pulled the blankets over her, wriggling to find a comfortable position on the unyielding surface. Her fingers touched the hard butt of the revolver and shrank back.

Her eyelids refused to close. She stared at the glow of coals and the darkness beyond them, trying to force her thoughts to an innocuous subject that would lull her to sleep. There didn't seem to be one.

. . . Was she to think about her father? The cruelties he had seen as justice? His death, unfair whatever the wrongs he had committed?

. . . The murderer, quite possibly a man she knew and had trusted?

. . . Luke, the only man she dared trust now, her bulwark, who would be leaving her when spring opened an escape from these storm-locked islands?

. . . Or should she think about her own course come spring: the lonely, possibly impoverished life that seemed more frightening the closer it came? Ought she stay in Victoria, which had the virtue of familiarity? Or would she find that women were treated with greater equality in America— in San Francisco perhaps, or Boise, or even Seattle? If there was need for a photographer . . .

She pushed back her panic and counted the weeks left to her. It was nearly Christmas. By late March or early April at the latest, the first steamboat would call at Skidegate and Luke would be ready to take passage, satisfied with his winter's work. Thanks to him, she would have a small nest egg and the luxury of a few weeks, or even a few months if she was careful, to find herself a means of earning a livelihood. The world was changing; she must believe that. Increasingly, women were being employed in capacities that were not traditional. Why would anybody be offended to discover that a studio photographer was a woman?

The life was one that had attracted her only a short while ago. She had imagined the freedom, the self-reliance, the end to mind-numbing idleness and lack of purpose. That it would be a trap of a different kind had not occurred to her then. Now she foresaw the penny-pinching, the equally mind-numbing repetition: one well-fed, complacent family after another, all posing stiffly, quibbling over her fees; the time she could devote to experimentation with her camera shrinking until she no longer had the curiosity to care.

Was this how Luke's wife had felt? Had she been terrified of going with him, but equally frightened of staying behind in the genteel society that must have dismissed her art as a charming diversion? Why could he not see that any woman of spirit and intelligence would gladly risk all to accompany him on his travels, to share the challenges and dangers, the excitement of discovery, and the pity and regret felt for what could not be salvaged? Did he know how rare was his willingness to admit a woman as peer?

Kate was still awake when he came in, shaking the mist off his hair. She lay very still, watching through her lashes as he stood above her for a long moment before beginning his preparations for bed. His back to her, he tugged off his boots, then shrugged out of his shirt. Kate was horrified with herself for watching, but guilty curiosity kept her eyes open. She was half-relieved and half-disappointed when he stripped off his trousers to reveal a gray union suit. Despite the places where it bagged, the thin wool was form-fitting enough to show broad shoulders and a strong back that narrowed to lean hips and legs.

Kate made an involuntary sound. He turned, and she was forced to pretend to sigh and roll over, as though unconsciously seeking greater comfort. Lying there with her back now to him, every muscle in her body was rigid as she imagined him staring at her, perhaps even taking the few steps to loom above her. She felt as a rabbit must feel when trying to stay immobile to avoid detection by a hunting owl. The urge to open her eyes, to *see* where he was and what he was doing, was nearly unendurable.

The silence continued; her nerves screamed for release. Kate held out for as long as possible, but eventually she had to turn again, opening her eyes just enough to see through the dark fan of lashes that he was wrapped in his blankets on his own mat, his back to her. With outrage, she saw that he was taking long, even breaths. He was asleep already!

All of her suffering had been for nothing. He hadn't suspected that she was awake, wasn't gazing at her with longing, wasn't lying sleepless with unrequited passion.

Kate was infuriated with herself yet again. Her aunt had been right to remind her of how foolish romantic notions were for a young woman in her position. She would only become bitter and unhappy if she let herself dream that this voyage would have such an unrealistic end. She must concentrate on practicalities and leave starry-eyed fictions to sheltered young ladies who would never be required to make their own way in the world.

Kate supposed that sleep had come. Why else was she so disoriented? Her head ached, her eyes struggled to focus. It was daylight, she could tell that much. But who had awakened her? She heard an outburst of familiar swearing, and a body thrashing about.

"What the devil . . . ?" Luke reared up, hair tousled and expression wild, the blankets around his waist.

The sound of angry shouts from outside removed any question of what had awakened them. Luke snatched up his pocket watch.

"It isn't much past dawn!" he said incredulously. He reached for his trousers. "I'll give them a piece of my mind. What infernal lack of consideration . . ." The crack of a gunshot was evidence that the argument—for such it seemed to be—had escalated at an alarming pace.

Kate was already pulling her dress over her head by the

time Luke shoved his feet into his boots. "Stay here," he ordered, seeing her head reemerge through the neckline of the gown. "It may be dangerous."

"You'll need me to translate," she reminded him.

He growled, "Don't you ever take orders? No, of course not! Imagining that you would was naive."

"You make me sound like a disobedient child." She hastily tied the laces of her boots and shrugged her braid over her shoulder. She had to run to catch up with Luke, who was already pushing through the blanket that covered the doorway. He had not bothered with a shirt, and above his unbelted trousers, the union suit was only half-buttoned. "Where are Gao and Kun taos?" she asked.

"God knows."

Outside, the shouts were easy to follow. A crowd was clustered around a fallen mortuary pole, decorated with Bear and Killer Whale. Kate had photographed it only yesterday, while it was still standing.

Jarvis stood astride the pole. In one hand he held a revolver pointed at the sky. He waved it at an Indian. "You speak English, damn it! Tell them I bought this pole, and by God, I'm taking it. I'll shoot the first man who gets in my way!"

Chapter Fifteen

Luke shoved his way through the crowd. Kate followed in his wake.

"Tell them I bought it!" Jarvis was bellowing.

Kate was not surprised to find that Gao was one of the combatants. It was at his chest that Jarvis now pointed the barrel of the revolver.

Gao folded his arms, his face impassive. "The man who sold you this pole did not own it. He had no right to sell it."

"He said it was his grandfather's. He took my money. That's good enough for me."

Voices rose all around, demanding in Haida, "What did he say?"

Gao translated. The result was so many angry shouts that it was difficult to make out who was a principal in the argument.

Luke stopped at Gao's elbow. "What the hell is going on?"

Jarvis snarled, "Stay out of this, Brennan! I was a gentleman the last time you interfered with me, but I won't be again."

"Gao?"

Ignoring the private collector, the guide rapidly explained the situation. Jarvis had indeed paid for the pole, and for the services of several men who were to take it down and float it to the steamboat. The supposed owner had even agreed to secretly bury the remains of his grandfather. They had intended to have the pole gone before most people woke up.

The moment Gao finished, voices of the disputants erupted again. A few spoke in favor of the man who had sold the pole. Kate assumed they were the ones who had been hired to do the job, and would thus profit from the sale. The rest were solidly on the side of an old man who claimed the occupant of the pole as his uncle. The crowd had splintered into a number of combatants, all of them shouting as their contribution to the din. In the meantime, Jarvis looked around wildly, pointing the gun at whoever stepped too near.

Enlightenment came suddenly to Kate. In a low, urgent voice, she said to Luke, "I believe the difficulty here lies in their traditional rules of inheritance versus our way. If the man who sold the pole is a Christian, he may have been persuaded that inheritance ought to be patrilineal."

Jarvis aimed above the crowd and pulled the trigger again. The deafening crack and the puff of black smoke from the barrel brought immediate silence. "Enough!" he snapped. "You." He waved the gun at one of the men he had hired. "And you. Let's get busy. Now!"

One of the two took a step forward; the other didn't move. Luke said loudly, "Do you plan to shoot every one of them if they don't get out of your way?"

"This is none of your business!" Jarvis's bearded face was flushed and his eyes glittered. "Do you think I'll let you talk me out of this pole so you can steal it from under their noses?"

Luke's words sounded like ice being chipped off a block. "*I* make damned sure when I buy something that the seller has clear title to it. I may occasionally offend sensibilities; I don't steal."

Jarvis showed his teeth. "Why accuse me of wrongdoing?

He claimed he had the right to sell it. I paid good money. If there's a problem, it's his."

Luke raised a sardonic brow as he glanced toward the fraudulent owner and the old man, who were nose-to-nose, arguing so intensely, they were impervious to all else. At their feet was the mortuary box, which had cracked open and spilled out the remains of their relative. Jumbled bones were made real and human by the black hair.

"I would guess he has a problem," Luke remarked. "So do you."

The private collecter swung the barrel to point at Luke again. "I have matters under control," he snapped. Sweat formed a sheen on his face. "If you don't want trouble of your own, you and that tame Indian of yours had better clear out!"

From the side of his mouth, Luke hissed to Kate, "Go get Richardson. And don't come back!" Then he said calmly to Jarvis, "Why not try to negotiate with the real owner of the pole? It's already down, chances are that raising it again would require some kind of ceremony he won't want to pay for. He may be angry only because he wasn't offered a share of the profit."

Kate retreated under the cover of his pragmatic speech, though she had no intention of retiring to safety. She feared that Jarvis might truly be dangerous. How could he gracefully back down now? Even if his intention had only been to bully the Indians, the animosity he felt for Luke had changed everything.

Ought she try to find Richardson, as Luke had ordered? Surely the missionary could persuade his fellow traveler to settle the dispute without violence. Unfortunately, she didn't know where he was staying. Even if she could find him quickly, he might still be sleeping. The time it would require to rouse him, to persuade him of the urgency of the situation, to wait while he dressed . . . No, impossible! Jarvis might shoot somebody before then. She would not let herself think about *whom* he might shoot.

He must be made to give up the gun.

Her hand was slippery with sweat as it grasped the rough-textured butt of Luke's revolver, hidden in the folds of her skirts. She had grabbed it on impulse and had meant to offer it to Luke, but how could she have done that under Jarvis's eyes? And what good would it have done anyway? The two of them, stubborn males both, might have stood there until doomsday, guns pointed at each other.

She circled the crowd, keeping a wary eye on Jarvis. He didn't even glance her way. Why should he? She was only a woman, no threat to him.

Edging into the crowd, she reached a position just behind the collector, who still stood astride the pole, booted feet planted firmly apart. Swallowing hard, she lifted the revolver and wrapped both hands tightly around the butt, finger on the trigger.

Luke and Gao saw her at the same instant. Identical expressions of alarm persuaded even Jarvis to take a hasty look over his shoulder.

"Set the gun down very carefully," she said loudly. Indians nudged each other and abandoned their own arguments once they saw the more interesting drama unfolding.

Jarvis half-turned. His wide mouth curled in a sneer. "You don't expect me to take this seriously?"

Her voice shook only a little. "Indeed I do. It is loaded, I believe."

Though she didn't take her eyes off Jarvis, she saw Luke's half-step forward. Gao hadn't moved, but she knew him well enough to see the tension in his bearing, the way he was balanced on the balls of his feet. Jarvis swung the gun between the two men and her.

Kate repeated, "Put your gun down."

"You wouldn't shoot a man." He wanted to believe it.

"I don't think you'd shoot a woman, either."

"A little lady like you, I don't figure you'd even know where to start." His confidence was growing.

"I aim and manipulate a camera rather well," she said, as coldly as she could manage. "I think I could learn. It has something to do with this trigger . . ." She aimed well above his head and tightened her finger. She was startled to discover that the mechanism pulled more easily than she had expected.

The recoil jolted her back two full feet. Indians scattered.

"What the hell?" Jarvis took an involuntary step back and teetered in space.

He never fell. Luke and Gao closed in, Luke taking the revolver and Gao twisting the man's arms behind him. Kate closed her eyes and released the breath she had been holding. Before she could open her eyes, somebody had snatched the gun from her hands.

Luke's face, flushed with fury, was inches from hers. He shouted, "What kind of idiotic performance was that? You didn't *think* he'd shoot a woman? Tell me, was that an educated guess, or did your feminine intuition inform you as such?"

"It worked, didn't it?"

If anything, his voice rose a notch. "So would calm reason have worked! He was bluffing, no more. He's ruthless, not dangerous!"

"Are you so certain?" From his expression, she could tell that he wasn't. "Hah!" she exclaimed in triumph. "Admit it! As a woman, I was far safer confronting him than you would have been."

"Bah." He wheeled around, then whirled back to face her. "Can you stay out of trouble long enough for me to deal with Jarvis?"

"What will you do with him?" Over Luke's shoulder she saw Jarvis's glower as he waited, pinned in Gao's grip.

"Nothing more than see to it that he makes a quick departure," Luke said curtly. "What else can we do? There's no magistrate to be had, and what crime did he commit anyway? He can claim he bought the pole in good faith, even though you and I know he was as good as stealing it. He'll play the gentleman for Richardson, and they'll proceed to the next village and stir up trouble that will be waiting for us when we get there."

He was right, she had to admit, but the ending struck her

as anticlimactic after the high drama of the morning. She left him to deal with the collector and Mr. Richardson and went back to Peaceful House, where she started over with her toilet.

While she was dressing, Kun taos returned. When she told him about the morning's events, he expressed his sorrow at having missed the excitement, but remained in good humor because of his own morning's success: He had caught and killed a small devilfish. While she re-braided her hair and packed several holders of fresh plates in a leather case, he roasted a tentacle under hot stones. Though she had never developed a taste for this member of the squid family, she wouldn't for anything have offended him by not eating the treat he eagerly served.

She had vaguely known Kun taos during her years here, but not in the same way she'd known Gao. Kun taos was just a boy amidst a pack of others, then a young man who was well-liked but without status because his parents had none. He lived with a maternal uncle, who, in the way of the Haida, was "nobody important." Neither the uncle nor Kun taos were Christian; she wondered, with some shame, whether her father or Mr. Richardson had made any special effort to convert them. Was there more glory in winning a chief over?

Kate tried to chew the squid without breathing, so she wouldn't have to taste it. Quickly, she swallowed and chased the bite down with a sip of Haida tea.

Poking at the next chunk of devilfish, she asked, "Have you been to the west coast, Kun taos?"

"Yes, but only to Kaisun and Chaatl. It's possible still to find otter there," he answered readily enough.

"You must think we're crazy to want to travel in winter."

"It is the only way. Otherwise, everybody would be gone." His teeth flashed in a cheerful smile. "*Dancing Canoe* is strong."

Kate knew he wasn't married, but sudden curiosity made her ask, "Do you have somebody—a woman—waiting for you? Are you promised?"

He laughed merrily. "No, no, not me! Someday maybe, but why would I want a wife now? What's the hurry? Then there would be little ones, and I would have to work much harder to feed them. How could I have come with you this winter?"

"Why did you want to come?" She supposed that was the question she had been driving at all along. Even Gao's motivations she questioned, though she refused to believe him a murderer. But from Kun taos's point of view, the winter would be long, separating him from his family and from the ceremonials he might normally play a part in. This journey might even be dangerous.

But the young man shrugged again, so blithely she felt certain he didn't believe in danger. "I don't like sitting around making fishing nets or mending tools," he said. "This way, it is as though I were a nobleman. I will pay somebody else to do the work for me. Who knows, maybe I can even potlatch!"

His voice held childish delight, and Kate was stabbed by pity. She had always been aware, of course, that the Haida class system was nearly as rigid and hierarchical as was its English counterpart. Worse perhaps, because like all the Northwest Coast tribes, the Haida had held slaves, won in battle with the Kwakiutl or the Bella Bella, or even with the Salish to the south, who were not nearly as warlike. She had always regarded the institution of slavery with repugnance, but she had discovered that even before her father's advent, captives were no longer held in large numbers. And really, the slaves were not treated so badly, or so differently from the lower-class Haida like Kun taos's family. It was theoretically possible for nearly any Haida to amass enough possessions to rise in status by potlatching, but in fact, it was as unlikely as a common foot soldier becoming a general and achieving a dukedom. Ironically, what chance Kun taos had was thanks to the disruption brought by white men.

Kate thought she had eaten enough of Kun taos's offering to avoid hurting his feelings, so she rose and shook out her crumpled split skirt. "Where did you catch the devilfish? Are there tide pools exposed?"

"Yes, that way." He gestured. "The other bay behind the village is rockier. I climbed over the next point. But the tide is coming in, so if you want to hunt for chitons or crabs, maybe you should wait until this afternoon."

"No, I thought to take some photographs," she explained. "I want to record Haida Gwai the way it is, without people."

The challenges of nature photography were very specific, and therefore interesting: The sky and clouds were particularly difficult and often required touch-ups in the developing process, but nearly as elusive was the definition that would show the texture of the cliffs or the detail of the tide pools. She had photographed everything in Skedans; she might as well indulge her own interests this morning.

"I'll go the way you did. Would you tell Luke where to find me?" Kate asked.

Kun taos agreed, and she shouldered her camera and a box of extra plates, tucking the folded tripod under one arm. She was scarcely aware of the weight; compared to the days of having to pull along a darkroom on wheels, this was freedom. She felt just a little guilty about using even six or eight plates, considering her limited supply, but so far, they had traveled well. She might find a few of them broken when she unpacked in Skidegate or Victoria, but the bentwood-cedar boxes were amazingly waterproof, and the plates themselves were packed in holders in light-tight boxes.

She went out the front door and followed the path to a track cutting between two houses. It led across the low neck of the peninsula to a north-facing bay that backed the village. The still-low tide revealed the treacherous rocks that studded the rugged cove.

Setting down her apparatus, Kate hiked up her skirts and crouched to take a child's pleasure in the sea creatures temporarily revealed: sea stars in orange and purple and black, the latter reminding her of bats clinging to the rocks; green urchins, closed tightly; blue-black mussels and goose barnacles anchored in place; a slick of brilliant green sea lettuce, and the bulbs of kelp, which she had taken delight in popping when she was younger. The smells and sounds were so familiar, part of the life here that would soon be lost to her. The heady tang of salt and drying seaweed filled her nostrils, just as the constant sigh of the long ocean swells that shattered into creeping fingers of foam filled her ears.

Kate took a look at the mouth of one of the caves that riddled the porous limestone cliffs, but she had no intention of entering one. She knew that some were used for burials, and the coal mines at Cowlitz had rid her of any desire to discover human remains in dank, dark places.

Instead, she set up her tripod, mounted the camera near the foot of the cliffs, and began to compose a photograph of the peninsula. Leveling the camera on such rocky ground required time and patience; she could later trim the print to remedy an image where the horizon tilted slightly, but a larger error would spoil the photograph, whatever its other virtues. The advent of small, hand-held cameras gave her hope that the day would come when field cameras, which took superior photographs, would also be more compact, eliminating the need for a tripod. If only the body of the camera and the plate-holders could be made light-tight, so that the black cloth, too, could be dispensed with.

Surely the streamlining of equipment would change styles as well. So much that was presently admired in photography was contrived, rather than natural. Portraiture was a case in point; invariably, the subjects were stiffly posed against an artificial background, and the photograph itself would be retouched. It had to be if it were to please the eye. A painter could abolish a subject's discomfiture with one sweep of the brush; the camera's unemotional judgment allowed no such accommodation. Kate had experimented with catching a child at a spontaneous moment, or her cousin Alice with her head bent over her needlework. The results were graceful, with an emotional content she found missing in the studio portraits, where all character was lost admidst the props and artificial lighting. Such natural portraits took longer, of course; one had to wait patiently until the subject forgot the lens aimed at her and reverted to normal behavior and posture. Would it be economical to take so much time when she might depend on studio work for her livelihood?

Today she was in her element, free to photograph whatever pleased her without reference to anybody else's preferences. She was determined to enjoy what might soon be a luxury she could not afford. As she pulled the black cloth over both herself and the camera, it was as though she were shutting out the many stresses of the last weeks and her fears for the future, narrowing her concentration to the satisfying task she had set herself. She carefully fitted the plate-holder into its slot. As was her habit, she had already scribbled a quick note to herself on the exposure she had chosen for this particular plate; it was too easy to forget, and thereby repeat errors.

Just as she bent to peer through the viewfinder and prepared to squeeze the small rubber bulb that operated the shutter with a puff of air, Kate heard the crunch of a footstep on gravel close behind her. She felt a stab of resentment at the distraction and the loss of her solitude. Had Luke felt it necessary to check up on her? But she heard nothing more; no one called out a greeting. Perhaps a rock had been dislodged from the cliff, or a Haida woman was shyly slipping past with the intent of digging clams.

In nearly the same instant that Kate released the shutter, something crashed down on her head. She knew that both she and her camera were falling, even as the blackness snatched away her awareness.

Luke was possessed with no sense of urgency. Caution alone had him strolling to find Kate; she ought to have the intelligence not to wander off by herself under the circumstances. Kun taos had insisted that he would have gone with her, but clearly, he had not offered. His laziness was beginning to irritate Luke, though he knew the feeling to be irrational. He hadn't intended, nor was he paying sufficient, to hire a body servant. On the other hand, the four of them were in this together, but Kun taos was the only one who was rarely to be found if work needed to be done.

Well, instead of feeling annoyance, perhaps he should be grateful that one member of this expedition lacked the complexity—and the complex motives—of Gao and Kate. At least Luke knew why Kun taos had come, and could thus predict his behavior. He was good-natured, and uninterested in Luke's activities. Luke could purchase, even steal, anything at all, and Kun taos wouldn't bestir himself to protest. He was exactly the kind of guide Luke had originally hoped to hire.

But Gao had interested Luke, who was convinced that the Haida culture had evolved because of men and women like him. When Gao told the old stories, he seemed to personify the subtle humor of them, the stoicism, even the anger. And the way his hands transformed crude lumps of slate or wood into the faces of Beaver or Hawk or Dogfish was well-nigh miraculous. Just the day before, watching in fascination, Luke had asked him how he decided where to cut, without patterns to guide him.

"The stone or the wood tells me," Gao said simply. "I see what lies within. It is as though—" he paused in thought "—as though the slate is a stream and I see a face just below the surface."

Kun taos, sitting comfortably on the other side of the fire, had unexpectedly contributed to the conversation. "I think he must have a spirit helper who aids him to see, as the *skaga*'s spirit helper lets him hear."

Gao had had to translate this; even he had looked surprised. "It might be that way," he conceded, after a long silence.

Without Gao, Luke might have been able to buy more, but he would understand less. And, contrary to Kate's unflattering opinion of him, Luke's greatest desire was to understand. The objects he bought were an aid to understanding, not an end in themselves, as they were for idiots like Durham.

Still recalling the conversation, he crossed the narrow, wooded neck of land to the other bay, followed by the voices of two quarreling women. He made his way along the difficult footing of the beach, scanning the cliffs with half an eye as he looked for Kate. He had noticed that fewer grave-houses were clustered behind the village than were at Cumshewa, for example. The readily available limestone caves would be a logical alternative. He had nearly reached a rocky outcrop that might have blocked his way had the tide been higher, when he heard a muffled crash.

A thrill of alarm seized him and he shouted "Kate!" even as he began to run. In seconds, he had rounded the outcrop and saw the heap beneath the black cloth. He felt the same terror he had when he'd turned and reached for Mary . . . too late. Not again! a voice within him howled.

Chapter Sixteen

Luke fought the urge to sprint to Kate's side. Instead, he paused to listen, watching for motion. Nothing. For an instant, he thought he heard the sound of rocks scraping together, but with the ever-present *whoosh* of the ocean, it was difficult to be certain.

Even as he reached the pathetic heap, it began to writhe. He wrenched the black cloth off just as Kate sat up, clutching her head. Blood oozed beneath her fingers, and her face was pale. Her dress was bunched above her knees. The tripod lay half across her, the camera still attached.

Luke dropped to his knees beside her. "What happened?"

"Luke?" She blinked hard, as though unable to focus. "I don't know. Something hit me . . . My camera!"

"Forget the camera!" he snapped, lifting it off her. "Look at me."

Had she ever obeyed an order in her life? Without another thought for herself, she knelt to tenderly lift the enormous rosewood camera body with its leather bellows and brass trim. "It's splintered," she said, in the stricken tone another woman might have used for her child's broken arm. "Look."

He did look. It didn't appear to him that the damage to the finely finished wood would affect the camera's function. "It took some of the blow," he observed. "That may be all that saved you. I wonder . . ." His immediate anxiety for her quieted, he sank back to his heels and studied the crumbling rocks in their vicinity. "I suppose you were struck by one of these." This wasn't the moment to discuss the natural corollary: Had the rock fallen by chance? He couldn't accept such a coincidence, and his brief scan of the cliff face offered no answers.

Kate bit her lip, and her fingers stilled against the camera's battered body. "I thought I heard something." He could see the effort it took her to remember. "A footstep . . ." She started to shake her head, but he saw that the small movement had hurt. In a whisper, she finished, "It might have been a shower of smaller rocks before the larger one fell. I can't be sure."

Had *he* heard rocks scraping together, within seconds of his shout? The temptation to mount a search was enormous, but he dared not leave her. Given the rocky outcroppings everywhere, the caves, and the ancient forest that climbed steeply from the water, the chances of finding somebody who sought to hide would be small in any case.

"Let me look at your injury," he said, and cupped her face with one hand to tilt it up.

Kate gazed up at him with wide eyes as softly gray as the mist that so often concealed the mountainous heights of these unexplored islands. Missing was her usual look of irony, which protected any vulnerability she might have felt. In its place was perplexity and entreaty. Her mouth trembled, and blood trickled down her high, curved forehead.

He wiped the blood off with his fingers, trying to concentrate on a medical diagnosis all the while that rage and fear wreaked havoc in his stomach. He couldn't lose her—the thought was unbearable—but how could he protect her? They were trapped here now for the winter.

Her pupils were equally dilated; he recalled otherwise as being an alarming symptom of head injury. When he felt gently with his fingers, he found that an enormous egg had formed on her scalp, just beneath one of the thick braids coiled around her head.

"You were lucky," he said. "Not only the camera, but the cloth and the thickness of your hair protected you from greater injury. Tell me how you feel."

She pressed her lips together. "As though I must . . ." She fought free of his hand. "Must . . ."

Just in time, he helped her turn, so that she expelled the contents of her stomach on bare ground rather than on herself. Feeling utterly useless, he patted her back until her shoulders ceased to heave.

In a dreary voice, she said, "Poor Kun taos."

"What?"

"He was so pleased with himself for having caught a devilfish, and so desirous that I eat some of it."

Relieved that she made sense of some sort, when he had feared lest her mind be wandering, Luke said, "Forget Kun taos. He can cook you some more for supper."

She sighed. "And I detest it so."

Luke felt a peculiar twist in his chest: relief, and something more complex. This was his fault. If he had not brought her . . .

"Can you walk?" he asked, more abruptly than he had intended.

"Yes, of course." She let him help her up and gave him instructions for packing away her equipment.

He swung the heavy leather case over his shoulder and wrapped his other arm around her, his hand at her waist. For a moment, she was stiff, but her head must have pounded infernally, for she relented enough to lean against him. The sensation was bittersweet, and he cursed himself for taking any pleasure in the feel of her body . . . while for her part, she was accepting his arm willingly only for such a reason.

They met no one on their return to the village, and Peaceful House was empty. Kate had made no effort to talk; instead, she had leaned heavily on him, her face increasingly pale.

"Let me unroll your bedding," he said brusquely. "You should lie down and rest."

He'd anticipated an argument, and her meek "thank you" alarmed him. She accepted the cold compress he applied to her head, her lashes fluttering shut. He changed the pad several times, with no visible reaction from her; eventually, her even breathing persuaded him that she was asleep. He stood looking down at her—at the pale curve of cheek, the stained fingers curled loosely beneath her chin, at a dark wisp of hair that stirred slightly when she exhaled—and he was reminded of Mary.

Dear God. Fear struck, and a sound of animal pain escaped his throat. What if today had ended differently? How could he live with himself? He knew suddenly that his selfishness was even greater than he had imagined; he had not coveted only the photographs for his museum, he had wanted Kate herself. It was just as it had been with Mary.

Luke bowed his head. How could he so easily have broken his own vow? He had deceived himself once that women could adapt to the rigors of these expeditions. What further tragedy would it take to convince him otherwise?

Of course, Kate's injury was not quite the same as Mary's fatal fall. Kate had been assaulted by a murderer whom she was trying to flush from hiding. Her death, unlike Mary's, could be prevented.

His emotions at last controlled, he left her thus and sat just outside the door, where he could hear her if she became restless. The scene that lay before him was uncannily normal. It was as though white men and the trouble they brought had never existed. Fishermen were unloading halibut from a canoe, while two women dug clams on the horseshoe-shaped beach. Two toddlers played at the edge of the water, and an older boy chased a girl who was shrieking for her mother. Not far away, a man was engaged in patch-ing a canoe. Fresh red cedar made plain that he had cut out a section and replaced it; now he was sewing the patch in place with spruce root. Beside him was a bowl of pitch that would complete the job. Only the fallen pole remained of this morning's dispute.

In contrast, Luke's thoughts were bitter fare. Barring the possibility that Kate's injury was the result of unlikely mischance—which he didn't for a moment believe—today's events increased the probability of what he had long suspected: The murderer of the Reverend Hewitt must be one of four men. Gao, Durham, Richardson, and Sims. Sims topped Luke's list.

Perhaps illogically, he still didn't believe that the crime was one Gao would have committed. He had considered the possibility that Kate's father had not been killed because he stood in the way of someone peddling artifacts stolen from graves, as Kate had concluded, but rather because he himself was doing the peddling. The Reverend Hewitt could have justified it with his conscience on the grounds that the money was being used for the benefit of the descendants of those whose skulls filled the bentwood boxes. Looked at that way, Gao's motive for a murderous rage could be understandable. And yet, Luke found it hard to see his Haida guide as a cold-blooded murderer. Gao was an intelligent, thoughtful man, who saw the road that lay ahead in a way his compatriots didn't. That very self-awareness made it unlikely he would have committed such a crime, for the murder had obviously solved nothing. Men like Jarvis would keep coming, no matter who was here to help or hinder. However villainous any one man had been, his death could not change the march of history. Gao might accept the knowledge with bitterness, but he would not be foolish enough to deny it.

On the face of it, Richardson was an even more unlikely candidate. He was eager for the Indians to rid themselves of anything carved with crest figures, yet the contempt—even the dislike—in which he held the Haida made it doubtful that he would care enough to murder for his cause. Too, he appeared to have abandoned the Reverend Hewitt's expensive plans that were intended to help the Haida achieve economic independence. Richardson was determined to build a more commodious church, but would one missionary kill another only to gain the money to erect a larger House of God?

Luke would have liked to take Durham seriously as a suspect, but the force of his previous objections still held. A collector could become fanatical, even rabid—witness Jarvis's behavior of this morning. But Jarvis had not shot anybody, either. No sensible man would risk imprisonment, or even execution, merely because he coveted some fine Northwest Indian artifacts.

Sims, on the other hand, was an admittedly violent man who had disliked the missionary. Who knew what the final spur might have been? A woman whom the miner had coveted persuaded to be chaste? Support for Indians determined to expell the miners from their land? An attempt to arrest Sims for trading in whiskey—for Luke seemed to recall that Hewitt had been a magistrate, too, as Duncan was at Metlakatla. Iyea and Xaosti, murdered in turn because of what they knew, might well have been confederates of a man such as Sims.

Luke had become so engrossed in the inexorable path his thoughts followed that he was startled when Kate suddenly appeared in the doorway. She swayed, one hand pressed to her head, and Luke leaped to his feet to grasp her elbows.

"You're on the verge of collapse! Why did you get up?"

She let him help her to a seat on an upturned log. "Oh, my head aches so," she said fretfully. "And once I began thinking . . ."

Being no fool, she would have arrived at the same conclusions he had.

"Do you believe I was attacked again?" she asked straight out.

"Yes." His voice was as grim as his reflections.

Her thoughts were still moving more slowly than was their wont. "Then my father's killer is one of only . . ."

"Four men." The sight of her strained, pale face reawakened his memory of that instant when he thought he might be too late, that history had replayed itself. He forced himself to continue: "Kun taos could not have passed me, and must thus be eliminated."

"Gao, Durham, and Mister Richardson. Who else? Oh, I suppose you mean Sims."

"He is certainly in the vicinity. I don't even know whether he was with some Indians or on his own. He could have beached a canoe anywhere."

Luke could tell that she conceded the point with doubtfulness. She didn't want to suspect the miner, and this reluctance would make him a greater danger to her.

"I suppose some enemy of yours among the Skidegate Haida could be following us," Luke said, determined to be fair. "Though I have seen no familiar faces."

They sat in silence for a moment, until he became aware that she was gazing at the fallen pole. "I didn't think to ask . . . what did Mister Richardson say about Jarvis's conduct?"

Luke's tone was dry. "He was convinced that the Indians' savagery had driven Jarvis to defending himself. He thought the dead man's relatives should have been happy to bury the bones in keeping with Christian tenets. Why would they object to having them spilled onto the ground? Richardson was good enough to inform me that even though the man had not been a Christian, he would offer to say a few words over the grave, should his family choose to have a small ceremony."

"I don't know how Father endured him as long as he did!"

"Because they had a great deal in common."

"Did they?" she asked thoughtfully. "I begin to think that Mister Richardson was less than candid in those days. Either he hid his own opinions, or they were only just forming."

She had reminded Luke of something he had been meaning to ask for some time. He would have preferred to discuss this when she was closer to recovery, but he respected her determination to face the unpalatable.

"What did your father say about him in that last letter?"

"Not enough." She sighed. "Only that Mister Richardson loved his own comfort too well and his work too little. You must understand that Father was unsparing with himself and never understood the minor failings of others. But he also said he had discovered reason to doubt Mister Richardson's calling. He stopped short of saying why, I suppose until he was sure. I assumed it to be some ecclesiastical dispute, or perhaps an inappropriate interest in a woman that Father didn't like to mention to me."

"Would it have been so bad if he had married a young Indian woman?"

"Do you know," she seemed now to be gazing at some scene less concrete than the present one, "I don't believe Father would have minded. I used to wonder . . ." she stopped.

"You wondered?"

"Whether Father himself visited a woman, or . . . or at least cherished an interest in one."

Luke was intrigued to see that pink stained her cheeks, but any opportunity to pursue the subject was lost when Gao approached.

His gaze went directly to the torn strip of white shirt that Luke had used for binding Kate's wound. "You are hurt?"

Her eyes met Luke's in silent question; without giving himself time to consider, he nodded. Gao knew about the other attack on her. Why attempt to keep this one from him? His dismay looked real, but then, had he been the assailant, he would be dismayed as well. Though Luke's arrival had broken off the attack, the villain must have hoped the one blow had been adequate.

Gao's first remark after her explanation interested Luke without reassuring him. "That Jarvis, could he have been so angry he would have wanted to hurt you?"

Kate looked faintly startled. Luke, who had considered the possibility, couldn't help but wonder if Gao was trying to divert attention from the more logical motive . . . assuming that anything about this affair could be thought logical.

One of the principal difficulties was in understanding why her father's murderer wanted to kill Kate as well. Did she know something of which she had not yet grasped the significance? Had hate felt for Hewitt been so acute that his daughter, an extension of him, must suffer, too? Or was it enough that she was asking questions, reawakening memories? Had the murderer thought himself safe until she arrived, determined to know the truth?

Kate turned to Luke. Her face betrayed fresh confusion. "Had you not just left Mister Richardson and Jarvis when you came looking for me?"

"Unfortunately, no." Luke grimaced. "I saw Jarvis off, but the missionary needed to pack and talk to some people, so the canoe was to come back for him. Instead of waiting, I went to meet a fellow who had indicated an interest in selling a set of gambling sticks and a mat. Richardson had apparently convinced him of the evils of gambling. I was probably there by the time you set out, I suppose in full view of the world. Unfortunately, I can't vouch for when Richardson departed, or whether Jarvis might have come back. I should have been more vigilant."

"That's easy to say in retrospect," Kate said. "You had no reason to anticipate an attack on me."

Luke grunted. Attempting to sound casual, he asked, "Gao, did you see Kate go?"

The Indian shook his head. "I went to talk to the one who owns the pole, to see if he will stand it up again."

Luke had no doubt that if he went inquiring, he would be told that Gao had indeed talked to the nephew of the man whose bones currently lay in full view on the beach. The trouble was, that conversation might have taken place an hour ago, or ten minutes ago. The Haida didn't yet carry pocket watches; time was fluid.

Aloud, he said, "Unfortunately, anybody who has seen Kate at work would have known what the equipment she carried meant."

"That I would cover myself with a cloth, so that he could safely approach unseen." Wincing, she reached up and touched the lump on her head. "But Jarvis has never seen me work."

"True," Luke said, "but Richardson might have told him about your skill."

"You mean my hobby." It was her turn to sound dry. "I suppose the end result is that we know no more than ever."

Luke glanced at Gao. "I wouldn't say that. We've certainly narrowed the field of suspects. Assuming, of course, that Jarvis didn't go after you in a homicidal rage."

Gao's face showed nothing. Unfortunately, it rarely did. Luke wondered if his Haida guide had any idea that he was one of those suspects. But Gao's next remark indicated that at least some of the implications had not escaped him. "I will ask whether the missionary and the miner are the only ones who have recently come from Skidegate."

Luke nodded. "Good idea. But you think they are, don't you?"

"Yes," Gao admitted. "There would have been talk had there been others. But I will ask."

Gao was glad that the day was a good one for travel. Northwest Wind had blown away the clouds that The-One-in-the-Sea dressed up in. Always, Northwest Wind brought cold. He lived in the northern mountains and liked it that way.

When Luke found out that Durham had already left for Tanu, he had decided they should go on, too, even though he had not bought as much here as he wanted to. He blamed Jarvis, who had made everyone angry when he tried to take the pole away so early in the morning that Raven had not even called.

Gao still wondered why Luke had stopped Jarvis. Was it because he and that man Jarvis were enemies? Or had he thought that if he stood against Jarvis, people would like him then, and sell him their things?

He had talked about buying only things that the seller truly owned. Did he think that made him a good man, and Jarvis a bad one? But Gao remembered the bag Luke carried and the way he always told people that he would hide what he bought so no one else would know it had been sold. Was he not telling people to come to him secretly? Many nights he slipped out of the house after he thought the others were asleep. He came back with that bag full. Gao had looked in some of the boxes where Luke put the things he bought. There were masks and cedar-bark rings and dishes used in ceremonies.

Already this winter, Gao had seen one potlatch where the chief was giving away parts of a whale that had washed ashore on his beach. He had used high words about how great he was, to give away so much. His hands were cupped and he said to each house-chief, "This bowl in the shape of a grizzly bear is for you; this bowl in the shape of an eagle is for you." But his hands were empty.

Sometimes Gao's stomach felt sick and his head seemed to have an angry fight inside it. Then he stopped himself from casting everything he found on the fire only by remembering what Luke said about the museum. Maybe the *yetz haada* would see the things there and no longer look at the Haida as if they were common mosquitoes to be slapped with no more thought than one gave to defecating.

Now the ocean was choppy and the air so cold it hurt to breathe, but even the tops of the mountains were clear, shining with snow. They stayed as close to the shores of the islands as they could; Luke wanted to see the places they passed. Though snow was not melting, waterfalls still leaped over cliffs. Near Talunkwan Island they passed a rock covered with sea lions. There were so many that the rock seemed to be moving, like the reef called Woman-Shakes-Under-People that was on the west coast. Suddenly, above the voice of the sea lions, Kate called, "Oh, look!"

Gao turned his head to see the shining black fin of a killer whale, and then another, and another. All these were black; he could see no white, which meant that they were Ravens. A friend of Gao's had drowned just last winter, and everyone knew that those who drowned went to the house of The-One-in-the-Sea, where they were fitted with fins so they would appear as killer whales. The drowned friend had been a Raven, come to Skit-ei-get from Skedans. Maybe he was showing himself here now so people would know what had happened to him.

Kun taos hurried to put grease and black-and-white flicker feathers on the paddle and offer them. Even a brave hunter was wise to fear killer whales. Kate told Luke that Killer Whales were the greatest of the supernatural beings who live under the ocean.

"We see them as killer whales, but in their villages under the ocean, they supposedly look like people."

"How do you know all this?" Luke asked.

"There is a story," Kun taos said after Kate had translated. "Once a man in a canoe passed a killer whale. He threw a rock and struck its fin. The next morning, he saw smoke coming from a point that was near his village, and he and some other men went to see who was there. It was a man mending his canoe. The man called out to him, 'Why did you break my canoe?' From that, they knew that killer whales are only the canoes of the Ocean People.'"

Luke made a pleased noise. "Remind me to write that down."

The whales separated to go around the canoe, one long body passing so close that Gao could have touched the glistening black hide with his paddle, if he had been foolish enough. It was not the canoe that interested the whales, but the sea lions on the rock, which they began to circle.

"The sea lions are safe, aren't they?" Kate asked. She watched as though she could not look away. "If they stay on the rock?"

Gao did not answer; he knew what would happen. He had seen it before. He and Kun taos pulled hard to be sure *Dancing Canoe* was a safe distance away.

Over his shoulder, he saw when a killer whale leaped high enough to snatch a sea lion off the edge of the rock. The huge black body splashed down, and spray shot into the air. Kate made a sound and half-rose in the canoe. The roar of the sea lions became as great as if Thunderbird had rubbed

his feathers together, and the rock began to shiver as the animals panicked and leaped off into the water. The other killer
whales were waiting. The blue waves broke into blood-red
foam where they struck the rock.

Kate pressed her fingers to her mouth and sank back to
her seat on a thwart. Nobody said anything. What was there
to say? Killer whales were the most powerful beings in the
ocean; even the Haida would not hunt them.

Not very much later, Luke asked, "That land ahead, what
is it?" He looked at Kate, and Gao could tell that he was
talking so that she would think about something else.

"Kunga Island," Gao said. "See, beside it, that is Tanu."

Both islands reached high out of the sea, Kunga the most
steeply, but all the land down here was mountainous and
covered with dense forests.

The village was called after *t'anu,* a kind of sea grass
found nearby. It faced two separate bays and was split down
the middle by a rocky shoal. Some of the poles here were the
most skillfully carved that Gao had ever seen. There were
maybe forty houses in two rows. The town-chief's house
was so large that each side had its own name. One side was
called Rock-Slide House, because so many trees had been
cut down to build the house that it looked as if a rockslide
had happened.

More canoes were drawn up on the beach than Gao had
seen since leaving Skit-ei-get. Many people still lived at
Tanu, though he had heard that last winter, the pestilence
had killed a hundred or more. They had not listened to the
missionary very much here, and didn't want the vaccine.
Many went to Victoria every year—it was not so far for
them—and they had brought the disease back with them. It
was said that people had died so fast, they were all piled into
one grave. Gao was glad that he didn't know many people
from Tanu; it would have made coming here hard if he had
had to find out whose souls had flown away and who was
lucky enough to live still.

Children and dogs and a few adults came to meet the
canoe when they landed. Luke helped Kun taos drag the

craft up to the grassy crest. Kate waited a few steps back, while Gao said what they had come for.

An old man leaning on a stick spat on the ground. "The missionary was here with that other. After he was gone, we found the gravehouse of a *ska-ga* split open with an ax and everything gone, even the bones. Then another *yetz haada* came yesterday. He said he wants to buy things, too. Nobody will talk to him. You shouldn't have brought still another one."

Gao nodded. He was not surprised by the old one's story. Part of him hoped nobody would talk to Luke, either, but a different part of him knew that the things would be sold anyway; if not today, then another day, if not this winter, next. Would there be anybody better to sell to than Luke? Nobody else had promised to go home and say, "See, this is how the people there live. This is what they believe." Nobody else had promised to write the stories down so that they would not be forgotten.

So he said, "This man that I brought is called Luke Brennan. He kept that Jarvis from stealing an *xet* at Skedans. Luke knew that Jarvis had not bought it fairly, and even though the man had a gun, Luke Brennan made him leave without the pole."

Within the old man's wrinkled face, his eyes were small and dark, like berries. For a long time, he looked toward Luke, who stood up the beach by the canoe. The others who had come to greet them waited for him to speak. He must be one who had earned their respect.

At last he said, "Does he pay good prices?"

"Yes," Gao replied. "Sometimes he buys things that should not be sold, but he gives what things are worth."

The old man shrugged. "I will tell people. Right now, most everybody is at Property House. The chief's son there, they say his soul is about to fly away."

"He is ill?"

A younger man said, "No, his canoe split when he launched it. The waves were too high. He was swept out. We pulled him from the water, but he was in it too long. His family just asked the *ska-ga* to come, but he says they should have called him sooner. He is powerful, but what can he do so late? He said he would try, but he thinks that even his spirits cannot help now."

"The white man will want to see him acting as a shaman." It was to the old man Gao spoke. "Would this *ska-ga* say a *yetz haada* cannot?"

The one who had earned respect spat again. His face creased so that his eyes could not be seen. "He is very strong. He acts like a shaman all the time. I think he would say anybody can see him."

Gao bent his head respectfully. Then he went to help unload.

They had done this so many times that they were finished soon. After Kun taos had gone to find firewood, Luke said, "Well, shall we go introduce ourselves?"

Gao told him what the old man had said.

"Ah." Luke had looked tired before, but now he was like a hunter who has seen his prey and feels strong again. "Kate, bring your equipment," he ordered. "We may not get a chance again to photograph a shaman at work."

Gao would have said something, but Kate talked fast. "I can't come."

Luke drew his brows together. "What?"

"I'm a woman. I can't come."

He spoke quietly, but in a way that told Gao he was angry. "In God's name, why not?"

For her sake, Gao said, "Women have power that might take away the medicine man's. After a girl changes into a woman, she must be careful."

"Changes?" Luke sounded sarcastic. "Do you mean when they start tempting men?"

"Haida girls go through *tegwena*—puberty seclusion," Kate said. "After that, they are thought to be powerful until the change of life, after which they can have no more children."

Gao said, "There is a story that a girl stopped a dog that was rolling down a hill, just with her eyes, she was so strong."

"What if the man who is dying wants his mother or wife with him? The medicine man says no?"

Kate looked at Gao. Her eyes begged him for help. He said, "The medicine man might let a woman stay if it is not her time of the month."

"Fine!" Luke said in an impatient way. "Since it's not . . ."

She said nothing, but a red flush crept up her neck to her cheeks.

Luke's mouth opened, then closed. At last he made a noise like "Harrumph."

Hadn't he noticed the rags she had washed and dried by the fire? Gao and Kun taos had been careful to leave their fishing and hunting equipment outside the house once they knew it was her time. Otherwise, they would have been unlucky.

"I'm sorry," she said. Her eyes were looking down and her voice was soft. It was the way Gao would like his wife to speak when she had disappointed him.

Luke made a noise in his throat again, then said, but not strongly, "I don't suppose you'd consider slipping in? If you lurked under the black cloth, he might not even realize you were female."

Now she looked straight at him. "I cannot ignore their taboos. Not when it comes to something that is life and death."

Gao waited, glad that she did not laugh at beliefs that were not hers. He would have refused to take her to Property House, but this way was better.

Luke's mouth twisted as though he were sorry, but also glad, at what she had said. He gave a nod and said, "Gao, tell Kun taos to stay here. I don't want Kate left alone."

"If you just give me the revolver, now that I know how to shoot it . . ."

Gao remembered that shot, which might have hit a raven if one had been passing over. "I will tell Kun taos," he said.

Luke lifted his eyebrows, as though he had been waiting for Gao for a long time. "Then let's go."

Chapter Seventeen

"Well, he's dead." Luke flung himself down on his mat with a sigh. "Poor devil. I don't suppose he could have been saved in Boston, either."

Gao was quietly spreading his own mat for the night. After a few words, Kun taos had vanished out the front door.

"Had he contracted pneumonia, do you suppose?" Kate asked. As if it mattered—she supposed she was making conversation to preserve a semblance of normalcy after her earlier absurd display of self-consciousness.

"I couldn't guess. I have the impression that he capsized only a day or so ago. The strait is too cold for anyone to survive immersion for long. He might have had too much water in the lungs. I'm not sure he was even aware of the medicine man working over him."

Just as well, Kate would have said, had it not been for Gao's presence. Her father may have been right when he argued that the medicine men only worsened any illness or injury.

"Rest is crucial," he had declared. "Can you imagine the

effect of having men constantly dancing over and around you, uttering wild cries, a drum pounding near your head, teeth or bones tied to the apron clattering, and half the village crowding in to see the 'cure'? What is truly a miracle is the fact that any patient has ever survived such treatment!"

Kate had seen such scenes while she was still a girl. Her preconception colored by her father's prejudices, she had expected to be appalled by the wretched condition of the patient and the treatment meted out to him. She had assumed the shamans to be selfish, even cruel men who had, with sleight-of-hand and deliberately obscure talk, convinced the ignorant that they could do them some good.

She had seen things that ought to have convinced her of her father's point of view. She recalled an occasion when the *ska-ga* supposedly sucked the illness from a patient's body, after which he triumphantly removed a wad of blood-soaked eagle down from his mouth and held it up for all to see.

Kate had protested scornfully to Martha, who was not yet a convert of the Reverend Hewitt. "He must have already had the down in his mouth. I suppose he bit his cheek or tongue to make it bloody. Was anybody really fooled?"

Martha—Gaudgas, then—had remained serene. "The spirits told him to show us in that way what he removed from that sick man. How else could we see it, when our sight is so dim?"

Of course, if the medicine men had always failed, they would not have been respected. Kate had seen one of the successes, though she had not thought of it in years.

The young man who was ill had been a friend of Sarah's brother. He had seemed to have the wasting sickness. The Reverend Hewitt was resigned, ready to consign him to the Heavenly Father. The family was not so willing. They called in the *ska-ga*, who was the Reverend Hewitt's worst enemy.

Without her father's knowledge, Kate had slipped in with Sarah. Sticks beat the floor to summon the spirits, and the *ska-ga* shook a rattle in the form of a bird, dancing around the fire, left hand toward the middle of the house as he tried to find his power. It was as though he were a blind man, groping for an unseen object.

His hand remained empty. The family offered more blankets.

Over the next few days, he fasted, she heard, then went out into the woods to try to recover the lost soul. Sarah came running to fetch her when he reappeared, the soul cupped in his hands.

The patient was covered with a mat, while the people sang and beat time. The *ska-ga* had truly looked barbaric: long hair twining like snakes around him, his bare chest so emaciated one could see his ribs, his eyes so fierce and wild that she had shuddered when they looked through her. With a great cry of *"hwu, hwu, hwu, hwa!"* he flung the soul back into the young man's chest.

The patient had stirred and opened his eyes, to the general amazement and satisfaction of the audience. Later it was said that he had been allowed a first meal that night, starting with the tail of a salmon, then the next day, the chest of the salmon, until he ate the head and was recovered.

Kate's father insisted that it had all been trickery, that the young man and his family were in league with the medicine man to fool everybody into thinking the *ska-ga* was more powerful than the white man's god. Reason told her that the soul could not be touched or handled or compelled to go to this place or that. And yet a part of her wondered, for the Haida believed in much that was unseen. As Sarah put it with a graceful shrug, "Who could know?"

As the years passed and her father's vaccines and insistence on antisepsis humiliated the medicine men, her own certainty had hardened. She had nearly forgotten her awe when the young man moved and opened his eyes for the first time in days. How could it be explained?

Well, she had seen her own mother wish herself to death. The body must follow where the mind led! If a direly ill person believed with all his heart that the spirits had drawn the sickness from his body, was a physical rallying so illogical?

Luke spoke up, oddly echoing her progression of

thoughts. "Gao, how do you see the god we white people try to foist on you? Is he an enemy? A fabrication?"

Kate had to translate some of this. The silence then was long. Gao lay on his back, staring up at the darkness amid the massive timbers that supported the roof.

Finally, he said, "Sometimes I think maybe he is the same as Power-of-the-Shining-Heavens. But we revere him in our own way. Why should we have to go to your church?"

"Good question." Luke sounded wry. "What do you think, Kate?"

She frowned. "I think maybe he is the same, whatever we call him. Why would he have revealed himself only to us?"

Gao turned his head to look at her, his gaze sharp. "The missionaries, they say we shouldn't believe in the supernatural ones, that your god would be angry if we didn't believe only in him."

Slowly, putting into words the thoughts that were just now coalescing, Kate asked, "What if you and Kun taos and Luke and I all saw a grizzly bear, but each of us saw only a part? Would we know that the sharp claws you see and the hump covered with hair that I see belong to the same creature? Could they possibly go with eyes so small and the stub of a tail? We might call them The-Clawed-One and The-One-with-the-Great-Hump. If we had never seen the whole, how could we know that we saw parts of the same creature?"

"A philosopher." Luke's tone mocked, but he was smiling.

"Of course," Kate admitted, "Mister Richardson would not agree with me."

"That goes without saying," Luke muttered.

Gao gave a nod. "I will think on it."

They lapsed into silence until Luke said, "Gao, you know I've been intending to give a potlatch. I figure I'd better hurry up and do it, before Jarvis shows up again or something else happens to tar my reputation. What do you think, would I offend the family of the man who died tonight? Do we have enough food to put on a modest feast?"

"If we fish, maybe. And dig some clams." Gao sounded less grudging than Kate would have expected. Perhaps he thought such a feast would be only common courtesy. "No, I think the family would not be insulted."

"Then let's get busy. First thing tomorrow, we'll issue the invitations."

It went without saying that Luke had no idea of how to cook, or of the quantities of food that would be required. At Gao's suggestion, Kate enlisted the help of several women who dug clams. Gao made clear that this was women's work, just as fishing and hunting were men's. The latter was true because of women's supposed supernatural powers; should a woman attempt to fish, she might drive away the salmon altogether. If she caught an octopus near its den, the den would be abandoned forever. Kate had a suspicion that men's unwillingness to gather berries and dig for clams had more to do with the repetitive, unexciting nature of the work than it did with any taboos.

The same women agreed to help prepare and serve the feast; they would roast salmon, halibut, and seal over great fires built on the beach. In return, they were able to choose first from Luke's selection of calico. Resigned to her role as chief hostess and cook, Kate spent hours planning the quantities of food needed and purchasing what they did not have. She wondered, just a little acerbically, what Luke would have done if his original photographer had come. The four men might have been forced to don aprons, figuratively speaking of course.

A good deal of her time was spent hunting down one particular necessity. A potlatch would not be a potlatch without grease, the Haida's principal condiment. She was able to trade for a sufficient stock of it, but the price was high, and understandably so. *Taow,* the grease extracted from the tiny oolachen fish, must be traded from the Tsimshian Indians on the mainland, for the oolachen did not live in the waters around the Queen Charlotte Islands.

Gao and Kun taos provided some fresh halibut, the seal, and a few birds, as well as another devilfish that Kun taos triumphantly contributed. Even Kun taos was drafted to reluctantly scrub the interior of House-Dressed-Up, their current abode.

Kate was still bothered by what she knew Luke's motivation to be: He hoped to use the Haida's own customs to weasel his way into their confidence, and thus inveigle them to show him ceremonial items normally kept hidden from white men. She might have refused her assistance, except that even Gao, still deeply suspicious of Luke's intention, considered it only good manners to put on a potlatch. Too, she was brought back to her usual dilemma: Was Luke right in thinking that the Haida culture would one day vanish completely and that only what was held in museums would remain?

Luke invited the leading families of Tanu. Much to Gao and Kun taos's merriment, he practiced his speech several times beforehand. He had memorized several sentences in Haida, which Gao drilled him on. The remainder, Gao would translate.

The guests were punctual, filing in with polite inclinations of the head. All were dressed in their best, though that, of course, had changed. Kate remembered stories her father and the Reverend Collison of Masset told about the unusual garb the Indians wore on special occasions in the early days: magnificently patterned dressing gowns, counterpanes fastened about the waist with ropes, even a jester's costume fringed with bells. Somehow, a medicine man in Masset had acquired a white surplice, in which he came attired to a Christmas service. Coupled with the long hair rolled around a pair of caribou horns, he had made a truly demoniacal appearance, the Reverend Mister Collison had said reminiscently.

But those colorful days were gone. Now the women wore dark, high-necked gowns, the men boots and dark trousers with frock coats. The chiefs had added headdresses or woven hats and Chilkat robes to the conventional garments beneath. A few naval uniforms were in evidence, but the same could be said of any gathering in Victoria. Of course there were remnants of former days: labrets in the lips of the older women, silver bracelets, tattoos.

Once the house was full and the most important guests seated to each side of Luke at the rear, he stood and waited for the hum of talk to die. He was several inches taller than any of the Haida. Despite the endless rain, the bronze on his face had faded little, while his hair had grown to a length that curled over his collar. As she had come to know him, Kate had realized that he was eminently civilized, but tonight he did not look it, despite the newly applied polish on his boots and his clean-shaven jaw. He was magnificent, more savage than the natives who surrounded him. Perhaps it was the Chilkat robe he wore over his more sober garb that lent him an air of primitive dignity.

The robe was not as fine as the one he still hoped to buy from the chief in Haina, but he had little faith in the promise made there.

"I refuse to go home without one!" he had said back in Skedans, showing her his new purchase. "I would have been satisfied with this one if I hadn't seen the other. I'm regarding this as insurance. I'll have Gao offer this one to Durham if I'm able to acquire the one in Haina. Durham admits he hasn't found one yet. Who knows, I might even make some money on the transaction." The thought of palming a second-rate specimen off on his rival was obviously gratifying.

Standing before the assembly, Luke began his speech with the obligatory apologies for the modesty of the feast. "I have only small gifts for you," he continued, inclining his head respectfully toward his nearest guests. "I have come from far away and could not bring much. What I have may be useless to you, but perhaps the cloth or the mirrors will please your women. You have been generous in welcoming me. I wish only that I had something to give you in return that was worthy. But I hope you will accept what I do have and know that my thoughts were good."

Several chiefs in turn stood to thank him for his munificence. They had never seen cloth so beautiful. The feast was so large, they might eat all winter and still not finish what he had served.

Like any anxious hostess, Kate waited impatiently through the seemingly endless courtesies. They had discussed the guest list at some length, but the house seemed more crowded than she had imagined. Were there only a hundred guests here? What if there wasn't enough food for everyone? Might it seem to be a deliberate insult if some chief found that the devilfish or salmon or whatever he fancied had run out before he could be served?

Eventually, Luke got around to securing permission for Kate to photograph what she saw during their visit. "Using her box with windows, she can write pictures on paper. If you dance, on the paper you will be dancing. It is as if she is copying from a patternboard onto a woven mat, but faster."

They agreed that they had seen a photographer at work before. George Dawson had been to Tanu two years earlier and photographed the village, though he had been interested more in houses and poles than in people. Others of the guests had seen photographs in the windows of a studio in Victoria.

Luke explained that unlike Mr. Dawson, who had still been working with wet plates, Kate would not be able to develop her photographs here for them to see. There was not room in the canoe for her to bring everything she needed.

"But the images she sees are stored on these glass plates, just as you press berries into cakes to save them for the winter." He handed around an exposed glass plate, as well as several photographs. "These she took in Skidegate."

Murmurs of pleasure and sidelong glances of envy ensured their agreement. If those families in Skit-ei-get who were nothing, not worth even noticing if one met them, had their poles and houses written on paper, the noble families in Tanu wanted at least as much.

Luke distributed the gifts and then invited the guests to eat. Soon all lined up to be served at the several fires outside, where food was steaming. The earlier drizzle had decreased to little more than a damp feel to the air. Sparks shot up into the darkness. To Kate's relief, the guests took modest portions; they must guess that the visitors had limited resources. Laughter and animated voices reassured her that a fine time was being had by all.

Unavoidably, among the guests was James Durham. Kate had just brought out another enormous wooden dish of crab apples swimming in grease and was on her way to one of the fires to be sure that food wasn't running short when she passed so close to him that courtesy compelled her to pause to greet him.

"I wish I'd thought of having a potlatch," he said good-humoredly. "The Indians seem satisfied with the merest fripperies, and now they'll look at Brennan as one of themselves. I suppose your guide suggested it?"

"No, I believe Luke came prepared. Our load will be considerably lightened from here on out."

"Do you still intend to go up the west coast?" He sounded more than curious, though she was unsure of what gave her that impression.

"Yes, why?"

"Richardson railed at some length about the dangers. He had enough hair-raising stories to persuade me. I gather that the coast there is exposed to brutal storms and pounded by enormous waves. He claims that even the Haida avoid it, and in winter most of all. Such a journey is foolhardy at best! If Brennan insists on being an adventurer, won't you, at least, return to Skidegate with me?"

Kate was surprised at his passion—no, that was hardly the right word. Intensity, perhaps. Something compelled her to lay a hand on his arm, which felt unexpectedly muscular. "Thank you for your concern," she said gently. "I must be foolhardy myself, because I have always longed to visit the mysterious west coast! It must be one of the wildest and least-known spots on the globe. How can I resist the chance to see such a place with my own eyes? I prefer to think that I, too, am adventurous rather than foolish."

"Well, I tried!" he said.

Kate found herself wishing that the night was not so dark, that she could see the expression in his brown eyes and that his full mustache did not disguise the twist of his mouth. That last remark could be taken in two ways. What if she had agreed to take advantage of his chivalrous offer, transferring herself to his protection? Might an accident have befallen her before they reached Skidegate?

He must have said something additional, she realized suddenly, for he was looking at her expectantly. How detestable it was to be listening constantly for shades of ominous meaning, to suspect everyone, even old friends! How ludicrous it was that she knew almost nothing about this man, and yet she found herself studying his hands, noticing that they were larger than she had realized, more capable. He certainly had the strength to have bludgeoned three men to death. But did he utterly lack conscience? She had accepted Luke's dislike and her own distaste, making no attempt to discover what kind of man James Durham really was.

"Do you know," she said, as though musing on a surprising fact, "I just realized how little I know about you personally. You've never mentioned a wife or family, for example. Do you miss your home?"

"Abominably!" The word came out with such force that even he looked surprised. A sizzle of grease poured on the nearest fire presaged a leap of orange light that allowed Kate to see how rueful as well as charming Durham's smile was. "You struck a raw nerve," he said simply. "This is the longest I've been away from home since I married two years ago. I miss my wife very much."

"What is her name?" Kate asked.

"Clara. She's young and very pretty, with a laugh that never fails to make me smile." A muscle in his cheek twitched. "I've been grateful for your presence, Miss Hewitt. A woman's gentle words soften the loneliness."

Kate was smitten by a pang of guilt. "Perhaps you should take your Clara along the next time you undertake an expedition."

"She is no Amazon like you," he said, his lack of tact

promptly smothering Kate's guilt. "Why, she would barely come to your shoulder. Her skin is so pale, I doubt she could withstand a harsh sun. She is easily shocked or horrified; even her appetite is delicate!" He appeared to indulge in fond recollections for a moment, then shook them off. "It had never occurred to me to take her. I must confess, however, that I have envied Brennan. Not that I am implying anything improper about your relationship!" he hastened to add. "I would be content only to have Clara's companionship. To see her smile occasionally, hear her laugh . . ."

"Women are rarely as fragile as they appear," Kate suggested. She couldn't decide whether to be furious or amused. Was he truly unaware of how insulting his comparison was? On the other hand, he was jealous of Luke, which must imply *some* admiration of her. Or at least of the *idea* she apparently exemplified.

"But Clara has little in common with you," he protested. "Her girlhood was sheltered, she was not forced early on to adjust to a harsher life."

"And so you think her incapable of doing so? Perhaps you don't give her enough credit."

"What if she came to be in a family way on an expedition such as this?" He sounded genuinely desperate.

"That might be inconvenient," Kate admitted. "Although I repeat my earlier remark; women look more fragile than they are. Pioneer women have had babies with scarcely a pause on the trail. If that possibility worries you, however, you could enjoy her companionship without taking any greater risks."

It took him a moment to understand her delicate suggestion. When he did, Durham cleared his throat. "Yes. Well. Of course. I apologize for venturing into such an intimate topic. I fear I was tempted, despite your unmarried state, because you, too, are gently bred, and yet you seem to positively relish this peculiar life."

Kate thought again: How could any woman of spirit not relish such a life? Yet she had probably already said too much. She was not like other women; she had long ago accepted that. His Clara most likely had more in common with Alice than with Kate. Despite her respect for the steel that lay beneath Alice's tender exterior, Kate could not quite picture her gentle cousin braving storms in an Indian canoe or eating roasted octopus tentacles—or sleeping in a single room with three men, two of them "savages!" She shouldn't raise Mr. Durham's hopes. Clara might run sobbing to her mother at the suggestion that she actually accompany her husband on his trips to primitive, even dangerous, parts of the world.

So Kate said only, "You might ask her at least. She may be longing for you as much as you are for her."

"Yes." He bowed his head; his voice sounded repressed. "Thank you, Miss Hewitt."

As Kate murmured something about her duties as hostess and moved away, she pondered the unexpected conversation. She would not be able to look at James Durham in the same way again. He had revealed a deeper part of himself. It did not allow her to like him, precisely; how could one like a man so insensitive to the feelings of others? But it was much harder to *dislike* a man who had expressed such loneliness, who had confided in her, and listened eagerly for nuggets of wisdom.

It was also, she discovered, much harder to imagine him as a murderer.

Luke hunched his shoulders in an instinctive effort to keep out the rain, but what was the use? He was soaked already, and blasted cold. There was no escape: They bobbed on choppy, iron-gray water that was almost indistinguishable from the low clouds and steady rain.

Kun taos and Gao paddled uncomplainingly. Lord knew, they were probably used to this incessant downpour. Kate had begun the day clutching her umbrella, but it did so little good that she had abandoned it several hours since. Her bedraggled hair dripped down her neck and onto her face; she huddled miserably inside sopping garments.

He might have delayed departure from Tanu if it had been raining this hard two days ago, but then it had only drizzled and Gao had agreed that it was safe to travel. Luke cursed his decision; would that he had been blessed with foresight!

The scenery during these three days of travel was magnificent, but unvarying: great forests of spruce and cedar plunging down to rocky shores. Reefs and islands interrupted the coast, and long inlets vanished into the mist. Occasional streams issued from mossy shadows or fell in long cascades from cliff faces. Though this southern portion of the islands was little more than a mountain range rising from the sea, the heights remained obscured by gray clouds.

Seabirds were everywhere, and seals and sea lions. A day out from Tanu, they saw their first otter, once so common but now nearly obliterated by the Haida, who sold the furs to the white traders greedy for the valuable pelts. On the second day, porpoises chased the canoe for some time, arching out of the water just beside the dipping paddles as though they wanted to see this creature more closely. Gao said that black bears were so common in these parts that one could scarcely pass a beach without seeing one. Now, of course, they were hibernating.

The journey had included one pleasant interlude: a small island known for its hot springs. Kun taos was uneasy about landing there; he called it The-Island-of-Fire. Gao shrugged and said, "The waters are said to cure almost any kind of sickness. I don't know. They feel good."

"By all means, let's stop," Luke had agreed.

A bright green mossy sward could be seen from some distance away. Once the canoe was beached, all they had to do was follow the hovering steam. One bubbling stream was scalding, but another issued into a pool that was of perfect bath temperature. Luke suggested, "Ladies first."

Kate looked rueful. "Since there are three of you, I ought to insist on waiting, but I won't. To actually immerse myself, to wash my hair in hot water . . . Please say we can stay long enough to do laundry as well."

Luke investigated and found—just downstream from

where Kate could be heard splashing and singing in a clear soprano that was pleasant but uncertain of the tunes—a spot where he and the two guides could scrub clothes. The water had a faint odor and left a whitish deposit on the banks, but served nicely for their purpose. Considerably later, they traded places with Kate.

Luke stared when he passed her and could not seem to make himself look away. Her skin was usually so pale, but now her face was pink. Her hair hung dripping to her waist, laying wet patches on her dress so that it clung to her figure. Her eyes sparkled more green than gray; she was softer somehow, as though an invisible tension had been relieved. He would have given almost anything to have seen her floating in the hot water, her dark curls spreading like kelp around her, steam rising over her white breasts and belly and thighs, concealing and intriguing, revealing just enough.

Good God! His reaction was as strong now, remembering, as it had been two days ago when he watched her vanish downstream to wash her own clothes. He could scarcely look at her anymore without imagining her unclothed. It was torment at night to see her shake her hair free from its braids, to watch her run a brush through the wiry curls until they crackled, to lie there in the darkness conscious of her sleeping only a few feet away—or restlessly awake, as he was. He had never considered himself to be driven by physical needs; for hours at a time, he could ignore hunger or tiredness if satisfying either would take him away from the patient unearthing of an ancient burial, or stories or dances, or even unpacking a shipment of artifacts from one of his correspondents around the world. He could remember deluding himself into believing that he would forget she was a woman; she would become an adjunct to his work, possessing no more personal power than her camera. Hah!

It would have been easy to regret bringing her. She had been trouble from that first dinner on board the *Skeena*, when he had suspected her motivation for coming. He had never before been in the position of having to play bodyguard to a fellow traveler, not even his wife.

Had Mary lived, she would have been sitting just so in the canoe. She had never complained, either, about her fears or the discomfort. These days, memories of Mary came to him constantly. Whatever Kate said or did, he wondered whether Mary would have done the same; whenever he lusted for Kate, he remembered heated lovemaking with his wife. The circle was one he could not escape, for then he would wonder whether Kate would hold him or touch him in the same way; whether she would be gently accepting as Mary had been, or more passionate.

Yet he could not altogether regret hiring Kate. True, her undeniable photographic skill was an asset, but perhaps also it was not a bad thing that she had reawakened his memories of his wife. Forcefully expelled from his thoughts, Mary had become a ghost that haunted him. His guilt had not let him reconsider his responsibility in her death. Kate had compelled him to do just that.

He remembered the passion and bitter resentment on Kate's face that first day at her aunt's house. This winter, she must often be physically uncomfortable. She must fear for her life, miss the security she had left behind. Yet he did not believe that she had ever regretted coming, even for an instant. She was not just a strong-willed young woman who had disliked being dependent on her relatives. She was also an artist who was being stifled.

As Mary had been. He heard Kate again: *Your wife was not just a woman, but an artist as well. How could you not love that part of her?* Had Mary, too, accepting the risks, chosen freely a life that allowed her to use a gift denied to a mere woman? Had she felt as he would if someone told him he must give up his museum work and become an accountant, closed in an office all day, tallying up figures?

Or was he constructing an elaborate justification that would allow him once more, selfishly, to pursue his heart's desire?

He knew how selfish he had been that night when the four of them huddled under the rotting planks that formed the roof of a house that had probably been abandoned sixty years or more ago. Gao called the town Kaidju, Songs-of-Victory Village. Here, several houses still stood, while the poles leaned or had already fallen. The dark, dripping forests had nearly reclaimed the village site; velvet-green moss had crept over everything, while spruce trees split open the poles and timbers they had rooted within.

Thank God, Gao knew the location of long-deserted villages such as this one, where they were able to find refuge of sorts when darkness fell. The shores were so rocky, so broken with inlets and points and islands, that just finding the occasional small beach of coarse gravel where the canoe could be pulled out of the water required prior knowledge.

During that day's travel, Gao had pointed out other ancient village sites. He said that in Skincuttle Inlet alone, there had been ten villages, all of them belonging to the Raven Crest people known as Middle-Town Haida.

The incessant rain had hardened as the day went on until now it dripped through cracks between planks, sizzling as drops struck the feeble fire Gao had coaxed into being. Luke looked at Kate, who sat on her mat with her hands held out to the inadequate warmth, several miscellaneous woolen garments draped over her. She had not even tried to wring her hair out or to get dry, but instead, she shivered every so often and spoke only when necessary. She had begun coughing as the day progressed and the dampness reached into her lungs. He was wet and cold himself, but his greatest discomfort came from his awareness of his own selfishness.

Should they turn back now, or do so after they saw Ninstints? Ought he risk her life, too, in his pursuit of the unknown? Durham had cornered him at Tanu to reproach him for bringing Kate on a journey certain to be dangerous. Luke could not tell Durham why he dared not accept his offer to return Kate to Skidegate. Even if he could have been certain that Durham was trustworthy, he could not depend on him to protect Kate from her father's murderer. Durham was not a self-sacrificing man; common decency would make him chivalrous up to a point, but Kate's welfare would not be so essential to him that he would risk himself.

Richardson, too, had been extraordinarily insistent that Luke release her from her promise so that she could return with him. The missionary had declared his intention to speak with her one more time, but presumably he had not located her before the canoe returned for him. Or he *had* found her, and struck her over the head with a rock. Luke would have been more suspicious about Richardson's vehemence, except that it was characteristic of him, and even understandable. This *was* a dangerous journey for a young lady.

Thinking thus brought Luke back to his earlier preoccupation, for Katherine Hewitt's welfare had become all-important to him. He must admit as much, if only to himself. The question was: Would she be in more danger from the Reverend Hewitt's murderer, should she again be within his reach, or from nature's violence on the exposed west coast of Haida Gwai?

They spent the night, just as they had the last one, fully clothed, all lying head to toes as close as they could to the fire. It was not restful.

The rain pelted down as hard in the morning as it had the previous day. They could reach Ninstints today, where Gao was certain the houses would be habitable. One day forward or two back; the issue was decided for Luke.

The day was interminable, as wretched as the one before. They were wet and cold within an hour of launching. They must pass through a wide channel between Moresby Island, which formed the main spine of the Queen Charlottes, and Kunghit Island, the southernmost of the chain but for some rocky islets. The tide raced through here, and Gao insisted that they wait until the ebb so that they were not fighting it. They found the merest toehold in which to wait the tide out; the mountains and hills rose steeply from the shore. The trees here were stunted from the ocean storms and grasped at bare rock with their roots.

By the time they were able to get underway again, Kun taos was sulking.

"We sat like old women in the rain, when we could be halfway there! What was there to be afraid of? A little current? We are Haida, not seaward people. You think *Dancing Canoe* is not strong enough? You carved it yourself."

Through blue lips, Kate translated the part of this that Luke hadn't understood. The rain still drove down, but it was mixed with sleet, adding bitter cold to the wet. It was no wonder that Kun taos resented the delay, doubting Gao's judgment as he did.

Gao reacted with unusual anger. "We just saw a man die because he launched his canoe when he should not have. It is better to be cautious."

"He was careless," Kun taos said with a shrug. "Anyway, Raven has already decided how long we should live. Why should we worry about it?"

Luke had heard Gao speak of Raven, who, in one form, determined the length of each life. When a baby was born, Raven heard the cry in his aerial mansion; he would reach without looking and withdraw a stick from a bundle. If it was short, the baby's life would be correspondingly so; if it was long, so would be the life.

Gao drove his paddle with unusual force into the gray, choppy water dented by rain and sleet. "Anybody could make his life shorter by foolishness. Do you want your soul to go live with the killer whales, or to *Taxet*'s house? How could you be born again?"

Kun taos shrugged again. "Today you are like an old woman. Will you be a coward, so that you do not need to fear becoming a killer whale?"

"Only fools are not careful," Gao said shortly. "The world is as sharp as a knife."

"It is not so hard to walk on an edge." The exercise of paddling had warmed Kun taos; he sounded his insouciant self again.

Gao's voice was biting. "You know the story of the one who mocked the saying."

Kun taos laughed. "My soul is still with me, is it not?"

When Gao didn't answer, Luke asked, "What is the story?"

Kate answered, "It is said in Masset that a father once told his son that the world was as sharp as a knife, and that if he did not take care, he would fall off. The son laughed and said the earth was broad, that one cannot fall off it. While he was talking, he kicked at a stump. He ran a splinter into his foot and died. Thus the Masset people know the saying is true."

She coughed then, and fell silent. Her back was to him, so he couldn't see her expression, but he could imagine it. Sleet must sting her face as it did his. The perpetual gray everywhere—water, sky, sleet—had leached the color from the forest, even from their clothing. Its depressing effect was undeniable.

Sleet alone fell by this time, though it seemed to Luke that it was letting up some. The tide, ebbing into the Pacific Ocean, had picked up speed. Anthony Island, where Ninstints huddled in the lee of a tinier island, lay just ahead when they emerged from the wide channel.

Despite the ebb tide, the waves were noticeably larger. Anthony Island was exposed to the power of the Pacific, though the village was on the eastern side, cradled in a small, curved inlet. To the Haida, this was Red-Cod-Island Town. The white men had called it Ninstints, after the name of a prominent chief.

As they entered the narrow entrance to the harbor, rounding the rocky isle, and Ninstints came into view, Luke thought for an instant that it was inhabited after all. It looked no different than Tanu or Cumshewa; twenty houses or more sprawled in the usual uneven line, a gray forest of poles rising in front of them. And yet, something about it spoke of its emptiness. A moment later, he realized what was missing: the canoes that ought to be drawn up where now sea grass grew thick. It didn't seem possible that a village this size was entirely deserted, a ghost town.

Dancing Canoe lifted on a wave that swept them onto the beach. Gao and Kun taos drove with the paddles to get as far from the water as possible. When gravel scraped under the hull, Luke jumped out to help drag the craft higher. He was so cold and stiff that it was all he could do to grasp the gunwales.

Luke raised his voice. "Let's find the driest house and hope to God we can find burnable wood."

Many of the houses looked habitable; from only a few had the planks been taken to be used on new houses elsewhere. Too many stood in solitary dignity, waiting for the beat of drums, for smoke to drift skyward, and for the laughter of children. It was an uncomfortable place, too recently abandoned. Had the people died so fast?

They all grabbed as much as they could carry and started toward the closest lodge that appeared sturdy. They had nearly reached it, their heads bowed against the sleet, when a hoarse cry was followed by the very air shivering with the beat of black wings. Ravens rose into the air from everywhere—from the roof ridges and gravehouses and poles—so many that the gray sky turned black momentarily as the birds wheeled and lifted and croaked warning of the intruders.

"Damnation!" The hair on the back of Luke's neck lifted. "Where did they come from?"

Of course he didn't need an answer. He simply hadn't looked closely, none of them had. Kun taos said something; Gao grunted. It was too cold to linger in wonder or superstition. One by one, they stumbled through the oval doorway into a house. Inside, gray light barely filtered through cracks and the smoke hole. Two levels were excavated below ground. Steep stairways still felt solid when Luke tested them cautiously.

The rocks surrounding the fire pit were white from bird droppings. Luke didn't give a damn. He looked around in assessment. What could they burn?

In one corner rested a dusty heap of poles that had probably been used to hang halibut and salmon to dry over the fire. While Gao broke those into shorter lengths, Luke tore apart shelves and several screens on the upper levels. A few bentwood boxes, empty and cracked, could be burned if need be; the back stairway could go as well.

He was desecrating this place, but their urgent need overrode any qualms. Gao was already on his knees coaxing flames from the brittle but damp bits of wood. Kate had disappeared with Kun taos, presumably for another load from the canoe. He knew how useless it would have been to suggest to her that she leave what needed doing to the men. She would probably be warmer moving about anyway.

They returned to report that the sleet had quit. "I saw stars," Kate said, "but it's getting colder."

It must have been half an hour before the fire put out any discernible warmth. By that time, Luke had rigged a dressing room, and all had changed into almost-dry clothing. Even Kate's wool skirt, taken out of a box, steamed gently, showing how the damp penetrated everywhere. Overcoats were soaking, and all four used Hudson Bay blankets tied around the shoulders in their place. Gao put water in a kettle over the fire to heat, and eventually they had both Haida tea and coffee to drink with a cold supper.

Night had fallen, and not even Luke had any desire to explore. To Kate, he said quietly, "Shall I lay your mat out? Would you prefer us to leave to give you a few minutes of privacy?"

"Thank you," Kate said, "but you don't have to leave." As the fire grew, she had gradually emerged from the blanket that had been clutched around her shoulders, but her voice was dull, her face unanimated. "I don't intend to take a stitch off."

He cleared his throat. "Do you need to go out?"

He thought for a moment that she hadn't heard him, but at last she stirred. "Oh, I suppose."

Gao rose far more gracefully than Kate did. "We will go find more firewood. We must keep the fire from going out."

Luke nodded, appreciating his tact. He knew that Gao would stay away, and keep Kun taos with him, until he was certain Kate was abed.

The two Haida went out the front door. Taking the lantern, Kate followed them. Without removing planks, there was no back entrance in this house. She would need to go around the side for privacy. Left alone, Luke began rummaging through his bag in search of his toilet articles.

When he heard the first scream, for a fraction of a second, he thought it to be the screech of a bird. Even before his brain concluded otherwise, he was moving.

Chapter Eighteen

K ate!" he roared. He was barely up the two levels and out
the oval doorway before he collided with her. Instinctively, his arms closed around her. She was gasping for
breath as she clutched him, her body shaking. The lantern
she still held swung, flinging crazy patterns of light and
shadow over the house and the poles.

His arms tightened. "What happened?"

A shudder went through her and she pushed away from
him, her breath still rasping. Luke let her go but for a hand
on her arm. She tried valiantly to sound as if she had recovered her composure. "I . . . oh, I'm being absurd. Something
lashed against my face. When I held up the light—" She did
so again.

He, too, saw the long, black hair swinging free from the
grave box atop the mortuary pole. The strands brushed the
huge, uncaring eyes of the carved eagle on the pole below
the box.

Swearing, Luke steered her inside the house. There, he

snatched the lantern from her and set it down. When he pulled her into his arms, she stood stiffly.

"For God's sake, just once let yourself have hysterics!"

"I . . . I am incapable of hysterics." He could barely hear her, she spoke so softly; her mouth was in the vicinity of his throat.

"At least relax, damn you!"

For an instant, her muscles became if anything more rigid, but then she sagged against him. He held her and felt her tremble, moved his hands soothingly over her back. He closed his eyes and laid his cheek against her hair. Even still damp, it was springy, as determined to go its own way as Kate herself was.

Slowly, her shudders ceased, until she rested peacefully against him. His hands refused to still, savoring the line of her long, slim back, the delicate bones of her shoulders. He knew he ought to let her go before she noticed how his body was reacting, but his pleasure was too intense.

When she lifted her head, his hands tightened on her shoulders. What light there was pooled at their feet. Her eyes were dark and shadowed when they searched his. The silence was a part of the texture. What was she thinking? Feeling? Another shudder rippled through her, but this time, he sensed its difference.

He bent his head so slowly that she could have evaded him. Never a coward, she chose not to. Instead, she closed her eyes and lifted her face to his.

He ought to have made the kiss gentle, something both could later pretend had been no more than reassurance. But it was impossible. He had been restraining too many feelings for too long. His mouth took hers hungrily; she answered him the same. He groaned, she sighed. One of his hands cupped her breast; his other hand was spread at the small of her back to press her closer. She felt so good against him; not soft and pliable, but rather like a lock of her hair, which would spring free sooner or later but was temporarily willing to curl about his finger.

The image was so erotic that he was shocked into awareness. Good God, what was he thinking? Drunk with passion, still he became suddenly aware that his leg had insinuated itself between her legs, that his thoughts had progressed beyond bounds of decency.

He groaned again and lifted his head. Her dark lashes fluttered up and she looked dazedly at him.

She was dependent on him, his conscience reminded him. He couldn't take advantage of her! Yet another part of him wondered: Would she let him do just that if Gao and Kun taos could be escaped? But what if she became pregnant? What if she wanted to say no, but feared to? What if . . .

"No!" The word was torn from his throat. "I'm being a cad! I beg your pardon."

Sounding uncomprehending, Kate echoed, "You beg . . ." She broke off, and he saw her spasm of understanding. The silence bristled with all that was unspoken, and then she straightened her shoulders and lifted her chin.

"I am as much to blame. Perhaps it was inevitable that a kiss or . . . or something should happen, given our enforced proximity."

"Proximity be hanged!" He grabbed her upper arms. "I kissed *you*, not the only available woman."

"I *am* the only available woman."

He was shaking with frustration. How had this degenerated into a childish argument? "I've been wanting to kiss you for weeks. Months. But this is not the time or place . . ."

They both heard the voices just outside. Gao and Kun taos would be upon them in seconds. Reluctantly, Luke let her go. She showed her perturbation by stumbling toward the fire pit without picking up the lantern first.

Luke grabbed it and followed her, but she had already vanished inside the makeshift dressing chamber.

Damn! How was he to talk to her now? Would he have to wait until tomorrow? What would he say then? I didn't mean it? That would be worse than the truth. I want you desperately? He was gentleman enough, thank God, to refuse what she hadn't even offered. What made him even think she shared his feelings? One passionate kiss? She might be a passionate woman—*was* a passionate woman. Perhaps from her point of view, proximity alone was responsible.

Unutterably depressed, he greeted the two men and then prepared for bed. Wrapped in a blanket, Kate scurried to her mat without looking at him. Gao watched her oddly, but made no remark; in fact, he and Kun taos were both unusually silent. It was a long while before Luke slept, but Kate was so still that he couldn't tell whether she was wakeful as well. She was a quiet sleeper at any time.

One of the four roused often enough during the night to keep the fire fed with bits and pieces. Morning arrived, bitterly cold but crystal-clear. Luke clutched his blankets around him as he moved crablike to build up the fire. Even so, his toes curled away from the icy plank floor.

One by one, the others awakened. Kun taos was irritatingly cheerful, given that Luke's head felt as if he had been soused last night. Kate seemed much as usual, though she still avoided Luke's gaze.

She was dressing behind the screen, the men by the fire, when the harsh call of a raven announced morning. Supposedly, the supernatural beings were out and about at night, but they must return to their own villages before Raven cried morning or fall down dead—or whatever the equivalent was if one were not quite human to start with.

Strangely, this raven kept calling. The sound was the familiar croak but was held until the note undulated, then repeated. Curious, Luke shoved his feet into his boots and hurried out. Gao was right behind him.

In front, Luke looked up. The largest raven he had ever seen sat atop the frontal pole, which, coincidentally, depicted a raven. The live one was glossy and black, the rays of the rising winter sun shimmering in iridescence on its feathers. The bird tilted its head and looked down at them, pausing in its vocalization as if to contemplate them. When it called again, its voice resonant and penetrating, it half-spread its wings and fluffed up its feathers, as though attempting to appear larger than it was to frighten them.

Gao made a sound, and Luke turned to look at him. The guide was staring at the bird as though it were the creator, The Trickster himself.

"Is it trying to tell us something?" Luke asked.

Gao seemed to wrench his gaze away. He appeared frightened, Luke saw with sudden disquiet. "It is said that when the raven calls for a long time, there will be a death in the village." Gao's throat worked. "When a raven ruffles up its feathers to look big, the death will happen soon."

The clear skies accompanied by cold lasted for several days. Ice lay in thin sheets on the upper reaches of the beach, and in the early mornings, frost glistened on every coarse blade of sea grass. The mountainous slopes to the north and west were dusted with white.

Luke wanted to stay long enough to study the village in a way impossible with the inhabited ones. Here, he could see the interior of every house, poke into abandoned cedar boxes, take without objection from Gao the household implements and fishing nets and hooks that had been left behind. He grilled Gao and Kun taos on the meaning of the figures painted on house walls and boxes and incised into poles.

The weather was perfect for photography. In no other sense could the time at Ninstints be considered an idyll. Kate did her best to avoid Luke, an effort doomed to failure considering the circumstances. If only he had cooperated! But no . . . if anything, he stalked her.

Inevitably, he cornered her. She was setting up to photograph an interior house pole that interested him. This particular house was not excavated within; the space was all on one level. Against the back wall stood a magnificent pole, carved from floor to roof. At the top, a human embraced a hawk and a bear cub; below, a bear held a human between its paws, while frogs emerged from the bear's ears. Protected from the elements, the paint was still vivid, a fact that made Kate regret the fact that photography did not allow the reproduction of color. Would there someday be a way?

Gao had explained to Luke how the different paints had been made, before the coming of white men. Charcoal, crushed clam shells, iron oxide, and copper ores, ground and mixed with salmon eggs, gave black, white, red, and blue. Some colors could be made from a fungus that grew on the hemlock, and from a moss. Gao used paints made in the old way, he said, which had not surprised Kate. He was of the temperament to be a purist; compromise was not in his nature.

Today Kate had waited to photograph inside until the sun was at its zenith, so that the greatest possible light poured into the smoke hole and through the cracks.

When she heard footsteps behind her and turned to see Luke standing in the open doorway, sunlight streaming around him, her heart lurched. Before he could speak, she asked, "Do you suppose we could remove some planks to provide more light?"

The quirk of one eyebrow suggested that he knew quite well why she had rushed to ask for assistance, but he said willingly enough, "I don't see why not. I'll ask Gao if he'll help. It shouldn't be difficult to replace the planks."

"Would it matter if we didn't?"

He was staring at the painted rear wall and the pole in the middle. For a moment, she almost thought he had forgotten her. When he answered at last, his tone was melancholic. "No. I suppose it wouldn't, but all this would vanish even sooner if we exposed it to the weather. I must do what little I can to preserve even what is impossible to take."

Again she had a peculiar sensation in her chest, as though a hand had squeezed her heart. It occurred to her what an inconvenient organ her heart had become. It existed solely to move blood through her veins, not to remind her painfully of her every emotion!

Well, she had wanted to know how it felt to be attracted to a man, to know his touch and desire. In her foolish curiosity, she hadn't guessed the power one kiss could have. How could she have known that she could feel so intensely, that she could want on such a primal level to be joined to another soul? No wonder women had so few defenses against men! If Luke had not let her go that night . . . But, thank God, he had.

Now he suddenly swung to face her. It was at moments like this that she was reminded of how brilliant a blue his eyes were; they were so clear, so penetrating, she wished she wore a veil.

"We must talk," he said.

"No." Instinctively, she fought him, though she had never believed in postponing confrontation. When had she turned into such a coward? "We are forced to work together—more than that, to live together—for another two months. Please . . ."

"We should clear the air."

"We should agree to pretend it never happened," Kate said stubbornly.

"I have no wish to pretend any such thing!" His vehemence shocked her. "If the timing were different, you must know—"

"I know nothing." She bent and peered through her camera's aperture, though she might as well have been looking up through the smoke hole for all she saw.

"Blast it! This is not like you." He took several steps closer. It was all she could do not to shy away.

She closed her eyes, balled her hands into fists. Somehow, she must sound composed! Amazingly enough, she almost did. "Uncomfortable things are better said when we are nearer escape from one another."

Luke drew in an audible breath; a minute must have ticked by in utter silence. At last he spoke, his every word icily polite. "If I understand you correctly, then I must apologize. My intention was not to prey upon you when you're at my mercy." Only then did his voice alter, become rougher. "I cannot forget what happened, but you ask for pretence. That at least I can grant you." Out of the corner of her eye, she saw him retreat. "Now, I'll find Gao and see about bringing more light in."

He was gone. Kate sagged, resting her forehead against the cool, sharp edge of her camera. Oh, Lord, what had she done? Why hadn't she at least let him speak?

Of course she knew the answer. She had feared the worst: not that he regretted what had happened, but that he would feel compelled to pretend it meant something more to him than it did. She had no doubt that he wanted her; the tension had been building for too long. God help her, she had even goaded him! Her face burned at the memory of the nights when she had brushed her hair with slow, luxurious strokes, long past any need. Glorying in her unaccustomed power, she had reveled in the knowledge that he watched.

Somehow, she had never realized what the end result must be. Would he believe how innocent she was? How inexperienced? Perhaps she had thought—hoped—that he might take her away when spring came, a gallant knight on his white charger. Exactly the kind of nonsense she had imagined Alice thinking, and tried to discourage.

She guessed that he was willing—indeed, felt *obligated* —to rescue her. Well, she wouldn't let him! She owed him that much. Right now, she was his entire world, as he was hers. Matters would look different when they returned to Victoria, when he saw her again as she really was: an awkward, unfeminine, outspoken spinster, who had only her photographic skill to recommend her. Any man would want considerably more in a wife. Nor did she want a husband who had married her out of pity, to save her from a bleak life.

If she was wrong, if he truly wanted her, he would surely speak again. In the spring, she would let him.

Her eyes stung. She knew better.

Their meals consisted almost exclusively of what they had brought with them: smoked sockeye and dog salmon and halibut, dried berry and root cakes, seaweed and preserved herring spawn, crab apples with wrinkled skin that always made Kate think of Sarah, whose cheeks had been so rosy. Occasionally one of the men shot a bird of some kind, which they steamed by pouring water over hot rocks. Gao had lowered himself to joining Kate to dig for clams; chiton could be pried off rocks for variety. The diet was monotonous, but standard for the Haida. The quantity of food required to feed only one family for the winter was staggering; preserving it consumed most of the summer and fall for the women.

Tonight they were eating mashed potatoes—thank heavens for the potatoes they had dug up in an abandoned patch near the village—with grease rather than butter, along with fresh halibut caught today by Kun taos. Kate was beginning to sympathize with Mr. Richardson's viewpoint, though she had never minded the diet when she lived at Skidegate. Her father had always made sure they had flour to last the winter, and the cow had provided milk and butter. They'd had chickens as well; Kate had never been able to kill one, but she had cooked them when the Reverend Hewitt became aware that his daughter had served fish for countless nights in a row. And then there were the eggs . . .

She sighed. The three men looked at her, then quickly away. The meal was being eaten in silence. She knew, of course, why Luke avoided meeting her eyes and had little to say. But Gao, too, had behaved oddly since . . . Well, she wasn't sure when. At least since they had arrived at Ninstints. He had been quiet, even grim.

Did he fear the next leg of their journey? She remembered Kun taos calling him an old woman who let his fear of *Taxet*'s house make him a coward. The Skidegate Haida believed that most people went to the Land of Souls at death, but drowning victims went instead to live with the killer whales, while those who died violently went to *Taxet*'s house, somewhere up in the sky and said to be an unpleasant place. Its greatest disadvantage was the fact that being reborn from there was difficult, if not impossible. There were other destinations: If you died from a fall, you went to House-Hanging-from-the-Shining-Heavens; its owner, Great Shining Heavens, was said to have little people dangling headfirst from his eyelashes. Shamans went to the Shaman's Country.

Was he afraid? She began to watch him covertly, for what good that did; he ate with his head bowed, his thoughts turned inward. Kun taos glanced from face to face, his own perplexed.

Kate was as startled as the two guides when Luke set down his wooden bowl with a decisive air. "I think we should turn back when we leave here, rather than go up the west coast."

She was the first to speak. "Why?"

"It's dangerous." He looked at her unemotionally. "What seemed like a fine idea when I conceived it back at the museum has begun to sound foolhardy. I have more than my own safety to consider."

Her eyes narrowed. "You mean mine."

"I mean all three of you."

"You know Kun taos is eager to go!" she cried.

Poor Kun taos was listening without the faintest idea of what was being said. She was too upset to translate; fortunately, Gao took pity on his friend and did.

Then Gao fixed Luke with steady, dark eyes. "It is impossible to run away from something that is foretold. Whoever sent the omen has thought of what you might do. It—" he groped for a word, at last said something in Haida that Kate translated as fate "—it waits no matter what way we go."

"Omen?" she echoed.

"We saw a raven. It sat on this house and made itself big."

Kate knew what that meant, and she had a momentarily dizzying memory of her vision, eons ago in Victoria, when Raven had spoken to her. Was he warning her alone now, or had he lured her here and now mocked her? But *why*?

"Why didn't you tell me?" she asked, yet knowing all the while what the answer was, and resenting it.

"Omens be damned!" Luke stood and began to pace restlessly. "The weather on the way here made me understand what we might face. What if that drenching downpour had been accompanied by high seas? I'm told there are few landfalls on the west coast. We might easily be caught between by a storm."

"I have been there," Gao said. "If we are careful, the danger is not so great."

Luke betrayed himself then by a glance at Kate. "I still say—"

"I will never forgive you if you change your plans for my sake." Kate kept her voice steady and calm. "Why should I be any more vulnerable than the photographer you meant to hire?"

"You are a woman . . ."

She waited.

"Damn it, Gao, tell her!"

Gao shrugged. "If something bad happens, we will all die. It does not matter if we are men or women."

"See?" she said childishly.

Luke flung up his hands. "Very well! On your own head be it!" With that, he stalked out, leaving renewed silence in his wake.

They stayed at Red-Cod-Island Town for several more days, during which Gao and Kun taos told what stories they knew about the Kunghit Haida, the southern tribe. Their language had been different, Gao said, just as the Haida around Masset spoke a dialect unlike the Skidegates'. They had inhabited as many as two dozen villages. As their numbers shrank, one village after another was abandoned, until only this one remained. The last smallpox epidemic had left so few, the survivors had moved to Skidegate.

Behind were left not just the lodges and the mortuary poles, but also the more homely evidence of human habitation: a shell midden, the potato patch, and several apple trees, whose apples had been eaten by the birds or fallen off the trees to rot. Nearby caves served as burial houses for those not important enough to have a mortuary pole raised to hold the remains.

More than bones would have been left in the caves. The dead were enclosed in handsome boxes that might also hold prized possessions. Since Gao was to accompany Luke to

view the caves, Kate decided to go, too, out of curiosity—
though she was more interested in the two men's relationship than she was in the objects.

. On the way, Kate had time for reflection. How they had
all changed in the six weeks since they left Skidegate! Gao,
for example: He had been an angry man, fiercely certain that
he could stave off the inevitable, or at least that it was right
to try. He had been prepared to hate Luke, perhaps to hate
any *yetz haada*. Now he had come to see how little he alone
could do. He had to know that a hundred years hence, this
place, and all like it, would have been swallowed by the forest and the sea. It might be haunted forever, but there would
never be a potlatch here again; visitors would not arrive in
canoes with white sails like sea birds, they would not dance,
coppers would not be thrown into the sea. No pole would be
raised; the ones here would crack and rot within until the
eyes of Killer Whale and Grizzly Bear and Raven could no
longer see. But had Gao yet recognized the struggle that was
ahead of him? Had he begun to wonder where he would fit
into this new world?

For Luke, this had begun as a competition. His convictions had been sincere, Kate thought, but all the same, the
expedition had been a game to him. He must have bigger
and better than Durham, or Jarvis, or any other collector.
How often had she seen that covetous gleam in his eyes?
When had she last seen it? He was torn now, she thought—
still believing in his mission, but conscious of the violation.
He felt the oppressive atmosphere now, heard the voices and
the beat of drums that whispered at the edge of Kate's
awareness. She had seen how feverishly he wrote down the
stories, heard the passion in his voice when he urged her to
photograph everything, to miss *nothing*. Only yesterday,
they had found a doll just inside a house at the end of the
curved beach, left on the floor as if forgotten in the haste of
departure. Skillfully carved from cedar, it had fur for hair, a
tiny cedar-bark dress, and an expression of benevolence. It
must have belonged to a child. Luke had picked it up and
stood staring at it for a long moment. And then he had

crouched to lay it back down in the precise position he found it in, his hands oddly gentle. A moment later, he turned abruptly to brush past Kate and leave that house.

Of course he would be back; in the end, he would take the doll, to put in a glass-fronted cabinet in the museum, where children would stare at it and wonder about the child who had once cradled it. But Luke would not take the doll lightly; he no longer saw it as a prize he had won.

And her? She, too, had started out with a straightforward goal: to find her father's murderer. She had thought she knew her father; though she had not liked some of the consequences of his mission, she had admired him for his dedication and agreed with most of his goals. She had long since forgiven him for his neglect of his responsibilities toward her and her mother. She supposed she had been so angry at her mother that she had placed the blame for her unhappy childhood there rather than upon her father.

Perhaps it had been inevitable that she would discover he was not the man she had thought him, would begin to see him with some objectivity.

In truth, "confusion" was probably a better word to describe her emotions! Slowly, she had realized that avenging his murder was no longer her only aim in life, either. It was Luke who had somehow become central to her existence, though she hardly understood what she felt for him. Physical awareness, certainly. Liking? Most of the time. Gratitude? That was one of the least comfortable of her emotions. Nor did she always know where her attraction to him stopped and her envy of his life began. Did she love him alone? Would her feelings for him allow her to become a comfortable, domestic sort of wife, if that was what he wanted?

Even there, she was dreaming! She was glad to be distracted from her reflections when Gao stopped at the opening to a wide cave shaped like an inverted V. Tree roots twisted on the walls to each side. Luke advanced within, while Kate paused at Gao's side. He said nothing when Luke began to poke around, glancing up at Gao often. The

Indian's stance was not that of the implacable guardian she remembered from the shaman's burial. Instead, his expression matched the one Luke had worn yesterday when he gazed at the interior house pole. Sorrowful.

Luke lifted the lid off a box and appeared to contemplate the contents. From where she stood, Kate could just see the smooth knob of a protruding bone and some tattered wool fringe. Luke asked, "Gao, once the soul leaves the body, do your people believe there is any attachment left to the bones themselves?"

After a pause, Gao said, "There is a story from around here. When the people of a village were all out hunting, the dead rose from their grave boxes and went into the chief's house. There they danced. One of them stepped on a salmon skin. It stuck to him. Another pulled it off, but then it stuck to him. While they were trying to pull the salmon skin off the second man, the sky opened and Raven cried. At once, they all fell down. When the hunters came home, the chief's house was full of bones."

It was absurd, of course, a tale to frighten children. But Kate couldn't help glancing around uneasily. One box had been opened, perhaps by souvenir hunters, and the skeleton within had collapsed into a heap of bones. On top was the skull, the eye sockets staring owlishly up at her.

Luke said suddenly, "You know that all of this will disappear one of these days, when Jarvis or one of his kind makes it here." It was to Gao he was looking; his eyes held a challenge.

Regret, bitterness, sorrow . . . Kate could see all these on Gao's face. His mouth twisted. "Maybe they will not find every place."

"Maybe not."

Now Gao's gaze challenged in turn. "If I were not here to see, would you take everything?"

Luke sank onto his heels beside a painted cedar box; faded red and black graphically depicted a frog. In one hand, Luke held pitchwood that burned with a flickering orange flame. "Yes," he said bluntly. "Not the bones, but the other things. They would be safe in a museum. Here, they are not. One by one, they will be taken by people who think of them as curiosities, people who, once home, will stow them in attics and never look at them again. In the museum, they will be seen and admired; the stories will be written down, so that your children's children may go there and see the things and know what they mean and why they were made. I think that the dead will not miss these things."

"I will not say it is right to take things from the dead," Gao said with the fierceness of a sudden squall. "But I know I cannot stop them all from coming and taking. Even you I cannot watch all the time." He turned so abruptly that he bumped Kate, but without glance or apology, he strode away.

She recovered and stared after him. Luke came to her side and did the same.

"Was that a warning, or tacit permission?"

"I'm not sure," she said slowly.

"In his heart, he knows I'm right. So why am I not rejoicing?"

She looked at him. Brows knitted, he was still gazing after Gao.

"I don't know. Why aren't you?"

"I have the feeling he's lived on anger so long, he doesn't know any other way."

She was disconcerted to have him make an observation that so exactly paralleled her own thoughts. He was too perceptive; did he read her as accurately?

"I must go," she said quickly. "I'd like to finish photographing the poles and house fronts today."

Of course he knew perfectly well that she was fleeing him; one sardonic glance told her as much. But when she took a step forward, he stayed her with a hand on her arm. Kate looked down at the hand, strong and brown and at the moment, a little dirty. She had a dizzying recollection of the first time he had stopped her so, that day in her refuge behind her aunt and uncle's home. His offer then had changed her life—whether for better or for worse, she didn't yet know. What would he ask this time?

But Luke was not even looking at her. He was still frowning in the direction where Gao had disappeared. Sounding unusually hesitant, he said, "Do you think Gao would accept more or less permanent employment from me? If I made him my agent, he could purchase artifacts that would be sold in any case. And instead of trying to overcome the difficulties involved in buying a pole, I'm considering hiring Gao to carve one or more. I'd like a handsome canoe, too. He speaks English well enough that I see no reason he couldn't even handle shipping from this end, if I've made prior arrangements. What do you think?"

"You must know that it is a splendid notion," she said, her tone constrained. Somewhere in the midst of Luke's speech, she had been stunned by the knowledge that she did indeed love him. How could she help it? So few white men would have considered hiring an Indian, much less trusting him with the museum's money. Mr. Duncan had insisted that after a winter here, Luke would share his opinion that the Indians were like children. He had been wrong.

And she knew perfectly well that Luke would prefer a pole of some antiquity to the newly made. He had run into frustrations, but ultimately, somebody in Masset or Skidegate would have been willing to sell one, and Luke could have arranged for its shipping himself in the spring. No, this idea was conceived for Gao's sake, not Luke's.

Quietly, she said, "I have no doubt that Gao would be trustworthy. You're a generous man."

He looked uncomfortable. "Self-serving, rather."

"You can't fool me, of all people!" She had to say it. "After all, I myself am the fortunate benefactor of just such a generous impulse."

"Pah!" His hand left her arm and he stalked back into the cave. Over his shoulder, he snapped, "If I were less selfish, you would not be here. You may yet regret my supposed generosity!"

Kate didn't attempt to argue anymore. He would never admit to being motivated by anything other than self-interest. She knew him too well to need such an admission.

"Do be discreet," she suggested. "Gao is a man at war with himself. You could easily give him cause to regret his impulse."

In the act of wedging the torch into a crack so that his hands would be freed, Luke looked up. His expression was wry. "So much for the high praise. Do you really think I'm idiot enough to antagonize Gao at this point?"

"No, of course not. I only thought . . . never mind." She was the one to feel like an idiot as she fled. She had spoken without thinking, picturing the old Luke, the one who had wanted her to distract Gao on the *ska-ga*'s burial island. She had wondered even then if he was serious. It would be like him to pretend to be ruthless, even while his better emotions motivated him.

How ironic that he encouraged her to think the worst of him, and yet was hurt when she did!

They left Ninstints on a morning like so many that had come before. A gray mist hung low, obscuring the mountains to the north. As the canoe sliced through the kelp at the narrow mouth to the harbor, Kate looked back at Red-Cod Island Town. It was a forlorn sight: empty houses, a pole that listed, another split open by a seedling. Lidless eyes staring blindly from the carvings. Gray, rocky shoreline and a dark, dripping forest behind. The ravens had returned to fight bitterly over some dead thing down the beach. Kate had to turn away quickly, before the tears that burned in her eyes could fall. Only a minute later, she turned back again for one last glimpse, but already, tiny Anthony Island was lost in the mist and drizzle.

In her cheerless mood, the endless gray seemed to symbolize this winter. She had come imagining that she was called, that she could make some difference. She had discovered that she was alone in her search for her father's murderer. She had deluded herself that the Haida would care, that they would see what he had tried to do for them, even if much of it had been left undone. Instead, her presence was unwelcome; she had brought shame to people she loved, and for what? She was no closer to knowing who had killed the Reverend Hewitt than she had ever been; spring would be for her a season of defeat, not hope.

She was not alone in feeling somber. Gao and Luke were silent, Gao broodingly so. They talked little that first day, spent skirting the reefs and rocks lying offshore of the southwestern coast, heavily forested and forbidding. Only Kun taos looked around with cheerful curiosity.

Shortly after leaving Ninstints, they passed the reef the Haida called Ki'l. When all the world was water, legend said, this reef alone showed. There the supernatural beings waited for the waters to subside. Gao's tone was matter-of-fact, taking for granted the truth of legends and the existence of unseen beings. That shrubby islet and the kelp lying over submerged rocks were so ordinary Kate had a peculiar, unsettling sensation as she gazed at them. If they could be seen and touched, was it any more fantastic to think one might meet Property Woman on the beach, or see The Singers coming through the air in a canoe?

Luke paddled, too; though the swells were long and slow, they were still powerful, and Gao was determined to stay well off from the shore. There were several points known for their vicious riptides, and jagged rocks could extend well out. Kate noticed that for all his earlier contempt of Gao's caution, Kun taos did not argue. Had the raven frightened him, too?

They slept that first night in two tents rigged from the canvas sails, one tent for Kate alone. Rain, seeping through the green canopy above, pattered softly on the canvas over her head.

For a few hours the next day, the clouds lifted, allowing them to see the forbidding landscape. The country was more mountainous now, with rocky shores rising vertically to snow-clad peaks three thousand feet or more above sea level. Stunted trees clung to the slopes, scarred here and there by recent landslides. The surf crashed in white foam against gray cliffs. High, flat rocks, rising above the swells and streaked with white, must be rookeries; on others, sea lions watched them pass.

They stopped early that night, at a tiny gravel beach within a basin concealed behind a protective headland. Mountains rose all around it, the lower slopes heavily forested. Everywhere Kate looked, cataracts plummeted from rocky faces. It was a secret spot, gloriously beautiful, if also too harsh to be considered welcoming.

There they found crude bark shelters left by fishermen. Gao built a fire and they laid out clothes and blankets to dry. They might actually succeed in the endeavor, since for once, it wasn't raining.

Luke wandered, finding several fossils along with some rotten timbers that had once supported a lodge. His enthusiasm leavened Kate's gloom, and even, it seemed, Gao's. With nightfall, the fire leaped higher, crackling and popping as the damp wood burned. As was his habit, Luke pressed questions on Gao, who answered willingly enough, sometimes consulting with Kun taos.

Tonight Gao related the story of how Shining Heavens had caused himself to be born, found by a chief's daughter in a cockleshell. She raised him as her son, using moss for a soft bed. As he grew, he hunted birds and used their skins to cover himself and become as the sky.

The fire was burning low, its coals glowing in the darkness; even in translation, Kate heard the cadence of a story told many times.

"Then Shining Heavens said, 'Mother, I shall see you no more. I am going away from you. When I sit in front of Q!anan in the morning, there will be no breeze. Then people can catch their food.' "

Gao fell silent at last. Luke stretched. "Well, Gao, will tomorrow be such a morning?"

"I do not think so," he said. The worry was in his voice again.

Chapter Nineteen

Kate lay sleepless, alone in her shelter, listening to the last popping sounds the coals made as they settled, and finally, to the snores from the other shelter. Once she would have sworn she heard a disgruntled, "Damnation! Turn over," followed by a short silence. She had to smile when the snores resumed. Was it Gao, or Kun taos?

She slept eventually, but fitfully. The light was pale, almost opalescent, when she slipped out of her shelter in the morning to find that Gao had preceded her. The fire leaped eagerly over broken branches, though the eternal dampness made them hiss and steam. He turned and nodded, his eyes grave.

Kate held her hands out to the flames and studied him. In a low voice, she asked, "What is it you fear?"

He bent to poke the fire, his eyes evading hers now. "Nothing. I am being foolish. An old woman, as Kun taos said."

From that stand, she couldn't budge him. Luke emerged from the other shelter a minute later, groaning and raking his fingers through his hair until it stood up straight. Even as he shrugged on his coat and headed for the fire, his clear gaze went first to Kate, unreadably, and then to Gao. There it rested for a moment, unnoticed by their guide, and Kate knew that Luke sensed, as she did, Gao's disquiet.

By the time they launched *Dancing Canoe,* a drizzle had begun and the ocean was a dark, turbulent gray, the crests of the swells ruffled with spray. A wind had sprung up that clearly worried Gao. Southeast Wind, who lived under the sea and had many brothers, such as He-Who-Rattles-the-Stones, was one to fear.

They passed spires of limestone rising from the sea, and had been on their way for less than an hour when the drizzle turned to rain, a driving downpour that slanted across the bow. The waves rose and the troughs between them deepened. The wind lashed the crests until they began to break, whipping cold spray over the canoe.

Gao and Luke took down the sails, a task made dangerous by the sheer weight of the soaked canvas and the pitching of the canoe. They had to shout to communicate with each other, and even then, their words were snatched away by the wind.

They had hoped to reach Kaisun today, but now Gao cupped his hands and bellowed in Haida, "We must make for Tasu Harbor!"

Kun taos agreed; even the most foolhardy could see that these pounding seas were too powerful to defy. Rolling and groaning, the thirty-five-foot canoe felt as fragile as an eggshell. Hollowed from one log, the wood had little give; it was not uncommon for one to split asunder when stressed so severely.

Kate had automatically begun to bail. She was nearly blinded by the cold rain, and could only pray Gao would be able to see landmarks. Flecked with foam, waves towered above them, twenty-five feet high or more. The canoe scrambled up each one, then pitched down the other side, leaving Kate's stomach behind.

Despite her bailing, Kate was kneeling in six inches of

cold water by the time Gao gave the shouted order to make for the narrows that led into Tasu Sound. Through the gray curtain of wind-driven rain, Kate saw the opening, surely no more than a third of a mile wide. *Dancing Canoe* felt as tiny as a child's toy when it was lifted and flung past the forbidding headlands to each side by the foam-crested waves. Surf thundered just behind them, and rain stung their faces.

Yet, within minutes, the sound of the surf was muted and the waves crested without breaking. The surface of the sea was still choppy, dotted with whitecaps, but the wind no longer buffeted them, shielded now as they were by the mountains that rose to each side.

Kate continued to bail, but with less sense of urgency. Behind her, Luke set down the paddle and bowed his head. As she watched surreptitiously, she saw him rotate his shoulders and utter a stifled groan. His muscles must be screaming in protest. The Haida men, nearly all of them fine seamen, were known for their powerfully developed arms and shoulders, a necessity when so much time was spent paddling.

The narrows widened into a large sound. Kate could see little beyond the dark forest that reached the unforgiving shore. The rain still made a gray veil, and the clouds hung low. Under Gao's direction, the canoe followed the northern shore, which curved into a long bay. One of the many long-abandoned villages had stood there: Singa, or Winter Village. When they landed, they found little trace of it but for a few mossy timbers and fallen poles, rotted beyond recognition.

A stream emerged from beneath the dripping, gloomy cover of spruce, cedar, and hemlock. Ferns, bowing under the weight of rainwet foliage, trailed fronds over the banks. Fallen trees, draped in moss, made green bridges set at odd angles. Bark shelters here had decayed and collapsed long ago; this damp climate ensured a short life for anything susceptible to rot.

The wind was still cold and bitter. Luke suggested they retreat well under the woodland canopy to set up camp.

Though the wind was checked there, the slanting rain still made its way through in a steady drip from every leaf and needle and branch. The ground was saturated; water had collected on the broad, shiny leaves of salal and seeped from the balls of moss that hung from branches. To every side were the enormous trunks of unimaginably ancient trees. It was quieter here in the forest, and darker, even a little spooky.

Wet sails made uncomfortable shelters, and a reluctant fire offered little warmth. Fortunately, the bentwood boxes and tightly woven baskets that held their food, blankets, and clothing were waterproof, so Kate was able to change—though the wool jacket and skirt were her last dry clothes. She felt selfish for worrying when she realized that Gao and Kun taos had no dry clothing; they seemed to exchange one blanket for another, hanging the wet ones in the feeble hope that they might dry.

As they all hovered around the fire, Gao told what he remembered hearing about the long-extinct Haida tribe that had inhabited these western shores: the Pitch Town People. Supposedly, they had originated the art of tattooing during a potlatch here at Winter Village, celebrating the wedding of a Raven chief to an Eagle woman from Cumshewa. From here, the art had spread throughout Haida Gwai.

"I have heard there are burial caves," Kun taos said, either not seeing or ignoring Gao's hand, raised as though to check him.

Feeling something of a traitor, Kate opened her mouth to translate, but Luke had understood. His grasp of the language had grown at astonishing speed, though he spoke it brokenly. Gao sat back resignedly as Kun taos added helpfully that he thought the caves were out on the eastern point of the bay.

Like Kate, Luke held a blanket draped over his head and shoulders. In disgust, he gave it a shake, scattering droplets in every direction. "Perhaps it will quit raining by morning," he said, without a great deal of hope in his voice. "We can go take a look then."

If anything, it was raining harder when, feeling as sodden as the ground underfoot, Kate emerged from her tent in the morning. Overhead, the trees moaned in the unseen wind. Luke sat on his heels by the fire, shielded from the rain by a jury-rigged lean-to. When she sighed and sat down on a moss-covered log that squished underneath her, Luke gave her one of those inscrutable, yet oddly searching, glances.

Color rose in her cheeks, but she said lightly enough, "I'm beginning to wonder if I'll ever be truly dry again."

He grunted. "I know what you mean. No wonder the Haida have dreamed up so many forms of indoor entertainment for winters." He lifted the kettle. "Coffee?"

Kate accepted the steaming mug, taking care not to touch his fingers with her own.

"Where are Gao and Kun taos?"

He nodded toward the tent. "Kun taos is still snoring away. Can't you hear him?"

"So he's the one," she said in amusement. "I wasn't sure."

"Laugh, will you." Nonetheless, Luke's mobile mouth relaxed into something approaching a smile. "You may sleep with him tonight."

She might have taken offense; the subject was perilously close to the one they were avoiding at all cost. But somehow, these last few days, sometimes frightening, always uncomfortable, and yet exhilarating despite all, had freed them from some of the constraint. So Kate merely smiled. "Thank you, but no."

Both looked around when a branch cracked. Gao was approaching from the bay side. He said, "We must remain here. The wind still blows hard."

Kate would have stoutly resisted any attempt to launch *Dancing Canoe* today. She was not ordinarily afraid of sea travel, and had firmly put from her mind memories of the vicious storm in Hecate Strait. But yesterday's towering waves had been a fresh reminder of how frail human beings were when at nature's mercy.

The morning proved to be oddly peaceful. The three men went to see the burial caves, leaving Kate to her thoughts.

She had been aware for some time that she might have a decision to make. Her father had taken her once to Kiusta and North Island and shown her a cave. It was a miracle that it had not already been plundered, but the Reverend Hewitt thought it was not well known because Kiusta itself had been abandoned so many years earlier. Kate had never forgotten the sight: In the flickering light of the torch, she had seen the painted boxes that held as many as thirty Haida, along with the traditional sprigs of myrtle. Each bentwood box was filled to the brim with household objects, the copper neck- and knee-rings, and the ceremonial masks that covered the sightless faces.

Of course she had wondered from the beginning whether the riches within the cave might have had something to do with her father's murder. But especially she had wondered since discovering the cache of skulls in the coal mine. She could think of nothing else about Kiusta or its near neighbor, Yaku, that would have explained even a visit there, much less passionate feelings. The last inhabitants had left Kiusta to its solitude nearly thirty years ago. Brush had overgrown the sheltered village site.

The burial cave lay across the watery passage and up a steep gully from the shore. Would Gao and Kun taos know of its existence? Would Gao say even if he did know? Ought the fragile cedar objects be left to rot undisturbed, as was meant? Or did they belong in a museum, as Luke believed?

Of course the decision might well not be hers to make. If the cave had something to do with the murder, it had likely been stripped already. But who could have bought the contents, with James Durham and Luke already departed from the Queen Charlottes? Her father had not mentioned any other collectors.

By the time the men returned several hours later, Kate had come to no conclusions. She still had time; they would visit Sims at Kaisun first, and probably at least two other ruined villages north of it.

The rainfall abated by afternoon, becoming a soft drizzle.

The water was still choppy, but when the tide went out, Kun taos decided to hunt for crabs or urchins, or even for a small devilfish, in the tide pools. Luke wanted to search the strip of forest along the shore for signs of the old village.

To Kate, he remarked, "Early Europeans buying furs from the Haida didn't mention poles. Are they a post-contact phenomenon, or did the explorers and traders never leave their ships? So many of the villages are sheltered from the open sea by small islands or the arms of a bay—it may be that many of the Europeans never saw a winter village." He was developing his thesis with his usual enthusiasm. "Then, of course, they may have encountered the Haida at their summer fishing camps, rather than at the permanent villages. I've asked Gao if he knows how far back such carving dates, but oral history is so imprecise that he isn't sure. A remnant of a carved pole at a village of this antiquity would establish their existence long before they were recorded in the journals of Europeans."

Kun taos departed happily, picking his way across the rocky beach, slick with green seaweed, toward the low-tide line. He carried the sharp-pointed, barbed lance used for hunting devilfish. Kate and Gao were recruited by Luke, who suggested that each carry a small knife to scrape off the moss covering any likely appearing downed logs.

A few that Kate found might have been house timbers; most were only fallen trees. When Luke called out, she wandered over to see his discovery. She glanced idly toward the inlet, where Kun taos crouched over something out toward the rocky point.

Beside Luke there was an enormous, decaying log that had been partially hollowed out. Beneath the canopy of spruce and cedar, moss had crept over it, and smaller trees grew along its length. When he peeled back some of the moss, charring could be seen. A craftsman had adzed both ends to points and roughly gouged out the interior, then used hot rocks to burn away more of the heartwood, sealing and hardening the wood at the same time. Normally, the unfinished canoe would have been skidded down to the water and towed back to the village for finishing. The maker of this one had never returned.

Gao pulled off a crumbling bit of the rotting cedar. "Who knows why?" he asked. "Maybe he didn't like the tree after all. Maybe he died."

A distant yell brought Kate's head around. For a moment, she was only puzzled when she didn't see Kun taos. Perhaps the voice had not been human. The sound might have been an eagle calling to its mate, or the bark of a seal. Neither man beside her gave any sign of having heard.

But where *was* Kun taos? It had been only moments since she last saw him. Could he possibly have gone far enough to have disappeared behind the point?

A certain disquiet made her say, "Gao, did you see where Kun taos went?"

Both men turned sharply, searching the craggy stretch of tide pools and rocks, with gravel pockets in between. Luke muttered, "Where the devil . . . ?" but before he finished, Gao had taken off at a run. Abandoning speculation, Luke was close behind, but Kate hesitated for a moment. If Kun taos had fallen into a deep tide pool, they might need something longer than an arm to extend to him. She snatched up a good-sized branch and dragged it behind her.

Well ahead, Gao was half-scrambling, half-running, directly toward a point near where she'd seen Kun taos last. Had he heard another cry? She saw a splash and something briefly surface—an arm? Her heart was in her throat as she slipped on a thick, slippery piece of green seaweed, caught her footing again and raced on. Gao knelt, shouted something. He lifted a big rock and hurled it down. On what?

Luke reached him, then swung around with wild eyes. He ran to meet Kate and grabbed the thick branch from her hands.

"What is it?" she cried, but he wasn't attending.

She fell once more, skinning her knee on a jagged rock, before she reached the deep tide pool. It was churning, the water peculiarly opaque, almost black. A leg kicked to the surface; it was Kun taos, held by something!

Luke flung the branch to Gao before diving to his stomach and grabbing Kun taos's foot. He pulled. The water foamed, and an enormous tentacle appeared, suckers all along the underside. Gao slammed the branch down on it, and again on a second one. There were eight, each ten feet long! Was it possible, a devilfish so large?

"It's stronger than I am!" Luke bellowed.

Kun taos's lance must be at the bottom of the pool. Kate picked up a rock and threw it as hard as she could, then another. Tentacles writhed and the water roiled, black with the octopus's ink. Gao held the branch poised above the water, waiting for an opening. Luke gave a powerful yank and gained a few more inches of Kun taos's leg. Kun taos was still thrashing, but surely he would drown if they couldn't pull him out soon.

The hideous reddish-brown head and body appeared, the small eyes set high amid the wrinkled skin. Gao saw his chance and brought the branch down with such force that it cracked and shattered. Blood spurted red into the inky pool. The monstrous creature lurched, agitating the water.

"Pull!" Kate screamed, and Kun taos popped free. Gao helped haul him from the water, frighteningly still. When Luke slapped his back, water gushed from his mouth, but he hung senseless.

Kate cast a wild glance at the pool, but there was no sign of the devilfish. It had retreated to its den in the depths.

Luke dragged Kun taos to the nearest pocket of gravel and turned him on his stomach, then straddled his back. He shoved forcefully on Kun taos's back, and Kate thought she saw a tremor of movement. Luke shoved again, and again. Water trickled from Kun taos's slack mouth; his cheek was ground into the gravel. Luke was swearing, a litany.

Gao, who had knelt beside his friend, rose suddenly with a violent motion. He lifted his arms and glared at the sky. In his own language, he shouted upward, "Power-of-the-Shining-Heavens, look upon me! Save my friend!"

Kate felt sick. It had all happened so fast. The edge of the world was indeed as sharp as a knife, and Kun taos had fallen off.

Even though he was angry inside, Gao sang the crying songs for his friend so that Kun taos could hold up his head proudly wherever he had gone. Even now, he might be at the house of The-One-in-the-Sea, being fitted for a killer-whale fin.

Luke helped him set Kun taos's body up inside the shelter. Gao looked through Kun taos's things to see if he had finer clothes, but everything was wet and wrinkled. Kneeling there, Gao bowed his head, fighting the tears and the anger that made him want to scream out in defiance. Kate touched his shoulder and he gripped her hand. She knelt and wrapped her arms around him. He hardly knew when Luke turned and left.

He should not be thinking such thoughts! Even when Gao didn't speak them aloud, Power-of-the-Shining-Heavens knew them. He might be angry in turn. He might say, "The stick that Raven drew for your friend was only so long." Or, "Kun taos was foolish. Did he think he alone could best a devilfish so many times his size?"

Another hand touched him, and Gao looked up.

Luke held out the Chilkat shawl. He was wet, from the rain and the fight. "Kun taos should wear this, if he would not be offended because the crest figures are not his."

The tears fell then, hot on Gao's cheeks; how could he help it? "Some are his," he said. "Raven and Frog. I think he would be glad to wear this."

So they dressed him up in it. They talked about Kun taos: the times he had made everybody laugh when they were wet and cold and tired, the uncle who would mourn him, the way he had fought death for so long today. First Kate, then Luke, left to sleep, but Gao sat up all night with his friend. When the first light showed, pale gray, Gao went down to the edge of the sea. He built a fire there, and sang more songs.

What medicine shall I use in my grief?
What medicine shall I use?
There is nothing I can use.
I long for your dear face.
If I could see the trail of the dead,
I would follow it.
Friend, I long to see all of you.

And then Gao put tobacco and food into the fire, grease and salmon and berry cakes, so that Kun taos would have plenty wherever he was. The flames leaped hungrily at the grease, and Gao smelled food cooking, as though a feast were being prepared down below.

When he turned, Luke and Kate stood silently behind him. They each put food in the fire, too. At last Luke and Gao carried Kun taos's dead body to the burial cave, where they bent his knees and back to put him in a painted box. Curled inside there, he was not Gao's friend anymore. He was only a shell. Soon he would be one amidst the ranks of skeletons here, those whose threads of life had long ago been cut.

Kate adjusted the Chilkat shawl. Luke lifted the lid onto the box. Gao turned abruptly and left, but he heard her murmur something.

"Our Father Who art in Heaven . . ."

Back at the camp, they packed, saying as little as possible. Gao saw Kate check for dampness inside a box that held her glass plates, as she often did. But her face was stricken when she set the lid back on it. "I never photographed him," she said, and Gao knew that for her, this was a great loss.

Luke took Kun taos's place with the paddle, so they had to take rests. He was not used to the rhythm, and his arms tired. The rain was cold, the seas leaden gray, but Southeast Wind no longer blew. Nobody spoke much. Gao could tell that these two white people mourned his friend and were not just being respectful.

They passed many story places: Gul Island, where it was said no mice could live; Hole Island, where lived the strongest of all Ocean People around here; the narrow cleft where Standing-Shining-in-the-Ocean cured himself of disease by swimming through the fissure and scraping his body raw on the barnacles. There were hidden reefs here, and tiny islands. Many-Killer-Whales Island lay at the opening to Kaisun Harbor.

The village stretched along the gravel shore. Forest grew behind, rising to a steep hill. Poles stood tall and gray, some of them leaning. Sea grass engulfed the houses that were left. It was flattened from the rain, but Gao did not want to wade through it. He looked for a trail or a canoe. The miners who still thought they would find more gold in this inlet must use the village for a base.

He saw no canoes, but smoke drifted in a thin line from the smoke hole of one house, called Thunderbird. A trail led from the gravel beach to the door. He and Luke pulled *Dancing Canoe* above the high-water line and then followed Kate to the house. Her dress was so wet that she tried to wring out the skirt. Her hair dripped down her back. She knocked beside the hide-covered opening, but when only silence answered, she pushed it aside. Gao was right behind her, and Luke behind him.

"Hello?" she called. Her voice sounded thin. But by the time she moved forward, Gao's eyes had adjusted to the dimness. The fire had burned down to coals. Near it, dirty blankets were heaped on two mats, and a makeshift table had been constructed of boards propped across upright logs. Clothes dried on poles, and food-encrusted dishes and pans were piled on the table. Gao could tell that no woman lived here.

"Well." Kate's head turned as she looked around. "I suppose we could find our own house . . ." She stopped and pressed her fingers to her mouth. Gao followed the direction of her shocked stare. Beside one of the mats, there was a crate. On it, a photograph leaned against a small bowl carved in the shape of a sea otter.

She took two quick steps and picked up the bowl. The

photograph of Kate as Gao remembered her long ago fell flat. Both her hands cupped the bowl as she turned it to examine it closely.

"What's wrong?" Luke asked.

She spoke in a choked whisper. "This bowl was my father's. It was . . . one of my favorite pieces. He would never have given it to Sims! So how did Sims get it?"

We got us some company." Kate didn't recognize the voice that penetrated into the lodge, but she knew the one that answered.

"Unload while I find out who . . ." The hide was pushed aside, his huge frame silhouetted by the gray light behind him. A few long strides and he reached the fire.

Sims' brown eyes went directly to the bowl. The silence was thick; neither Gao nor Luke said a word, though both men watched keenly.

Kate slowly lifted the bowl in her cupped hands, forcing Sims' unwilling gaze to follow it. "I always thought this carving had great charm," she said musingly. "The style is unusual."

"You recognize it." His tone was resigned. "I shouldn't have kept it."

"Or you should have hidden it. I would never have searched your things."

His eyes at last, in alarm, met hers. "By God, you don't really believe I had anything to do with the Reverend's death!"

"Is such a supposition so unreasonable?" Was that her, whose voice was so hard?

Without once looking away from Kate, he spat a brown stream at the fire, where it hissed on contact with the coals. "I may have killed a man once, but I was drunk and so was he. He was a bastard who was asking for it. I didn't have any reason to kill the Reverend."

Kate gazed down at the graceful sea otter whose belly

formed the bowl. She had to bite her lip hard to hold back the tears that were stinging her eyes. "You must have made a fair amount of money on what you stole."

Sims gave a gusty sigh. "There's no way to make it right, I shouldn't have done it. But . . . damn it, I was broke! I was at Skidegate, word came that the Reverend had been found dead. Richardson was nowhere around. You'd told me about the collection. Durham had tried to hire me to buy for him. I said I wasn't interested, but he'd left his direction. Here it was, an easy way out of my trouble." His mountainous shoulders jerked. "I took what I could carry, hoped you'd never miss it. Shipped it off, and he sent me a draft. By then, I didn't need it quite so bad, but it was too late. How could I tell you?"

"Why should you?" she asked bitterly. "I suppose you thought you'd never see me again."

His beefy hands dangled impotently at his sides as he nodded at the bowl. "Couldn't bring myself to sell that one. It was in your bedroom. Made me think of you."

The tears still hadn't spilled over, but they blinded her. Kate whispered, "You were my only friend."

He sounded almost angry. "The Reverend warned you about me, didn't he? I never pretended to be any good. You were the one who wanted to be underfoot all the time!"

"But you were kind to me." She looked at him beseechingly. "You could have chased me away, or been cruel. Instead, you told me I was pretty. Do you know what that meant to me?"

Sims stared at her, and beneath the untrimmed beard, she saw his throat work. "You were pretty." He sounded gruff. "Are pretty. I may not be worth much, but even I know that."

Emotion swamped her, and she was suddenly that girl again, one who thought herself as homely as an eagle's awkward offspring. In his crusty way, he had taught her to spread her wings. Why, all she had to do was to listen to him now! He would not defend himself, but he rushed to defend her.

Kate smiled through her tears, hoping her mouth did not tremble noticeably. "What nonsense. Just as big a nonsense as telling me you're not worth much. You were more a father to me than my own! Of course you didn't murder him. I never really thought you did, you know."

He glowered at her. "You're too trusting."

By her side, she heard muttered agreement from Luke, a silent bystander until now.

Her smile began to feel more natural. "I prefer not to be as great a cynic as all you men."

"Katie Rose . . ." The miner grimaced horribly, and she guessed that he sought to hide some excess of emotion. "I had nothing to do with the Reverend's death. I swear it. I'd been in Skidegate for days, you can ask anyone. Gao, you must remember that dust-up I had with Wadatstaia. Caused enough of a stir." When Gao nodded, Sims turned back to Kate. "At the time, I thought—" He broke off.

Kate felt a chill. "You thought?"

"Wondered about that Durham fellow."

"But he was gone."

"Maybe. But the steamer he left on was headed north."

Sharply, she asked, "You mean, it was to call at Masset? Could he have gotten off there?"

Sims said with obvious reluctance, "Don't know. Just wondered, that's all."

Beside her, Luke said grimly, "If so, he could have hired the two Indians to fetch your father. All they'd have had to do was complain that Durham himself was desecrating graves. Which would have brought the Reverend running."

"Yes." The possibilities unfolded in Kate's mind. How easily it could have been done! This answer did not explain why the Reverend Hewitt had not left word of his destination, but the villain could have contrived even that. Perhaps Iyea or Xaosti had been charged to deliver a message for him. Only . . . "Why would Durham want to kill him?"

"Maybe he didn't want to," Luke said slowly. The others were staring at them. He ignored them, as she did. "Maybe he only sought to trick your father into showing him something—who knows what? But then if your father threatened Durham in some way, perhaps declared his intention to write the museum trustees . . . a moment of fury, or fear for his future, and the deed would be done."

It made a dreadful kind of sense. Kate found that she didn't want to think about James Durham in such terms. Poor Clara, so gentle and pretty, waiting at home!

"I suppose there is nothing we can do now."

"Except that we'll be in Masset ourselves within a month," Luke said. Any awkwardness between them was forgotten. How little she deserved such a staunch ally! "If Durham got off the steamboat in Masset, we ought to be able to find out."

"You intend for us to go on, then?" Kate asked. "I thought perhaps, without Kun taos . . ." She glanced at Gao.

So did Luke. "Gao? What do you think? Is it safe to proceed, or should we cut through the channel to Skidegate?"

Gao's gaze had flicked from face to face as they talked. He had probably not understood every word, but certainly enough. He nodded now, somberly. "If you will paddle, we can go on. We will be careful, and watch the sky."

Luke's eyes, clear and compelling, met hers again. "I assumed that you would want to visit Kiusta. Was I wrong?"

"No," she said steadily. "I must see it for myself."

He inclined his head. "Then so be it."

Chapter Twenty

The next few weeks assumed a dreamlike quality for Kate, as though she lived in a sort of limbo. She had been freed of her worst fear: that Sims had murdered her father. Of course she had resisted any such notion from the beginning, but that didn't mean she hadn't been terrified that it might be so. She had seen Sims in a temper and knew him to be capable of violence. He would seem from the outside to be so much likelier a culprit than James Durham or Mr. Richardson—each unarguably civilized. And yet she knew what kindness and tenderness Sims was capable of feeling.

They had stayed in Kaisun for three days. When the time had come to say good-bye to him, he gave her one of his bear hugs and said gruffly, "I'll make a point of needing supplies in time to see you off at Skidegate in the spring."

"Oh, will you? Thank you, Sims. For everything."

"Did you get that damned bowl?"

"No." She smiled through her tears. "I left it to remind you of me. Along with the photograph."

It had both touched and alarmed her to see that photograph, one she had taken herself only to find out if she could do it. She'd given it to Sims on impulse, before one of her departures for Victoria. Perhaps she had melodramatically imagined she would die in a wreck at sea and thus never return. She wondered uneasily whether the fact that so many years later, he still kept it prominently displayed implied something about his feelings for her. She almost hoped that she was wrong.

The photograph itself showed a girl of sixteen years, as tall as she was now, but still gawky, angular, all legs and elbows and cheekbones. And that hair! A wild, dark mass, it had stuck out in every direction, overwhelming the pale face and narrow shoulders. How Sims could ever have called her pretty would forever remain a mystery.

Luke, too, had picked up the photograph, which she had repropped against the sea-otter bowl. He studied it for a long moment, then glanced up with a quirk of his mouth. "This is something like I've been imagining the Creek Women look."

"More like one of the Wild Men," she retorted.

"No, definitely not a man, despite the lack of . . ." He cleared his throat. "But there is undeniably something untamed and elusive about this girl." His vivid blue eyes lifted to her. "Hard to imagine she was ever coaxed into a bustle and hairpins."

"I fear," Kate said ruefully, "that I was dragged rather than coaxed. And see how quickly I've abandoned both."

He smiled, his eyes warm. "I've noticed. You are an adventuress to the core."

Something had changed between them. He had not mentioned the kiss again, but he had also ceased to pretend that it had never happened—if that made any sense! She was becoming convinced that at the time, she had hurt him; in her own fear of being wounded or humiliated, she had not stopped to think of what *he* might be feeling. Somehow, in the days and weeks since, he had quit believing that she did not care, that his embrace had left her unmoved. Several times she had looked up to find him regarding her with a faint smile and a dark hint of something more tumultuous in his eyes. And yet, he was a gentleman; she had asked him not to speak of the matter until spring, and he would keep the promise he'd made her.

If only she had not insisted upon it! A need was growing in her to discover whether he would ever again look at her the way he had that day, as though she were not just pretty, but beautiful, even desirable. She longed to feel his touch again, his lips. The one kiss had happened so quickly, so unexpectedly; she had still been caught by the horror of being lashed by the hair of a woman long dead, and was therefore off guard. She had since thought back so many times, trying to recall every instant, every sensation. She ought to have been shocked. She did blush. But nothing he had done—no place he had touched her—felt wrong. Just by remembering, a peculiar warmth crept through her and she was a little weak, if pleasantly so.

What would he think if she hinted that another kiss might be acceptable? Would it stop there? Could *she* stop it there? Did she want to?

Was this how a woman ought to think about a man she might contemplate marrying—if only he asked her? Heavens, had her mother and father ever felt so? That question answered itself; they must have, else why had each chosen so unsuitably? The Reverend Hewitt must have known how little-fitted Amy Stapleton was to be the wife of a missionary. And surely she had feared, in her heart, the life that lay ahead should she wed a man dedicated to such a cause. But they had married anyway, despite the disapproval of her family. And look at how it had turned out!

Yet Kate remembered a certain look she sometimes saw on her invalid mother's face. Kate could on occasion persuade her to talk about the Reverend Hewitt. He visited perhaps once a year; Kate knew her father's appearance, his dedication, his personality. But she did not know *him*. Rarely sensitive to her daughter's needs, in this one way Kate's mother seemed to make an effort for her sake. But her mood would vary. She might be resentful, petulant, wistful. In mid-sentence, she would pause and gaze at the far wall of her bedroom for the longest time. Kate had not understood then. Now she wondered. Had her mother still loved her husband? Did she long for him? Remember his touch? Know that she had exiled herself from it?

Of course, such musings were useless. Kate would never know the answers. She had not had the courage to ask her father why he had abandoned his wife and child, why he had not pressed Kate's mother to try again, or himself chosen to minister to the Indians at the camps around Victoria, if that would save his marriage. Perhaps he had not cared by that time. He might never have truly loved young Amy with all her frailties; he could easily have imagined her to be someone different, stronger. Perhaps his love had died when she could not measure up to his idealized image of her.

On one occasion, Kate had especially ached to ask. About the time that she had taken that photograph of herself, when her own interest in the opposite sex was stirring, she had walked in on her father with a young Haida woman. It was an odd scene; his hand rested on the curve of her neck, and his thumb played with the corner of her mouth. The young woman had stood quiescent, but her inner self seemed to strain away from him. He had looked angry, desperate, supplicating. He clearly wanted something of her, something she could not, or would not, give him. Kate must have made some sound, because his hand dropped to his side and he turned quickly to face her with his expression much as usual. The young woman slipped away, just as Kate's courage did. She had married shortly thereafter.

Might the Reverend Hewitt have loved the young woman? Of course, Kate would have been fiercely resentful if he had married again. Only two years after her mother's death, Kate was still torn between her mother's narrow, frightened view of the world and her father's equally narrow, but confident view. She hated now to think that she had stood in his way. Had he sensed her feelings? Would he have allowed them to influence him?

Well, it might be that she had misinterpreted the entire

'scene. The young woman was a convert to Christianity. If the man she intended to marry was not, any self-respecting missionary would have disapproved. Perhaps the Reverend Hewitt's touch had been fatherly. But Kate didn't think so.

As if it mattered anymore. The memory was only one of many that, together, had changed the way she thought of her father, that had begun to meld into a whole she could understand, even love, but no longer idolize.

The day she, Luke, and Gao left Kaisun, they proceeded only the short distance to Chaatl, another ghost town that lay on a large island at the western end of Skidegate Inlet. There was evidence that a fire had swept through the village within the past few years. Freestanding poles had survived the inferno and now rose gray and eloquent from the scrubby shore vegetation. Several small houses had been built and maintained for seasonal use; otters and seals populated these western shores more thickly than the eastern, bringing hunters.

They stayed only one night. The landscape was majestic, the village looking southward across a narrow channel to steep, forested hills. Conscious of her dwindling supply of plates, Kate took only one photograph. Afterward, she watched as Luke sketched individual poles.

He didn't argue at her decision not to waste more plates. She briefly wished that she had known what a complete photographic record Luke had hoped to compile, then realized that it would have made no difference. She had brought what plates she had, in addition to the quantity she'd been able to purchase in Victoria. Without time to plan, where else could she have obtained more?

Gao had withdrawn into a gloomy silence and kept very much to himself. He had little to say about the history, and seemed deliberately to deny himself even the small pleasures of a story or a laugh. He ate only enough to satisfy the worst hunger pangs, and no more. He did continue to carve, completing the miniature pole in the dull, black stone—a tiny, perfect gem—and starting a statue of what appeared to be a mother, seated and nursing a child, but the child was a bear cub. All was not clear yet; perhaps the mother, too, was a bear.

At bedtime, Gao announced that he would not sleep inside the house. He would wrap up in blankets without, he insisted, and would not be dissuaded.

Luke gave Kate no chance to be uncomfortable at their privacy. He sat outside with Gao until she had completed her toilet and cocooned herself in her bedding. He took such care not to catch her unaware that her tension had relaxed into near sleep by the time she heard him come in without the aid of a lamp and find his own mat. He had given her no chance to do anything as reckless as tempting him. Which was just as well! Even assuming the results were not so dangerous, her experience in such a feminine art as seduction was nonexistent. She would no doubt blunder horribly.

The next day, they continued up the rugged coastline, standing well out from several points known for their vicious crosscurrents. Huge beds of kelp betrayed the presence of reefs beneath. Twice, Kate caught a glimpse of the charming face of a sea otter peering at them. Many of the rocks were populated by sea lions, and also provided home to gulls and cormorants.

That night was spent deep in the shelter of an inlet at Moving Village, where the decrepit remains of several lodges offered shelter. Again, Gao would not sleep with them. When he stoically departed, the silence he left behind was awkward. At last, Luke asked in a low voice, "Do you suppose he's suffering guilt because he wasn't able to prevent Kun taos's death?"

"I don't know," Kate answered. She concentrated on rinsing off the tin plates with water Luke had hauled in and heated. "The Haida believe in denying themselves as a form of mourning, but usually only when it is a husband or child who dies, I believe. Gao took it hard."

Luke grunted. After a moment of silence, he said, "Well, I suppose we might as well turn in."

"Yes." She sneaked a peek at him, then reached up and began pulling pins from her hair. She had just picked up her brush when he rose to his feet with such haste that he knocked his shin on the crude table they had built. "Confound it!" he growled, but didn't pause in his flight.

It was with a certain amount of satisfaction that Kate brushed her hair. She took her time undressing and carefully laying her gown out, as though it made any difference if a few more wrinkles were added. She had barely lain down on her mat when Luke stumbled back in. Through lowered lashes, she saw him shake the rain off his clothes. He stood beside his own mat on the other side of the fire for the longest time. She couldn't quite see his expression, but he was certainly gazing at her.

"Damnation," he muttered at last and sat down to kick off his boots. Kate was embarrassed to realize how disappointed she was that he didn't disrobe before lying down with a sigh and yanking the blankets over himself.

She slept well, but in the morning, Luke was obviously out of sorts. His clothes and hair were rumpled, the lines of his face weary. Gao looked just as bad, so the day was begun in surly silence.

This coastline was riddled with caves. They stopped to see several, one with stalactites and another with an entrance at least a hundred feet high. Far inside was driftwood that must have been flung there by waves so much larger than any she had ever seen that Kate could scarcely envision them. She realized how fortunate in the weather they had been; despite the endless rain and occasional gales, this winter must be mild compared to some.

By the middle of the afternoon, it was obvious that Luke was exhausted. Kate could imagine how much his male pride must rebel at admitting that he couldn't continue, but at last, he called, "Gao? Is there a place where we can stop soon? My shoulders are sore today."

Kate had already noticed a point ahead. Somewhat uneasily, wondering what Gao intended, she had watched the approaching line of white spray and breakers that extended far beyond the tip of land.

Gao rested his paddle on the gunwale. "There is a way

through," he said after a moment. "It would be safer to go around, but far. Can you paddle hard when I tell you?"

"If it saves us going miles out of the way, yes," Luke said. He rolled his shoulders with a grimace of pain and followed Gao's lead, thrusting the painted paddle back into the rolling gray water.

Without a word, Kate picked up another paddle and joined them. If she were Haida, she would be as competent with the paddle as any man. As it was, she did her best when the need was for speed and great exertion, but she tired quickly.

Now the spumes of water neared, and she could see the black rocks that formed the half-hidden obstacle. Gao directed the canoe straight toward a line of breakers that rose and crashed in a wall of white that disguised what lay beyond. The canoe shot forward, Gao calling instructions.

He lifted one hand. "Wait!" *Dancing Canoe* slowed. Spray was wet and cold on their faces, and the roar of the surf filled their ears. Kate's heart was in her throat as, kneeling, she held the paddle poised above the water. A wave lifted the canoe, tossing it forward. "Now!" Gao bellowed.

They paddled furiously, driving the canoe ahead on the crest of the wave. Her arms protested, then screamed in agony, but vicious black rocks to each side and swirling white water allowed no pause. It seemed like an eternity, but it must have been only seconds before they were catapulted out the other side as though they had shot over a waterfall. They paddled until the roar began to recede and the white foam turned to gray swells.

Kate sagged onto the thwart, and Luke laid his paddle down with a groan. "Thank God you know this coast!" he declared.

A half-smile, rare these days, lightened Gao's broad face when he turned his head. "I have been here only once, when I was a boy."

"Then how the hell . . . Never mind." Luke shook his head. "I don't want to know if you're making wild guesses."

They resumed paddling, crossing a broad bay with inlets

that vanished into the mist that hung low over the mountains. On the other side, facing south in one of two tiny coves, stood Tian, or Slaughter Village. The site was fronted by rocky islets that would presumably break the force of winter gales and stormy seas. The name had its origin in the fact that sea lions often covered the rocks and were thus readily hunted. Only one house stood in usable condition, though the corner posts and timbers of others remained like the bones of great beasts. The one house was at the west end of the village. It alone had an excavated house pit, indicating that the several levels found in the occupied villages might be a relatively recent phenomenon. Its gabled roof was so low that it would not have been possible to stand upright were the ground not dug out.

Kate and Luke unloaded the canoe while Gao started a fire in the corner where the roof timbers seemed to leak the least. Kate was carrying one end of a cedar box containing food supplies, Luke the other end, when he abruptly stopped halfway up the rocky beach. Kate almost dropped her end. She opened her mouth to complain, but what was the use? He was frowning at the skeletal remains of Tian.

"Do you know, I don't see a single house frontal pole. I wonder when this village was built. I must ask Gao. It would seem to bear out the theory that the poles we see elsewhere are indeed of recent vintage."

"Maybe the villagers were merely lazy," Kate suggested frivolously. "Or perhaps Tian was never meant to be permanent."

He had given her a scathing look after her first remark, but her second turned his expression to thoughtful. "I can't decide whether you have the logical mind of a scientist or simply enjoy demolishing my arguments."

"Are the two mutually exclusive? You can't tell me that eminent scientists don't enjoy demolishing each other's arguments. After all, I heard you and Mister Durham."

Luke snorted. "He's not a scientist, he's a fool!"

Kate shifted her grip on the box. "If we don't start moving, I'm going to drop this on your toes."

"What?" His gaze dropped to the box. "What the devil are we standing around for?"

Kate rolled her eyes.

On the next trip, he tried to stop again to contemplate the carving on a mortuary pole that was splitting with age. On the box supported by double poles was incised a crude figure that Kate guessed to be a grizzly bear. It was odd, she thought, that the grizzly figured so largely as a Haida crest when there were none on the Queen Charlotte Islands, only black bears. These islands were distinctive for the lack of other mainland animals, too: deer, wolves, squirrels, or mountain goats.

This time, she succeeded in keeping Luke moving while he remarked on the primitive style of what carving there was. "Which would argue for the antiquity of the village, rather than for a lack of permanency." He sounded triumphant. "I doubt that carvers could be persuaded to do less than their best work simply because they didn't intend to live here long."

"Oh, I don't know. Don't you labor harder over an article intended for a prestigious magazine than you do over one written for a minor quarterly that hardly anybody will see?"

"Blast it, woman . . . !" But they had entered the house, which required that they duck, and there was Gao, crouched by the fire. He didn't even look up. His still presence discouraged any desire for light conversation. Luke and Kate set down the box, and she began studying its contents.

What she would give for fresh baked bread with a dollop of melting butter! Or strawberries, or eggs, or a glass of milk. Medallions of beef in a thick sauce, or roasted turkey, or crisp bacon. Why hadn't she at least insisted that a supply of flour be brought, to vary their diet?

Kate sighed and went back to debating between dried halibut or dried dog salmon as the entrée.

It had become their custom to put small amounts of everything they ate into the fire, whence it would go to Kun taos. Doing so had become automatic, and curiously comforting.

After their unsatisfactory meal, Gao sat chipping away at

the soft slate, his head bent. His answers to Luke's inquiries were brief. The village had been abandoned for a long time, since before he was born. It had been Raven, owned by the same lineage as Yaku. He knew nothing else.

Finally, he set aside the sharp tool and the small statue. "I will go to my mat. Do you want to leave tomorrow?"

"How far are we from Kiusta?" Luke asked.

"We can reach it in one day."

"Hmm." Luke gazed into the fire. "Let's wait and see what the weather's like. I wouldn't mind a day's rest."

Gao nodded, appearing indifferent to the decision. Kate wondered whether he looked forward to returning home or dreaded it now that he had to inform Kun taos's family of their son's death.

Luke said abruptly, "Gao, this may not be the time to discuss this, but I want you to think about something."

Gao waited.

"You know I've failed to buy a pole or a canoe. I'd like to hire you to carve me both, maybe even several poles. An example of each kind: a mortuary pole like you did at Haina, an interior pole, a memorial pole . . ." When Gao said nothing, he went on. "More than that, I'd like you to be a permanent agent for me here. If you would buy objects for me that were to be sold anyway, together we could build a fine collection. I know your scruples, and I won't ask you to go against them. I hope by now you realize that I am sincere in my intentions. I understand that you would rather keep the pieces here, but you must know that you are fighting a losing battle. At least in my museum, the heritage that you value so greatly will be preserved for the future. And I would be glad to buy much that is newly manufactured by you or other carvers you can recommend. Perhaps in that way, I can help maintain your traditions."

Some of this, Kate had to translate. She had wondered why Luke had waited to ask Gao, but of course there had been no hurry; they still had all winter and a long journey ahead of them. How like Luke to speak now, at the moment when Gao, although past his sharpest grief, most needed hope!

Gao listened, firelight playing off his enigmatic face. It might have been a mask, with broad cheekbones and straight nose, lines carved deeply beside the eyes and mouth.

When she finished translating, Gao turned his gaze to Luke. Kate would have twitched under his scrutiny, but Luke had the self-possession and patience to bear it.

"It is a good speech you make," Gao said finally. "I will carve poles and a canoe for you. The other I will think on."

"That's all I can ask," Luke said, inclining his head. "Why don't you sleep here tonight?"

"To have respect for myself, I must be alone to feel grief for my friend," Gao said simply.

How could one argue? Gao departed, leaving behind him the tension that seemed greater each night. Kate would have sworn it was not all on her side. Tonight Luke looked at her quickly, then back at the fire.

"Would you prefer to go on to Kiusta tomorrow?"

She had waited so long that she hardly knew how to feel about the fact that so soon she would be there, where her father had died. She was almost afraid. Would his brutal murder at last become real to her? Would that violence permeate the place, give her nightmares? Worse yet, what if she felt nothing? What if he was no more there than he had been at Skidegate? She would be forced then to accept the fact that he was gone, that he had left his mark nowhere.

"I'm unlikely to learn anything there," she replied. "Another day makes no difference."

Luke nodded. A burning branch snapped, making her jump. Ridiculous that she was so self-conscious, only because they were alone! They had spent all winter together, slept within an arm's reach on occasion. Where had the easy relationship gone? She sneaked a glance at him, to see his brows drawn together as he looked broodingly into the fire.

Her voice sounded too loud when she said, "I believe I'll go out now, before it starts to rain again."

"Here, take the lamp." His fingers grazed hers when she took it, and she felt as if she had mistakenly touched the hot glass. He sucked in an audible breath at the same moment she jerked back. They stared at each other.

"I . . . I'll be back," Kate said inanely.

The drizzle was no encouragement to linger outside. When she went back into the lodge, Luke accepted the lamp from her, taking care that their fingers made no contact again. He disappeared in turn, and she began her preparations for bed.

With her back to the door, she might not have heard him enter had he not bumped his head on a roof timber and cursed. "Were they pygmies?" he grumbled.

"Hard to imagine how they bore living in houses with roofs so low that they couldn't stand upright," she agreed.

Luke grunted and set the lantern on a trunk. He stood there for a moment as though not sure of what to do next. Kate had already brushed her teeth and changed into her voluminous nightgown, and was presently loosening her braids. She hoped that he didn't notice how her hands shook. At last, he sat down on another box and began removing his boots.

Kate took a deep breath. "I've been thinking."

Another grunt. "Do you ever stop?"

She shook the last braid out and chose to ignore his ill-tempered remark. If he was disgruntled for the reason she hoped—even prayed—it was easily forgiven.

"Father took me to Kiusta once. He showed me a nearby cave."

"We've seen many caves this winter."

"This one was . . . different." She pressed her lips together. "Extraordinary."

One boot in his hand, he looked up and said dryly, "And you've just recalled the sight."

Kate felt the flush creep up her neck. Stiffly, she said, "At first, the cave didn't seem . . . important. I didn't make a connection until we found the skeletons at Cowgitz. And then I hesitated because I didn't like to think of it being ransacked."

"*I*, of course, was the despoiler you feared."

He was not making this confession any easier. She forced

herself to meet his angry gaze. "I didn't know you very well. And I've made no secret of my reservations concerning your purpose here."

"Which would all be very well if your life had not been in danger." Luke rose and began to pace within the limited space allowing him to stand upright. "Or were you so confident you could unmask a murderer on your own?"

"You make me sound remarkably selfish." His pacing was unnerving in the firelit circle. He cast an enormous shadow on the timbered wall, and she wondered if he was aware that he was stepping in rain puddles with stockinged feet.

"Foolish, rather," he snapped. "As independent as you're determined to be, you ought to have been born a man." Before she could form an outraged protest, he added in a peculiar tone, "Though thank God you weren't."

He had quit pacing; his back was to her. Kate lifted her chin. "And what is that supposed to mean?"

Luke turned to face her, his shoulders squared. "You know very well," he said, that same odd note in his voice. His mouth was twisted, rather like Sims' had been when he strove to hide deep emotion.

"No," she whispered. "I have sometimes thought . . . But I have so little experience."

"Even a complete innocent can hardly fail to notice when a man forces an unwelcome kiss on her."

Losing courage, she stared down at the hairbrush in her hand as though it were a foreign object. "Not exactly unwelcome," she said, hoping she was speaking clearly enough; her heartbeats sounded so loud that she couldn't judge for herself. "I was . . . unsure of how to interpret your motives, you see."

"Good God!" The next thing she knew, he crouched on his heels in front of her. With one hand, he gently removed the hairbrush from her grip, while with the other, he lifted her chin so that she was forced to meet his eyes. "How could you possibly misinterpret my motives?"

"I thought," she forced the words out, "it was possible that the very fact I had agreed to come, unchaperoned, with you, might lead you to believe I would welcome some sort of . . . physical relationship."

He actually laughed. "If I had thought such a thing for a minute, why in God's name would I have waited *months*? Do you know how I have suffered?"

Kate could only shake her head.

"Tell me the truth." Luke's gaze commanded hers. "Do you share my feelings?"

He had said nothing about marriage still, but was he cad enough to imply that he loved her, without his intentions being honorable? Her confidence in the answer made her feel foolish for her doubts.

"Yes," she said, almost steadily. "I have long wished that I were the kind of woman a man like you—"

He interrupted, "You are exactly the kind of woman most calculated to make me forget my common sense."

Kate was taken aback. "Is that intended as a compliment or an insult?"

His voice roughened. "Most definitely a compliment. Despite your cruel rejection of my one attempt to speak my mind, I had begun to think you might actually enjoy sharing my travels."

"You won't attempt to leave me behind?" she asked.

He smiled. "I believe you would have trod right on top of that snake."

She smiled back—triumphantly, shakily. "You are the only man I have ever met who would regard that as a virtue in a woman."

"Then we are surely meant for each other." Though he had not moved, she felt the new tension in him. "May I kiss you?" he asked gravely.

"Please do."

They looked at each other. How awkward this was, Kate thought. Why had he asked permission? If only he had just swept her off her feet!

His hands grasped her forearms and he stood, pulling her with him. Her blanket dropped to the floor. For the first time, Luke seemed to realize that she wore her nightgown.

"Are you cold?"

She wanted to scream. She sincerely doubted that she would be cold once he embraced her. If he intended to.

"No," she murmured.

He bent his head. His mouth was a hairbreadth from hers when he paused. "I shouldn't do this. How can you trust me to stop? Good God, I don't know if I can!"

Kate had never knowingly been brazen, but it seemed that the desire to be had been lurking in hiding, waiting only for an opportunity to spring forth. For she opened her mouth intending to say something reassuring, but what came out was, "Why should you?"

For a moment, she thought she had shocked him. He lifted his head and stared at her. But then he said thoughtfully, "We are not married."

"Are we to be?" She was only a little apprehensive.

"Of course we are! What did you think, that I proposed hauling you around half the world as my mistress?"

"Very well, then. Would you discard me if you decided I was not satisfactory?"

His brows drew together in a familiar scowl. "You don't believe that!"

Kate smiled. "No, I don't. So what have I to fear?"

"There can be—" he cleared his throat "—consequences. We won't be back in Victoria for several months."

"Then we can set an early wedding date."

"I intend to do that in any case. I must return to Boston, and I want you with me."

"Then?"

"You have persuaded me." And it seemed she had, for his mouth captured hers with all the ardor she could have wished. He pressed her up against himself so tightly that she discovered things about the male anatomy she had never known. When she felt his hand on her breast and his tongue sliding along hers, Kate nearly panicked, her boldness exposed for the sham it was. She had been kissed only the once before; this was too much, too quickly!

But it was really very easy to quit thinking at all. There

were so many new sensations. If she moved so, she could make him groan. Her touch made his muscles ripple beneath her hand, a novel experience. Of course, she had wanted for a very long time to see him undress.

Naturally, by the time she did, it.was much too late to cry halt. Even assuming she had wanted to.

Chapter Twenty-one

Luke had gained new respect for the Haida's seafaring skills these last days. Gao paddled without cease hour after hour, never showing a sign of tiredness. He had been up this coast only once before, and yet he knew every feature of it. To Luke, one line of breakers was like another, one rocky shore or cave inseparable from any other. His muscles had begun to protest the exercise from the minute he picked up the paddle that morning. By now, he was in agony, matching Gao's rhythm only with the greatest effort of will. To think he had dismissed Kun taos as lazy! Thank God he had something to occupy his mind, or he might have crumpled to his knees hours ago.

Ahead of him, Kate sat on one of the narrow thwarts, her back straight and her head lifted impatiently to catch a first glimpse of Kiusta. They had rounded the wave-swept northwest cape of Graham Island and approached several reefs that Gao regarded warily. To the northeast lay the low, densely forested island that was the northernmost of the Queen Charlotte chain. There, ocean swells crashed in surf against the rocky shore. But the canoe had entered the passage between islands, and as it rounded the kelp-marked reef that Gao called Kah'dea, the force of the open ocean was blunted.

"There you will see Yaku," Gao called, gesturing.

They had decided to continue the short distance to Kiusta, perhaps coming back to visit the village of Yaku another day. Little was left there, Gao said. Only fallen poles and house beams.

The blasted rain descended in its usual fine mist. No wonder moss covered every surface of these wet islands, and the magnificent poles and houses rotted so quickly. Luke had thought he was mentally prepared for the infernal weather, but day after day of dismal, damp gray skies had an undeniably depressing effect. If only he'd had the sense to ask for Kate's hand in marriage weeks ago, he would have had no need to be depressed at all! Richardson could have married them, and Luke would have had innumerable nights as satisfying as the last two to counteract the lowering effect of the weather.

Ah, well. With a degree of smugness, he contemplated the elegantly straight line of her back, the escaped wisps of wiry dark hair, the curve of her cheek when she turned her head. At least he had seen the light in time.

Of course, a gentleman shouldn't have taken advantage of her innocent generosity. God knows, he had tried to resist—for all of thirty seconds. He had become weak after a winter spent battling temptation. And she had made splendid sense; why wait for the formality of wedding vows?

Had he not wanted her so badly, and found her offer so touching, there might have been an element of humor in the scene. There she was, swathed in heavy white flannel from neck to wrist and ankle, her gown surely designed to repel men gripped by their baser appetites. Her words said one thing, her eyes another. He had quickly discovered how nervous she was. Lord knew, he'd been nervous himself, afraid that he might frighten or shock her, wishing there was a soft bed to lay her on, wishing that he'd had a bath, hoping that he could be sure his physical needs were not pushing him to do something she would regret.

Well, if she regretted anything that had passed between them, she had not shown it. Once past her first fear, Kate had been as passionate as he could wish. She had touched him with innocent curiosity, held him tightly, uttered small cries he had smothered with his mouth so that Gao would not hear them through the walls. Remembering the softness of her lips, the dreamy look in her eyes, the weight of her breasts in his palms, was enough to make his body stir now, despite his exhaustion. For once in his life, Luke could summon very little curiosity about yet another village, even one endowed with a spectacular burial cave. His interest was solely in nightfall, and in whether Gao would feel that his self-respect demanded he sleep separately for another night.

Somehow, Luke felt sure the Haida would. In fact, Luke had begun to wonder whether Gao hadn't absented himself only to give them privacy. He hadn't the personality of a martyr. What possible good to Kun taos would be accomplished by Gao's sleeping out in the rain? On the other hand, Gao knew white people well enough, and Kate in particular, to be aware that they were considerably more inhibited about sex than were the Haida. Heaven knew what conclusion Gao had come to about the relationship between his fellow travelers. Perhaps he was only doing his part to effect a resolution.

If Richardson did not turn out to be a murderer, perhaps Luke would ask Gao to stand up for him in a wedding ceremony at the Mission House in Skidegate. Luke thought that Kate would happily trade having her aunt and uncle there so that she might feel her father was present in some way. Beyond that, Luke's imaginings of the future were vague, but pleasant: in tandem, they would explore primitive parts of the world, Kate's photographs the perfect complement to the artifacts he collected for the museum. If children intervened, they would of course be equally interested in the past, miniature scholars and adventurers—or adventuresses —stepping carefully in their father's footsteps as he explored tombs, or peering through the viewfinder on their mother's camera.

His agreeable daydream was interrupted by the sight of sandstone bars exposed in the reef that extended northeastward between Yaku and Kiusta. Gao had said that it acted nearly as a breakwater for the site on which Kiusta, or End-of-Trail Town, had been built. Thank God they were nearly there. Luke's shoulders and arms were groaning.

A sandy beach fronted the ragged remnants of a village. Behind it grew forest, but the land was low-lying compared to that farther south. Even before landing, Luke could see that the trees here were larger than any along the west coast, where growth was stunted by winter storms.

Kate was gazing toward the village with an expression that gave away much of the complexity of her emotions. She must be weary; she had spelled him on occasion that day, and neither of them had had much sleep these last two nights. She had anticipated this moment for so long; *here* her father had been struck down, *here* she thought to find a part of the truth. Yet she must be apprehensive, too. The violence of the death had probably seemed abstract until now. At Kiusta, it would become real.

Did she know where his body had been found? Would she look around and imagine that here a canoe had been pulled up on the beach, there he had walked, perhaps eaten, or even slept? Did she *want* to see the exact spot where his battered head had struck the ground, where his blood had drained into the soil?

By the time they dragged *Dancing Canoe* above the high-water mark and carried their possessions to shelter, the gray light was fading. Night came early during the winter this far north. Not just selfishly, Luke was glad to see it. In the morning, Kate would find it easier to confront the past.

Kate dreamed of her father that night. Of course, the happenings were nonsensical, as dreams usually were. He was behind the pulpit giving a sermon, and she couldn't quite make out the words. Yet she saw him as clearly as though he stood in front of her: curly, grizzled dark hair, gaunt face, piercing eyes. There was something peculiar about his stance, however, and his hoarse voice rose until it was harsh, even angry. Of a sudden, he picked up a mask and donned it, so that in her dream, Raven was giving the sermon. Her father's angular body had changed, too: His severe, black frock coat became a shredded-bark costume; then that gave way to glossy black feathers and the thin, black legs of a bird.

She awakened with a start to the loud cawing of a real raven, close outside. A shudder passed through her. Had her mind transformed her father for a reason? Had he imagined himself as godlike as Raven, who decided the span of all men's lives?

No, ridiculous. That wretched bird's voice had penetrated her sleep, that was all, intruding into her dream thoughts.

She relaxed, comforted by the warmth of Luke's arm draped over her waist. He still slept soundly; his even breathing tickled the back of her neck. Kate closed her eyes and willed herself to sleep again, but without success. She was too unsettled, both by the dream and by her knowledge that here her father had died. Would she feel his presence, as she had not in Skidegate?

Finally, she slipped out from under Luke's arm and quietly dressed. Not wanting to disturb him, she didn't even attempt to build up the fire. She braided her hair by the pale gray light that slanted through cracks and the smoke hole. As she pushed aside the blanket Luke had hung over the doorway, she became aware of the silence. Missing was the incessant dripping of rain from the sky and branches. Kate paused just outside.

The tide was low, exposing rocks and pools and slippery seaweed. How delighted Kun taos would have been! she thought with a pang.

She saw no sign that Gao was awake yet. She would have

time to wander around on her own then, even to shed a few tears without either man knowing.

Kate had just taken a step forward when the raven called again, the caw so loud and close that she started and began to turn. Out of the corner of her eye, she saw the huge bird launch itself from the house pole. Had she not ducked, its black wing would have brushed her face. When she straightened, her heart was pounding. She must have cried out, too, because behind her, she heard Luke's voice.

"Kate?" It rose to a near roar. "Kate!" His mutter was still distinct. "Why the devil does that woman never wait for assistance?"

Resignedly, she turned back. So much for her few precious moments of solitude.

Over breakfast, all three agreed that the first order of business ought to be the cave. Luke anticipated exploring the village itself; a surprising number of possessions had been abandoned here. Huge serving troughs, piles of cedar boxes, fishing equipment—all had been left as though the owners thought they might return. Rooting around in the corners of this house while he waited for water to boil, Luke had even found a mask of a human face. But as the morning wore on, Kate's sense of urgency increased. If the cave had been stripped, she could feel sure that the desecration was the cause of her father's death, or at least the reason he had come to Kiusta. If it was intact . . . but how could it be? She could think of nothing else in the vicinity that could possibly explain his presence.

The cave, known as Skungo-nah, actually was tucked in a cove on North Island, across the passage from Kiusta. Kate's father said that it was named for an ancient hermit who had once lived there.

On North Island, Kate directed the men to beach *Dancing Canoe* around the point from the peculiar rounded rock, with trees atop it, that sat for all the world like a giant flower pot on the beach. A shaman's grave was reputed to be sheltered amidst the trees there.

Her recollection was that the cave was at the head of a steep gully leading perhaps five hundred feet from the shore.

"I believe it was this one," she said, gazing upward. Pushing aside wet undergrowth, she led the way, the men at her heels.

Behind her, Luke asked, "Gao, do you know this cave?"

In his usual measured way, their guide said, "I have heard talk of it. I did not know where it was."

Eagerly, yet fearfully, Kate had taken only a few steps when her brain at last processed something her eyes had seen.

She stopped so suddenly that Luke ran into her. "Look," she whispered. Ahead of her, where she had not yet stepped, was a newly trampled trail. Broken stems oozed pale green, the heel of a boot was stamped clearly in the mud.

A party had been there ahead of them. The tracks couldn't be more than a day or two old, if that. Yet nobody had been camped at Kiusta; no canoe other than Gao's was drawn up on the beach. Where had they come from?

Luke held up a hand in silent command. All three stood very still, ears straining. From the forest came a woodpecker's sharp *tap, tap, tap;* from nearer, something scurried beneath the undergrowth, and yesterday's rain dripped from leaf to leaf.

At last, Luke gestured to Gao, and the two men passed Kate. Luke waved her back, but she stubbornly stuck to his heels. How typical of a man to be certain one minute that she would be too brave to quail at an adder, and in the next to be equally determined to make sure she never had the chance to prove it!

Despite the fact that others had preceded them, leaving a clear trail of broken branches and stems, the three, with Gao in the lead, still had to push through thick, wet undergrowth. Dripping branches slapped at their faces, and vines tangled around their ankles. Once Gao stopped. Like a tiny flag, a shred of red flannel dangled from the sharp twigs of a huckleberry.

Kate had forgotten that the mouth of the cave was obscured by a high lip of loose rock. For a moment, she thought that she—and those who had trampled the path ahead of them—had mistaken the gully, that it was a dead end. But no, there the cave was, well-hidden: the tall, narrow opening to a rough-walled chamber eroded out of conglomerate. A few small ferns grew inside the rocky entrance.

The gray daylight penetrated only a few feet into the darkness. Even that was far enough for Kate to see some jumbled boxes, splintered open, and a bone. A human thigh bone, she thought, unable to tear her eyes from it.

"Hell," Luke said softly. He took time to light the lantern he carried and held it high as he stepped into the cave. The others followed. They didn't have to go far to see that they had come too late.

Once this cave had held as many as thirty boxes, many of them handsomely carved or painted, all neatly stacked, each holding the remains of a man, woman, or child. Now the few boxes left were shattered and the bones scattered, some separate as though they had been kicked aside. Delicate ones were splintered into fragments where booted feet had trod without care.

There was nothing else here. Only broken, plain boxes; no copper neck- or knee-rings, no ceremonial masks. Worse yet, Kate realized after an appalled instant, was the fact that there were also no skulls.

"James Durham," Luke said grimly.

"Or Leland Jarvis," Kate felt compelled to add. "Would Mister Durham's guides have allowed him to do this?"

"Maybe he left them in Masset and hooked up with someone less scrupulous. A couple of miners out of pocket. Why should they care what he does?"

All the while, Gao had stood rigid beside her. In this light, his countenance could have been the mask she had earlier imagined, but now it was an angry one. His lips drew back from his gritted teeth as he gazed around.

"Didn't you say there is another village nearby?" Luke asked. His voice sounded hollow, its resonance swallowed by the walls of the cave. "They might have camped there instead, might be there still. If so, by God . . ."

Gao spoke for the first time. "I think they are gone, but I would like to be wrong."

"Let's go."

They returned to the beach far more quickly than they had climbed from it. Anger made even Kate heedless of the difficult footing. Gao and Luke launched the canoe with dispatch, long strokes of the paddles driving it silently around the rocky point separating the cove from the village site of Dadens.

Once prosperous, the village had been destroyed long ago by a fire. Since then, a few small houses had been built for seasonal use. The beach was deserted, Kate saw at once. When they landed, Gao pointed out a wisp of smoke that rose from the ash of a fire in front of the best-constructed of the houses. He bent and stirred the coals with a stick, then looked up. "It is still warm. It burned yesterday, or maybe even today . . . if they left very early."

Luke grunted. He prowled the beach, though an incoming tide would have washed away signs of what kind of boat had been pulled up here.

Kate looked around with a sickening feeling of failure. She had to remind herself that the cave might have been stripped a year and a half ago. She had expected that it would be. These visitors could have been innocent of the depredations, whatever their intentions had been.

And yet, she didn't believe that. The way the wet undergrowth had been beaten back and the numerous prints of booted feet suggested many trips to and fro. The ivory-colored edges of the splintered bones made her think the damage was recent.

Kate was turning toward Gao when her eye caught a glimpse of white. She pushed back the wet frond of a fern to expose a human skull, lying on its side. It had been kicked here unnoticed, silent proof of what her instincts had known.

"Look," she said, vaguely surprised to hear how angry she sounded.

Both men turned as she knelt and held up the skull. It was small, belonging to a young child, poignant evidence of some family's tragedy long ago, renewed now by the violation of the burial. Gao took it from her and for a moment, looked down at it, cradled in his strong hands. His head was bent, his mouth twisted.

He looked up at last, his expression tortured. "We must return it." He went directly to the canoe and waited there, his back to them.

Through a tight throat, Kate said, "But it will be alone there . . ."

Luke wheeled on her. "For God's sake, the child has probably been dead for a hundred years!"

Of course he was right, though she suspected he shared her feelings of pity. Kate took a deep breath and had herself in hand again when she asked, "Did you find any trace of a boat?"

"Nothing." He turned, scanning the beach and the crude houses for one last time. "It is acts like this that give all of us a bad name."

In silence, they paddled back to the cove. Gao alone followed the beaten path back up the ravine.

Waiting below, Kate imagined Gao gently setting the small skull on the floor of the cave. Would he try to find the bones that might belong with it?

Renewed pity, mingled with horror, stirred within her again. She said fiercely, "Taking the entire skeletons would have been better. To remove only the skulls and to treat the other bones so carelessly demonstrates terrible indifference to the susceptibilities of the Indians. Or are they supposed to have no feelings?"

Luke made a rough noise. "Someone of Jarvis's ilk doesn't care. Why should he? He'll be on his way soon, with no intention of ever returning to the same locale. He doesn't dare, he's left such a trail of outrage behind. Durham may be more discreet, but he does much the same."

Kate plucked her wet skirts away from her body. She was soaking and should have felt chilled, but her emotions were in a turmoil too great to allow for awareness of petty discomforts. Mixed with all else was guilt. But why? Because she would have stood aside and let Luke do the same?

She felt compelled to speak her troubling thoughts aloud. "I hardly know anymore what is right. I told you about this cave, aware that you would want to take some of its contents. What is so different about this?"

She heard the long breath he exhaled. "God knows," he said heavily. "I tell myself that my scientific purpose justifies much that is distasteful. How can we know the history of mankind without studying their past, and how else can that be done? Yet common decency surely demands that we make our studies in a less offensive manner. A year ago, I might have acted the same, given the opportunity. Now . . ." He grimaced. "Now I wonder if we couldn't measure the skeletons where they are and leave them. Do we really need ten cedar boxes when one, or two, or five would do? And yet, I keep coming back to the central issue: What we don't take or study now will soon be gone, snatched by souvenir hunters, rotted, or its purpose and symbolism forgotten." He shook his head. "What is right? I have no more idea than you do. I believe I have confused even Gao."

Kate nodded, grateful for his honesty, at least. Whatever Luke might say, she didn't believe that he would ever have engaged in such wholesale plunder, guaranteed to offend the descendants of those buried here.

A few articles could have been taken without the loss ever being noticed. But this outrage would certainly sour relations between the Haida and any museum or private collectors. Rancor might well make impossible the kind of collecting and photographing she and Luke had done this winter.

Gao returned, his posture stiff, anger still radiating from him. He passed Luke, who said quietly, "I'm sorry."

Gao gave a jerky nod. Kate reached out and touched his arm, but she could not speak. He looked down at her hand where it rested on his arm, and then raised his head. Their eyes met and searched; at last, he nodded again. Not another word was said as they made the return journey to Kiusta.

The two men went ahead of Kate into the house, ducking to enter the low portal. Kate heard them talking, but made no move to follow them. She knew both of them well enough to guess that they would decide to pursue the thieves in hope of catching up to them. This might be her only chance to look around and wonder. Where had her father's body been found?

It would have been nearly impossible to make her way from house to house without the aid of a scythe, so overgrown by shrubbery was Kiusta. Even since she had been here, perhaps three years ago, more beams and poles had fallen or been swallowed by the lush vegetation. She was unlikely now to have time to photograph, but in any case, it would scarcely have been worth wasting the plates.

Two, perhaps three, houses were clearly used as shelters on at least an occasional basis. Faint tracks led to them. If the Reverend Hewitt's body had not been in one of those places or on the beach itself, it would never have been found. Kate guessed that although Kiusta had acquired its name from a trail that went overland from here to a wide bay on the west coast, the land route was seldom used now.

Perhaps her father had been struck down even here, just in front of her, where the path led up from the sandy beach. She took a few steps forward and closed her eyes. *Father!* she cried silently. *Are you here? Speak to me.*

She strained for something, anything, but felt only the slam of her heartbeat, her wet, chilled skin, her fingernails biting into her palms. Nothing. "Father, please," she whispered, and waited yet again. But he was not here. It was as though he had never been.

Kate bowed her head, fighting tears. What came to her then was completely unexpected. An odd calm stole over her; her tension and frustration melted away. How often her father had warned her to think carefully before she wished for something . . . because one often received what one had wished for. Had she *wanted* to find him here, some ghostly wisp of the man he had once been, now trapped in a spiral of betrayal and pain?

He had believed with all his being that earthly pain was fleeting, the salvation that lay beyond it, eternal. The Reverend Hewitt had trusted in his Heavenly Father to wrap him in an embrace. It was she whose faith had been lacking, she saw suddenly. Her father was at peace. And so, too, could she be, if only she accepted her loss.

By the time she heard Luke crack his head on the door frame and swear as he exited the house, she was sufficiently composed to face him. "Do we depart?"

He reached out and touched her cheek, where there might be a tear stain. "We can come back should you feel the need."

Kate stepped forward and leaned against him, rejoicing in the strong arms that encircled her. "No." Her words were muffled by the wet wool of his coat. "I'm satisfied. There may be ghosts here, but they are not his."

"Your father was far too forceful a personality to end up as something so insubstantial."

"He was, wasn't he?" She was able to smile and straighten. "Well, are we leaving?"

Two days later, the three arrived at Masset, the largest and most highly populated village remaining. Any hope of catching Durham or Jarvis sooner had been erased. They had stopped briefly at Yatza and then at Kung, finding not a soul at either village.

Yatza had been established as recently as five years ago by Chief Endenshaw, once hereditary chief of Kiusta. The lodges were crudely built, the poles few and relatively primitive. Still, it was obviously inhabited. Gao guessed that the villagers had gone en masse either to Masset or Yan for a potlatch.

Kung was otherwise. Houses were decaying though still habitable, but in some cases, the split-cedar planks had been removed from the walls and the only possessions left were those too large to bother taking: empty cedar boxes, long troughs used for feasts, and stone mortars. Like so many other villages, but more recently, Kung had been deserted.

It was impossible to tell at either place whether visitors had come and gone in the past day or two. The fire pits were cold and blackened, and there were no signs of a camp having been set up outside. At Kung, little remained to take, while at Yatza, much could have been pilfered from the empty houses without being obvious to the unfamiliar eye.

Masset was familiar territory to Kate. She had been here three or four times. Her father had liked to visit the Reverend Collison, whose interests had been so similar to his. The line of houses jogged around the peculiar little hill that had given the town its original name: White-Slope Village. The land hereabouts was otherwise low and densely forested, a contrast to the mountainous country they had left not so long ago.

At nearly the exact center of Masset stood the enormous residence of Chief Wiah. Collison had measured Monster House, as the building was called, and insisted that it was more than twenty-one meters wide. From its front entrance, a ceremonial boardwalk extended down to the beach. Important visitors would not have to wade through damp grass or wend their way around canoes or drying racks.

Although some of the houses here, too, appeared to be empty, a great number of canoes were drawn up along the beach. Signs of European influence were more noticeable than in other villages; many houses had sashed windows, and already one house had been torn down to make way for another, this one in the style of the white people's.

The Hudson Bay Company maintained a store and residence here, surrounded by a picket fence. Mr. McKenzie, the company's factor in Masset, would undoubtedly be courteous; he was new here, and probably had not even been acquainted with the Reverend Hewitt. Still, the HBC and Kate's father had been bitter enemies. The holders of a virtual monopoly, the company paid the Indians ridiculously low prices for furs, keeping the people under its sway by allowing them credit at the store. The Reverend Hewitt had hoped to free the Skidegate tribe, at least, from economic dependence by buying a steamboat and taking the furs directly to Victoria for sale, bypassing the HBC altogether.

The arrival of two white people created enough of a stir to bring children and dogs running to meet them. It was at Kate's suggestion that they proceeded directly to the Missionary Society House, where she hoped to find the Reverend Collison. The children ran ahead, so Kate and the two men had scarcely entered the narrow lane between tidy fences and hedges when an unfamiliar-looking young man came hurrying out, still shrugging into his frock coat.

"Why, I didn't believe them! But it is indeed a white woman!"

Kate took his extended hand. "Yes, although appearing less than her best, I fear. I'm Katherine Hewitt, my father was the missionary at Skidegate." She introduced Gao and Luke, then asked anxiously, "Is the Reverend Collison here?"

"Dear me, no. The Church Missionary Society insisted he return to Metlakatla last year to assist Mister Duncan. You weren't aware?"

"No," she said slowly. Surely if Collison had been at Metlakatla, they would have met him. She knew Mr. Duncan to be increasingly at war with the Missionary Society; were they attempting to replace him with Collison? Perhaps Mr. Duncan had managed to send his rival missionary up the Nass or Skeena, well out of his way.

The young man peered from face to face. "I don't believe I introduced myself. My name is George Sneath. I am doing my best to continue the work so ably begun by the Reverend

Collison. I trust you'll be my guests tonight. I have company already; perhaps you know Mister James Durham?"

"Then he's here!" Luke exclaimed, triumph and a kind of bitter pleasure in his voice. "We have a great deal to discuss with him!"

"Indeed? I've counted myself fortunate to have his company. I confess I will be sorry to say good-bye to him."

Luke snorted, but Kate gave him a repressive glance. She felt Gao's tension, just as great, although he waited in silence. More calmly than she felt, she said, "But didn't Mister Durham just arrive? We thought he was close ahead of us."

Sneath's eyes widened. "Why, no. He's been here for a week or more. I suppose you know he works for a museum. I flatter myself that I've been of some assistance to him in purchasing what artifacts the Indians are willing to sell. Did Miss Hewitt say that you, too, are here on behalf of a museum, Mister Brennan?"

Luke ignored him. "Blast it, if Durham has been fixed here, who could possibly have been at Dadens?"

"Dadens? Then you haven't just come from Skidegate?"

"No, we've circled the islands," Kate said. "We were disturbed to find the burial cave at Kiusta ransacked. Anything worth money was taken, even the skulls, and bones were strewn everywhere. It couldn't have happened more than a day or two before our arrival."

Gao spoke for the first time. "It was not right."

The young missionary's brow crinkled. "But who could have done it?"

"We were hoping you would tell us," Luke said grimly.

The answer was slow. "Another gentleman was here recently, with his own steamship. A Mister Jarvis. I believe he was buying things as well, but surely . . ."

Luke was not slow to express his feelings. "He's a scoundrel of the worst stamp. But tell me, did he have Haida guides? The cave is unlikely to be found by chance."

Sneath frowned. "I'm not certain, he was here so briefly.

He wouldn't have had time to hire them here. I was sorry the stay was so short, because Mister Richardson accompanied him. Jarvis had been good enough to bring him. Richardson wasn't aware that I was here; he'd been told that I was transferred. He very kindly decided to visit those Christians among the Masset band and give a sermon in my absence. When he discovered that I was here after all, he elected to continue with Mister Jarvis, perhaps spreading the word of the Lord in Yatza or any other inhabited villages. I hoped they would stop for a longer visit on the way back."

As he spoke, his voice seemed to recede, until it sounded far off. Kate felt suddenly detached, as though she watched the scene through the viewfinder of her camera. She was still in this state when Luke turned to face her.

The lines beside his nose and mouth were carved deep; the intensity in his eyes succeeded in piercing the bubble of unreality that had surrounded her. Luke said bluntly, "He must have shown the cave to Jarvis."

"Yes." A man of God. Was it possible? What could be his motivation? Of course he was eager to see the Indians sell anything with crest figures on it, but to aid in the desecration of graves was another matter altogether. When such things happened, her father had been shocked and angry. How could another missionary not only excuse such a violation, but participate in it?

Luke's thoughts must have paralleled her own, for at this juncture, he said quietly, "We've heard several times that Richardson presses the Indians for donations. Would he consider this a reasonable sacrifice to acquire the means to build a larger church?"

No! It was inconceivable! She must give Richardson the benefit of the doubt. Perhaps he did not know what Jarvis was like. He might have innocently pointed out the sights. As events followed their course, he would have been able to do little but protest.

She had created a reasonable scenario, but she did not believe it. For the Reverend Hewitt had been murdered, and though the hand that did it might not have been a white man's, the motivation behind the act must surely have been.

If it followed that her attacker was also the murderer, he could only have been one of the four men who had left Skidegate and been in the vicinity of Skedans when the last assault on her was made. The Indians had assured Gao that no other visitors had arrived from Skidegate. Of the four men who had, they had been eliminated one by one as suspects in the two crimes: Sims and Gao had been in Skidegate when the murder occurred at Kiusta; James Durham could conceivably have been the murderer and her attacker, but he could not have ransacked the cave—and therefore, why commit the murder? Only her father's successor could have committed all three acts.

But why? *Why?*

Chapter Twenty-two

"They haven't been back here?" Luke demanded of the young missionary.

Wide-eyed, he shook his head.

"Then perhaps they continued around Cape Knox to Tian, or went north to the Prince of Wales Islands."

"What do you propose we do?" Kate asked with some asperity. "Chase them around?"

"I propose that we depart promptly for Skidegate. They must return there eventually, if they have not already done so." Luke's voice was hard.

Guilt obliged her to protest. "But you had intended to stay in this vicinity for weeks!"

"We can come back easily enough, once you have your answers. This may be your only chance."

"I . . ." She would have felt even more guilty had she not been certain that he was as determined as she to follow this hunt to the end. "Very well."

Looking from one to the other, the missionary said, "This

outrage should certainly be reported to Mister McKenzie. He is a magistrate, you know."

Kate hadn't known, but it was quickly agreed that Gao and Luke would speak to the HBC agent.

"You intend to leave in the morning?" Mr. Sneath inquired. "But you will dine with me and spend the night?"

"Yes, thank you very much," Kate said.

"And your chaperone . . . ?" he inquired delicately, glancing around as though another woman would pop out of the hedges.

Kate's mouth went dry. She had not thought in a long while of such matters as propriety and reputation. The Haida had either been uninterested in her marital status or indifferent to it; Mr. Durham, to his credit, had never expressed any shock or dismay that she traveled alone with men; and while Mr. Richardson had expressed both, she had felt confident that he would guard her reputation nevertheless. But here, at last she was faced with the way the rest of the world would regard her winter's journey.

Before she could summon an excuse, however weak, Luke said coolly, "Unfortunately, Miss Hewitt's chaperone became ill some way back and had to return to Skidegate. Miss Hewitt is a very fine photographer, you know, and was determined to complete the task she had promised to undertake. I expect her photographs to educate museum goers in a way the artifacts alone, out of context, cannot. Have you ever seen her work?"

"I'm certain I should admire it, but I cannot approve of an unmarried young woman continuing on once her chaperone became ill. It was imprudent, at the very least. Why, if Miss Hewitt's conduct should become known, her reputation would be irrecoverable!"

Luke leveled a gaze on Sneath that had the man shifting uneasily. "It will reassure you to know that I intend to make Miss Hewitt my wife as soon as possible. I'm sure we can rely on you to say nothing that would damage her reputation."

"Naturally, though I cannot like . . ." The missionary faltered under Luke's cold stare. "I could conduct the service before you leave," he offered. "Once you are husband and wife . . ."

Pride had kept Kate's head high, though she was both coldly angry and bitterly aware that Mr. Sneath was right. Her selfish desire to shake off the shackles of society would reflect badly on her aunt and uncle, and even on poor Alice, if Kate's adventures became known in Victoria.

Luke interrupted brusquely. "We can't afford the time. Now, are you certain you have room for us?"

"Yes, yes, but I must find a woman to share . . . How shall I explain . . ."

They left him mumbling to himself. Kate walked with dignity beside Luke, but felt the heated flush in her cheeks. Torn between anger and humiliation, she was grateful for Luke's defense, but also burningly aware of how smoothly he had intervened. It was true, of course, that he intended to make her his wife, so why had it sounded like a lie? Had he anticipated this moment and planned ahead what to say?

Dear heavens, had he felt obligated to ask her to marry him because he had known what she would encounter on her return to civilization?

She was appalled by the realization that she might indeed have misunderstood his motives. He had admitted from the beginning to feeling responsible for her, because she was his employee. Did he feel responsible for her endangered reputation, too? Had he already guessed that she would not be welcomed back at her uncle's home?

Kate glanced sidelong at Luke, who looked much as usual, if more raffish than when they had begun their adventure. His dark, wavy hair badly needed cutting, his clothes were worn, his boots scuffed, and she knew his hands to be blistered and callused. He was talking to Gao about tomorrow's departure, apparently unaware of her churning emotions.

She would leave it that way for now. Pain stabbed somewhere in the region of her heart, for Kate knew that before spring, she would have to give him a chance to withdraw from his offer of marriage.

Balancing Rock appeared off the starboard bow. Mist swirled around it like ghosts dancing in the rain. Huddled under a blanket in the canoe, wondering if she would ever be truly dry again, Kate watched it vanish as mysteriously.

They had pushed hard to make it here so soon. Luke in particular must be exhausted, yet he drove the paddle through the water without cease. Only his face, set in a grimace, betrayed his pain. Disregarded, rain dripped from his nose and cheekbones and hair.

There the forest of poles rose ahead; the long beach came in view, the white spire of the Skidegate church.

Kate had been just as wet, just as weary, all those months ago when they had crossed Hecate Strait through a squall, but then this had been a homecoming. Now she knew better. She had learned too much about her father and herself. This place and these people were part of what she was, but only a part. She did not belong here, any more than did most of the manifestations of the white man's presence.

How could the neat, framed houses with their picket fences, the narrow church with a spire, and the cemetery of white crosses ever look natural at the edge of the living stillness that was the forest? The Haida crest poles were made of the very fabric of the dark trees and represented creatures that lived beneath their shadows or in the stormy waters that separated these islands from the rest of the world.

No steamboat was anchored offshore. The canoe was lifted by a last swell; with guttural cries, the two men drove hard with the paddles and leaped out the moment the bow scraped on gravel.

Kate dropped the blanket, lifted her skirts, and scrambled over the gunwale of *Dancing Canoe*. As the men pulled the craft high up the sandy beach, she gazed toward the Mission House. The door was shut, the windows dark. No smoke drifted from the chimney. Her heart beat a little faster at the thought of rummaging through Mr. Richardson's possessions, which, once out of the Reverend Sneath's presence, Luke had suggested doing.

"Something might be found to settle the business of your father's death one way or the other," he had pointed out. "If we find nothing, he need never know we have looked."

Shivering now, Kate didn't know whether to hope that she found something, or nothing.

They had arrived almost unnoticed. The mist hung low, the drizzle discouraging anyone from loitering outside. One boy did call out to them, then ran with the agility of a mountain goat toward Thunder-and-Lightning House.

She turned when Luke said, "Gao, while we search the Mission House, why don't you find out what you can about Richardson's whereabouts. If you would prefer that we come with you to speak to Kun taos's family . . ."

"No," Gao said. "They will be afraid when they hear we have come and he is not with us. I must tell them."

Kate seemed to be seeing everything through new eyes. Gao had aged, she observed with shock. He was thinner, the lines on his face deeper, the young man's fire in his eyes damped. The passion and anger had died along with his friend. No more than Luke or Kate did Gao know what was right or wrong where ambiguity was possible.

But two wrongs would not be disputed: murder, and the desecration of graves. A man guilty of both deserved no pity.

Luke stopped beside her. "Shall we?"

Kate pressed her lips together and nodded. Behind them, a dog started barking, and then another; far down the beach, a voice called a greeting to Gao. But she and Luke walked silently to the Mission House.

To her surprise, the front door was not barred. But inside, the musty smell of a place that has been shut up assailed them. Kate looked around, noting anew how bare the front room was. Where would Emmet Richardson hide something?

"It would help if we knew what we were looking for," she said. Her voice was too loud in the quiet room.

"Artifacts he hasn't sold," Luke suggested. "Or money. More than could reasonably have been collected for the new church. He might have kept a notebook of transactions, or receipts of some kind." Already he was scanning the books in the one case. "Blast it, I wish I'd thought to ask Durham if he's bought from Richardson."

"I suppose I'll start in his bedchamber."

A grunt was her answer. To overcome her reluctance, she reminded herself of the careless—even the deliberately destructive—way in which her own trunks had been searched. It helped that Mr. Richardson hadn't moved into the room that had been her father's.

His bedchamber was as stark as the front room. The sturdy spool bed had been there since the house was built. It was topped with a worn churn-dash quilt in faded blue and white. Beside the bed stood a marble-topped stand, holding pitcher and bowl, like that in her bedroom. Her father had always kept a Bible near at hand, but she saw no books in here at all.

Otherwise . . . She turned slowly. The wardrobe looked to be the most promising. Its oak-paneled doors squeaked as she opened them. Inside, it was nearly empty. Two muslin shirts hung beside a shabby coat. A faint odor of mildew clung to the fabrics.

The first drawer on the bottom contained two shirt collars, neither one laundered even to her standards, much less to Aunt Grace's, and a pair of suspenders. A set of summer undergarments, a plain wooden cloth brush, a tie. Nothing here was inappropriate to his station. Kate began to feel squeamish.

Nonetheless, she made herself open the second drawer. It seemed heavier; she had to tug. Before she had reached farther than the striped nightshirt that lay on top, Luke entered the room.

"Find anything?"

"Nothing so far," she said. "Have you tried the kitchen?"

"No, this room is a better bet. Remember that he has help in the kitchen." He opened the drawer on the bedside stand and began rummaging through its contents.

Kate ceased to pay attention once she lifted the nightshirt, for beneath it was a good-sized metal box, secured with a locking clasp. The keyhole was empty.

"Luke."

At her tone, he turned immediately. In a stride, he was beside her. "That's more like it," he said softly.

It was obvious when he lifted the box that it was heavy. He set it on the bed and jiggled the clasp. Without looking up, he asked, "May I borrow a hairpin? I'll bet I can pick this lock."

She snatched a pin from her hair and handed it over. He poked it into the keyhole and with seemingly limitless patience, made tiny probing movements. Kate wanted to scream at him to hurry. The silence was oppressive, unnerving. What if the missionary returned and caught them in the act of breaking into his strongbox? Nearly anything else could be explained, but not this.

Her anxiety was stretched so thin that she imagined she heard a bump in the kitchen, a footstep. But the doorway remained empty. They should have closed it, she thought suddenly. If Richardson returned unexpectedly, he might not come in here, but he was certain to if he saw the door standing open. Instead of closing it, however, she dithered. This way, they were more likely to hear somebody coming; she didn't feel quite so trapped.

"Ah." The sound was one of satisfaction.

Kate looked back to Luke, to see that the clasp had popped open. He laid down her hairpin and with both hands lifted the metal lid of the box. She quit breathing as she watched.

It was filled with small cloth bags. The clink of coins sounded as soon as Luke picked up the first one. He undid the drawstring and poured out a stream of gold onto the faded fabric of the quilt.

Kate could only stare down at it. He emptied a second bag, a hillock of gold beside the first. A thick wad of U.S. currency joined the fortune already spread on the shabby coverlet. But most shocking of all was the next item Luke tossed aside as he lifted another bag.

A watch. Her hand reached out unbidden to pluck it from the bedcover. Her fingers knew the scrolling, the ornate shape of the letters: E. H. Edward Hewitt.

She must have made a sound, because Luke's sharp gaze lifted, going from the watch in her hand to her face. "What is it?"

In her mind's eye, she saw again the way the gold chain had trailed from her father's pocket. Nearly every hour through the day, he would dip into the pocket, pull out the watch, nod with satisfaction when he noted the time.

She clicked open the case, just as he had always done. It had not been recently set or wound; the hands pointed to 12:36. Kate had the sudden, macabre fancy that the watch had stopped at the instant her father died, that it had not run since.

Luke took the piece from her unresisting hand. "Your father's?"

Now, of all times, she had to cry! She took an angry swipe at her tears, but she had not succeeded in answering when a voice from the doorway did it for her.

"I should have sent it to you." Richardson stood stiffly in the opening. He looked much as always but for wet shoulders and pale hair darkened by rain. Even his ordinarily well-tended side-whiskers shed droplets. "I apologize. I didn't realize the sentimental attachment you felt for it."

Kate was stricken dumb. Did he hope to pass off his possession of the watch as an oversight? Ought she pretend that she and Luke had wandered in here by chance, were poking through his things . . . why? she wondered wildly. Because they were concerned about his absence?

Beside her, Luke said coolly, "Would you care to explain how it came to be in your possession?"

That was when the missionary lifted a revolver, held

without the slightest tremble, so that the barrel pointed directly at Kate. "Once I had done a dreadful thing, how could I let it be for naught? The watch would have lain in Miss Hewitt's drawer. I at least could sell it. It's a very fine one, you know."

"Why?" Kate whispered. "Why did you do such a thing?"

"I never intended to. I'm not a madman." His brown eyes entreated her to believe him, as though it mattered. Perhaps it *did* matter, for he must eventually face judgment. It might be that he imagined her forgiveness would weigh on his side. "He brought it on himself. Nothing would do but that he must see the cave! I tried to dissuade him, but he was inflexible."

She couldn't yet think clearly, didn't dare to look at Luke. What did Richardson intend to do to them? Her instincts told her to keep him talking.

"What did you tell Father?" she asked.

His tone aggrieved, the missionary said, "How was I to know the cave was on North Island? Everyone spoke of it as belonging to Kiusta. The Indians all claimed to have forgotten, or they wouldn't tell me. When I asked your father, he insisted on a reason for my curiosity. I told him I'd heard that it had been ransacked. How was I to know he would be so outraged that he would insist upon journeying there? He wouldn't delay even for a day; we must leave by dawn."

"And so you had to kill him?"

Kate stole a sidelong glance at Luke, who had straightened and now watched the missionary dispassionately. He had managed, unnoticed, to back up a few feet, so that the bed was no longer between him and Richardson. Surely he didn't intend anything as foolhardy as flinging himself directly at a man with a gun!

How could he? she thought more realistically. She was between the two men. In fact, she was so near Richardson, he could have reached out and grabbed her arm.

The entire scene had an air of unreality. How long had she known and trusted this slight man with the receding hair? Yet there he stood, his voice as well-modulated as when he gave sermons, explaining very reasonably why he had murdered her father. She kept expecting him to say, *Don't be ridiculous! Of course I didn't kill anybody.*

But no. He continued quite calmly at first. "When we found the contents of the cave intact, we proceeded to Kiusta for the night. He confronted me, said that he thought I was not suited to this kind of work. He asked if I was dealing in artifacts. Whatever my answer, it was not satisfactory; he thundered a denunciation of me. He declared that I should pack and leave the minute we returned to Skidegate; otherwise he would notify the authorities."

Richardson's prominent Adam's apple bobbed. Sweat beaded the high dome of his forehead, and his voice began to shake. "I could not—would not!—go back in disgrace, without adequate means of earning a livelihood. But even so, I did not plan to injure him. I swear to you! It was the way he spoke, so entirely without sympathy. He felt no understanding for anyone weaker than himself. After all I have suffered on these accursed shores, I could not bear it! He turned away from me in complete contempt. I snatched up a rock and swung in that moment of rage." He shuddered. "The sound it made when it struck . . . I hear it over and over. You cannot imagine my grief, my regret . . ."

His speech would have been pitiful had he not uttered it while holding a revolver in a very capable hand. Like him, Kate could not help herself.

"Yet you murdered two more men."

In agitation, he said, "My conscience must suffer no matter what. Unless I were to turn myself in, I had to kill them—else all would have been for nothing. They would have witnessed against me!"

Kate gazed at him in wonder, and with the beginnings of fear. For of course he must kill her—and Luke, too—or all would still have been for nothing. How could the outside of a man be so deceptive?

"But why?" she whispered, knowing that their only hope lay in delay. If he could be persuaded to keep talking, might somebody come? Better yet, could his conscience be awakened? He had killed for the first time under emotional duress; the next two murders were cold-blooded, but he despised the Indians. From his warped viewpoint, killing a white woman might be another matter. Look at the perspiration dripping from his brow, the way he pleaded with her! She continued: "I don't understand. Surely you were once sincere in your calling!"

"Of course I was!" He was beseeching her still; how ironic, a killer who cared what his victims thought and felt about him. "I was convinced that the Lord would lead me out of poverty and uselessness, to a life that had meaning. I would not be another wretched clerk straining his eyes to record other men's documents, whose hopes for a greater life were doomed." He blinked rapidly; his free hand clutched a handkerchief he used to dab away the beaded sweat—or was it tears? "I thought with my own strength to lift a whole nation from the debasement of the brute to the dignity of the sons of God. I would not be a mere drop in the sea of humanity, but rather, one of the waves that would roll their healing floods over every part of the globe.

"But do you think the rest of the world cares what happens here? We have been cast to the four corners of the earth, lost, forgotten! The natives themselves are ungrateful. They would rather sink back into sloth and lawlessness. I have done all I can! Any blessed fruit that grows here rots before it can be plucked."

The floor creaked behind her; Luke was moving surreptitiously. Kate said hurriedly, "But Father often said that the Lord tries our faith and patience to test us. He claimed that we must answer any disappointments with more earnest prayer, more humility, more faith."

"My faith has waned. No, it has been drowned by endless rain!" He sounded nearly hysterical. "But I tried, I gave all I could to savages who never appreciated my sacrifices. It is only fitting that they repay me with the means to start elsewhere."

Kate stole a glance at Luke. *Tell me what to do,* she pleaded silently, but though his eyes met hers, she could not read his expression. Oddly, she thought she saw a flicker of movement outside the small window, but how could that be? Gao would have no reason to follow them so quickly, and who else was there to come to their rescue?

Behind her, Luke asked in a tone of careful reason, "Why did you wait so long to sell the contents of the cave?"

"How could I offer them to anyone once the body had been found nearby? I was shaken up that day, or I would have hidden it. As it was, I fled in shock and horror, unable to think selfishly. Once I had time for reflection, I realized that Iyea and Xaosti could not be trusted to stay silent. I didn't need them once I was within a day's reach of Skidegate. Then I was forced to wait until a collector came who had never heard of the murder."

"Jarvis."

"If only I could have left with him." Richardson looked directly at Kate. "But he was determined to go on to Sitka and Wrangell before proceeding down the coast. I could hardly tell him how great was my need for secrecy and rapid flight. I feared you would take the risk of crossing the strait to intercept me or to contact the authorities."

"And so you have justified everything," Kate said, that sense of unreality still swaddling her.

"You know, don't you, how little I desire to hurt you?"

Luke snorted. "Yet you have assaulted Kate twice!"

The missionary's mouth tightened. "The first time, I hoped only to frighten her into giving up her foolish hunt for the murderer. It is her stubbornness that brings us to this!"

Kate felt dizzy. "And what is *this?*"

"I must ask you to step outside with me." Too quickly, he grabbed her arm and yanked her up against him. The barrel of the revolver pressed into the soft skin of her temple.

In sudden terror, Kate looked at Luke, who had lunged forward but halted when he saw that he was too late. In his blue eyes she saw terror to match her own, but his was not for himself. It was her he feared for, though he must know that Richardson would kill him, too.

"Go ahead of me!" Richardson snapped. "I will kill her here if I must!"

Luke's hands curled impotently into fists, but he carefully circled within touching distance of Kate and went ahead. Through the wavery panes of glass in the front room, Kate saw the gray shore and one end of the village. It might be her last glimpse of them. Out back was the forest, which she had once feared so much. How odd that she might, after all, die there.

The kitchen stove, enormous and black, was cold. The back door stood open. Beside it was a scuffed leather trunk. Had it been here all along? If only they had glanced in the kitchen!

Two steps led down to the footpath. The henhouse was here, a mere lean-to. As Kate felt for the first step, which creaked beneath their combined weight, she heard a soft cluck from within. If she reached in right now, she would find warm eggs beneath the hens, cushioned by the moss she had always used in place of straw. They could have had an omelet for dinner, and biscuits. And milk.

Her foot found the second step, then the muddy path. She let herself be urged forward, toward the deep shadows of the forest. The missionary was no taller than she; his body hadn't the muscular strength of Luke's. But that cold metal grinding into her temple was persuasive.

They must do something; anything! She would *not* walk unresisting to her death. If she struggled, would he be willing to shoot her now, where he might conceivably be seen and heard? Could Luke do something amidst the confusion?

Luke looked over his shoulder as though he had heard her thoughts, and he gave a brief nod. Without delay, Kate acted. She let herself slump, almost breaking Richardson's grip. He swore; she hadn't known he ever did.

"Don't make this harder than it must be!" The barrel left her temple, wavered toward Luke, who had leaped toward them. "Get back!"

Luke froze, then turned his head. Somebody was coming around the back of the house. Who . . . ? Kate had hardly recognized Gao before the others appeared behind him. Samuel and Martha, their son, even the young daughter-in-law. There were men she hardly knew; Annie; Qawkuna. They came silently, implacably.

The missionary backed up, dragging Kate with him.

Luke followed, within an arm's reach. "Let her go, Richardson. Don't make things worse."

She felt her captor's head turning wildly, knew the instant he saw the Haida who were behind them as well as in front. Nengkwigetklals with that evil scar; one face after another, some she knew, others strangers.

"I'll shoot her!" Richardson screamed. "Damn you all, I'll shoot her!"

But of course he didn't, couldn't. What good would it do him now? Bodies pressed close, jostled. Luke seized the moment and snatched Kate away, swinging her around to shield her with his body. The missionary turned the revolver toward Luke, but it was knocked from his grasp, trampled underfoot.

Richardson was raging, but to no effect. Just as the forest inexorably swallowed the silent sentinels of the Haida past, so he vanished among the savages he despised, who judged him and found him wanting.

The next thing Kate knew, Luke crushed her in his arms. She could scarcely breathe and her face was flattened to his chest. But, oh, it was so comforting! The slam of his heartbeat, his sweat, his strength—she had never known such joy as that which followed on the heels of despair.

For she knew now that he loved her, and how much. And she knew that another kind of love had saved them. They had come, these saviors, not for her sake, but for her father's. She was not alone after all, and would never be alone again.

Epilogue

With a certain amount of satisfaction, Kate emerged from under the black cloth. She was seldom mistaken when she felt the tingling that told her she had composed a superior photograph. This Inca fortress of Sacsahuaman in Peru was unusually challenging. Planes of finely fitted rock walls contrasted little with the sparse vegetation and dry hills, which in turn merged with the great vault of sky. But she had chosen her time of day carefully; shadows lay just right, creating sharp outlines on the throne carved out of solid rock. Steps led up to it; below was the parade ground, where the troops were reviewed, and beyond zigzagged the triple walls built of individual stones far taller than a man's head, all fitted so tightly by those ancient peoples that nowhere could a knife be slipped into the joins. How had they done it? she marveled anew.

Kate had begun dismantling her camera when she noticed the nearing cloud of dust on the road up from Cuzco. Visitors? Perhaps curious tourists? The bellows on the camera collapsed and she fitted its rosewood body into the case.

From habit, her fingers traced the scar in the fine wood. Better there than her head, Luke always insisted, but she still resented the damage.

The cloud of dust coalesced into four mounted burros and two heavily packed llamas. She shielded her eyes and studied the riders. In the lead was a familiar-looking face, as broad and dark as Gao's, beneath a gaudy cap with earflaps; it belonged to a guide she and Luke had decided not to hire. Behind him was another Peruvian; the brilliant colors, worn by even the men, were unmistakable.

Whether from inadequate nutrition or heredity, the Peruvian Indians were stocky and short. But the next rider, swaying awkwardly on the bony, narrow back of his burro, was a head taller and dressed in gray. There was something familiar about him: dark hair, a luxuriant mustache, a peculiarly elegant carriage despite his undignified position . . . Good God, was it possible?

Kate did not know whether to be amused or alarmed. Poor Luke, off happily excavating, would return to find he must entertain his rival, a man he cordially despised—James Durham.

How many years had it been? She calculated quickly. Four. Though the two men had continued to compete, they had not chanced to meet again; Durham was in the Yucatan when Luke and Kate had mounted an expedition to China. When they traveled the Nile, Luke's rival had been investigating the American southwest.

Still shading her eyes, Kate was overtaken by an unexpected flood of memory. She had last seen Durham in Masset, on her and Luke's return after the confrontation with Richardson. Poor Mr. Sneath had been obliged to entertain them all again. He had also married Luke and Kate, laying any potential scandal quietly to rest, so she supposed she must remember him fondly. Gao, of course, had stood up for Luke, and had since proven to be a reliable agent for the museum, within the limitations imposed by his qualms. He now had a wife and children to support.

On that return to Masset, she had expected to find Mr.

Richardson in custody, awaiting a steamer to take him to Victoria to face murder charges. But Mr. McKenzie was surprised; he had not heard that Richardson was even suspected of such a vile deed. The Indians deputed to deliver the missionary to him had never arrived.

In the years since, Richardson had never been heard of again. Had he been flung into the cold water, or abandoned on a barren rock where death might have taken days to find him?

The gold was left for the Haida, a bitter replacement for what it had bought, but they were its true owners.

If she had learned nothing else, it was how inseparable were the good and ill her father had done. Right or wrong, it was too late for the Haida to turn back; the cruel, inexorable flood of the white man's progress had swept them up in its currents. Perhaps the Reverend Hewitt had hastened the loss of all that made them a people; but he had meant well, which was more than could be said for most of the white men in their dealings with the Indian. Her emotions surprisingly buffeted by the reawakened memories, Kate thought now that it was a modest epitaph, but perhaps enough: *He meant well*.

The visitors had passed the walls and approached the campsite. She really ought to go greet them. Kate was folding her tripod, idly watching the column, when for the first time, her eye was caught by the rider of the fourth burro. Were those skirts bunched up? Was it possible . . . ? The burro stopped; the rider swayed and pushed aside a veil, revealing a young and quite charming face.

It could only be Clara, Kate realized in delight. So James Durham was educable after all! Well, it just went to show that anything was possible.

Author's Note

As novelists sometimes must, I have occasionally altered history to suit the demands of the story. Most notably, I have placed a white missionary in Skidegate long before one was there. In fact, the first missionary to the Queen Charlotte Islands was William Henry Collison, who came to Masset on the north end of the islands in 1876. The Skidegate Haida asked William Duncan at Metlakatla to send a missionary to them as well; Edward Mathers, a Tsimshian Indian, was sent, but the Haida were resentful as they had hoped for a white man, and Mathers did not stay long.

I'm indebted to Douglas Cole for his fascinating book, *Captured Heritage: the Scramble for Northwest Coast Artifacts* (1985), which, along with the work of Franz Boas, launched me on a journey in search of the motivations and insights of the many nineteenth-century men who wrote about the Haida Indians. Of those men, I'm most grateful for the work of John R. Swanton, whose *Contributions to the Ethnology of the Haida* (1905), *Haida Songs* (1912), and

Haida Texts and Myths, Skidegate (1905) did the most to preserve the customs and beliefs of the Haida.

More recent work that was valuable to me includes *During My Time: Florence Edenshaw Davidson, a Haida Woman,* by Margaret B. Blackman; and the several books of Kathleen E. Dalzell, who lovingly writes of the history and geography of her home. Particularly helpful was *The Queen Charlotte Islands: Of Places and Names.*

Any mistakes are, of course, my own, and I hope do not detract from the story.